EARLY PRAISE FOR THE BOOK

'Past and present bounce off each other to fascinating effect in a novel that combines an unusual and disparate set of ingredients, producing from them an irresistible Rampuri korma.'—**Anuradha Roy, author of *Called by the Hills*, *All the Lives We Never Lived* and *Sleeping on Jupiter***

'In her languid, capacious and sensitive novel, Khan explores what it means to be a woman, both in the nineteenth century and in the modern day, when so much of the world is stacked up against the expression of a woman's desires and her ambitions. Patiently, verse by verse and with infinite care, Khan uncovers the hidden heart of the tawaif Munni Bai, and also the stifling and casual claustrophobia of a modern marriage.' **—Ira Mukhoty, author of *The Lion and the Lily* and *Daughters of the Sun***

'Tarana Husain Khan deftly weaves two love stories across time: the openly celebrated romance of poet Dagh Dehlvi and the famed tawaif Munni Bai "Hijab", where the veil becomes a paradox of revelation, and the clandestine affair of a present-day writer and her confidant, a passion that must remain hidden in the shadows. Together, these parallel tales illuminate how love moves between secrecy and disclosure, voice and silence, across centuries.'—**Rana Safvi, author of *A Firestorm in Paradise* and *In Search of the Divine***

'A lost love legend, which is one of Urdu literature's unexplored heritage treasures, weaves its way through a story of contemporary challenges and pressures and a quiet love. Tarana Husain Khan achieves a fusion of recreated time and real time with flexibility and finesse.'—**Neelum Saran Gour, author of *Requiem in Raga Janki* and *Three Rivers and a Tree***

'Between multiple locations of space and of time, *The Courtesan, Her Lover and I* deftly interweaves the telling of the tale and the tale itself. A contemporary story of unfulfilled love deepens the drama and heartbreak of Munni Bai Hijab and Urdu poet Dagh Dehlvi's tragic love story. The framing device—letters and Urdu couplets—give the book an interesting, unusual narrative structure. With its wealth of detail about the enigmatic figure of the late nineteenth-century courtesan, there is plenty here to beguile and ensnare!'—**Sara Rai, author of *Raw Umber***

'At the heart of this textured and quietly intriguing narrative stand Hijab—a courtesan of rare wit—and her lover, Dagh, Mughal Delhi's last classical Urdu poet. Drawing on Dagh's letters, Tarana reimagines their relationship with intimacy and nuance, allowing archival traces to take on emotion. Threaded through their story is her own—a personal journey into their world and the questions that drew her in. *The Courtesan, Her Lover and I* takes a bold approach to exploring how romance and literary history intersect, and how the past is not distant but remains alive and breathing in quiet and subtle ways.'—**Saif Mahmood, author of *Beloved Delhi***

ALSO BY THE AUTHOR

FICTION

The Begum and the Dastan

NON-FICTION

Degh to Dastarkhwan
Forgotten Foods

THE COURTESAN, HER LOVER AND I

TARANA HUSAIN KHAN

First published in India in 2025 by Hachette India
(Registered name: Hachette Book Publishing India Pvt. Ltd)
An Hachette UK company
www.hachetteindia.com

1

Cover design by Amit Malhotra and front cover illustration by Rishika Kapoor.

Drop cap, 'Goudy Initialen No. 296' by Frederic W. Goudy.
Drop cap 'Zallman's Caps 1991' by D. Rakowski.

Section breaks and dingbats: 'Bergamot Ornaments' by Emily Lime Design;
'Eutemia Ornaments' by Bolt Cutter Design-Industrial Strength;
'Printers Ornaments One' by Michelle Dixon.

Endpapers: 'Guest-house – Fort in Rampur, Uttar Pradesh' via Wikimedia Commons

Hardback ISBN 978-93-5731-287-5
eBook ISBN 978-93-5731-397-1

Hachette Book Publishing India Pvt. Ltd
4th & 5th Floors, Corporate Centre,
Plot No. 94, Sector 44, Gurugram 122003, India

Typeset in EB Garamond 11.5/16 and Minion Pro 11.5/15
by R. Ajith Kumar, New Delhi

Printed and bound in India
by Manipal Technologies Limited

For the tawaifs, the 'atish e parkalaas'*—flames who danced, burned and were forgotten.*

Maza yehī hai ke tarfain se ho bechainī
Merey taḍapne ne unko bhī beqarār kiyā

An exhilarating restlessness mirrored in our hearts,
My tormented state disquieted him.

—MUNNI BAI HIJAB

Tum kehti ho ke mujhe bhool jao... achha tum yahan aa jao phir hum dono ek doosrey ko bhoolney ki koshish karengey.

You ask me to forget you... alright, come to me and, together we shall try to forget each other.

—DAGH DEHLVI in a letter to MUNNI BAI HIJAB (1902)

Contents

Dagh's Letter to Hijab

O cruel one,

After our meeting, you stayed with Nawab (Haider) for two days. My heart was beset with great sufferings. I cannot believe that you were constrained or compelled. In this princely state of Rampur, there are many god-fearing women who would never succumb to the snares of the rich even for thousands of rupees. They remain loyal to their oath of fidelity. On one side are the riches and luxuries of the Rampur State; but your lover has no outstanding qualities, except that he can lay down his life for you. Can my rival do this? Do you really believe so? If not, why do you forsake Dagh to get involved with him?

I write this with immense pain—if you don't want our relationship to end why have you deprived me of even seeing you?

Tum jāno tumko ghair se jo rasm o rāh ho
Mujhko bhi pūchtey raho to kyā gunāh ho

It is your wish to seek the company of others
Would it be a sin to inquire about me too?

This lover writes to you not to reproach but in the hope that you will meet him and assuage his pain.

Dagh Dehlvi
Undated letter

فیصلہ

1

Faislā (Decision)

AFTER A WEEK BRACKETED BY TWO SUNDAYS, I ADMITTED TO myself and to my husband, Faraz, that I wasn't going back to school. Until then, my resignation, which I had handed to the principal with aplomb, was a piece of paper I could crawl back and retrieve. Faraz didn't ask me why—it was my choice to go and teach at the local school and my decision to leave after six months. He prides himself on being a non-chauvinistic Rampuri, a rare breed.

The decision has solidified into a daily routine of rising late, coffee on the porch and the bliss of watching the bilious yellow school bus carry on without me to the dull grey building. The first day, the bus stopped and honked at the gate as usual. I sent Meezan Bhai, our cook, to tell the bus driver that I had left school. The school was an obnoxious, unsurvivable riot, but the children were amazing, though a bit unruly. I think of my students, wonder about the half-stories I left behind and resist the urge to message them. I will, someday. I was just a new teacher with a fresh outlook and stories from another part of the world. There were a lot of we-will-miss-you-ma'am and please-don't-leave; they will forget, as teenagers often do. I had celebrated my 'liberation' with a hearty kofta and kardhi lunch—a strange Rampuri combo that comforts and satiates at many levels—and was beset with calorie-guilt. We really need a word for that angst, guilt, anger and apprehension one feels after a high-calorie lunch.

I have to tell Baba, my father-in-law, about my decision. He might have heard about it already—he has an uncanny instinct of smelling out everything in our lives. Baba, as if waiting for confirmation, comes immediately, leaving his patients. I ferry the arguments and my defence around in my head. The job that Baba got for me—taking me to the school principal like a child seeking admission—was supposed to be a stopgap arrangement until we settled down in Rampur and I could orient myself to our new reality. Faraz always accuses me of being too eager, rushing on without giving much thought and then regretting. Some days, I inhabit this light, frivolous being and feel weightless, almost feathery.

I'm on my second cup of black coffee, standing on the porch, waiting, when Baba arrives with an impatient blaring of the car horn as Meezan Bhai rushes to open the gate. I gulp down the dregs of coffee, wishing I had something stronger. I imagine Baba's reaction to the out-of-work daughter-in-law greeting him with a brandy-infused, half-drunk smile. I have plans, I have answers—difficult ones but clearly vocalized in my mind.

Baba gets out of the car, side-hugs me and pats my shoulder. At least he isn't angry. I relax and ask Meezan Bhai to get Baba's Lapchu tea with freshly-baked brownies. He settles down in his favourite chair and remarks that Faraz must be sleeping late as usual. Faraz was, in fact, lolling in bed, leaving me to face Baba-music. I was annoyed with him, and we had a mini-argument, but he just wouldn't budge. While stirring the teapot to make the liquor stronger—twice clockwise and twice anti-clockwise—Baba asks me casually when I last had my period. I assure him I am not pregnant if that's what is worrying him. He is, after all, a gynaecologist and this is his first thought-reaction to any aberration related to women; for unmarried women, he prescribes marriage as a cure-all. He shakes his head and says, 'It's your menopause.'

I lie to him that I just had my period. What did that have to do with anything, anyway? Baba takes a sip, dips the wet spoon in the sugar bowl, taking out a carefully calibrated minuscule amount, and stirs it in his tea.

'Rukmini, my darling child, menopause is a process that starts in your forties. It's a difficult time; there is a lot of hormonal disturbance. Hmm?'

Wait, did my father-in-law just blame my decision to leave my teaching job on a hormonal fit? I was prepared for anger or persuasion, but this—this was literally below the belt. Plus, he implied that I was on my last dregs of youth. Akriti, my closest friend, says it's creepy to have a father-in-law involved with my uterus. Baba, the doctor-patriarch of the family, was into everything—medical and personal—right from the beginning. After years of taking his advice, opinions and medications, now it feels like an intrusion.

'Baba, I resigned from my job because I hated it.' I flatten my sentence and try to unclench my teeth.

'Never mind if you hate it. You go to work; that's how it is!'

If Jumbo, Baba's beagle, were here, he would have barked in my defence. He hates loud voices. Feeling bad at his outburst, Baba puts on his calm doctor voice. 'It's okay to take a break and get back to work later.' He suggests gently that I could think of starting a school, a small one; then it would grow, and people would flock for admissions because of my Dubai teaching experience. He even offers to take a loan on his precious orchard to cover the cost of setting up the school. I can see his plans for me expanding in his imagination. I know Faraz will say that it shows Baba's trust in my abilities; he never made the same offer to Faraz.

'I'm not going back, and the idea of starting a school here horrifies me. Everything is so disorganized, so… so casual here.' I try to burst his bubble and end up sounding like a teenager. The good doctor morphs back to being Baba.

'So you want to sit at home? Can you afford to?' I hope the antique teacup has resisted the shock of being slammed down. It is one of the several precious crockery pieces Baba bestowed upon me after our return.

I break the real bad news—I have decided to get back to writing. Before Faraz and I got married, I was a features writer writing about the food scene in Delhi—there wasn't much food writing at that time, just restaurant reviews and an odd column on a cuisine—and human-interest stories for a national daily and doing well. For me, the one positive when moving back to India from Dubai was the possibility of taking up journalism again. I was inside my head already. But Baba found me the job and advised me to let things settle down and then think about it. I should have protested then, but things were so uncertain, and I thought I could start testing the writing space again while still working. He had always looked down upon my career and was quite happy when I gave it up after marriage to look after Gul, our daughter.

'You want to become a journalist and go around asking people for interviews! And… and write what exactly?' The temperature of the air he was breathing out and the elevation of his eyebrows were building up into a quintessential Baba tantrum.

'Articles…'

'On what? Crime, rape!' Crumbs from his third biscuit splutter out. Jumbo would have gone berserk licking them up from my too-plump sofa, transposed from my Dubai home; it looks incongruous beside the ornate wooden chairs, the original inhabitants of the colonial bungalow, our new home.

Baba jumps up, pacing around the table. I know he is imagining me wandering in the tiny gullies of this small town, meeting random people, inviting censure and gossip—totally unacceptable for a Rampuri daughter-in-law. I had expected all this; I'm prepared to weather it and put a stop to his plan B for me.

'I can write about Rampur, the city. People hardly know about

Rampur, Baba.' I try to be gentle but firm—maybe only in my head. Recently, an online magazine published my article on Rampur Raza Library, and the editor wrote to me saying that I had a wonderful voice. Reassured, even though it wasn't a reputed media outlet, I had enrolled myself in an online writing course that cost me half a year's pay and tried to juggle school, online classes and writing assignments.

'Don't you dare write about me before I die!'

I assure him that I shall wait for all the family members to die before writing about them.

'You and Faraz think you can leave work and live by selling off land!' Baba sits down with a thump and shakes his head.

'Meezan, get me some water!' he yells. He knows Meezan Bhai is lurking in the corridor listening in on our conversation, very much a part of our life's travails.

Baba gulps down the water, takes out the prescription pad from his bag, scribbles something, tears it off a leaf and hands it to me—medicines for my incipient menopause. He calls it 'perimenopause', which somehow sounds like a flighty, shifting state.

'Your mother was sweating so much at your wedding, remember? I knew it was menopause.' He cheers up at his past diagnosis. As we walk out to the driveway, Baba delivers a quick lecture on menopause—as though we didn't live in a Google-world where we are condemned to know—predicts a tough time for me, pats my back reassuringly and drives off in his battered Maruti to his waiting patients.

Baba comes from a long line of practical, imperturbable hakims and doctors who went to work without a day off. I picture his grandfather and great-grandfather riding in a carriage to the Nawab's bedside, feeling the veiled begum's pulse through a perforated sheet, and bandaging sword wounds after epic battles. Rampur was, after all, a princely state under colonial rule till Indian independence and people still harbour a hangover from the Nawabi era, cradling heirlooms and memories.

I return to the drawing room after seeing him off to find Faraz peeping out from the bedroom door and throw a cushion at him.

'Faraz Khan! You left me alone out there. How could you!' Faraz laughs and starts making comical Baba faces.

'I stood with you when he came for you! I'll never, ever, ever be there for you!' I scream, throw some more cushions and collapse back on the sofa with him, laughing. Suddenly, we are the way we used to be, when everything was a big adventure and a laugh. He tells me it's my fault for getting bullied into taking up teaching when I really wanted to write.

'You don't understand. It's not so easy. I haven't written a single line in eighteen years!' Nothing that could be called consequential at any rate. I wrote two articles for a friend's food blog and got some likes and shares. Parameters of success and readability have changed drastically in the screen-obsessed, share and follow world. I'm told we only have two seconds to catch the audience bent on the endless scroll.

'Did I ask you to stop writing?' Faraz snaps.

'I'm not blaming you!'

Everything becomes about him in all our arguments. Maybe I'm overcritical and it drives up his defences. His mobile pings, and he turns away with a shrug.

I miss my old life, I miss us there, and I miss Gul. It has been a year now—nine months, almost a year—since our return from Dubai, and things seem suspended and splintering on the edges. Sometimes, there is nothing to cling to.

What will you do today? What will you write? Who will publish it? Baba's voice in my head has now mutated into my thought-voice.

تلاش

2

Talāsh (Search)

APPARENTLY, UNLIKE JANE AUSTEN'S SINGLE WOMAN, AN ambitious woman is a problem to be solved. It infuriates me that Baba and Faraz have probably had this 'man-to-man' conversation behind my back on how best to 'handle' me and my resurrected writerly ambitions. I know them so well that I can almost see them in their usual roles. Faraz rooting for a 'let her be' approach—his normal stance, more out of exhausted indifference than faith in my abilities. Probably after a huge argument—since all their exchanges these days end up like that—Faraz has been entrusted with the task of introducing me to Daniyal Khan—a high-brow culture vulture vetted and endorsed by Baba. It's typical of Baba to take charge, point me towards cultural relics, curtail my potential meanderings in the town, suggest that I write about Rampur culture while slyly hoping I burn off my writerly dreams and come home. He is hardly subtle, and this makes me even more adamant to succeed. My usual response is resisting Baba's suggestions, which are actually decisions, like a rebellious child; but I agree to the scheme to maintain peace. I can understand Baba's frustration—I have unsettled his carefully calibrated equilibrium. He had set up Faraz in a mango trading venture, me at a job and Gul safely lodged in a medical college. Now I was wilfully unemployed with impractical and potentially unprofitable plans. Not that I earned much when I was teaching, but it was enough to 'put food on the table', as Baba says. Most of the time, Faraz takes care of the daily expenses, and we live in a rambling colonial bungalow, a British-era club that Baba had bought years ago.

As we drive out to the old city area, Faraz briefs me that Daniyal Khan comes from a family of scholars, is very well-read and has a library with manuscripts inherited through generations. He doesn't know much about Daniyal's education or career, just that he would be the best person to assist me at this stage—at least Baba thinks that this scholarly rendezvous with a possibly priggish custodian of Rampur heritage will help or, hopefully, discourage me.

It has been more than two months since I left my job. My table is littered with half-finished articles while I aimlessly net-surf under the pretext of research and detest myself for it. I fed my anxiety by asking Meezan Bhai to prepare his specialities, stress-eating and slumping into post-eating despair. The only bright spot was supposed to be my Stanford University online writing course, but I was falling behind on the assignments. What should I write about? A bored housewife? Displacement? Life in small-town India? I was drawing a complete blank, paralysed by writer's block in anticipation of mutating into a writer.

I have hardly been to the old city around the Rampur Fort. We live on the edge of Rampur, right where the highway hits the town. Baba's house is the only place we visit in the walled city besides a few relatives on Eid or for some special occasion. The ancient geography of the town, encircled by centuries-old walls and gates, unspools in Faraz's commentary. He points out the neighbourhoods named after Pathan chieftains of yore, who settled down in Rampur when it was established in 1774. Some are even named after trees—peepal wala gher, Imli Asmat Khan—or landmarks. I laugh over 'Inayat Khan ki seedhiyan' (Inayat Khan's stairway) named after some person immortalized for building a two-storied house. The houses are arranged in clusters called ghers, with a common courtyard, a mosque and a cemetery. You don't have to go far for weddings, festivities, prayers and burial; the circle of life is transcribed within the mohallas. Faraz points at the place where there used to be three magnificent stone gateways leading to the Raza Library, the erstwhile durbar of the Nawabs. The famed ten gates to the city have been demolished in the name of crafting a 'smart city' by a local politician. I can still see some crumbling old houses with clay-tiled khaprail roofs. They will soon be sold off and replaced by new, uninspired structures in greens and pinks. 'New money', as Baba says, or simply a result of old families getting rich again from sons working abroad or the inevitable division of old kothis. The weddings are no longer held in common courtyards. There are several banquet halls where we have attended marriages, receptions and other celebrations. The food is unerringly fabulous, exclusively carnivorous and centred around the awesome trinity of qorma, kababs and pulao. I dress up and zero in unabashedly on the eats. My devotion to food became my redemption in the eyes of the Rampur relatives who had raised their collective eyebrows at our marriage. Marrying a Hindu woman at that time was not politicized but still unacceptable on religious and cultural grounds.

We navigate into an ever-narrowing gully with busy drains on both sides and houses squeezing against each other. I look up at the balconies jutting out, almost meeting over our heads, the web of electric wires slicing the blue sky. There is a small mosque tucked in a corner as we turn into a brick-lined lane. I can feel Faraz getting irritated. He clicks his tongue and gestures to a guy sitting on a motorcycle and chatting to a friend. The man gets off and tilts the motorcycle, and we just about manage to pass through without scraping it.

'We should have walked,' I say.

'And have these louts gawking at you!' Sweat beads dot Faraz's forehead. I hand him a tissue, which he rejects with a grunt.

'I could have worn an abaya and scarf if that would make you comfortable.' The thought of wearing the abaya brings on a suffocating, unbreathable feeling.

'I just want this mess to be over!'

I clamp down on my words and endure his silent, martyr-like annoyance. He would have never come if Baba hadn't forced him to. Still, I'm thankful for his help—anything to jolt me out of the place I'm in now.

The car stops at the end of the lane in front of an ancient, ornate archway. I gasp at the architectural magnificence of the carved stone pillars and the scalloped arch towering over us. Thankfully, it's not painted in whitewash like other gates and extravagantly displays its open brickwork and red sandstone carved with intricate vines and floral arabesque—typical late Mughal architecture. A massive wooden gate embedded in the arch is opened by an old servant who bows and salams as Faraz parks his car in a vestibule area, which has another car under a tarpaulin shroud.

Faraz tells me that Daniyal's ancestors were Rohilla Pathan chieftains who came with the original settlers and later became officials in the court of the Nawab.

'We are also Pathans from Swat, but we came in later,' he adds, unbuckling his seat belt.

I nod; I have heard the story of his pure Afghan bloodline narrated by the relatives with the silent rebuke against my Hindu 'taint'. Baba often laughs and says hybridization creates naturally superior survivors.

We walk through a smaller arch into a garden, which gives way to a brick-lined courtyard. A lemon and white painted double-storied haveli, which can easily be classified as a mid-sized palace, regal and suspended in a colonial past, towers beyond the courtyard.

A tall, spry man in a crisp white kurta pyjama is standing somewhat ceremoniously with his hands behind his back at the edge of the garden. He touches his forehead, acknowledging me and hugs Faraz in a formal manner reserved for acquaintances through a web of generational ties. Daniyal Khan. I remember meeting him at our marriage reception. Inquiring politely about Baba, Daniyal leads us up three steps to the courtyard and through the mosaic veranda into the roundish drawing room—the archetypical gol kamra. It is a study in carefully preserved colonial opulence with vintage pictures in silver frames on ornate tables, porcelain vases and a grand piano at one end. A painting of Nawab Raza Ali Khan in full royal paraphernalia over the fireplace looks down at me, weighing my value against his Rampur legacy, heightening Daniyal's subtle dismissal. An alcove in the wall has a marble bust of some ancestor. A huge chandelier hangs over the ostentatious centre table. Curlicued cornices, hand-painted wallpaper and wainscoting complete the British-style colonial decor. The room is lit up with side table lamps even during the day, giving it a sepia-toned, ancient feel. We take our seats on brocade upholstered sofas around a defunct fireplace.

Faraz starts talking about my decision to take up writing and my interest in 'documenting Rampur culture'. It is completely normal for women to be referred to in the third person in their presence and their thoughts and ideas mansplained in menspeak. Women in Rampur generally do not initiate a conversation with unrelated males, fade into smiling silence and wait for the right cues to step in. I'm used to it and play along, trying to hide my discomfiture. I wonder if Daniyal even knows my name. Most women go as wives, mothers and daughters of male members. But Daniyal would, of course, remember the great controversy over our marriage. Eighteen years ago, marrying a Hindu only worked out if there was a formal 'conversion', and then, everything was just great. So I had transmogrified from Rukmini to Rukhsar, at least for the purpose of the nikah. I was still Kuku to everyone, which worked for both my names.

Finally, Daniyal half-turns towards me and asks which aspect of culture I would like to work on. I can discern the line he has already drawn from his patronizing tone. He clasps his hands, his elbows resting on the armrests, his eyes half closed as he leans back, awaiting my response. I tell him that I had started reading up Rohilla history. The 'reading' was mainly on Google—articles, websites and features. Basically, I could name the ten Nawabs and had some idea about their reigns.

'The history of Rampur has never been written properly. Google sites and all the articles on Rampur are not based on facts,' Daniyal interrupts, his smile feline; I must be looking Google-guilty.

'Most people don't know much about Rampur, but recently, there has been a lot of interest around Rampur cuisine and culture,' Faraz says and gets up to inspect the brass fire poker set near the fireplace. A servant brings tea on a creaking trolley with finger sandwiches, Rainbow Bakery biscuits and pakodis. Daniyal pours from the silver tea service and hands the cups to the servant to pass to us.

'You see, the Nawabs were smart enough to support the Britishers in the revolt of 1857—they didn't have much faith in the rebels and were more inclined towards self-preservation. That's how we were able to preserve and rescue manuscripts from Delhi, Lucknow and other cultural centres. They were great collectors, and when they first settled here, they set up their library—the present Raza Library houses their collection. Also, Rampur became a place where poets and artists flocked, especially after the downfall of the Mughal and Awadh kingdoms.' Daniyal coughs, takes a sip of tea and continues his lecture on the cultural movement in Rampur. Maybe he doesn't get an opportunity to speak on the subject. In the dull light of the drawing room, he appears sepia-toned and ancient as the rest of his paraphernalia.

'I recently wrote an article on the Raza Library,' I interject as soon as I get the opportunity.

'Ah, good.' His lips curve into an indulgent smile over the teacup.

'Kuku has a master's in English literature.' Faraz defends me, picking up his third Rainbow biscuit. We had mutually decided to stop bingeing on the calorie-heavy cookies from the princely era established Rainbow Bakery. The Nawab had sent the baker, Irshad Khan, to Paris to learn the art of French pastry making. My mind is a repository of disjointed scraps of oral history narrated by Baba.

'Unfortunately, English Literature is not native to Rampur. We have only Urdu poetry and dastans.'

'Literature is not confined to any language; and I can read Urdu.' I'm gratified by his look of surprised interest. I'm no longer dismissed as a touristy outsider wanting to dip a toe into his fiercely protected, crumbling Rampuri culture.

I'm not fluent in Urdu, but I can make sense of the script after painstaking effort. After our marriage, while I was learning to read the Quran, I had asked the old maulvi to teach me Urdu as well since the script was the same. I will get Maulvi Waheed Sahib back, that is, if he is still alive.

'No wonder your accent is good...' Daniyal trails off and withdraws from our exchange. He could have completed the sentence—in spite of being a Hindu. I'm the Other, the outsider forever.

Faraz and Daniyal get into the various court cases Daniyal is fighting to keep his lands. I'm excluded and feel like a child left to wander around while grown-ups speak of pertinent matters. I walk with my cup to the bay window, sit on the window seat and gaze at the garden with a fountain at its centre. The fountain is probably redundant now, and the edges of its marble basin are streaked with blackish lichen. Unpruned English roses grow wild in their beds, and splashes of yellow crocuses enliven the overgrown grass. It's still a pretty picture in the setting sun. An Urdu book lies on the seat. I pick it up and read the title: *Dagh Dehlvi Bahaisiyat Masnavi Nigar*—Dagh Dehlvi as a Composer of Masnavis. I know that masnavi is a longish Urdu poem about beauty, love or maybe battles. The cover has a black and white photograph of the poet seated on a plush chair dressed in a dark, presumably gold-embroidered cloak with a sash and a white turban. It looks like an official court dress. The intent, almost proud gaze in the close-set eyes draws me in.

'Dagh Dehlvi was also, in a manner of speaking, from Rampur—a Rampuri.' Daniyal tentatively settles down on the window seat at a respectable distance from me, his back stiff with propriety, and continues. 'He came here when he was just four. He had lost his father; he lived in Rampur for about twenty years. I believe the environment of the Rampur durbar had a profound influence on his writing style.' He coughs, which I realize is a precursor to his learned exposition. I nod and put the copy down. I don't want him to feel that I was showing off and pretending to read Urdu—maybe I was, a little. He carries on about Dagh's life at the Rampur court and how, in the 1860s and 1870s, he spearheaded a literary movement and laid the foundation of the Rampur school of poetry. I set aside the book and tell him I'm not interested in Urdu ghazals.

'Study him for his love of life, for his love for Munni Bai Hijab—the greatest literary love story. What else is there to write?' His eyes smile at me with teacherly indulgence.

'How can I write about a poet without studying his works?' Do I look the kind of writer to him who would write historical romances about these poets and their muses.

'His poetry is simple, from the heart. You would understand it immediately.'

'I'm not into poetry; more of a prose person.' I feel tempted to reel out my former writing credentials.

'I believe that every writer is a poet.'

Unbelievable! How can this man tell me what a writer is supposed to be; this is my territory.

'Not me, sorry.' I shrug and get up. I want to get out of this dark, cavernous, overly opulent room. Exit left. Scene ends.

He offers us a tour of the house. I'm tempted, and Faraz has an eager look.

'Some other time. Baba had promised to drop in.' I demur, reluctant to give him the pleasure of showing off. His smile recedes, but he accepts the excuse with a faint nod. We thank Daniyal, and I feel happily bitchy at the snub.

Outside, Faraz tries to back the car out of the gate into the tight lane with the help of the old doorman.

'You were rude!' he snaps as soon as he has negotiated the tight turn and we are on a more breathable by-lane.

'Well, he shouldn't have been so disdainful… uff, such a snob.' I certainly didn't need Daniyal's approval or his hand-holding. I'm simmering and vaguely exhausted.

Faraz tells me Daniyal's family was married to the Nawabs' and they would have been Nawabs from another line. That is, if the eldest son had died or something. So, they are almost might-have-been Nawabs. Whatever. I go back to Daniyal's words and subtle gestures. Would he have suggested Dagh's love story if I were an established journalist or a male writer?

'Daniyal is a great scholar of Rampur poetry, has knowledge of Rampur history and has this wonderful library. He would have been of great use to you.' Faraz shakes his head, negotiating the gullies with the impatient blaring of the car horn. His job is done, and he can report back about its failure to Baba.

There are four missed calls from Gul and where-are-you's on WhatsApp. I dial Gul to come up against a sorry-will-call-you-right-back message. *Are you ok?* I text. Everything for Gul is an emergency. Faraz had no calls. 'Calm down,' he says. 'It's probably nothing, or she would have called me.' The 'what ifs' silently convolute my brain; I try to breathe through the anxiety, suddenly drenched in sweat. I should never put my phone on silent. Faraz always feels I overreact where Gul is concerned. Poor Gul was suddenly bundled off to a med school on a Non-Resident Indian (NRI) quota. I don't know if she even wanted to become a doctor or was just influenced by Baba's desire to carry on the family legacy. It is a posh kind of med school with air-conditioned dorms, so at least she is comfortable. Gul has lived in Dubai since she was two. India was just a month of summer-monsoon holidays.

I call her again. *I'm okay, I'M OKAY!!* She message-yells. Probably in class, says Faraz. At this time? I'm relieved to be out of the clustered mohallas. I breathe. It's nothing. Mamma never, ever missed a call from me. She answered on the first ring as if waiting for me to call. Was it guilt or love, I shall never know. But she was right there even though I didn't need her.

I finally get to speak to Gul later in the evening. The hated anatomy professor had ridiculed her, she nearly broke down in class and was sick of cutting up dead men. The hostel food was lousy, she was surviving on McDonald's and was sure the numbers on the weighing scale were scaling up. Stop whining, I tell her, my mother's voice superimposing on mine. Gul is in this lovely, though dangerous, city. She should explore with her new friend, Rita. They could be touristy together and Insta the hell out of old Delhi monuments. She negotiates a late evening out. I tell her to call back when she returns and once again remind her of the imminent danger of getting raped. She had always lived in such a safe environment that she couldn't sense danger. At one point, I had even thought of shifting to Delhi till she found her Delhi legs, but she made friends and seemed to be revelling in the freedom of being away from close parental control. Faraz is sure she will go wild. I have other terrors.

I'd thought that I would miss Gul terribly. My life had been all about her since she was a premature baby, born about eight months after our marriage (more raised eyebrows and whispers). I even took up a job at her school to be close to her in case some disaster befell her there. Surprisingly, I find that I relish the mind space when I'm not obsessing about her physical safety. Mothering is done over one or two calls or a video call if Gul is in the mood. There is no empty-nest syndrome for me; I must be an unnatural mother. If she missed classes, we would get to know about it because the college belongs to Baba's Rampur friends. So I can focus on my work till Gul's college hours. After that, I try to squeeze in an evening Zoom call, which she detests. Above all, I want her to be honest with me. I had been terribly dishonest with my mother—running off with Faraz to romantic gardens and having long lunches in restaurants during college hours. Faraz says that we can invent any system, but Gul will lie and deceive. It is only natural for a teenager to misuse the sudden freedom. We can only hope she doesn't get into trouble. He means boy trouble, and I can only think of rape and murder. The subliminal fear that people are ready to jump her while she is walking, eating or sleeping in the hostel never leaves me.

I don't think my mother ever thought so much about me. She was a professor at Delhi University, and her teaching job was more real to her than my life. When I told her I wanted to marry Faraz, her only remark was that it was a strange choice to bury myself in a conservative Muslim town when life held so many possibilities. After my nikah—which she attended in a sleeveless, backless blouse and a large, black funereal bindi, causing everyone to gape at her and ignore me, the bride—she told me I would get bored and leave Faraz soon.

Daniyal, in deference to Baba's request and our visit, offers to take me to Raza Library to see the 'Rampur ke Shora' (Poets of Rampur) exhibition. I'm surprised. I had made it pretty evident that I didn't care at all for Urdu poetry. Maybe Daniyal wants to oblige Baba, and I decide to play on—it's amazing how often I do that. Faraz drops us at the library gates on his way to meet a mango vendor. Walking up the grand sweep of the library steps to the main building, the erstwhile durbar of the Nawabs, always uplifts me. We used to frequent Raza Library with our Delhi friends, who dropped in to gorge on Rampur kababs. Recently, I returned to research my article and had introduced myself to the crusty librarian as the daughter-in-law of Dr Musheer Khan.

Daniyal is waiting for me at the entrance. I almost didn't recognize him in his casual dark blue cotton shirt with white fish print splattered all over. We greet each other with a light touch of our respective foreheads, and I thank Daniyal for taking out time for me.

'Fish is the symbol of Rampur State,' he tells me, noting my appraisal of his outfit. Faraz says that I have a disconcerting habit of looking at people too intently.

I step into the library with a confident air, greet the librarian pointedly and exchange greetings with a research scholar who had helped me with my article. I barely glance at the Italian marble statues of goddesses and shepherdesses lining the gallery or gape at the exquisite stained-glass windows. I'm not a wonder-struck tourist—maybe an insider-outsider now.

The Durbar Hall is busy with local citizens peering into glass cases with exhibits and speaking in hushed, reverential whispers. The towering pillars with gold leaf capital and the sheer magnitude of the hall illuminated by sparkling hundred-bulb chandeliers have the effect of quietening the general chatter. An odd child cries or fusses and is comforted by the abaya-clad mother. Almost all the women are dressed in abayas and accompanied by male members of their families. They are humble citizens eager to relive their grand collective past.

Daniyal points at a facsimile of poet laureate Mirza Ghalib's corrections of Nawab Yusuf's poetry. I look at the remarks in the margins, very like our modern editing process. Despite my indifference towards poetry, I'm drawn into his whispered narrative of the poet's life after the devastation of 1857, his closeness to Nawab Yusuf Ali Khan and how Rampur supported him through years of deprivation and penury.

A life-size cutout of Dagh Dehlvi, an enlarged copy of the picture I saw the other day on the book cover, stands on the marble platform where the Nawab sat on his gold throne. The poet's gaze is even more piercing, a forbidding look, but for a strange mixture of pride and sensuousness. Daniyal informs me that the library has copies of Dagh's letters, especially the ones he wrote to his lady love, Munni Bai Hijab. We edge ourselves to look into a glass case where Dagh's handwritten letter to Hijab is on display. Daniyal reads out, his voice gravelly and soft in my ear.

> *'O cruel one,*
> *After our meeting, you stayed with Nawab (Haider) for two days. I cannot believe that you were constrained...'*

The yearning words and Daniyal's hushed tones give me goosebumps. I busy myself tracing my fingers on the glass case over the curving Urdu alphabets like a child phantom touching a delicious treat. As we walk out of the hall, Daniyal explains that Munni Bai Hijab was a tawaif from Calcutta, invited to perform at the Jashn e Benazir, the royal festival, by the Nawab's brother, Haider Ali Khan, in 1881.

'Dagh fell in love with Hijab immediately. Maybe Hijab reciprocated or played along like a tawaif.'

'In the letter, Dagh seemed to be very hurt, and he is sort of... shaming her for going to Haider,' I remark.

'Munni had to stay with Haider because he was her host and patron. But she met Dagh secretly and broke the tawaif code of honour in a way. It was a dangerous affair. Dagh, who worked for

Nawab Kalb e Ali Khan, could have lost his job, and Munni could have been imprisoned.'

We are out of the hall, the spell is broken, and we find our normal voices as we gaze at the rose garden in front of the library in the harsh, punishing sunlight. Daniyal has streaks of grey in his thick hair, which highlight the soft waves. I try to guess his age. He is definitely older than Faraz because he calls him Daniyal Bhai.

'Did tawaifs have affairs? I mean, I thought one paid for the services.'

Daniyal laughs. 'Tawaifs were human after all and probably did indulge in secret liaisons. Dagh was never her patron; one can say a mentor-cum-lover. You see, Munni Bai Hijab was an emerging poetess at that time; Hijab was her pen name, or takhallus, which she used in her ghazals. She was just nineteen and had published a diwan, a poetry collection.'

'Oh. Did she succeed as a poetess?'

'She became quite renowned in Calcutta for some time. However, she's mostly famous as Dagh's love. Some biographers even allege that Dagh wrote her ghazals.'

'How typical... even for women writers today if they get involved with great male authors. So did they get married? I mean, how did it end?'

'Apparently, their affair continued for nearly twenty years, documented in his passionate letters. I won't tell you how it ended. I mean, you can think about writing about it—if you want to, that is... I'm sorry, I do go on and on about this because it is so much a part of our forgotten history.'

'Any letters from Hijab?' I ask.

'Only one, it seems.'

The romantic liaison between a poet and a tawaif is hardly novel, yet something about Dagh's longing and the way he chides Hijab in his letter intrigues me. How did it work out between tawaifs and their lovers at that time? Did Hijab make a mark as a poetess in a male-dominated writing world—at least I presume it was male-dominated since most of the Urdu poets we have heard about were male. On our way out, I buy the slim volume of Dagh's letters, *Khutoot e Dagh*, from the library bookshop.

Munni Bai Hijab
(1881)

HIJAB, AT NINETEEN, YOU HAD ACHIEVED MORE THAN AN ordinary woman could aspire to—a beautiful tawaif, a published poetess, with a diwan to your name, you were perched on the precipice of fame. A new century was about to begin; the stories of mutiny against the angrez, the lived histories of the apocalyptic revolt of 1857 against British rule—vivid narratives by Apa, your mother, and Khala, your aunt—were all in the past now. The survivors, displaced and ravaged, had fashioned new ways to live out their lives. Company Raj, the rule of the East India Company, was over, and the rotund and remote British queen ruled from 'Englistaan'. The world, resurrected and new, lay at your feet. Even the esteemed tawaif, Malka Jan, noticed you and had invited you to her daughter Gauhar's birthday celebration at her grand Chitpur Road residence. Malka Jan, half-European, with her impossibly fair complexion coveted among Indian tawaifs, reigned over Calcutta with her words and music.

'Malka Jan is a half-breed, and her mother, a Hindu, had left the profession to become the bibi of a white man, only to return to it after he divorced and discarded her. I think Malka just wants to see the competition; be careful of her,' Apa had snorted. You were a khandani courtesan, shaped by generations of women honing their art, folding heritage into layers of their dupattas and the beat of their anklets. Blood, art and coquettish adas passed on from mother to daughter.

Malka Jan, once your neighbour in Colootola—though she didn't visit your family then—had bought a two-storied house in upmarket Chitpur Road for an exorbitant 40,000 rupees just three years after moving from Banaras with her little daughter, Gauhar. This move was a symbol of her newly minted grandeur, an attempt to rewrite herself. She had started learning the trade but lacked the maturity of ancient tawaifs. Apa was right—you could sense Malka Jan's tremulous jealousy flickering beneath her effusive compliments. She was just a few years older than you at twenty-five but, as Apa said, motherhood ages a woman by years. You and your sister called your mother Apa, elder sister, instead of Ammi—a custom in your community to evade the aging mantle of motherhood. Still, it was thrilling to be recognized by Malka Jan as competition. You complimented her in turn and told her that you had memorized all her ghazals.

'This is where I will live one day,' you told your sister, Hameedan, on your way back. Your Colootola house, overlooking the bustling bazaar, seemed diminished and insipid despite the carpets, mirrors and chandeliers acquired over the years. Apa had bought the house after years of struggle for survival and recognition in Calcutta. She was one of the many tawaifs displaced after the violent suppression of the rebellion in Awadh. Initially, she bought the first floor and set up her salon there. There were just three rooms around the hall, which she used for her soirées. A balcony with wrought iron railing overlooked the street below. Later, as the girls grew up, Apa bought the upper floor from an old tawaif, and you, with Hameedan, Apa and Khala, moved to that floor. The lower rooms were set up with ornate furniture and chandeliers to entertain clients. The Colootola area was known for Muslim tawaifs from Awadh and north India, and Apa was happy to be there because she could still hear Awadhi and Allahabadi dialect on the tongues of old tawaifs; but it was plebeian, almost vulgar compared to Chitpur with its grand colonial buildings. Malka Jan's house, nestled next to the Nakhuda Mosque, was a mere turn and a short walk from your house but a world away. You would find your way there soon, you decided.

An invitation from Haider Ali Khan to present your ghazal at the Benazir Mela, the spring festival held at the princely state of Rampur, arrived in answer to your ambitions. A renowned patron of art and music, Haider Ali Khan, the brother of Nawab Kalb e Ali Khan of Rampur, was enthralled by your kalaam and your reputed beauty and voice. Flattered and ecstatic, you accepted the invitation. Apa said travel was the path to refinement for tawaifs and well-travelled courtesans drew rich and discerning patrons.

The train journey from Howrah to Lucknow was your first experience of train travel. Apa, Khala, Hameedan and your brother, Khuda Bakhsh, travelled with you along with four accompanists. Khala's son, Shafeeq, had been entrusted to look after the kotha with Maulvi Sahib, your old Urdu tutor, and his wife. Large columns of nashteydaans clanked with the richness of kababs, qeema, be-pani ka gosht, khade masaley ka gosht, stacks of roghani tikiya and puris; steel canisters filled with water were hauled into the compartment along with tin suitcases and bedding rolls. Khala, the master cook of the family, had prepared all the dishes in ghee with barely any water so that the food would be preserved through the long travel. Khala and Apa knew the secret Awadhi recipe of be-pani ka gosht—preparing meat curry without a drop of water. 'Three parts curd, four parts meat and ghee, and not even a drop of water —remember this, girls. You won't get to eat it after I die,' Khala said, claiming that it would remain fresh for fifteen days in summers and two months in winters. She said the secret was preparing the meat using a lot of thick curd and ghee and cooking it on low heat for hours. You loved the thick, rich curry of be-pani ka gosht, the perfect balance of sharp spices, tangy curd and the light sweetness of fried onions. You never ate the tender meat pieces, just gorged on the curry with parathas. The dish was associated with picnics near the Hooghly and rare excursions to the hills. Apa always got food prepared in Awadhi style, which she said was the best cuisine in the world. She was dismissive of Bengali food, saying the Bengalis didn't know the fine art of cooking till Nawab Wajid Ali Shah came with his khansamas and educated them. Awadh lived in her heart as the culture capital of Hindustan.

'We are dereydaar tawaifs from Awadh. We departed to Calcutta after our Nawab Sahib left Awadh.' You had often heard the story of the perilous journey Apa and Khala had undertaken on a bullock cart, dressed in sarees, pretending to be simple village women, their petticoat hems heavy with gold pieces and precious stones. It was because of the patronage of Nawab Wajid Ali Shah that the tawaifs and the culture of Nawabi Awadh had survived after being transposed to Calcutta. Apa used to sing at Nawab Wajid Ali Shah's soirées at Metiaburj. Initially, they had taken up residence in Bow Bazar with tawaifs from Awadh, Kashi and other cities. Calcutta was now a hub of seasoned tawaifs. Malka Jan and Hingan Bai ruled over the hearts of the bhadralok—the English-speaking elitist social class of Calcutta—and the Muslim princely classes.

Apa couldn't sleep with the racket and the jostling of the train, and it was with relief that she alighted at Lucknow after a twenty-six-hour journey. It was your first visit to Awadh, and Apa wanted to introduce you to everyone. You stayed at Apa's cousin, Jwahar Bai's house in Chowk Bazar for a week—a blur of visits to Apa's old friends and relatives, shared stories and tears. Apa showed you the kotha she lived in before the 1857 ghadar. After tearful farewells and sighs—Apa was sure she would never see her loved ones again—your entourage set off to Bareilly, a shorter six-hour railway journey.

'My ears have just stopped ringing from the vile chuk-chuk of the train, and you are taking me to that iron prison again,' Apa grumbled as the company settled down in the compartment with a replenished stock of food prepared by Jwahar Bai.

You were received at Bareilly station by Nawab Haider Ali Khan's musahibs and Rampur guards, who escorted the party in a phaeton to Rampur—a five-hour journey. It was a pleasant March, and the mango trees along the road were daubed with light lemon blossoms.

Shujaat Khan, a musahib, chatted incessantly about the grand palaces of Rampur and the preparations going on for the Benazir Mela to the enthralled girls. Hameedan giggled at something Shujaat said, and Apa told him, 'Hai, hai, beta, can you be quiet? My head is fit to burst with pain.' It was obvious to the old tawaif that the young man was a hanger-on—musahibs were paid companions and sycophants anyway—and was trying to ensnare the sixteen-year-old Hameedan. He could barely afford to sit in a mehfil.

You felt yourself dissolving and floating in the vast opulence of the mahals and gardens of Rampur. Haider Ali, a knowledgeable musician and a true connoisseur of your beauty and talent, hosted night-long mehfils in your honour. It seemed that all of Hindustan waited breathlessly for the Jashn e Benazir at Benazir, the summer palace of Nawab Kalb e Ali Khan, which drew singers, dancers, poets and guests from all over north India.

On the day of your debut at the first mehfil of Jashn e Benazir, you felt flamboyant in your peacock blue farshi pyjama and yellow short blouse, which exposed a slice of your waist, half hidden by a heavily embroidered gold tissue dupatta. You explored the bustling shops set up in the mango orchard around the Benazir Palace with Hameedan. The only women visible at the fair—set up inside the palace walls and along the road leading to the palace—were the tawaifs, randis and common women going about their menial tasks. The noble women, the begums, were sequestered away from the fun in the Badr e Muneer Palace inside the Benazir orchards, guarded by a mini army. You were far above the common randis in garish tinsel dresses with their untrained voices and titillating songs, ready to lie with anyone for a few takas.

Hameedan plucked some light green, still unripe jujubes as you held the thorny branches. You left the branches, and they swung up; Hameedan offered you some jujubes, but you refused.

'Let's go inside. My throat will suffer from the dust here.' Apa said train travel had thickened your voice; she made you drink a herbal concoction for your throat every morning.

'There is barely any dust, Aapi. Look at that male tawaif. I've heard about him. He is Ali Jan.'

You had never seen a male tawaif and stood giggling at Ali Jan's dance moves.

'Appi, Aapi, Dagh Dehlvi! He is looking at you,' Hameedan whispered.

It was unmistakably the famous poet. You had seen a picture of him. You became acutely aware of the searing gaze, of the light breeze blowing tendrils of hair on your face. You stopped giggling, adjusted your dupatta and pretended to look in the opposite direction, giving your profile view. Later, you would see yourself anew on that day in Dagh's masnavi composition, the *Faryād e Dāgh*, in which Dagh called you 'pari shumail'—a luminous fairy—and declared that he had fallen in love with you at that moment.

Nawab Kalb e Ali Khan inaugurated the first soirée with a performance by Hingan Bai. The hall still reverberated with her impeccable notes as you took your place at the centre and sang a thumri, '*Piya bin nahin aavat mai ko chain*' (I'm not at peace without my beloved), and a Holi song. Haider Ali requested you to sing your own ghazal. 'How can I dare to sing my ghazal before such renowned poets?' You touched your forehead and looked at Dagh, but Nawab Kalb e Ali Khan insisted that you must sing your new ghazal. You bent in salam, accepting his wish and sang:

Dil bahut bechain be-ārām hai
Kya muḥabbat kā yahī anjām hai

The heart is restless and fraught,
Is this the consequence of love.

The audience applauded your words with effusive 'waah-waahs' and called for an encore of the last lines. Dagh, seated next to the Nawab, seemed to be stilled by your performance. Nawab Kalb e Ali Khan turned towards Dagh as if to ask his opinion. Unlike his father, Nawab Yusuf Ali Khan, Kalb e Ali wasn't inclined towards poetry. He enjoyed writing nasr (prose) and listened to dastans, though he continued to support the highly recognized poets of the day. You watched as Dagh inclined his head, considering. Khuda Bakhsh, standing behind him, would later repeat Dagh's words: 'She is young, too young. Poetry demands blood and tears from several heartbreaks.'

You felt the weight of his judgement—a poet's wisdom layered with longing and regret. What did the great Dagh know of your heart's suffering. You had been warned never to fall in love, but sometimes, love's play became too real; every patron left a mark, tearing away a part of you.

To Hameedan, Dagh delivered his damning opinion, *'Unsey keh do ke mashooq ko bālā-e-tāq rakhein aur khud mashooq ban jayein.'* (Tell her to set aside her lover and become the lover.)

You were a guest at Haider Ali's haveli. For now, he had all the rights over your body and your voice—your patron in an endless line of highest bidders.

Become the lover.

Faryād e Dāgh (Dāgh's Entreaty)

Dekh kar us parī shamā'il ko
Reh gayā thā thām ke dil ko
Dil ko main dhūndhtā rahā na milā
Ānkh miltey phir patā na milā
Rang chehre se uḍ gayā kosoñ
Dil se maiñ mujh se dil judā kosoñ
Ābru kā lihāz o pās kisey
Hosh meiñ āoñ ye hawās kise
Yār o gham ḳhwar mūnis o humdum
Keh rahe the tujhey ḳhudā kī qasam
Dāgh tu mājra bayān to kar!
Tujh ko kyā ho gayā tu bayān to kar

When I saw the beauteous fairy,
My heart left my body entwined with hers,
Lost to me as our eyes met
I paled, unmindful of the mores of worldly life,
And struggled to regain my consciousness.
My friends and well-wishers kept asking me
What has happened to you, o Dagh
What has occurred to make you thus?

—Dagh Dehlvi (1882)

تبدیلی

3

Tabdīlī (Change)

WE WERE LOVERS—GENTLY AT FIRST, WITH GROWING PASSION, and then reverently as parental opposition coalesced us into a stubborn unit. Mamma, after her initial protests, was resigned, though she continued to barb me with constant harsh, bitter words. It was Baba who refused to budge for several years, hoping that we would break off when we completed college and became busy with our careers. I was secretly surprised at Faraz's tenacity. Maybe we had slipped into a habit of being together whenever we could. I don't think I had set out with marriage in mind. Rebellion, maybe.

Mamma's backless, sleeveless blouse and her page-boy haircut—she decided to cut off her longish hair for the wedding—haunted me for days after our marriage. Did she have to put so much of her flesh and bone on display and crown it all with a big, black gunshot wound of a bindi. She had decorously put the end of her saree on her head for the nikah and flung it away afterwards with a faintly amused, touristy expression. I could sense the darkness of her armpits, dreading the moment she would raise an arm, revealing the harsh, unshaven stubble with a wave of sweat and talcum smells. There was something defiant about her that day, as if she was daring people to question her. She was rewarded by curious looks and whispers. It was all for me—she wanted me to be focused on her throughout the event. I was on edge with a mixture of anxiety at what she might say or do and an unaccustomed protectiveness. I wouldn't put it above the women of the family to ask her to cover up. I was thankful when it all ended without any unseemly incident.

'Just sprinkle your sentences with lots of inshallahs and masallahs, and you're good,' Mamma advised me after our nikah. Her voice had carried a weary dismissal and the sense that she was seeing me go towards my doom; I don't think she cared too much about that, anyway. I decided to inhabit my new life more fully by learning to read the beautiful curling Arabic script of the Quran with incomprehensible sounds and even memorized the prayers. I loved reading Urdu, rolling the softness of the sounds on my tongue, so familiar and yet so refined—the 'sh', 'za' and 'kh' sounds coming up unexpectedly between words I had grown up with. I practised the words and the intonations and threw them at Mamma—it was shalwar not salwar, qeema not keema. I read some Urdu poetry back then, asking my tutor for the deeper meaning of couplets—it was in this new, timeless world that I wanted to reimagine myself. I dressed in shalwar suits and wore long-sleeved blouses over sarees, revelling in the newness of Rukhsar, my nikah name, which also conveniently shortened to my nickname, Kuku. Mamma said it was just a sham name, a show staged for the benefit of barely fooled relatives and Rampuri society. I was silly to take it seriously. For me, it was the final severing of the ghostly, strangulating umbilical cord. Faraz had asked me if I wished to continue with Rukmini Mathur or go for double-barrelled Rukmini Mathur–Khan. I wanted to slash it all out, but becoming Rukhsar Khan would require some legalities and a change of passport, so ultimately, I settled into being Rukmini Khan, which inspires barely concealed, surprised curiosity even after eighteen years. There is a moment when they wonder, questions brimming on their lips—how it felt to dwell in the twin worlds of the segments of my name. Actually, I didn't feel like a Rukhsar. Baba calls me Rukmini because he loves the mythology around the name—the faithful, loving wife.

I made a point of saying my namaz when Mamma visited. She would look at me with a pitying, exasperated look she had reserved for me during my rebellious teenage years. 'I won't study sciences' and 'I will marry Faraz' had been met with 'couldn't care less', 'go ahead', and then, prophecies of doom. The look played over and over during those brief, uninvited visits propelled me deeper into the Muslim world. She wanted me to feel the full weight of my choice.

Faraz was impressed by my zeal in learning prayers and reading the Quran, and so was Baba. They had not expected me to press on with the 'conversion' after the obligatory recitation of the Arabic kalima. Baba's fierce objection to the marriage, more cultural than religious, had transformed into a clannish protectiveness—I was now his bahu, his izzat. In his particular Baba-way, he welcomed me into the family with his open-hearted love and warmth. At best, I was expected to follow the socially accepted norms when in Rampur. Baba defined himself as a cultural Muslim, going occasionally for Friday prayers and the twice-a-year Eid prayers. He said it ensured that he would get a decent funeral prayer and be buried next to his wife. Apparently, if a person was never seen praying, the community might not recite his funeral prayers. Faraz had laughed and said that he had earned his Jannat by converting a kafir (non-believer). Yes, I was converted from being a casual agnostic to opening myself to occasional prayer. I would prostrate before a faceless god and sometimes be drawn towards ringing the bells of the temple to stand before my smiling Krishna. In Dubai, I had slipped between both worlds, each offering an unburdening and a surrender in a profound silence. In Rampur, I kept my Krishna in my bedroom—hidden away, yet ever-present.

During those early Rampur years, I was enthralled by my new life, insulated from all the noise in Rukmini Mathur's world. Mamma had once remarked that I had shed my skin like a snake. Yes, I had deliberately scoured off my outer shell and emerged new and shiny, my scales gleaming, my skin hypersensitive to everything around me. I had expunged all parts of me that were like her.

I visit the Raza Library with my dupatta swaddling my head loosely—a shield and an identifier that still feels strange. I'm the car-driving, Dubai-returned, Hindu-convert daughter-in-law of Dr Musheer Khan. The novelty and whispers wear off, and they get used to me pottering around. A junior librarian helpfully teaches me the categorization of books—tazkira for biographies, tabbakhi about food and so on—it's the strangest categorization, penned diligently in volumes of catalogues. There is an alphabetically ordered catalogue as well that I can search in library card cabinets or on the website, but all the titles have not been uploaded there. One can find a book catalogued in the traditional, as well as the colonial style, like two ways of being. There are still collections that have not been catalogued. Baba said that when the Rohilla Pathans under Nawab Faizullah Khan established the new city of Rampur in 1774, the first two public spaces they constructed were a mosque and a library. They came with their collection of books loaded (I presume) on horse carts and settled here; each successive ruler sent officials to different countries and parts of India to buy manuscripts and books to enrich the collection. They rescued hundreds of books from being burnt by the British after the Revolt of 1857. I feel swamped in the taxonomy of thoughts and lives, suspended in eras stretching back hundreds of years.

They allow me to sit and read in the scholar's section because of Baba. It is a sitting room next to the durbar hall, with hand-painted light green wallpaper, faded at places, a carved wood fireplace and plaster of Paris mouldings on the ceiling. Modern desks and chairs and glass-front steel almirahs bearing publications and catalogues line the walls, professing their indifference to the colonial decor. A ten-foot-high door leads out to the veranda, which runs around the structure. It used to look out at the gardens. They have cemented the side gardens to prevent seepage of water into the basements, and the veranda arches have been sealed with wrought iron grill to keep out the monkeys. I watch the shadows of iron lattice patterns across the marble floor elongate with the passage of the day. I think of the life of Raza Library as a grand durbar, the Nawab taking his seat on the throne, the people with their petitions and the British officers bowing not low enough. There is a balcony that runs on three sides above the hall where the women sat behind curtains, a view of the world through a veil; they looked down at the coronations, births, deaths—events which they had no control over. Their vision of the world outside the zenana was through a hazy purdah, in front of their eyes, tied to the windows of carriages, cars; the only thing in sharp focus was their life inside the zenana portions of their houses. They were unseen and unheard outside. Some survived in oral histories, even fewer were mentioned in passing in the written histories if they had birthed a royal child.

A chamber further inside the scholar's room is the manuscript room, where enclosed in the walls of steel and glass almirahs sits the chief librarian, commanding obeisance, which I slavishly offer—a salam, some minutes of light chit-chat, evoking gruff replies. He is the gateway to all manuscripts, I have been told by the young librarian who aspires somewhat hopelessly to the seat. The latter is still on probation after ten years of service; he is still kind and attentive. The position of the library director lies vacant after a dispute between the board members. The district magistrate is officiating as an ad hoc director, and the library ambles on with set patterns, hosting events and exhibitions covered by the local papers. Someday, the Ministry of Culture, under which the library is allowed to exist, will send a politically approved director, and things will become officious, lax or worse.

I had read volumes in Hindi on Rampur history and culture, which were published by the library. I now attempt to read about the Rampur school of Urdu poetry—the literary movement at the time of Nawab Kalb e Ali Khan—and about Dagh. Daniyal had dropped a brief, to-the-point email suggesting titles on Rampur's cultural history. Most publications and collections are in Urdu, and I have lost the ability to read it coherently. The script has no emphasis and sounds, just alphabets strung together, and you must know the vocabulary to read. There are so many unfamiliar words, which I try to vocalize and look up in Rekhta dictionary.

I confess to the young librarian that my Urdu is scanty. His gaze is gentle and forgiving—he didn't expect me to be familiar with the script—and helps me whenever he can by reading out research articles from the library journals. I thank him and ask him to suggest a tutor. He offers to come over on Fridays, his weekly holiday, for two hours. He tells me his wife consults Baba and he wishes to help me. I jump at the offer. He will help me stitch the words together into meaning and decode Dagh's poetry.

Munni Bai Hijab

(April 1881)

Kabhī sher o suḳhan kā charcha thā
Kabhi apney watan kā charcha thā
Rāt kaṭ-ti hañsī ḳhushi kyā kyā
Hotī rahtī khili dili kyā kyā
Ḳhāna-e dost 'aish-e ḳhāna thā
hā'e kyā din they kyā zamāna thā

At times she spoke of poetry and the arts,
At times of her motherland;
Such talks were close to her heart.
We spent nights in happiness and joy
My friend's house was our pleasure palace.
O such wondrous days and time.

—Dagh Dehlvi
Faryād e Dāgh (1882)

Dagh wrote to you, insisting you spend an evening with him. You refused, of course. You were bound to Nawab Haider during your stay in Rampur—his guest, his momentary muse and a temporary mistress. Nawab Haider was a renowned musician in his own right and a generous patron. The nights were long with performances and mehfils, sometimes ending in Haider's bed. You were elated by the adulation.

Thoughts of Dagh lingered in your mind even as you played your part in the musical soirées. Dagh Dehlvi, the greatest poet of the time, had declared your poetry too shallow. Does he want what all the men want from you—your voice and beauty to titillate and excite his imagination? Another letter arrived, bursting with compliments and insistence. 'Meet me just once at Khan Sahib's house; it's safe.' The immediacy of Dagh's yearning touched something in you. You know he could master words to create an illusion, but your curiosity and heady excitement bent you to his request. Hameedan and Khuda Bakhsh agreed to accompany you. Bundling into burqas, Hameedan and you slipped out unnoticed with Khuda Bakhsh and rode Khan Sahib's carriage to his house. It was the last part of the night, and you had just returned from Haider Sahib's mehfil. Apa and Khala had gone off to sleep. Your thrill was tempered with fear. If Haider Ali came to know of this meeting, he would create hell for Dagh and you. Hameedan asked if they would throw you in prison. This was a princely state; the laws were slaves to the whims of rulers. In Calcutta and British-ruled India, you could at least appeal for justice. Sometimes, a form of justice was granted. Apa would be livid. Your reputation as a tawaif would be destroyed forever. Maybe you were reckless to be pulled into this game. Just this once, you promised yourself.

Dagh was waiting for you in the guest room, his presence dignified yet gentle. His royal blood showed in his bearing, in the loose, languid grace of someone who has known power and loss. Yet there was such humility and kindness in his eyes that strangers would find familiarity and acceptance. You bent low in salam.

'If you were just a beautiful face with a lovely voice, I would have been besotted, but you are sukhan faham—understand art and poetry. Mirza Dagh is ready to declare his slavehood for you.' He laid out his words with a weight that felt real.

'Dagh Sahib, I thought you despised my poetry.' You smiled, softening the accusation and sat down facing him on the takht.

'My objection was that you haven't loved enough.'

'I'm a tawaif; loving well is a part of my repertoire.'

'Love as a deeply felt need, love in the form of eternal, spiritual love—ishq—is what I'm speaking of.'

'And you, Dagh Sahib? Have you been fortunate enough to experience this divine ishq?' You leaned back on the bolsters, cradling your face in your hand, the familiar notes of playful flirtation ringing your words. You knew the stages of love, the sufi ishq, from your lessons in Urdu shayari, and could recite them in your sleep—dilkashi (attraction), uns (attachment), ishq (love), aqidat (respect), ibadat (reverence), junoon (madness) and the inevitable maut (death). You had always managed to step back at the first realization of ishq.

'I'm an ashiq, a lover by nature, and I have loved several times.' His voice drifted to a soft cadence. 'My ishq is reflected in my poetry.'

'Your couplets penetrate my heart and live on the tongues of people. May I dare to sing your ghazal?'

'I want to listen to your words, not mine.'

You sang your ghazals for Dagh that night in a manner that felt like you were revealing a part of yourself which you rarely did. He praised some, frowned over others and held back his comments; at your request, he agreed to give islaah—suggestions to improve your poetry.

'At least till you are here, send your writing, and I will suggest corrections.'

Balancing meters and emotions within the boundaries of a ghazal was his expertise, and he was always generous in helping poets improve their art. A perfect couplet, whether it came from his pen or through others, was a great joy to him. You would come to know this essential grain of his persona through years of your association with Dagh; for now you were touched by his gift.

It was early morning when you returned. You changed into your night clothes and sat bent over the low table, scribbling, feverish with the desire to complete your new ghazal. Dagh's words echoed in your ears. 'I have played ishq-bazi, the game of love, several times, but when I look at you, Hijab, I feel uns for you—the stage of love that draws further into deep, spiritual ishq. I'm standing on the brink of ishq, which can only lead to junoon—a madness and death. These are the stages of love described by Sufi saints, Hijab; it's my inevitable fate that I will traverse them with you.' The candour of his words shook you to your core with an intimacy that went beyond mere seduction and the coupling of bodies. His eyes had sparkled with a mischievous glint, a warm acceptance, which seemed to say, 'I know *you*,' an understanding which, you felt, wouldn't shrink from your reality. Apa, finding you with your notebooks, asked you to rest and prepare yourself for the next mehfil that very night.

You, too, were adept at ishq-bazi, mastered for your art and survival. How could you be sure that he was not playing with you? He wrote to you every day—passionate and jealous letters—pulling you closer, convincing you that his devotion was genuine and not a fleeting infatuation. Flattered that this great poet loved you and was obsessed by you, you met him several times. His words and gestures revealed a fragile vulnerability and convinced you that your absence would devastate him, or so he made you believe. You had never experienced such devotion from a lover. Your time together was unmarked with demands, no obligations weighed on you; unlike Haider and other patrons, Dagh did not stake a claim on you. It was enough for him to be in your company, feeding on the few hours you could spare for him. He didn't ask for sexual favours; your relationship was never of a patron and courtesan. Lovemaking unfolded naturally and tenderly, a hesitant cadence of poetry growing between you, an expression, though not a vital part of the whole. He looked at you not as a tawaif but as a human being with wants and desires; you felt seen, not merely desired. Sometimes, you were beset with doubts. He would forget you when you left Rampur and fall in love with another tawaif and carry on his continuous search for a muse to pull his words together in heartfelt compositions.

Rampur was a small riyasat, and it was impossible to maintain this secret, precarious balance. At a private soirée at his palace, Haider Ali asserted his right over you in the most public manner. In the middle of your performance, he gripped your arm, pulling you towards him and forcing you to sit on his lap, his hold possessive and painful. You feigned a giggle, masking your anger, and got up, seething inside. How dare he treat you so brazenly, like a common prostitute? He wanted to put you in your place—a bought object. It had taken great self-control to continue your performance. That night, Haider's cruelty was punishing, stripping away your dignity; you had to beg him to be gentle. In Calcutta, you had started making independent decisions on where and when to sing and whom to bed. Apa would advise you, chide you for turning down a good offer and guard you, getting boisterous members in the audience escorted out. Here, you felt vulnerable, the entrapment gnawing at your spirit. After Haider's abominable behaviour, and probably licensed by it, his friends became bolder and lewder in their comments. Your joy at being appreciated turned to humiliation. Dagh's devotion and love was a salve to your wounded ego, even though you kept the ugliness away from him.

When Dagh came to know of the incident, or a version of it, he wrote a tortured letter, his blunt scorn slicing through you.

Oh unfaithful, feckless one,

Yesterday I sustained a deep injury. A gentleman spoke of your behaviour at the mehfil. How long will this state of affairs continue? How long can I listen to such talk? My heart is filled with deep, incurable wounds. I have lived through too many painful days and evenings when I know you are with him.

Tell me, has your lust increased or decreased? A man would be stone-hearted to not feel anything when he watches such a spectacle. There is no doubt in my mind that you have cavorted with villains like Yazid and the son of Nameer. My blood is boiling! Do you like being pawed and ravished by such people? What will be the outcome of all this? If you revel in such nights and days, then farewell. I will curb my burning heart and banish your name from my lips. There is a limit to shamelessness!

So this was how it would end. The ugliness of your life would destroy the self-confessed ishq of the great poet. He found you cheap and brazen. You thought he, of all people, would understand. His mother and aunt were tawaifs too, navigating life's hardships as best as they could. You had heard the story of his mother, Wazir Khanam, the most beauteous tawaif of her time, the widow of an Englishman, who married Nawab Shams Ali Khan of Faridabad Jhirka. The Nawab was hanged by the British for the infamous murder of William Fraser, a high-ranking British officer, who also coveted Wazir Khanam. Orphaned at four, Dagh had come to live in Rampur with his mother, where his aunt was a concubine of Nawab Yusuf Ali Khan. He returned to Delhi when Wazir married Mirza Fakhru, a son of Emperor Bahadur Shah Zafar. In those twilight years of the Mughal Empire, Dagh found tutelage and recognition. He was tutored in Persian and Urdu poetry, honed his art and presented his ghazals at poetic mehfils with the most well-known poets of the time at the Mughal court. Mirza Fakhru's death and Wazir Khanam's expulsion from the Mughal harem had set Dagh adrift again. Life for Dagh was marked by scandals, cruelty and loss. You thought he would understand.

The days that followed were a blur of hurt, anger and reconciliations. In the nearly two months of your Rampur sojourn, your bond with Dagh bloomed and frayed—the full breadth of a real relationship condensed into a few days. He was not your patron paying for your favours and wiles. You were always hot-tempered, only unleashing your fury on those close to you. With Dagh, you were always yourself, revealing the quicksilver of your moods, your fiery rage, your ego, your wounds and your tenderness—all the facets of yourself that you rarely laid bare to anyone. He showed his vulnerability, and his generosity of spirit enveloped you.

Apa came to know about the secret meetings because of Khuda Bakhsh's careless, perhaps deliberate, remark. Furious, she lashed out at you—a khandani tawaif didn't betray the patron like this. If people came to know about this in Calcutta, you wouldn't find good patrons and they would all starve; her warnings had an edge of desperation. You were always wilful. If Khala hadn't stopped her, she was ready to go back to Calcutta. She stopped eating with you or even talking to you. Khala, ever the mediator shielding you from Apa's wrath, gently reminded you that attachment and love could not enter a tawaif's life. Every tawaif looked for stability, a long-standing, generous patron who gave her a semblance of marriage and supported her family. She could perform at curated soirées, but it was an article of faith that she would only have sexual relations with her patron. There were many cases of Bengali tawaifs who had been killed or abandoned by jealous patrons. Apa had made numerous sacrifices to set you and Hameedan up as leading tawaifs and now was the time to reap the gains.

You courted danger, defied Apa and found yourself drawn to Dagh again and again, sharing with him stories from your life, the brutal edges of your world, your dreams and the fragile beginnings of your ghazals. Dagh was the most famous proponent of the Delhi school of poetry, and his style inspired the Rampur school of poetry. Together, you discussed styles of poetry as Dagh gently corrected your verses, guiding you away from the use of the ornate, idiomatic language, a hallmark of the Awadh school, and demonstrated the elegance of simplicity. He wanted you to reach deeper, express more honestly, to uncover something within you that you couldn't yet see. Your critics would later allege that Dagh had written your ghazals. You and your poetry would always be defined by those days with Dagh.

He also spoke to you of matters close to his heart, especially his poetic rivalry at the Rampur court with the famous Awadh poet Ameer Minai—the face-off of the Delhi poetic style pitted against the Awadh style. Theirs was a strange bond of love and rivalry. Dagh said that he loved Ameer Minai immensely, and if the latter fell ill, he would immediately go to visit him. If Ameer ever needed anything, he would turn to Dagh. Later, Dagh would live up to this trust by finding a place for Ameer at Nizam of Hyderabad's court when Ameer was in dire straits. That was Dagh—generous, loving, proud and competitive.

Dagh became distracted as the time for your departure drew near. He begged you to leave Calcutta and stay in Rampur. You could achieve fame and be near him. But Calcutta was your watan, your homeland; it was called *Fakhr e Hindustan*, the pride of Hindustan. Rampur could never aspire to the greatness of Calcutta. Your Apa had struggled to make a place for you and Hameedan in Calcutta. You had the spirited fire and talent; it mattered to you to make a name for yourself there and challenge the greatest tawaifs of the time with your voice and your poetry. You had been writing poetry since the age of five, had taken corrections from the famous litterateur of the time. Your life had just begun, and everything was leading towards a great career. Everyone said so. Dagh's humility and love had touched you. You felt certain that you could say or do anything and he would still be there for you. At least in that timeless period, in that borrowed house, you made promises to write to him and laid plans to come back to Rampur even though Rampur made you claustrophobic. You assured Dagh that you would return to Rampur for him and bade a tearful farewell.

اختلاف

4

Ikhtilāf (Conflict)

'WHAT'S SO GREAT ABOUT AN OLD POET AND A TAWAIF? NOT love—only lust meeting greed.' Faraz grumbles, seeing me bent over the volume of Dagh's letters on the dining table, which has now become my morning work desk. I know Faraz is struggling with his venture and try to ignore his remark. But I do feel a surge of guilt—he needs me, and I haven't been giving him time.

One of the reasons I had joined the school was to escape Faraz's moods. He can be volatile: have a fit of rage one moment, be calm the next. My days are being coloured by his moods again, lingering over me like a bad hangover. It disrupts my writing—the early sparks of it, anyway.

Of the three of us, Faraz found it easiest to settle back in Rampur. He began working on a new business plan to supply the city's famous Langra mangoes to international markets. Rampur is a mango-growing belt; the orchards hug the city like a half-moon. Mango trading seemed the most obvious business choice, especially because we have mango orchards. But Baba scoffed at the idea. In Rampur, mango orchards were leased to the thekedaars for the season, and they supply mangoes to Delhi's mandis. Breaking the system is nearly impossible and highly risky. After several discussions, Baba relented, allowing Faraz to handle our fifty-acre mango orchard for the season—the least expensive experiment—though it meant risking the sizable yearly income Baba got from the thekedaar. The mango season is nearly over now and so are his plans to make it big as a mango exporter. After a twisting path of several setbacks, we had ended with tons of rotten mangoes even after we had sent half of Rampur cartons full of Langras. I love mangoes, but I couldn't eat more than six Langras—that is more than two kgs! I didn't dare glance at the weighing machine out of respect for the mango season. Baba had cautioned me that menopause means weight gain as the hormones danced their way out. I will sort it out later. Faraz didn't touch the Langras even though he loved to eat them earlier.

Meezan Bhai prepares aam pulao with layers of mango pieces in sweet rice. The mango juice seeped into the rice layers, dying it ochre. He tells me it's an old recipe from my mother-in-law who used to prepare the pulao during season. I've had zarda and safeda sweet pulaos at weddings in Rampur. I'm not a fan of sweet rice dishes but the fruity zest of the mango is refreshing. Meezan Bhai says that they used to cook seb (apple) pulao and ananas (pineapple) pulao in a similar way. I put in a reminder to get those cooked, too, someday.

A rotting mango stench of failure filters into the corners of the house even though I had kept the mangoes in the old kitchen block outside the house to ripen in a paal. Akhtar Bai taught me to lay the paal with layers of newspapers cocooning the unripe mangoes. Every day, I go to check on them but the rot has set in and the sweeper throws away bucketfuls in the garbage.

Baba used to give us our share from the orchard lease. This year, since we didn't get our usual yearly income, we had to dip into our savings—what little we had left after our Dubai fiasco. It also meant that Baba had to depend on the earnings from the clinic, which I know couldn't be much because he barely charges his patients as most of them are from humble backgrounds. Faraz remains optimistic for the next season, determined to invest more of our savings into the project, which seems to be expanding in inverse proportion to failures. We are not hand to mouth, but the pinch has become a constant itch. The annual income from the orchard would have really eased things.

Faraz tells Baba that we are down a few lakhs and he needs to continue the venture for another mango season to make up the loss. Technically, it's Baba's orchard, inherited from his father. Baba explodes—ballistic at the failure, at being robbed of the steady income and at Faraz's insistence on carrying on with his business scheme. The I-told-you-so's and Baba's intense disappointment in his only son bursts out in a massive showdown.

'You won't succeed, ever. I can give it in writing. You-are-a-failure! It's better now to become a dependent on your old father and wait for your daughter to get a degree and support you,' Baba sneers. I can see the hurt in Faraz's eyes. I think every son needs appreciation from his father—a basic, sometimes unrecognized need.

Faraz shattered all Baba's dreams. Baba hopes to salvage the family medical tradition through Gul. I want to pull away from the father-son clash but watch, frozen in stupefaction. Meezan Bhai is listening in as usual, while Jumbo goes into a barking frenzy, adding to the confusion. I try to lead Baba and Faraz into the bedroom to argue privately, but they shrug me off, too busy hurling unforgivable words at each other. Baba's face is flushed so red that I fear he will collapse; his massive stomach jiggles with rage. Jumbo goes berserk, barking, and climbs over Faraz, who takes his paws and flings him away, infuriating Baba even more. I offer Jumbo a biscuit to coax him away, but he's now a part of the melée snorting, circling back and barking.

Baba is in no mood to allow Faraz another disastrous year. I don't blame him, considering the recent Dubai debacle, but expecting Faraz to make a profit in the first season is unfair. I'm torn. Suddenly, Baba turns to me with a 'tell me if I'm wrong'. I have this terrifying ability to hover between two diametrically opposite arguments even while speaking. I listen to myself fumbling, teetering between both sides, feeling powerful for a second with their attention, and then decide to hedge the question. Faraz glares at me, furious at my disloyalty.

Finally, Baba storms out, leaving Faraz seething. I try to sit with him in solidarity.

'Of course, you couldn't be successful in the first season. Listen, if Baba doesn't want you to continue, maybe we can explore Delhi for opportunities. Gul can also stay with us…'

'Just stop talking!' Faraz yells and walks off to the bedroom.

I should have left him alone, but then he'd complain that I was too preoccupied with my work to even bother about him. I feel colonized by his emotional needs.

I need a hard-hitting and practical Akriti talk. I call her and regurgitate everything. I can almost see her pursing her lips, holding back her remarks, planning their slow release.

'Kuku, you need to meet people and socialize. You are too lonely, and all this is pulling you down.'

'And you are a social butterfly? You barely come to the main city or even visit me.'

Akriti lives in Benazir Farms on the city's outskirts, and Faraz won't let me drive out there all alone. She has her plate full, so I can't expect her to rush over. She often says that she had consented to get married in Rampur to be near me and then I had abandoned her for Dubai. I feel terrible for not being a part of her journey, especially her struggles with Shubham, her son, though we did keep in touch intermittently.

'Okay, so both of us have a lot going on, but we need to chill sometimes.'

Akriti knows that I don't like socializing, but once I do, I flower in company. I have almost become a recluse, which is great for my writing, but I tend to get emotionally bogged down, like today. Akriti sets to work, sorting out my thoughts, putting things in their places and dusting out dark corners. I breathe.

'You need people to discuss books and share ideas. Maybe we can start a reading group or a book club?' she thinks out loud.

Do we even have a reading community in Rampur? Rampur used to be a renowned literary space till the 1950s. There are definitely no book clubs or reading groups here. Mushairas are often held during the yearly 'Numaish' Exhibition and at Raza Library. Once, right after we returned, I attended a literary gathering at the library to honour an old short story writer, Fakhrunnisa Begum, with a *Nishan e Imtiaz* award. All her works were in Urdu and published by the library. I watched the wizened old lady read out her story in a quavering voice. Nearly all of the audience was senior citizens; young people can barely read Urdu now, the librarian told me apologetically. I could follow the story because it was in simple language. The Urdu script is dying, but the language is surviving and becoming more simplified.

There are no bookstores in Rampur, only stationary shops with some odd English classics displayed in glass shelves, their covers faded over years of exposure to corroding sunlight. I had once bought a Jane Austen title to support them. I usually order books on Amazon or download them on Kindle; I miss browsing through bookshops. Maybe a book club, even if it is for a handful of English language readers, is a good, even a radical idea.

Akriti forwards an online guide to book clubs and promises to come by for all meetings—it is already a reality in our heads, and we keep discussing it over calls. We set a tentative date and try to think of potential members.

'We will start a book club even if it is just the two of us,' Akriti declares. Thank god for dear Akriti. We've been friends since school, and when I decided to marry Faraz, she said she would marry a Rampuri, too—and she did.

Faraz often calls me impulsive, impractical and impatient—he throws all the damning 'ims' at me—maybe I am, and why not. The book club is a great idea. It might help him, too, though he is not a regular reader, but he needs to get out of the echo chamber of those blessed mango vendors. Besides, he loves entertaining. We used to host some fabulous parties in Dubai when the going was good. It's painful to watch Faraz slump into failure again. I let him cool off for a few days, which essentially means following the old rhythms of living without talking much. I know he will come back with some optimistic, grand or impractical plan. I secretly feel that it's good that Baba is around to temper him down, even though it means almost irreconcilable fights, with emotions all over the place—a very Rampuri Pathan thing. Despite exchanging fire from time to time, they love each other too much.

The book club suddenly becomes the focus of my plans. Finally, I find Faraz on an optimistic upswing—he can salvage some of the losses with the late varieties like Chausa, of which we have a sizeable number of trees. He is connecting with some export leads. I tell him about Akriti's book club idea, which is now my idea, too, but I can't present it as such; not that I need his permission, but I don't want him getting all worked up whenever we have a meeting. Akriti says I suffer from troubleshooting love.

'Don't call your schoolteachers. They are all riff-raff,' Faraz mutters.

I bite back a retort. I hadn't made any friends during my brief stint at school. I suppose I still had that unmistakable Dubai air, though I tried to blend in. I joined for lunch, shared tiffin, tried not to cringe at hands dipped into my veggies and traded my multigrain rotis for greasy parathas.

Faraz comes up with his candidate—Shezray, a member of some offshoot of the Rampur royalty, a so-called 'Sahibzadi'—on whom he used to have a massive crush.

'Princess Shezray! So romantic and fairy-tale-ish. At least you'll join the club and maybe even read a book,' I tease.

'Never! It's too much of a girly thing to do. But I'll stop by for a quick hello.' Faraz almost smiles, gives me a quick hug and leaves to check the Chausa trees in Baba's orchard.

I ponder over inviting Daniyal to the club. He might view the Rampur Book Club (yes, it has a name now) as a posh, glam affair and too foreign to his precious Rampuriyat. But I don't want it to be a ladies-only kitty party type of set-up, so I finally write to Daniyal with an invite. It reads like a pitch, using tropes like fostering the reading community, etc. Surprisingly, Daniyal writes back almost immediately, saying that it is an excellent initiative. A book club would be a support to my writing career and a space to discuss other works. I ask him to read a passage from *Home Fire* by Kamila Shamsie, our first book club reading, at the meeting.

When I tell Faraz that Daniyal has agreed to join the club, Faraz replies that he had always suspected Daniyal of being gay. His unmarried state leaves him open to such accusations in Rampur. Faraz has always been unashamedly homophobic, like most Rampuris, including Baba. Faraz informs me that 'Sahibzadi' Shezray has honoured us by deciding to join the club. It looks like we can be defined as a small group of readers now. A beginning.

Dagh's Letter to Nishapuri
(1881)

Dearest friend Nishapuri,

She and her entourage reached Azeemabad (Patna) from Lucknow, and from there, a calamitous note, an apocalyptic qayamatnama, was sent to me. I'm still reeling from the effect of her painful words. Maybe some people here tried to create a rift between us. Dagh's temperament is such that he cannot take unreasonable anger from anyone.

Why did you send her my picture?

Please do not speak of my state to anyone, or I shall drown in humiliation. Today I'm not feeling well, or I would have given a fitting reply to her letter.

Yours, Dagh
30 April 1881

Munni Bai Hijab
(1881)

Chaltey chaltey kahā ḳhudā ḥāfiz
Ab tumhāra merā Ḳhudā ḥāfiz
Subḥ ko wo idhar sawār huey
Ham ajal ke ummīd-wār huey
Zindagi bhar ye kab huā sadma
Pehle kyā thā jo ab huā sadma
Go sarāsar malāl thā wo hijr
Uske āgey wisāl thā wo hijr

In God's keeping I leave you, she said,
Only God can keep us safe now.
The morning she left me, intent on her travels,
I prayed for death to end my misery.
Never in this life have I felt such agonising grief.
But beyond the remorse of parting
Lay the hope of reuniting with her.

—Dagh Dehlvi
Faryād e Dāgh (1882)

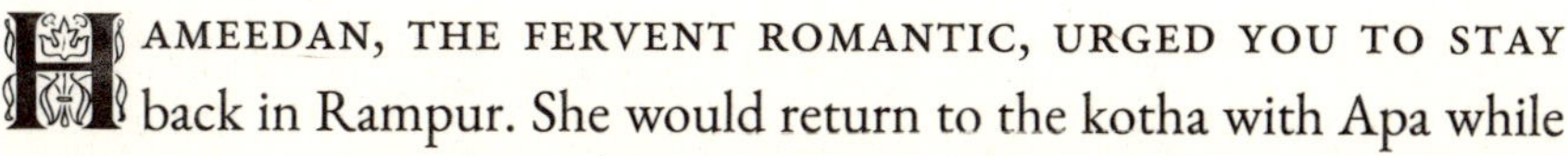

HAMEEDAN, THE FERVENT ROMANTIC, URGED YOU TO STAY back in Rampur. She would return to the kotha with Apa while

Khala and Khuda Bakhsh, who had developed a great fondness for Dagh, could stay with you. Rampur was beautiful and glamorous, but you felt stifled here—all your movements were reported to Haider Ali by his gossipy musahibs. Yours was the vastness of Calcutta, its clamour, its freedoms. Besides, Calcutta was the real challenge, and you had worked all your life to make an impression there. Dagh's love for you, his tears at your departure had melted your heart, but you were aware of the cracks in the relationship.

You felt relieved when you returned to Calcutta. You knew you were more fortunate than the others—the randis and veshyas huddled into cramped one-room hovels, entertaining customers to pay their madam. Apa called such establishments chaklakhanas, bawdy brothels where the poor locals and lower-rung British officers went to satisfy their lust. Your kotha in Colootola was a respectable locality, home to tawaifs from the United Provinces—Awadh, Agra, Banaras—famed for their learning and accomplishments. These women had worked hard to elevate music and poetry. Sometimes, you would stand on the balcony and gaze at the humdrum of the wholesale bazaar, at the rickshaws and carts, the labourers heaving sacks on their backs to the shops. You only came out occasionally, unlike Hameedan, who liked to sit there and watch the bazaar bustle.

One of your clients, Agha Sahib, a munshi at the governor general's office, had gone to Rampur with a missive for the Nawab. He came back and reported that Dagh had besieged him with persistent questions: Does she speak of me? Is she still passionate about poetry and the arts? Does she write? Who is she with these days? Whom does she entertain with her company? Then came the letter:

> *...If you don't reply immediately to my letter, I will buy myself some poison from the bazaar and lay down my life. I had made you promise, and you had sworn that, if not every day, you would write at least twice a week.*

Hameedan was moved to tears. 'Apa, please write to Dagh Sahib, or he will die! Oh, how can you be so stone-hearted?'

'I have seen many such ashiqs. What do you know of men, my little one? He'll find someone else to amuse himself.' You had feigned indifference, but you were tormented. You had written unforgivable, bitter words to Dagh because his stepbrother had behaved in a crass manner towards you at Azeemabad. You would always be a tawaif to them. Dagh had ignored your vicious outburst, though you knew it had wounded him, and persisted in his love. It was impossible for him to untangle his life from yours. You knew he was different from everyone who had ever courted you. That night, you wrote a consoling letter, promising to write more often.

Apa was happy to be back in Calcutta and convinced that what had happened in Rampur wouldn't affect your career here. Secretly, she felt that your association with Dagh had enhanced your poetry with strokes similar to his own—a popular, more accessible style, light in words yet deep in meaning. You had become the object of desire for the connoisseurs, admired for your sensitivity, charm and learning. At your mehfils, the audience would weep and sigh listening to your ghazals, bed you and pay you handsomely. It was the time to reap the years of investment in your tarbiyat—the years of learning music, literature and the etiquettes of a well-bred tawaif.

It was fortunate that both you and Hameedan wrote so well for it was the time of the tawaif-poetess. Malka Jan could ask the earth and would be granted that. Then young Gauhar would take over with her well-trained, melodious voice. Many famous tawaifs were earning well and were the highest taxpayers to the British government. You had a few more years to establish yourself and launch a plush salon in Chitpur like Malka Jan—an exclusive place where the nobility would flock. Maybe you would be invited to perform at Wajid Ali Shah's court, like Malka Jan, or receive invitations from nearby princely states. Apa had been invited to the Metiaburj soirées a few times when she was young and spoke with fondness of 'our Nawab Sahib' and his grandeur undimmed by exile. After Rampur, the world would take notice of you. You had another seven–eight years to make a mark among the shining stars. If you earned well in the next few years and invested in property, it would support you when your clientele inevitably dwindled. You had a melodious voice, though not as spectacular as Hingan Bai, but your compositions and your looks would keep you in high demand for a few years at least.

Apa ordered a new carpet for the mujra hall in a deep red hue, which reminded her of the soirées at Metiaburj. It was an investment in your career, which she was sure was on the verge of taking off. Everyone desired to listen to a well-travelled tawaif; her desirability abroad made her more saleable in Calcutta. The new carpet felt soft and silken under your feet as you twirled around experimentally. The evening sun filtered through the coloured glass of the arched doors opening out to the balcony, casting playful shadows across the room. You flung open the doors to relieve the stifling, heavy air. Apa was instructing the maid to dust the masnads and settle the bolsters. Her own masnad had a red velvet cover, where she would sit with her pandan next to her, her huqqa on a low table, touching her forehead with her bejewelled fingers and welcoming the guests. She was the chaudhrain, the head of the establishment, and had earned her position. After the performance, she would sit with Khala, counting the money, bestowing parts of the largesse to the musicians and keeping the rest safely in her wood chest with the large lock. The keys hung securely on the drawstring of her pyjamas. She had to be vigilant—Khala's son, Shafeeq, always eyed her treasure. He was assigned to stand at the doorway downstairs, enticing and ushering in guests up the wooden staircase into the salon.

Apa had been enthralled by the spread at Jashn e Benazir. 'Fifty types of pulao and so many styles of meat curries that I lost count; each dish had a unique taste and colour. The kundan qaliya was like eating shorba made of gold! Their masalas are very like our Awadhi masalas; only, they don't like to put kewra as much as we do. They say it's the water of their River Kosi that gives a unique flavour to their dishes. Here, I use the best masalas, but the water is nothing like our Lakhnau water—food never tastes the same,' Apa told her friend, Sughra. She marvelled at the Nawab's devotion to food. He had called cooks from Awadh and Delhi to teach his khansamas. She said Pathans only learnt to eat properly after coming to Hindustan. Nawab Kalb e Ali Khan was very fond of the halwa sohan made from samnak, wheat germ flour, and his khansamas had innovated several styles of halwa sohan—halwa sohan papdi was hard and biscuit-like, halwa sohan jozi was soft, halwa sohan maghazi had seeds, and halwa sohan doodhiya was milk-based. She had brought halwa sohan in large quantities from the mela bazaar outside the Benazir Palace, and the halwai had promised that the halwa wouldn't get spoiled even after two years because it was prepared with pure ghee and samnak. She tried to guess some of the ingredients of the light, shimmering kundan qaliya and asked Khala to cook it, but it never had the opulent flavour of the dish she had eaten at Rampur.

Your latest bhadralok patron—belonging to a wealthy, elite Bengali family—your 'Babu' was generous and kind. He was a lonely widower, and Apa was happy with the negotiations. Then there were the daily mehfils, which you loved and revelled in. Life was good. Apa told you that during her time, the angrez doctors could examine the tawaifs at any time and restrain them in the so called lock hospitals. Many a beauteous tawaif's career came to an end once it came to be known that she had the dreaded venereal disease. The draconian law had been abolished, but the spectre of disease still haunted you. Apa ensured that most of your patrons were from good families who didn't frequent cheap brothels.

When you were just fifteen, you had an abusive sexual experience with a fat and drunk Gujarati trader who had come on a business trip. Terrified, raw, you cried for days when passing urine. You begged Apa to take you to an English doctor, but Apa would hear none of it. If anyone heard of you going to an English doctor, they would suspect venereal diseases, so common among the randis. It would end your career, or you would be forced to entertain the not-so-well-off babus, the lowly clerks, who would bring in diseases. Finally, Khala called Kamla, a trained nurse, to examine you. Kamla assured you that you were fine and gave you angrezi ointment for the lacerations. You held her hand and cried. Sensing your fear and probably moved with pity for the life that lay ahead of you, she gave you a tube with a rubber ball at one end and taught you to do the deep wash if you wished to avoid pregnancies; she also advised you to wash with alum water every time a patron visited you. If you don't have alum, use soda powder, she said. You felt relieved and followed the practice meticulously through all your years.

You hadn't written a line since you came back from Rampur. Dagh, famously prolific, composed with effortless ease, and the words seem to flow from his lips in perfect meters. The last lines you composed lying in Dagh's arms had welled up perfectly scripted. It had never happened before; you got up and rushed to jot down the lines:

Bahār āyī hai sāmān-e chaman bandī hai gulshan meiñ,
Kali phūtī hai aks gul se nazārey ke dāman meiñ

Spring arrives as flowers spread out in the gardens,
The bud bursts open, mirroring the glory of the flowers.

He had asked you to substitute *shafaq phooti hai,* the morning rays are bursting, instead of *kali phooti hai,* buds burst open. It had changed the dimensions of the sher. You had got up, covered your head with a dupatta, bent and touched your forehead thrice—the mujra salam to a Nawab. Dagh had guffawed and folded you back in his arms. You are my pir, my spiritual guide, you told him. He had shaken his head and replied that his love, his ishq for you was like that of a Sufi for Allah. In the umbra of his loving gaze, you felt loved beyond reason. But those were the last lines you had composed. You planned to complete the ghazal after your return, but now you felt arid; the weight of your published diwan pressed down upon you. What if that was all you would ever write?

Did you love him the way he loved you? Could absences of 'hijr' (separation) define love more clearly than moments of 'wisāl', (togetherness)? You had asked Nishapuri Sahib to send you a photograph of Dagh. What did you feel looking at the intensity of those eyes, the proud set of the chin and the light smile on the lips? Then there was the gravelly timbre of his voice—lingering on the curves of each word, caressing the sounds and making them his own—which still echoed in your mind when you read any line touched by his voice.

دلکشی

5

Dilkashi (Attraction)

JULY TRUDGES ON, SULTRY AND BREATHLESS, HOLDING ITS oppressive weight as it awaits a relieving monsoon shower. I'm sure no one will turn up for the book club meeting. The sun persists with its relentless burn, unfazed by our plans. We shouldn't have agreed on 4 p.m. Papa was terrified that I would get a heat stroke and used to try and keep me indoors through the summer afternoons, anchoring me with stories. I switch on the AC—which will barely cool the cavernous drawing cum dining room—and recheck the Wikipedia 'checklist for a Book Club Meeting'. We have set aside barely two hours for the meeting before life reclaims us—cooking, tending to children, husbands and the inevitable phone calls.

I wear a deep red mulmul saree for the occasion. Unlike Mamma, I never pin the pleats or secure the pallu to crisp submission. My saree flows with me, moulded into my day—cocooning me around my shoulder, trailing with abandon on the floor, the soft pleats yielding to my steps. I had stopped wearing sarees when I left my teaching job; it was too much of an effort. But I missed the comforting awareness and the caress of the soft fabric on my bare arms and midriff.

Daniyal comes in first in his ancient Rolls Royce, which he seems to take out of its shroud only for special occasions. He is gracefully equine in his slightly festive kurta pyjama—beige with understated thread work. He wears his beauty so casually that he would be shocked and embarrassed to hear anyone mention it. I welcome him, and he quietly raises his hand to his forehead. He congratulates me on starting the book club and hands me a package. It's a book, of course—*Rise of the Rohilla Chieftains* by Iqbal Husain. He tells me that it's the only historical writing on the Rohilla Pathans who established Rampur and other cities of Rohilkhand.

'Why did we stop making cars like this?' I touch the gleaming bonnet ornament of the Rolls—a woman bending forward, poised to take flight.

'This is the "Spirit of Ecstasy". It represents a secret love affair between Baron Montagu and Eleanor, a commoner. The silver lady doesn't have wings, though it appears so; her garment is blowing back in the wind to resemble wings.'

'Beautiful, isn't it? I believe they made her kneel down and reduced her size in later models because she was obstructing the view.' Daniyal's eyebrows shoot up in surprise, and then, there is a faint smile that deepens the furrows on his cheeks.

'Umm... I love the silver and black of the car,' I smile.

'It doesn't belong to me. My father was the head of the maintenance department of the Nawab. So when the Nawab's properties were sealed in a court case in 1966, Papa kept this Silver Wraith, which had come in for repairs. There was no one to legally return it to,' he says with boyish mirth in his eyes.

'Lucky you!' I laugh. I turn as Akriti drives in. We wait for her to climb down from her jeep and I introduce her to Daniyal. She must have seen us laughing together for she whispers, 'He's hot!' when we hug. I smile at her cocked eyebrow. I wish we'd had a few moments before Daniyal arrived just to absorb her familiar strength and settle her tousled windswept hair—I always do that because she doesn't care about appearances. She loves to drive her open jeep and feel the wind in her hair, even in the blistering heat. We Indians are meant to work in the sun, she tells me when I ask her to take care of her weather-beaten skin. Wearing sunblock is out of the question. Daniyal decides to park his car on the other side of the driveway; maybe he feels the need to safeguard it, especially after Akriti's zippy entry.

'If the blessed Princess Shezray is fashionably late, we shall begin our meeting,' I say to Akriti as we start walking towards the porch.

'God, you're so territorial.' She knows about Faraz's crush.

'Of course not, just *bitchy*!'

I hope Daniyal is too busy easing his precious car on the gravel to hear us. Baba, too, has suggested candidates for the club—Dr Rishabh Gupta and his wife, Vani. Baba has never met the wife, who is 'from outside' and a nutritionist. He tells me that she is too sophisticated for Rampur and couldn't set up her practice here; she keeps running off to Delhi for her part-time consultant job at a hospital. Basically, he wants the too-cool-for-Rampur Vani to have a social circle as a favour to his colleague. I doubt if she even reads books. To Baba, nutritionists are just flim-flam for the wealthy; he extends this scepticism to most non-traditional therapies—homeopathy, acupressure and unani medicines are all khel, which don't even deserve his snort. Hard work is the cure-all therapy prescribed by him, and hardcore allopathy when required. If all fails, 'Open her/him up!' is his command. He saved my life with that when I had an ectopic pregnancy after Gul.

Vani comes in a rush of salon-curled, salt-and-pepper hair, which makes us feel like over-dyed cougars. She glows, the light literally bouncing off her pink cheeks—must be all the healthy eating. She has the enviable aura of being totally at ease with her body and its ageing and negates the general presumption that nutritionists should be reed thin. I can imagine her cooing to her clients, 'Love yourself, love your body' in a (for some reason) flowy ivory chiffon dress. She introduces herself, and we settle down in the drawing room to small talk. Vani's son studies at the Delhi University. Before we get sucked into parenting chatter, I gently pivot the conversation towards the book.

'Rishabh couldn't make it, but we read the book together!' Vani waves a copy of *Home Fire* as evidence. I'm fairly certain she has Googled the story, or maybe I'm just being my usual judgy self.

'Great, Vani!' I try not to sound patronizing and fail. Akriti admits she's only halfway through and begs us not to reveal the ending.

'So, Kamila Shamsie won the Women's Prize for *Home Fire*, and it was also longlisted for the Booker. The reason I chose it for our first meeting is her connection to Rampur. Kamila's maternal grandmother was the sister-in-law of Nawab Raza Ali Khan. Jahanara Begum wrote this wonderful memoir *Remembrances of Days Past*, set in Rampur; Kamila's mother is the remarkable Muneeza Shamsie, an award-winning Pakistani writer and critic.' I pause, feeling a bit like a teacher but pleased by the appreciation in Daniyal's gaze. I invite him to start the reading as planned.

In the middle of Daniyal's reading, we are graced with the arrival of Princess Shezray, apologizing for being late and begging us to continue as she settles into her seat. Daniyal continues to read, a faint line of irritation between his brows.

'So, this story is a modern retelling of *Antigone*, a tragedy by Sophocles,' I explain once Daniyal finishes.

'Oh no! I hate tragedies. Why didn't you choose a happy book, Kuku?' Akriti sighs.

'She chose it for the Rampur connection,' defends Daniyal.

'Tragedy lives longer with us, doesn't it? *Dr Zhivago*, *Gone With the Wind*. I was in love with Heathcliff,' says Shezray. She has that melancholic glamour of fading divas and seems to belong to another era that has just inexplicably ended, leaving everything around her stunted. I can almost see her in sepia tones.

'What a masochist. I hated him!' says Akriti.

'Yes, but what a story. Such love! Remember how he sat with Cathy when she died?' Vani breathes, hugging her book to her heart or the general region of the heart.

'And dug up her grave. The man needed a therapist!' Akriti retorts and gulps down the glass of water Meezan Bhai places on the table.

'This is a sort of a love story, too. Aneeka and Parvaiz are siblings raised by their elder sister, Isma. Now Parvaiz joins ISIS or is lured into it, and Isma tries to rescue him.' I firmly steer us back to *Home Fire,* anxious about following the Google-prescribed book club procedure.

'I think the central question that the book poses, like *Antigone*, is that should a traitor be given a decent burial,' offers Daniyal. He sits pin-straight on the chair, not tense but not evidently at ease. When was the last time he was with a group of women who were not his relatives?

'You might as well tell me the whole story. So, Parvaiz dies?' asks Akriti.

'Everyone dies in a terrorist attack! Bloody terrorists. They should be shot point-blank. My father was in the army, and he served in Kashmir. He said that local Kashmiris always sympathize with terrorists.' Vani rolls her hair up into an angry bun.

'What about the atrocities the army has committed against the innocent locals?' Daniyal glints.

'That's because they support terrorism.' Shezray glowers at Daniyal.

'You mean all Kashmiris are terrorists? Or all Muslims are terrorists?' Daniyal retorts a little too sharply for his usual calm demeanour.

Everyone starts speaking over and at each other in a muddled fury of Us vs Them.

'Hi, everyone! So how is it going?' I could have kissed Faraz for his perfect entry.

'You are brave for volunteering to be at a ladies book club, brother.' Faraz shakes Daniyal's hand and pats his back.

'So reading books is a womanly thing? And this is not a ladies-only club!' I jump in.

'Reading romance is girlish,' laughs Faraz.

'This is Kamila Shamsie!' I fall into the banter, grateful for the shift in energy. I leave Akriti to defend Daniyal's honour as I head to fetch tea and andarsey. We had decided that there would be no elaborate food distractions. I didn't want to be rushing around getting snacks served. But I felt compelled to serve deep-fried andarsey, my favourite monsoon snacks . They are an epicurean delight, with their crunchy, reddish-gold crust, freckled with crisp sesame seeds and fluffy, moist insides—the taste of heaven and earth after a monsoon downpour. Full-blown monsoons haven't started yet, but the street vendors have started frying andarsey. Vani has never had them and feasts on them with a delighted, 'Damn the trans-fats, darlings.'

After tea, I ask Daniyal to continue the discussion, but the momentum is lost. I try to hold forth on Anika's character and the choices she is forced to make, skirting the terrorism issue. Akriti, even though she hasn't read the book, joins in valiantly. I can sense Daniyal withdrawing, his eyes shuttered, his face a mask. Maybe he felt offended, he certainly looks the kind; I hope he doesn't opt out of the club. Shezray excuses herself—she has to run some errands. Soon, everyone remembers they have to be somewhere else and we are standing waving goodbyes.

'This was such a disaster! I should have never started the club.' I turn to Faraz as we walk back.

'You had Shezray and Daniyal in the same room…' Faraz smirks.

'So?'

'Old gossip—they were lovers.'

'Really! But you told me Daniyal is probably gay!'

'Maybe…'

'What do you mean? Just because he is single doesn't mean he is gay. I don't trust you any more with this!'

'One can be bisexual. Anyway, so the families intervened, and Shezray was married and packed off to Saudi Arabia. She has now separated from her husband.'

'Oh! No wonder there were such sparks and Daniyal looked uncomfortable. They'll probably get back together now; both belong to that old princely era. Hmm… a love story.'

Faraz turns and starts walking back to the house. I follow him unwilling to let the shared moment go. It almost feels like our post-dinner party conversations when we gleefully gossiped and analysed our fellow diners and guests.

'You know, Vani said to me, "I didn't expect Muslims to be so cool, but then, you're not really an M." What the hell!'

Faraz says that I'm overreacting to an off-colour remark. It happens to us all the time, and I should be used to it by now. I register the faint irritated click of his tongue, which could turn into a full-blown rant and walk off to the bedroom, suddenly enveloped with heat and the urge to fling off my saree and take a cooling bath. The build-up and excitement of the book club meeting has left me deflated. Was I expecting a sudden bonding of such diverse people? I should just focus on my writing. I go to sleep early with the failure of my book club. The intense complexity of the evening plays out in my fractured dreams.

Munni Bai's Second Visit to Rampur
(March 1882)

Jā ke ahad e shabāb kā āna!
Thā dubāra Ḥijāb kā āna!
Kyā merey dilistān kā āna hai
Ye to rūh e rawāñ kā āna hai...
Phir wahi sa'āt-e saīd āyī
Ki baras din ke ba'ad 'Eid āyi

Ḥijāb's coming back to me,
Was the return of youth
The return of my heart
The return of my soul
The happy moment arrived
As Eid after days and years.

—Dagh Dehlvi
Faryād e Dāgh (1882)

Dagh begged you to come to attend the Benazir Mela again; you wrote back, insisting you would only visit Rampur if the Nawab himself extended an invitation. It did not become a renowned tawaif like you to go uninvited. Yet you desperately longed to relive the magic of the Benazir Mela and Dagh's love; then you recalled his accusations of flirting with Haider—the labyrinthine connections and salacious rumours of your last visit still stung like a fresh slap. You were unsure, unable to decipher your attraction towards him. Yes, he stuck a deep chord, inspired you to believe in yourself, to write as he teased out the creases from your heart. Being with him was to confront yourself, to peel away the veneer and look unafraid at the sharp contours of self. He made poetry seem so effortless—now listen to this, he would say, and there was a masterful extempore sher plumbing the depth of emotions with an economy of words, the layers of meanings concealed in simple words. Like you, he had also been writing since childhood, but while poetry flowed naturally for him, for you, it was a painstaking labour. Words came like reluctant confessions, as though an invisible barricade curtailed their release. You licked your wounds with the fire of anger, which enflamed your words, and had to temper them into popular expressions of love, sorrow and heartbreak—who wanted to listen to an angry tawaif. You needed to be alone, undisturbed and at peace to compose; such places were few and far between in your clamorous life. For you, writing was a prayer, deep and intense; for Dagh, it was a living and breathing part of his life. You wanted to learn how to make your poetry live with your breath and he was your pir—your guide to this sensibility.

Displaced and shunned, Dagh had suffered as a child; his life was marked by the loss of people he loved. He carried his pain lightly; you were etched with suffering, bruised in many seen and unseen ways every day. You were damaged, and he was whole despite his trauma—that's what drew you to him. How could he retain his self in the face of such anguish?

The invitation to the Benazir Mela finally arrived to great excitement. Nawab Kalb e Ali Khan had himself written to you. Of course, it was Dagh's doing. The Nawab considered him his brother and was extremely close to him. Apa was furious at your decision to go to Rampur. What would you gain from this fruitless exercise? Dagh couldn't afford to be your patron even though he earned well. You were destined for Nawabs and princes, not for their poets and punitive employees. She suggested sending Hameedan in your place. Hameedan had also started writing poetry under your guidance, but her writing lacked your sensitivity. The fear in Apa's eyes was palpable; she couldn't risk you falling in love with Dagh, an older man, a poet—a reckless streak she knew you had. You were her prized jewel. Hameedan was opaque compared to you. Apa and the kotha couldn't afford to lose you.

Apa was afraid of ishq, the so-called eternal love that destroyed Khala's life. It was the dread of every tawaif and most grew up with cautionary family tales of such a love. Khala's love affair with a nobleman—who promised marriage and liberation from the kotha—destroyed her career, leaving her unable to accept patrons or perform. She would get hysterical when any man approached her and even lost interest in music. Khala and Shafeeq, her son from the nobleman, were now dependents on the earnings of the kotha; she served Apa and her daughters as they ripened into successful tawaifs. Do you want to become a dependant on Hameedan and her daughters? Always pretending to be kind and loving to Hameedan so that she could drop some food in your lap? In time, you should birth a daughter to carry on the legacy. That's the way it has always been. This kotha is your reality, accept it. Apa was brutal with her words.

'I shall go wherever I want to!' You capitalized on Apa's terror. It was important for you to meet Dagh again to untie the knot of your poetic voice; only Dagh could help you out of the despair that swamped you. You promised Apa you didn't love him—he was your teacher, your pir and spiritual guide. Apa feared your overemotional temperament, which made you, at times, withdraw from the glamour of mehfils into solitude. You would refuse to go for mujras, shun invitations drawing reprimands from Apa—we'll all starve to death if people knew how temperamental you were. 'You cannot afford to be vulnerable; cruel men will rape you and pick the flesh off your bones!' she used to say.

You wrote to Dagh and reminded him of the rumour-mongering by his friends, which marred your last meeting.

'They are not your friends. They are jealous of you and of our relationship. You are too trusting of them. I'm apprehensive about having such problems again,' you wrote. Dagh's letters revealed his anxieties, his fears that his rivals had supplanted him in your affections. After several letters and entreaties, you decided to accept the invitation. Apa displayed her annoyance by refusing to accompany you and sent Khala, Shafeeq, Hameedan and Khuda Bakhsh as your entourage. You wrote to Dagh en route from Banaras, picturing his happiness and impatience.

The mela was at its zenith when you presented yourself before Nawab Kalb e Ali Khan—bowing thrice and presenting a gold coin as nazar offering. The Nawab welcomed you, praising your talents, and remarked with a smile that you had left many hearts pining since your last visit.

'You are very kind to this humble tawaif. I hope I can please you with my songs at your mehfil.'

You greeted Dagh with stiff formality, your eyes skimming past his ardent gaze. His eyes dimmed as you turned away with the briefest of salams. He lowered his head and touched his forehead in respect, but you had already moved on. Did Dagh in his simplicity expect you to display your affection openly? You were surrounded by enemies—his so-called friends and Haider Ali's hangers-on—and had to tread carefully. You avoided him that whole day, then finding him sitting crestfallen like a child, went up to him.

'I have come to you, Dagh Sahib, out of my own free will. I'm eager to meet you alone, too, but I have to follow wazeydaari, the appropriate behaviour,' you whispered.

'Everything you say is right, Baiji. I'm aware of my wazey, my status.' Dagh touched his forehead. You had hurt him. He knew he couldn't afford to be your patron; it was foolhardy to expect love from a tawaif.

You had accepted Haider's invitation to live at his haveli and were afraid of showing any special favour towards Dagh even though he had requested Nawab Kalb e Ali Khan for the invite. The Nawab watched the two of you with some amusement and apprehension for his friend. Was this a game of love, or was this woman out to destroy Dagh's fragile heart?

Dagh attended all the mehfils where you performed. He was withdrawn and distant, precarious in his observation of courtly etiquettes. You didn't meet him for ten days—if he truly loved you, he could wait. After every mehfil, your thoughts circled back to him.

Dagh's Undated Letter to Hijab

Dearest of Dagh,

If you write to me that Nawab Haider had summoned Hijab and she was compelled to go; or that Nawab Haider had pursued her, it will be merciful for me. I'm not in possession of my senses. My wounds are innumerable, and every day rubs fresh salt on them, causing me great anguish. You and your family know the state of my affairs. I cannot compare to Nawab Haider; I can do nothing but roast like kabab in the fire of love.

Maybe you can tell the Nawab Haider that Dagh is in love with Hijab. He has others to amuse him, but if Dagh doesn't get Hijab, he cannot bear the pain engraved in his heart.

I wait impatiently for your reply.

Dagh

صدمہ

6

Sadmā (Grief)

I WAKE UP WITH THE UNMISTAKABLE BEGINNINGS OF A MIGRAINE and scramble out of bed to get black coffee with a double dose of paracetamol to hopefully stop it in its tracks. My mobile pings with a notification from a food and drink magazine where I had pitched an article on Rampuri cuisine. The rejection letter is so beautifully worded, delicately breaking the news that my heart keeps beating till the last line. I sit with my disappointment on the porch chair Faraz has painted fiery red. It reminds me of nursery class, of children pinned to their chairs. I hate the onslaught of the colour, especially today. Faraz usually gets up late. I treasure this quiet slice of time. Then there would be bed-tea for Faraz prepared by Meezan Bhai, the breakfast table, the quibble over too-soft eggs—another day as unremarkable as the others. Thankfully, it's cloudy, and I'm spared the glaring pincers of the sun. It starts drizzling; maybe the monsoons will grace us today.

There is a click at the gate, and Daniyal appears under a large, rainbow-hued umbrella; I almost smile remembering Faraz's insinuations. Daniyal folds the umbrella and says, somewhat apologetically, that he comes for his morning walk to Civil Lines and thought he would drop in. I can barely summon pleasantries with my impending migraine. Thankfully, I had changed into my shalwar kameez. I used to sashay around in my kaftan till Faraz told me that Meezan Bhai found it disrespectful. So I change into my day clothes before stepping out of the bedroom. I offer him tea, which he, perhaps sensing my lack of warmth, thankfully refuses and pulls up a chair. He asks me about my writing, and I tell him about the rejection letter.

'It's a long journey, Rukmini. There will be many more rejection letters. Save them; they are a part of your story.' I almost ask him to call me Kuku; he is, after all, a close acquaintance now, but I stop myself. He might think of me as being too forward.

I feel irritated at his dismissal of the damning rejection letter. Am I supposed to view the present as a past to laugh about in the future? For now, I just want to curl up in bed and let this day drift into oblivion. We watch the light drizzle unfurling into a rainfall. I could sit and watch the rain for hours; it feels like a celebration. I call out to Meezan Bhai for tea and cakes.

'Did you read Dagh's masnavi, *Faryād e Dāgh*, on his love for Munni Bai Hijab?'

'I'm reading it. Frankly, it goes a bit overboard, you know. A bit teenagerish, don't you think?' Love at first sight and the paean to the beauty of the beloved must have been a commonplace poetic theme at that time. It just feels so unreal.

'For me, it's the image of the poet writing feverishly; he completed the whole masnavi—838 lines—in just two days after his return from Calcutta after meeting Hijab. The masnavi narrates their love story. There is so much anguish in those simple, urgent lines.' Daniyal's hands skim the air, and I nod, caught with the imagery.

'But what of Munni Bai Hijab, the object of his passion. Did she really love Dagh, a fifty-year-old famous poet? Or was she just flattered?'

'Can we know if a woman really loves? We have no love letters from her addressed to Dagh. She was immortalized through his poetry. We see her through Dagh's masnavi and his letters.'

'But she was a poetess, too. What about her work? Was it not good enough?'

'She was highly acclaimed at that time, but sadly, only a few of her ghazals have survived.'

'So I'm trying to write Hijab's story, but the only lens I have is Dagh…' Munni Bai Hijab—what a name. Life gave her Munni Bai full of diminutive titillation, and she gave herself 'Hijab', veiling her body with a pen name. Her identity was a duality. Meezan Bhai lays out the tea and biscuits. We must be out of cakes, or Meezan Bhai decided that Daniyal wasn't important enough, or worse, disapproved of our meeting.

'If you read Dagh's letters and poetry you can visualize Hijab as a very strong and passionate woman. I don't believe Dagh's biographers when they write of her as a grasping tawaif out to ensnare an older, richer man. She had much richer patrons. It wasn't about money for her.' Daniyal sips his tea. Our eyes are riveted towards the dramatic escalation of rain and the dance of the trees. Meandering conversations while gazing away, looking at the road and driving, for instance, are somehow more in-depth and calming. Faraz and I used to have such long talks on our road trips.

'This could have an element of truth. He was about thirty years older than her. I mean, she couldn't be attracted towards him.' I muse. The pounding staccato of rain sends a light spray over us, and we shift our chairs closer to the centre of the porch; they are now angled towards the rain, but closer so we can hear each other.

'It's said that tawaifs were taught sixty ways of deception. There were many stories of that time about households falling into financial ruin because of them. But we can still consider the possibility that Dagh and Hijab found a higher love; they were both poets and had similar sensibilities. On the other hand, it might have been simply a carnal liaison. I'm suggesting that you unclothe your mind of the biases before you discover her—suspend disbelief.' Daniyal turns towards me, then starts scrolling on his mobile and says, 'Listen to these lines. This is the key to her feelings. Dagh writes in the masnavi that Munni Bai Hijab told him:

'Ham bhūkhey haiñ ādmiyat ke,
Ādmiyat ke sāth 'ulfat ke
Aisey waison se jī nahī miltā
Dāgh sā ādmi nahī miltā'

(I hanker for a humane, compassionate love,
I'm not attracted towards shallow mortals
Dagh's humanity is distinctive.)

I consider the reported words and think of Hijab's years of servicing naked lust, of getting paid, used and discarded. Perhaps she craved for ulfat, a humane, benevolent love; maybe Dagh held the promise of an enduring love and empathy.

'And what of the wives? They stuck to their philandering husbands?' I ask after a pause.

'What could they do? They had no agency and were forced to accept a social system where men went to tawaifs for entertainment and more. There were no movies or music systems. If you wanted to listen to music, you needed to go to the singers or employ them if you were rich enough. Besides, the tawaifs were trained in the art of lovemaking; probably the wives had no clue how to enjoy sex—maybe it was never discussed with them.'

The migraine tightens its grip, claws scraping around my right eyeball despite the paracetamols. I feel a surge of the angry heat of a hot flush—the bane of my life these days. How dare he be so presumptuous about the sexual desires of the wife?

'We cannot generalize, of course,' he concedes. I must be looking flushed and cross; I wish he'd leave.

I suddenly remember what woke me up so early today. The

migraine was triggered by a smell—the memory of hospital smells, disinfectants, bitter medicines and urine—hanging heavy over my lucid dream. The dream dissipated, but the pungent smells lodged into my right lobe, a dull ache building up to a full-blown migraine.

I never expected Mamma to be taken ill. Maybe a sudden death announced by a phone call; anything but the forced intimacy of caring for her body in the hospital. Her disintegration and dependence on me filled me with a thick revulsion. Akriti tells me that I'm still mourning for Mamma, that I have 'unresolved grief'. It's not true—I didn't love Mamma, and most of my life's decisions were inspired by this lack. But the hot mix of my emotions, some clearly etched, some nebulous, were ties after all, and maybe one needed to grieve when the attachment was no longer pinned to a living person.

'You are far away, already in another world,' Daniyal remarks.

I find myself telling him of my struggles with reading Dagh's letters in my stumbling Urdu. The masnavi is indecipherable to me at times. The librarian comes over dutifully every Friday, but I think I need more handholding.

'I read a page, then write it down in Roman script.'

'It will get better. Listen, I go for a morning walk at six. If you want, I can swing by around seven and help you out. I won't read it out to you but guide you along.'

'Umm... thank you, but I don't want to impose upon you. Maybe I'll hire a tutor. Maulvi Waheed used to teach me earlier.'

'He passed away. Look, I'll come for only half an hour, and then you can continue with your writing.' An incipient smile is teasing his cheek lines as he anticipates my answer. I feel that I'm doing him a favour by letting him be a part of my writing process.

'Thank you... that's so kind of you.' I watch the frown disappear and his lower lids ride up to crinkle into an eye-smile. He is the only person I know who can smile with his eyes while his mouth remains a straight line.

'My only condition is that you won't read the story online. It will fill your mind with biases.'

'You are a great one to talk about biases,' I say archly.

'Ah, and by the way, I'm in my fifties.' He winks, smiles and takes his leave. It is still raining, but he says he loves rain-walks.

'I don't think he has anything to do besides wander around in his haveli and go for court appearances,' grumbles Faraz when I tell him. He is in one of his dark moods since yesterday. It's impossible to get him to talk about it. Maybe his mood has seeped into my migraine. I contemplate taking the day off from struggling with Urdu; it will only worsen the headache. I want to run out somewhere now because Faraz is going to sit around and be all grouchy. The sharp hospital reek intensifies with my pulsating migraine. I decide to cook; maybe the smell of spices will dissipate the phantom stink.

I love cooking Kayastha dishes I learnt from Papa and some continental dishes I picked up over the Dubai years. Mamma never cooked; she considered food as an easily ignored element of existence. When Ayah ji went on her Sunday leave, Mamma asked me to make sandwiches and Maggi. After living through endless sandwich Sundays, I started cooking on my own as I grew older. I began every cooking session in a heat of anger spurred by the belief that it was my mother's duty to feed me. But by the time I finished a dish, I would calm down, feel the tangibility of flavours, the pleasure of satiation and a small sense of power. Cooking anchored me and made me feel independent of Mamma. I would try to recall Papa's gestures when he added the ingredients, the way he stirred the pot, the way cooking smells changed from sharp turmeric and garlic to a mellow medley of aromas. When the dish was ready, I would take a spoonful and close my eyes, comparing the accents and smells to the remembered taste of Papa's cooking. Faraz's first kiss was like smoke, like the smell of our home when Papa made kababs. I never told Faraz this, but his kisses were home.

I pop in a Brufen and head to the kitchen; it needs a good cleaning. Meezan Bhai completely ignores unwashed utensils and spills. He was Baba's old cook, and it was very generous of Baba to give him to us to make us comfortable, but I just can't deal with a messy kitchen. Today, I'm determined to learn the secrets of Rampuri qorma from Meezan Bhai. The curry of the qorma he cooks is smooth, slightly liquidy, topped with a reddish-gold layer of oil. His masterpiece is the fabulous bhuna gosht with the unachievable daneydaar, textured gravy. Whenever I ask him for a recipe, Meezan Bhai says, 'Dulhan Begum, till I'm alive, I will cook for you. Why bother?' He tells me Faraz doesn't like my angrezi cooking and prefers his qormas and pulaos. I have seen Faraz gorging on Rampuri food and putting on weight since we got back. We are devoted to Rampuri food.

I realize I have caught Meezan Bhai in a sentimental mood when he starts reminiscing about my mother-in-law, his Begum Sahiba. I know he wants to tell his stories and cook with me. I throw out some dusters, stiff with grime—which he says he has kept aside to clean the gas stove—and resist the urge to examine the array of plastic bottles with mysterious spices in the cupboard. We need more cupboards in the kitchen. I miss my Dubai cooking range with its sleek hobs and the gas oven. I wish I had fought with Faraz and brought it over. He said we could buy a new cooking range, which we never did. My expensive Dubai utensils, which I had refused to part with, are out of place in the kitchen, like my swanky sofas and laminated wood beds look flashy alongside the baroque antique furniture in the house.

Meezan Bhai starts narrating family stories and happily chopping onions for the qorma. The great thing about having a permanent cook is that you don't have to chop onions. He tells me that his father and grandfather cooked for the Nawabs. When the last Nawab passed away, Meezan Bhai's father came to work for Baba. Baba got him married and named the son 'Meezan', the weighing scale. True to his name, Meezan Bhai has the knack of knowing a near-perfect approximation of weights and can balance the flavours with his impeccable andaza.

I take out the meat from the freezer and put it into the microwave to defrost.

'Don't put it in the machine!' Meezan Bhai drops the knife and yells. Apparently, microwaves and all machines steal away the zaiqa (taste) from the meat. Meezan Bhai despises cooking frozen meat. I can't send him to the butchers every day. It takes him half the day to get meat; sometimes, he returns with no meat and a blow-by-blow account of how he outwitted the sly butcher. I persuade Meezan Bhai to let me defrost the meat in the microwave just this once. I take out my recipe diary. Meezan Bhai just might reveal his secrets today. He begins by simply pouring lots of oil into the cooker. No tablespoon or cup measurements for him.

'Dulhan Begum, qorma should be cooked in a degh over low heat. This pressure cooker is useless.'

I ask him to bear with the pressure cooker today. He fries the onions, and they emerge golden and shimmering on a plate. Next, he makes a mixture of ginger-garlic paste, onion paste, coriander powder and yellow and red chilli powder and sets it aside. I note down the measurements, asking him to slow down his hectic dumping of the ingredients. He fries the meat with whole spices—green cardamom, cloves, black cardamom and bay leaves—chatting all the while. I think he is trying to distract me. Then he dunks the masala paste, adds water and closes the lid for pressure cooking. The immediacy of spice smells and the pungent sting of onions have chased away the hospital smells. I rummage through drawers and shelves while waiting for the meat to cook. I discover several pudiyas—masala powders wrapped in bits of newspapers. He refuses to identify any of them but won't let me throw them. It's so unlike me to neglect the kitchen.

Meezan Bhai opens the cooker and informs me that the meat is done and we have to sauté the masalas some more till the oil separates from the gravy.

'You have to have strong arms to bhuno the masalas,' he tells me as I start stirring, and a garlicky-spicy aroma fills the kitchen. We don't even have an electric chimney, just an ineffective exhaust fan. My clothes will smell of garlic, and Faraz will make a face. I will shower and change later.

Papa used to cook on weekends with me as his sous-chef. He made the day feel like a celebration. We cooked elaborate, mostly meat-based dishes, and froze them to last through the week. Ayah ji cooked fresh dal, rice and vegetables every day. What would appear on the dinner table from out of the frozen meat boxes was always a surprise. Papa would often buy cookbooks, and we would decide on the dishes to try out. I would stand reading the instructions. He would pretend to mess up, and I would scream, 'Nooo, stop! Don't put that in!' He would act like an antsy French chef, would throw up his hands, pull his hair, fling away the apron and say, 'I burnt ze meat!' We would laugh and sing as Papa cooked through cookbooks.

Food became functional after he passed away. Mamma considered kitchen work as female enslavement, and I had to forage in the kitchen if I felt hungry. Ayah ji cooked uninspiring dishes with sullen reluctance. She felt cooking was not a part of her job description. She was hired to look after me. Soon, I started accompanying Ayah ji for monthly grocery shopping. Mamma had no idea about my food preferences or what was required in the kitchen. She would just alternate between yellow dal and black dal ad infinitum. When I asked for food, she would look affronted and challenged. She felt I ate too much, was obsessed with food and it showed on me. Unprovoked, thoughtless body shaming was an acceptable part of parenting at that time. I did think about food a lot—psychiatrists would decipher it as an attempt to fill a void and deal with grief—and missed those meticulously planned dining table dinners with Papa. I withdrew into TV meals, and Mamma would peck on tiny portions absentmindedly while correcting papers or reading something. We never had proper sit-down dinners after Papa. As soon as Ayah ji allowed me, I started cooking with her, then took over cooking dinner every day. It was a secret between us. Mamma believed women had come through a long struggle of emancipation from the kitchen and should stay out of it. Cooking was futile—everything was eaten up and you got back to cooking again.

'You will end up a housewife, living out your life serving your husband by making perfect rotis,' she would say with a cynical grimace if she saw me pottering in the kitchen. Food was the only tangible thing in my life; I craved the physicality of flavours on my tongue. I think now that my life revolved around absences, which I tried to fill with food and then Faraz's love.

Meezan Bhai adds some curd to the bubbling gravy, and I continue stirring. After a while, he puts in the fried onions crushed into a grainy powder. Then he takes out something from a pudiya and drops it in the pot.

'What was that?'

'Nothing, Dulhan Begum. Some garam masala powder.'

'It was a white powder! You are hiding something in that pudiya.' Here it was at last—the secret pudiya of the wily khansama. I grab it from his hand. It's a whitish grainy powder. I smell it, taste it and try to decipher it.

'Come on, Meezan Bhai. Tell me the secret! What is it?'

'Begum, this is char-maghaz powder made from four seeds—musk melon, watermelon cucumber and pumpkin seeds. Lo, now I have told you my secret.'

Another secret pudiya emerges out of an obscure corner with an aromatic mixture he prepares specially for qorma. I start jotting down everything. My Kayastha qorma is not a patch on his curry. Right at the end, he puts a huge dollop of ghee, seals the pan and takes it off the heat.

'Now when you open it, there will be taar.' Taar—the ghee drizzling down like golden strands with every nivala of the curry—is the measure of a perfect qorma. I'm already drooling with the qorma smells. I taste a teaspoon of the thickish gravy with its unerring balance of flavours and feel whole again.

Munni Bai's Second Visit to Rampur

(April–May 1882)

Boley merī balā qafas meiñ rahe
Ādmī kyun parāye bas meiñ rahe
Qaid ḳhāna hai Rāmpur mujhe
Jald ruḳhsat kareiñ ḥuzūr mujhey.

She couldn't survive this captivity, she said;
Why should a person be controlled by another?
Rampur is like a jail to me,
Bid me farewell soon, sir.

—Dagh Dehlvi
Faryād e Dāgh (1882)

FINALLY, DAGH GATHERED THE COURAGE TO SEND A LETTER requesting to meet you at Agha Sahib's house. You were incensed—Agha Sahib had poisoned Dagh's ears against you during your last visit. Dagh was trusting and loving towards everyone, even two-faced people like Agha Sahib. You wrote back a stinging reply, accusing Dagh of amusing himself with tawaifs in the past year, perhaps even using the very house. How could you expect him to be faithful? Dagh swallowed your insults and persisted in pleading through his letters, till you relented. After the Benazir Mela concluded, you and your entourage went to live at Agha Sahib's haveli, which he had so kindly allowed Dagh to host you in. Dagh was delighted. He greeted Hameedan and Khuda Bakhsh with genuine affection and ensured that everyone was comfortable.

'You are my guest. It is my honour to host you in this humble dwelling.' Dagh touched his forehead formally.

'I believe in wazeydaari; I observe customs and traditions. Such has been taught to us.'

'You speak to me of wazeydaari? If you were faithful to me, you wouldn't have stayed as Nawab Haider's guest.'

'My relations with Nawab Haider are older than my relationship with you—that is my wazeydaari. Now, since you had begged me to, I'm here.' You fanned yourself with the frilled hand-held fan.

'That's because I had asked Agha Sahib to convey to Haider Ali my involvement with you. He is a generous person and immediately told Agha Sahib that he would never stand in my way.'

'For you all, I'm a thing to be passed from one to another! You have the pleasure of having several tawaifs in your employ. Who amuses you these days? You wrote that nothing feels good. Maybe the tawaifs were the only way to cheer you up.' You smiled with mocking jealousy.

Dagh stood stunned. You had come to know that Dagh was famous for enjoying the company of tawaifs. You had overheard a recent bazaar saying, '*Jadi randi ko lag gaya hai Dagh*, Jadi randi has got a blemish (Dagh).' You thought for him, you were special. Maybe he wrote passionate letters to all tawaifs and satisfied his carnality with cheap randis.

'Of course, being with tawaifs is a part of your upbringing. It's home to you! Then you must be aware that we tawaifs charge for our company. Can you pay my nazrana? I have travelled for three days to meet you.' Your words were deliberate, twisting in the knife. Your reference to Dagh's mother, Khanum Jan, a famed tawaif, and his aunt, a concubine to Nawab Yusuf Ali Khan, was not lost on Dagh. His face paled with the insults; he couldn't utter a word to disrespect his guest. You clapped your hands, laughing.

'Ah, Dagh Sahib, look at your face—as if I'm asking you for a jagir! You don't have a jagir, I know. My fees are your islaah for my writing!' You placed your head on Dagh's chest, feeling his relief. Perhaps his heart still thrummed with the pain of your onslaughts. You would make up for the hurt by living with him for the rest of your time in Rampur. You needed to humble him before you could be convinced that he truly loved you—to slash open the depths of the relationship—only then could you reveal your love for him. He was, after all, going to be your lover, not a patron—a relationship of choice, not compulsion, which should rest on the foundation of love. Did he expect you to speak sugar-laced false words like his other tawaifs, the way you spoke your babus? Would that have pleased him?

You turned to him, and he set aside all your accusations and insults, becoming the ecstatic lover. This is what you craved—his gratitude, that incredulous wonder at the turning tide of love. His sense of self had to be destroyed and then miraculously resurrected by your love. How else could you be sure of him? Nights of love and poetry consumed both of you for two months; the town was alive with your love.

Later, he would write in his masnavi that your words broke him—a hurt he carried to his grave—'Hurt inflicted by words never heals; an honourable person dies of such wounds.' It was a relationship that began with fatal wounds and his realization that he had to bleed to carry on.

You attended mehfils, sang and recited your new compositions. Dagh helped you find words, weigh and place them to convey your feelings. His absorption with the language was intense. He coached you in the subtle difference in the usage of words by Awadh poets and Delhi poets. 'The word "jauban" is used by Awadh poets as a synonym for a woman's breasts, but for us Delhi poets, it signifies youth. *Ajab jauban barasta hai kisi se jab wo ladtey hain*—strange is the fire of youth when she fights with me. Understand that the physical is not so important as the idea behind the physical.' The lessons after your lovemaking carried a resonance beyond time. You would always hear his gravelly whisper when you wrote—his devotion to you transposed on his passion for words and language. He often spoke of the ongoing tussle between him and Ameer Minai—the battle for supremacy of Lucknow zuban versus Delhi zuban. He loved to say, '*Urdu hai jiska ka naam hamin jantey hain Dagh; Hindustan mein dhoom hamari zabaan ki hai.*' Only Dagh knows what Urdu is; Hindustan celebrates my language. It was said that people left with Dagh's couplets on their lips after Rampur mushairas because his compositions were so relatable and sublime in their simplicity.

After every mehfil, you returned to his arms, and he would plead, 'Live in Rampur. You will find many who will appreciate your talent—your qadardans. Your name will shine in the sky of shayaras (poetesses).'

But you craved a freedom that Rampur could never give you. In Calcutta, you could hire a phaeton and ride through the streets, go to the riverbank or wander the bazaars, bargain, laugh, talk in Bangla and Urdu. It was only at the Benazir Mela that you could walk on the paths and under the trees. You felt constrained in Rampur; you were a tawaif; people should look upon you and admire you. If you wanted to go out, a palki was brought and set in the courtyard by the kahars, and you crept in like a veiled begum. Its thick curtains smothered you and closed you off from the world; you longed to throw back the curtains and gaze at the streets and the people. Hameedan enjoyed the palki experience, but you missed the sweep of the wind on your face. You could walk down the street escorted by Khuda Bakhsh but had to cover yourself completely in a burqa. Soon, you felt tired of the unfree living and complained to Dagh.

You could feel Dagh sinking deeper into his ishq for you. He said that the next stage of his ishq was the insanity of the lover—the majnu. But you were not prepared for the intensity; his love's madness would surely throttle you. You told Dagh that it was not in your nature to be beholden to any man; you were a free woman and enjoyed the unique freedom that only tawaifs could have in society.

'Give me leave to go home,' you begged him and watched his crestfallen face—he had hoped for some more time with you, maybe a month more. But you were adamant—not a day more in this prison.

'Without you, I'll die of loneliness,' he said.

'Then come and live with me in Calcutta. You write, and I shall make your lines immortal with my singing. We shall be together.'

'You call this wazeydaari? You shall see my wafadaari (faithfulness) towards my Nawab. He is a generous employer and regards me very highly. He often refers to me as his brother. He gave me the honorary post of administering the stables when I had nothing. I cannot betray his unquestioning trust and love. I lack for nothing here. You know, when the Nawab lost his son, we sat and cried together; he was there for me when I lost my son. I have felt his pain, and he has felt mine. How can I ever repay him for taking me with him for the Hajj pilgrimage?'

'You say you will die without me, then why can't you live with me in Calcutta? I have enough for both of us there.'

'You mean I should live off your earnings like a pimp? Have you forgotten that I have a wife? What will be her position if I go and live with you?'

'You sell your shayari, and I sell my voice and body. I don't think we're very different. You, of all people, shouldn't have any qualms about living off the earnings of a tawaif! As for your wife, if it isn't me, it will be someone else. You cannot exist without entertaining yourself with tawaifs, and she must have made peace with it. Anyway, where would she go if she left you? If you so wish, she can come with you, too, and stay in your zenana. I wouldn't mind that.'

Dagh's first love and wife was his cousin, Fatima, his partner of thirty-four years. They had married as teenagers. She had his deep respect and the companionship of a life lived together. The loss of their infant son had brought them even closer in the past years. He would never forsake her. You knew and respected that. You were not dependent on any husband. Even if you sat back for months without a patron, you could live off the land you had bought on Apa's insistence.

Dagh had earlier been an absentee employee for eight years in the time of the former Nawab, Yusuf Ali Khan. He used to live in Delhi and come over to Rampur for mushairas and special occasions. His salary was sent to Delhi every month. If Dagh really loved you and wanted to be with you, he could persuade Nawab Kalb e Ali Khan to allow similar conditions of absentee employment. But Dagh refused to leave Nawab Kalb e Ali Khan. This was his wazeydaari and wafadaari—he threw your words back at you. What would you know about the meaning of those words? You changed patrons every few months, his tone seemed to imply.

Your time together was always fraught with familiar arguments. Your roles had been defined, the dialogues written, and you circled back to your parts. You wanted to escape the insidious staleness of the relationship, but knew that you would crave for his acceptance—the comfort of revealing your vulnerability and basking in his generous warmth, his all-forgiving love. Dagh's love had become the still point, the constant in your life that you had begun taking for granted. Sometimes, you were overcome with fear that this great, kind man would waste away because of his love for you. At such moments, you would soften towards him, regretting your words and stinging remarks.

As the day of your departure approached, Dagh stopped eating. Sometimes, his eyes brimmed with tears, and he clung to you like a child, already mourning the separation. He was living in the future, the loneliness of a time when you would no longer be by his side. In your young life, you had never seen such emotional dependence from a man. It was gratifying, and at times, strangulating. You were kind to him before leaving, begging him to come to Calcutta, extracting the promise of a visit. The departure was more fraught this time.

Teary-eyed, he said, 'You leave me at death's door. Khuda hafiz!'

أُنْس

7

Uns (Attachment)

'RUKH SE ZAHIR THA NOOR KA AALAM, AUR US PE GHUROOR *ka alam.* (Her face glowed with celestial luminosity/Framed by her haughty demeanour),' Daniyal recites. 'So, Dagh went to Calcutta to meet Hijab and after his return to Rampur, he wrote the famous masnavi *Faryaad e Dagh*. While he was writing it, he already knew that theirs was a doomed love. He was looking back with this lingering sadness for what could never be.'

'Why?'

'Because Hijab would never leave Calcutta to live in Rampur, and he couldn't leave his employment in Rampur.' Daniyal's T-shirt has dark sweat patches. He usually wears a T-shirt and joggers for his morning walk, which somehow make him look vulnerable. My mental image of him is in his starched formal kurta pyjamas, like some erstwhile royalty.

We sit on the porch, a table between us and a noisy, valiant table fan trying to fend off the creeping humid heat. These days, the mornings are tolerable, sometimes even cool, with moisture-laden breeze from the hills. Rampuris say, *Pahad baras riya hai*, the hills are raining. Looking towards the north, the vision unhampered by city constructions, one can see the mountains with paint-stroke smudges of grey clouds when it rains up there.

'We have these letters and poetry from Dagh, but what were Hijab's feelings? What did she truly want?' I offer him a cupcake. Meezan Bhai, resigned to Daniyal's daily visits, has started serving goodies. I believe Daniyal has charmed him—he takes care to greet him by name and indulges in chit-chat, sometimes even requesting him for tea. He is never condescending towards Meezan Bhai.

'Why are you rushing forward in the story? Why do you want to know how it ended?'

'You said it was doomed.'

'At the beginning, yes. But be patient with its journey. Dagh writes that though he had been in love several times, Khwaja Moinuddin Chishti and Hijab were his two enduring soul-loves. So, I do think he loved Hijab, but was his love reciprocated?'

'Maybe Hijab doubted his love. Even I doubt his rather extravagant and too poetic confessions of love.'

'Can people ever love each other equally? Perhaps we love an image of ourselves in the other—we never really know him or her. I think we invent the other as a version of ourselves, our desires or that part of ourselves we lack.' I tear my gaze away from Daniyal and muse over his words.

'Did Dagh really know Hijab, or did he love an image of her?' I murmur more to myself as we let our meditations hang in the air. We have become comfortable with our silences, breaking off and getting back to the strand of the discussion after long pauses.

Maybe Dagh never really knew Hijab; he just experienced her symptomatic personality—if there can be symptoms of the inner core—and wrote about them. Beyond her anger, flirtation, melancholy and expressions of love, who was she? Hijab tried to reveal herself to Dagh, but did he grasp her essential being? Do I know Faraz after all the years of being together? I know his feelings, his responses to things and often anticipate and hedge his moods. Akriti says that I should stop justifying his behaviour towards me. If you utter the words 'toxic relationship', I will stop talking to you about Faraz, I tell her. We are weathering tough times and will come out of it. It has been a long, difficult period.

'Was it difficult for women writers to get published at that time?' I ask after a lull during which Daniyal takes off his reading glasses and rests it on his lower lip.

'Hijab had written a diwan at nineteen. That must mean that she was good, or maybe it was self-published? I don't know the publication how-tos of the time.'

'I think there was a market for tawaifs who became poetesses. Malka Jan, the mother of Gauhar Jan, had also written a diwan a bit later. Perhaps they weren't as well regarded as the male poets. Unfortunately, Hijab's diwan hasn't survived. We have some of her compositions from the tazkiras, which is a collection of biographies of poets. Perhaps she wouldn't have even found mention in the tazkiras if it hadn't been for her association with Dagh.'

'So you believe women writers need—or needed—the endorsement of male writers to survive the test of time. What about talent?' I quip defensively.

'Apologies, I didn't mean to offend. I think there are a number of women writers today who will survive without male endorsement. Maybe Hijab was talented, but that didn't silence people who said that she was riding on Dagh's coat-tails, or rather sherwani tails. I wonder if she was as talented as Dagh. But I do believe that though there was space for women writers in the late nineteenth century, the publishers were still heavily biased towards male writers. Things are much better today.' I nod. I was, after all, a woman of the #MeToo era, quick on the defensive. How could I judge the realities of the late nineteenth century? Maybe at that time, it was crucial to have an influential male mentor to get noticed and published. Possibly her first diwan was published with the support of her tutor Nassakh who was an influential British official.

Our appointed half hour has extended to nearly an hour, and it is becoming hotter. I suggest we shift into the drawing room, but Daniyal says he needs to get back. Suddenly, I realize that over the past few visits, we have often overextended our time. My insistence on moving into the drawing room always makes him leave a bit abruptly. I don't want to disturb Faraz by having the discussion in the drawing room, and Daniyal has somehow accepted this tacit boundary. Actually, I don't want Faraz overhearing us, brooding over our talk and analysing it for me later. Akriti says I'm always anticipating trouble with Faraz and acting accordingly. Aren't we all troubleshooters in our marriages?

I search for the remains of Hijab's writings on Rekhta and transcribe them in my childish Urdu, tracing the meters as I vocalize them. I find four tazkiras with her biography, followed by her verses at the library, and note them down. I can safely say that I now have all her surviving compositions—there is barely a handful of them. The more recent tazkiras say that her diwan was lost. I try to decipher her feelings through her writings; I have to look up the meanings of some words in the online dictionary. Most of the couplets are filled with longing, love, melancholy, heartbreak and abandonment—the usual and accepted subject matter at that time. But you can't judge a writer by just a snapshot of his or her work; it is unfair. Besides, I cannot claim to be a good judge of ghazals.

I read her sparse biography in the volumes on women poets of the time. She is one of hundreds, distinguished only by her association with Dagh. All biographers concur that she was renowned for her poetry and singing, which is why she was invited to the Benazir Mela. Some critics debate Dagh's influence on her writing, some openly allege that her lines were practically ghostwritten by the besotted poet. But she had been composing and was a renowned, published writer even before she met him. She had other teachers—Abdul Ghafur Nassakh and Maulvi Abdullah Ansakh. Maybe they were her lovers, too. One critic somewhat condescendingly writes that though her poetry reflects Dagh's manner, the voice and rhythm are hers alone.

I look for chinks in her people-pleasing, performatory lines to find my Hijab—the quicksilver, temperamental, outspoken woman reflected in Dagh's masnavi; the woman who confounded him as he struggled to pin her down in his letters. Was she envisioning herself seated in a salon singing the soulful lines to a rapt audience? Or were the verses welling from a deep source, a translation of grief, unrequited love shaped into words?

Then I find the lines:

Hazrat e Nāseh na bak-bak kar phirayein sar mera
Qibla-e man chup hī rahiye bas nasīhat ho chukī

Mr Naseh your constant chatter makes my head spin
Be quiet, o learned one, enough of your advice (mansplaining)!

The sher was probably for a male friend; she'd about had enough of mansplaining. Here you are, Hijab!

Dagh's Undated Letter to Hijab

Dildar, dil Nawaz, O keeper of my heart!

How you have changed since you left! Have you forgotten all your promises and oaths? I sent you a letter, but you're too engrossed in the distractions of Calcutta to reply. Don't you ever think of my restless heart, or maybe, you feel I'm heartless? If you don't reply immediately to my letter, I will buy myself some poison from the bazaar and lay down my life. I asked you to promise, and you took an oath, that if not every day, you would write at least twice a week. It has been ten days since you left, and there is no news of you. If you couldn't write to me, at least you should have conveyed your khairiyat (well-being) *through somebody.*

Since you left, I feel lifeless. My heart cannot be at peace till I receive a letter from you.

Dagh
Undated letter

حَسَد

8

Hasad (Jealousy)

If I THOUGHT THE BOOK CLUB STORY HAD ENDED, I HAD underestimated Akriti. She called to suggest that we read Elif Shafaq's *Forty Rules of Love* this month. I connect everyone on a WhatsApp group, the Rampur Book Club, and decide to meet on the last Sunday of July.

Akriti: *You are writing a love story anyway—you need to know all about love-shove.*

Daniyal: *This book is a Western take on Rumi; like a brain candy. Let's read Rumi instead.*

Kuku: *You study Rumi and Shams, then, and give us insights at the meeting.*

Secretly, I hope he will opt out of the meeting and the book club. It's not intellectual enough for him, and I don't want him to sit there judging us with his brooding, inscrutable look. This meeting, even if it is around an alleged 'brain candy', is essential to cement the book club. Akriti says it's good that sparks flew at the first meeting; it became an icebreaker, and now we will settle into our roles and be comfortable around each other. All the sparks were there because of the ex-lovers, I snort. It makes the book club more exciting to see a real-life love story happening there, she laughs.

'Not all members are as profound as you,' I tell Daniyal when he arrives the next morning.

'So I'll keep my highbrow comments to myself.'

'That's not what I meant.' I look away and focus on the copy in my hands.

'That's exactly what you meant. I can leave the club if you feel I won't fit.' He has that still, watchful look as he awaits my reaction. I have seen it play over many of our conversations. Initially, I used to feel judged, but now, I just say what I want to, and he accepts it. I think he is done with appraising and slotting me in his mind and I can be myself.

'We want you there. You represent all the Rampur males. Besides, I need you to drive me to Benazir Farm,' I say lightly.

Daniyal eye-smiles. 'I thought you could drive.'

'I do, but never out of the city.' My driving circle is predetermined—home, school and the Civil Lines market. I know Faraz won't like my venturing alone so far and he's too busy to take me to the farm.

Daniyal and I drive to Akriti's farm for the meeting. The farmlands around the Benazir Palace were bought by Akriti's father-in-law after the Partition and named Benazir Farms. The family had come to Rampur as refugees from Pakistan. Nawab Raza Ali Khan had allotted areas inside the fort to settle refugees from Punjabi Sikh and Hindu communities. Some bought land and settled into farming while others took up trading. They were named 'sharanarthi', a prosperous hard-working community lending a vibrant diversity to Rampur's populace.

A dirt road turns off from the main road towards the farm. Daniyal slows and steers his precious Silver Ghost gingerly over the potholes; the silver lady on his bonnet plunges on head first. Acres of mango and guava orchards and fields verdant with the newly sown rice plantation stretch around us. Usually, Faraz likes to visit the farm and have a drink or two with Pradeep, Akriti's husband, but today, he is busy trying to salvage his mango venture. We pull up to the farmhouse, surrounded by manicured lawns. After a thorough inspection by, Snippet, her labrador, Akriti ushers us into her drawing room.

Vani is there with her husband, Ritesh, a petite, bespectacled generic specimen for 'the good doctor'. Vani seems to have dressed him to match her flowery lemon dress, which hugs her voluptuous frame unapologetically and shows off her sturdy legs. I have never seen anyone wear a dress in Rampur. Ritesh, despite his bright outfit, manages to fade beside Vani's garrulous radiance. I will probably forget his face after the meeting.

'So glad that Rampuri males haven't lost their reading abilities,' I greet Ritesh and welcome him to the book club.

'Mine has become too much of a farmer,' laughs Akriti. 'Pradeep is away in Delhi for work.'

'Mine too!' I add.

'Shezray is on her way, so let's wait for her,' says Akriti. I stifle my eye roll.

Akriti gets busy serving drinks, and I go to Shubham's room. Shubham is sprawled on his bed sketching something; he looks up in alarm as I enter the room, then relaxes with a tight smile. I know he hates crowds and has retreated to his room. I sit on the sofa and try to talk to him; he has become even more skeletal since my last visit about a month ago. They had to request long leave from school; he will only go for the exams. Shubham is about a year younger than Gul, and they used to be great friends as kids. He was such a bright, energetic kid that it's difficult to reconcile this quiet, shrinking boy as Shubham. I hear Vani's trilling laugh and tell Shubham that I should go. He stiffens as I reach to touch the top of his head, and I remember the no-touch rule.

Akriti glances up as I join them, and I give her a nod—he's fine. Despite her strength, Akriti is balanced on a precipice, living each day as it comes. She says the book club gives her a breather from the relentless stress. I'm seized with sudden guilt for not making time for her.

'Let's begin, people. The second meeting of the Rampur Book Club shall now come to order! We welcome Dr Ritesh to the club.' Akriti smiles.

Ritesh was assigned to introduce the book, and he has actually written down the introduction. I find that so earnest and cute. Vani looks at him adoringly as he stands and reads. 'Ella is a devoted wife and mother. But something is missing in her life. Love comes to Ella unexpectedly as she starts reading this book, *Sweet Blasphemy*. The book is about the love between Rumi and Shams Tabriz. Intrigued, she connects with the author, Aziz, and becomes intellectually and then emotionally involved with him. So the book is a journey of Ella towards true love, inspired by the teachings of Rumi.'

Vani claps and says, 'Well done, Doc! I toh loove Rumi, and this book really made it so easy to know his life and philosophy.'

'It's an "instant Rumi for all" kind of a book. But I liked the way Elif Shafaq had written about Rumi's life, his relationship with Shams and the times they lived in,' Daniyal interjects as patronizing as ever. I almost give him a 'stop-it' look.

'It must have been a dangerous life with the Mongols and wars. I think the women suffered the most as targets of violence. They were shut away—so claustrophobic,' I say.

'Maybe they preferred to be invisible and safe. You're right; the ancient tale is all about men, and the modern story is about Ella's search for love.' Daniyal nods.

'Adab!' Shezray arrives with a graceful apology for being late, arranging herself on a chaise lounge. Her purple dupatta unfurls around her, studded with intricate kamdani and edged with ancient silver lace; she has paired it with a simple ivory-coloured mulmul Lucknowi kurta and purple tanchoi silk churidar. As always, at least one article of her clothing looks vintage—about a hundred years old. Daniyal touches his forehead in a mute salam.

I continue, determinedly. 'So, search for love is the theme of the story. Yet here we are, all of us at midlife, in our comfort zones of being married or single. Every day is like the one gone before... Maybe I prefer it like that.'

'But Shams says that every day should be different, otherwise it's a pity,' says Vani.

'And so we should all go on a quest, a thrill? I find this idea of leaving family and responsibilities in the quest of love a very western trope,' Akriti frowns.

'I think the main point of the book was not Ella falling in love and leaving her family but the idea of love itself. Being aware of love all around you. Loving yourself and loving people—that's the essence of Rumi.' Shezray breathes out her words, or maybe she's still out of breath from her entry. Her under-eye concealer has congealed around her lower lids, making the dark circles ghostly grey in the harsh light. Ageing is always hard for beautiful women. Mamma used to say that I could at best be called charming—and only if I chose to smile.

'That's right. Rumi differed from other theologians of the time by focusing not just on the teachings of the Quran but also on love for fellowmen. In this, he was profoundly influenced by Shams,' Daniyal agrees. I notice that he doesn't look directly at Shezray, or maybe I was expecting their eyes to lock with mutual longing.

'I wonder if they were gay and if Rumi married his daughter, Kimiya, to Shams in order to silence people,' says Ritesh.

'I feel terrible for Kimiya and angry towards Shams. Why did he marry her if he was unsure of the marriage? What about the love he preached? He destroyed a life!' Dear practical, down-to-earth Akriti looks really angry with the book.

'I know, right! Kimiya loved Shams, and then Shams decides that marriage is not for him, and he has to conquer his desires. I mean, what the eff!' Vani exclaims. I revel in the heightened emotions of the members; I believe a book discussion should tear out your innermost feelings.

'I really believe that all these holy men sitting in one corner talking of love are selfish. They want perfection for themselves. Can I leave my son in search of perfection or... or because I found the perfect love?' Akriti bursts out, then stops and looks at me—*relax, Kuku*.

I feel breathless, my lungs wrung out. The best part of being married in this place is that no one knows my backstory, except Akriti.

'You are perfecting yourself by caring for your child,' Daniyal says gently. 'Submission and faith in our inner journey towards perfection are important.'

'Sometimes, choosing to stay single—like when I walked out of an abusive marriage—gives you freedom. But if you've been together for a long time, have kids, there's this shadow of the man in your life and in your children's, forever.' Shezray leans back, her eyes half shut. There is a beat of silence—we are unsure about how to respond to Shezray's sharing. I don't think Shezray is looking for empathy—at least not from us. Maybe she wants Daniyal to understand something between them or show her vulnerability.

'I'm gonna stick with my man; no worries, darling.' Vani threads her fingers through Ritesh's hand and smiles up at him. Ritesh squirms.

'Rukmini is researching this fabulous love story—Dagh Dehlvi, the poet, and Munni Bai Hijab, the tawaif,' Daniyal rushes in.

'And can you believe this—Dagh saw Hijab for the first time literally in Akriti's backyard, at the Benazir Palace, and fell in love with her!' I say, perhaps too eagerly.

'It was the greatest love story of that time,' Daniyal joins in.

'Dagh wrote a long poem about her and simply hundreds of letters to her...' I carry on.

'That's amazing! Let's go to the palace where it all happened.' Vani almost jumps up.

'Wait! Let's first have some snacks.' Akriti gets up to serve, and I join her. I'm not happy with the abrupt winding up of the meeting or my reaction to Shezray. I think it was brave of her to speak up. I'm usually quite accepting of confidences, and I want the book club to be an inclusive and supportive place; but somehow, I backed out and didn't give Shezray that space. Daniyal holds forth on Dagh and Munni as we have tea.

Edging Akriti's farm are the ruins of Benazir Palace. After a tea-pakora feast, we set off through the rice fields. There is a light drizzle, and Akriti hands each of us an umbrella. An octagonal structure with a dome crowned with a golden pinnacle comes into view.

'That's Qadam Shareef. People come here to pray for their mannat. It has the foot impression of Prophet Muhammad,' Akriti points out.

'It was bought by Nawab Kalb e Ali Khan from his Hajj pilgrimage to Mecca. The Benazir Mela ended with a procession to the Qadam Shareef and a fireworks display,' Daniyal adds.

'Wow! Can we make a mannat to find true love like Ella?' Vani giggles firmly holding Ritesh's hand, enjoying the romantic walk.

'You already have! College sweethearts,' says Akriti. 'But seriously, people say wishes do come true here, though I've never been inside.'

We cross the fields, skirting the monument, and reach the crumbling boundary wall of the Benazir Palace.

'These thin lakhauri bricks show that the boundary was built in the nineteenth century or even earlier,' Daniyal says as we walk through an elaborate archway. After last night's rain, the potholes on the mud road are filled with slush, making it difficult for Vani to walk in her pencil heels and ruining Shezray's embroidered jooties. I'm glad for my sensible flats; I knew we would end up walking around the farm. Mango trees form a canopy over us, and Daniyal points at a dry canal surrounding the palace. The canal water was sourced by French engineers from the Kosi River, he explains. We are walking in a loose group, with Ritesh supporting Vani through the mush. I notice that Daniyal always walks at a distance from Shezray; or maybe I'm just being hyper-aware of them. I glance down at the canal and see a rusted motorboat marooned in the undergrowth. Daniyal stops beside me and tells me that they used to have boat rides for the royal family and guests. I knew about the boat rides from my reading of the text on the Benazir Mela. They must have continued the joy rides on the canal till the motorboats came in. We walk over a quaint little bridge to cross the canal. The Benazir Palace rises before us, massive and resplendent even in its ruins.

'This was the summer palace of Nawab Kalb e Ali Khan in the nineteenth century. In fact, the canal and boats used to be there even when we visited as kids in the 1970s.'

Where did Dagh first see Hijab? At a mehfil inside the palace, walking around in the mela held around the palace, or strolling through the intricate paths in the orchard. I try to imagine the perfect setting for Dagh's love-at-first-sight episode.

Ten–fifteen steps lead up to what might have been the palace entrance. The iron bannisters on either side of the steps have been wrenched off, and the drooping ornate lamps are vandalized and eyeless. Akriti tells us that people started taking away fixtures from the palace when it became a contested property; the court case still drags on between the royal claimants. The high ceiling of the main hall collapsed a few years ago. Now, trees reach up to the open skies, their foliage thick inside the durbar hall. All the mushairas and performances must have been held there.

'Did Dagh really meet Hijab here?' asks Shezray. It has stopped drizzling, but she keeps her umbrella open, presumably to shield her outfit from residual drops from the trees.

'That's what he says in his masnavi,' Daniyal replies.

'And he fell in love with her forever? What happened next?' Shezray turns to me.

'I'm still researching. I don't know how it ended,' I say. 'Daniyal, can you access the masnavi on your mobile? Perhaps you could read a bit from it just to give context?'

Daniyal nods, sits on the steps, pulls out his mobile and reads:

'Ā gayā Benazīr kā melā,
Dil e pāband e waza khil khelā
Jalwa dekhā jo hūr e talat kā
Sāmna ho gayā qayāmat kā'

(Mela Benazir is in full swing again
The heart blooms with delight
Chancing upon the beauteous Hourie
I reeled with apocalyptic enchantment.)

Daniyal's voice, a tender baritone, lingers on the words, savouring their texture.

'Everyone just freeze where you are!' Vani positions her camera for a selfie. We capture the moment for the future and get busy posting it to the world. I realize that perhaps only Daniyal and I felt the impact of Dagh's words; maybe I shouldn't have asked Daniyal to recite it. Vani muttered something like, 'That was too much of Urdu.' Vani and Ritesh walk away towards a stairway, which Akriti says leads to the roof. We give them time to steal a kiss before ascending the roof behind them. We can see the whole orchard spread out around us from the roof. Vani is engrossed in clicking more pictures. We do another selfie, grinning at our images on the screen.

'I wonder if Hijab truly loved Dagh,' murmurs Shezray. She has wrapped her dupatta around her like a crinkled cocoon. Perhaps she felt the words of the masnavi, too, or she just wants to speak of the love story.

'Maybe they did love each other; or it was—what do you call it… 'situationship'. Tawaifs were the only interesting women—beautiful, well-read, accomplished, renowned for their intelligent repartee—the ideal muse for poets.' Daniyal sits on a low parapet.

'Sexually available, too,' Shezray remarks.

'Yes, that too.' Daniyal avoids the dark gravity of her eyes.

'A better idea than the boring middle-aged wife at home,' I retort, eyebrow raised.

'I believe Dagh loved his wife. It was a love match. They were both sixteen when they got married. Who says you can't love two women in different ways, or indeed men?' Daniyal replies.

'I think he was just a dirty old man amusing himself with tawaifs!' Ritesh smirks.

Daniyal shakes his head and gets up. I think he has given up the idea of the present company understanding the Dagh–Hijab love story. I also feel the need to protect the story from exposure to people with such a narrow viewpoint. Maybe we shouldn't have brought it up at all.

My phone buzzes in my hand. It is Faraz calling to ask what to get prepared for dinner and when I will return. He sounds irritated; the day probably didn't go well for him. His annoyance spills over, creeps up my skull and prickles at the roots of my hair. 'Skittish menopausal hormones'—Baba's diagnosis. My periods are delayed again, fulfilling Baba's predictions. Maybe I'm PMS-ing. I try to breathe slowly, calming my anxiety. I know Faraz wants me to sit witness to his mood and his suffering brought on by the current calamity, which he might not even discuss with me. I turn away from Daniyal's penetrating stare attempting to decipher me from the other end of the almost crumbling roof. It's nothing—just hormones; I'm a hormonal mess, I want to tell him. Mamma said women never had PMS till everyone started talking about it. It was a conspiracy to make women seem inconsistent and temperamental.

The drive back is quiet. Daniyal is sensitive enough to give me space. The sun has prevailed over the sheltering clouds, blazing feverishly.

I thank Daniyal for the ride and unceremoniously dump him with Faraz when we reach home. I'm in no mood for tea and chit-chat; I feel too exhausted to pander to Faraz. Maybe Daniyal and a few drinks will sort him out. Faraz and Ritesh are right—Dagh was just an older man lusting after a younger woman. Such liaisons are basically borne out of lust from the male point of view. What we delicately call love at first sight is merely sexual desire, a bodily response to stimulus. I'm writing a lust story. So banal, so transient and insignificant. I feel ridiculous; I'm pathetic.

Munni Bai Hijab, Calcutta
(June 1882)

Rasm e 'ulfat nibhātey ho agar
Jān kī ḳhair chāhtey ho agar
Uth ke sīdhey idhar chaley āo
Koī rokey magar chaley āo

If you are faithful to the norms of love
If you want your life spared,
Come immediately to me
Come, leaving everyone.

—Dagh Dehlvi
Faryād e Dāgh (1882)

IN THE NAME OF ULFAT, YOU COMMANDED HIM TO COME TO you. It had been a few days since your return to Calcutta. At first, you were relieved to be out of Rampur and its lazy, stifling lifestyle. The verve of Calcutta made blood flow with a sharp pang in your veins. The kotha was as intoxicating as ever with its jasmine and attar scents, the chandeliers and floor lamps casting lime green light on the tall mirrors all around the hall. Apa said it was important to have mirrors so that you would be aware of your attitude, your etiquette and your performance.

You loved to see your beauty reflected all around; it made you forget the crass desires in the eyes of men.

You had penned several ghazals in the two months you lived with Dagh as you tried to inculcate the impetuous flow of words, which only he had. Dagh said your poetry did not reflect your personality; that at times, you pretended a melancholic desolation that you didn't feel. He helped you expose your soul on paper. Only he understood that under the exterior of the vivacious, poetic tawaif lurked a viper-tongued, unhappy woman who lived to defend the sensitive poetess.

It was thrilling to sing your newly minted ghazals, to hear your voice tease the words into melody. Apa had accepted nazar, an advance payment for a mehfil from an important and rich zamindar babu who was bringing his angrez friend, Hewitt Sahib, that evening. She was excited about the mehfil and set about getting the kotha ready. She loved sitting on her special floor cushion, bejewelled, puffing on her huqqa, leaning back on velvet bolsters, her pandan close at hand to artfully prepare paan and proffer it to an esteemed guest. Years of toil, displacement and cavorting with men had won her this place.

Apa was relieved at your return and remarked that everyone was talking about your sojourns in Rampur and your association with the greatest Indian poet. You shone because of Dagh, but soon, people would know you for yourself. Every customer wanted to listen to a sensitive poetess, her tears and sighs emblazoned in poetry. Nawab Haider had complimented you, saying your poetry made him weep and stay up the night. You gave them what they wanted.

At the dazzling mehfil, beautifully curated by Apa, you sang the ghazal you had completed in Rampur. It had taken a full year to reach fruition. Zamindar Babu and Hewitt Sahib were enthralled. You knew the pattern—not content with listening into your soul, Zamindar Babu would want to possess your body for a few months, perhaps a year, and then move away.

Predictably, the next morning, Zamindar Babu sent a proposal for exclusive rights to your body. Apa, seated on her takht, offered a silver-foil-encased paan to the musahib and quibbled over the price with coquetry she played out for such occasions. The paan-stained teeth peeping out to support the enforced coyness nauseated you. You would become like her—a paan-chewing, corpulent negotiator for your daughter. In a few years, you would birth a girl; if it turned out to be a boy, you would try again. Girls ensured futures; boys were a burden, feeding off the kotha's earnings, like Khuda Bakhsh and Shafeeq. You didn't want the patronage of Zamindar Babu. At the mehfil, he had become quite drunk, and Hewitt Sahib had tried to grab you. Dagh never drank, and you would laugh that he had already committed the forbidden act of zina (fornication) with you and with many other women, so he might as well indulge in another haraam act—of drinking. He was a gentle lover, and his lovemaking was as passionate as his poetry. You felt precious and loved. With him, you had that sense of confidence that you could do anything and still be loved. Critics often accused him of having at least one tawaif in his control to entertain him and serve as his muse. Sometimes, you would feel intense jealousy for all those who had gone before and the ones who would surely follow you. You wanted to be enough for him forever.

Irritated by Apa's wheedling tone, you retreated to your room. It was midday, and you felt the hangover from the wine you drank after last night's performance. The mornings after night-long mehfils were always your worst. You called for breakfast and lay down again on the masahri. Dagh was the only person who could tolerate you in this mood. You missed Dagh's gentle presence, the generosity of spirit that made you feel like the most desirable woman in the world.

Apa came in, wreathed with the special content smile she displayed when she accepted a fabulously rich proposal. She sat down near you and started describing the terms of the proposal. You asked her to return the token amount. She was sharp with you—*How are we going to survive if you are so capricious?* She blamed it on the effect Dagh had on you. Last time you had returned from Rampur with your head full of Dagh and poetry. It was worse this time. You could feel Apa's fury and her intense desire to pull you by the roots of your hair and slap the obstinacy out of you. She had done it often enough in the past. There were beads of sweat on her lined forehead; a flush crept up her flaccid cheeks, and her teeth were bared like fangs. You did not get up in fear like you usually did but continued to glare at her—*Do your worst*. It had been years since those slaps, the sting of one superimposed by another, the scathing obscenities accompanied by pummelling and kicking as you were thrown on the floor. Khala would always throw herself over you and catch hold of Apa's hands. 'Forgive her! Forgive her!' she would scream. In hindsight, you now felt that Khala defended you not out of love but to be in your good books. After all, you were going to control the kotha ultimately. Apa was demonic in her anger. Her massive body, sitting inert for hours on the takht, would spring to life and become a tornado of raging retribution. She would fling off her dupatta, gather her trailing skirts on her arm, stand up to scream expletives and catch hold of the object of her anger, unleashing her fury—slapping, shoving and kicking.

You remembered the time Khala had caught you with Uttam, the son of the sweet maker. Uttam was beaten up by the kotha goons and thrown out into the street. Apa said she had saved you from getting spoilt, kharab. You realized later that what she meant was that she had saved your virginity for the highest bidder. That was the time your 'nath-utrai' ceremony was being planned where your nath (nose ring) would be taken off by the highest bidder for your virginity. It was a sort of temporary marriage to your first patron. They had stitched your trousseau in resplendent silks, with tinsels on the heavy embroidered dupattas and kurtas so tight that you could scarcely breathe. Apa had carefully chosen a handsome young boy, the son of a rich businessman. The first experience should be good but not such that you would fall in love. The young man was already married and going to be a father. Then there was Uttam with his adoring dark eyes lingering on you as he delivered the sweets from his shop. You called him to your room upstairs one afternoon, thinking everyone would be asleep. But how could they sleep, leaving the treasure unguarded?

'Apa, tell Zamindar Babu that I cannot accept his offer. Dagh Sahib is coming to visit me.'

'Oho, such airs! Your Dagh Sahib will never come, mark my words.'

You turned away from her. Let her beat you up, but you did not budge. If only Dagh could understand how fiercely you fought for your time with him. Dagh would come, he had promised. You heard Apa inhale sharply. Maybe she would smack your back in anger. You closed your eyes tight in anticipation. Apa put her heavy hand on your turned-away shoulder. 'Listen, my innocent doll, men never come back, or why would we be sitting here?' Her over-affectionate voice overlaid her rage.

You kept your back towards her. Dagh was not your customer; he was your pir o murshid and mentor, you asserted. Apa was flabbergasted at your attitude. She always knew you would fall in love, face desertion, then come to your senses and get back to work—the general pattern for over-emotional girls like you. They had a tough time with you after that disastrous encounter with the trader. It had taken months for you to get back to singing and a year to start receiving patrons. Apa understood that your involvement with Dagh was deeper than physical love. This would never do; they had a kotha to run, and you were the star. Hameedan imitated your poetic style and tried to amplify herself by outrageous flirtations, but you had the fame of being Dagh's lover and muse. Apa got up with a sigh and sent Khala to plead with you.

You came to an agreement with Khala, the peacemaker. If Dagh refused to come, you would accept the zamindar's proposal or any other patron Apa chose for you. Dagh would come; you were sure. He said the mouth of his grave opened when you left. You wanted him to see Calcutta, be enticed by its openness. You wanted to love him in the freedom of Calcutta. You wrote to Dagh: *If your ishq is true, leave everything and come to me or turn away from me forever.*

مُلاقات

9

Mulāqāt (Meeting)

Wo aur merey ghar meiñ chalein āyeiñ khud ba khud
Sar par merey Ḥijāb magar āsman nahīñ.

Him, and visiting my home is unimaginable
The sky is not my aegis, O Hijab.

—Munni Bai Hijab
Tazkirā e qadīm shairāt e Urdu

On impulse, I decide to visit Daniyal at his house to borrow his copy of Dagh's biography. He hadn't come over since the book club meeting nor had he excused himself from our daily appointment. I do miss our talks, delving deeper into Dagh and Munni's life, making that era alive for me. Meezan Bhai asks about him every day.

I call him up and invite myself over. He pauses and tries to keep the surprise out of his voice; we are both aware that this is culturally inappropriate—a woman visiting unrelated males alone in Rampur is unacceptable, even scandalous. I don't tell Faraz, to avoid his barrage of questions; he would insist on taking me, and it would have to wait till whenever he is free or in a better mood. I drive to Baba's clinic inside the city, park the car there and hire a rickshaw to Daniyal's house. Navigating the narrow gullies in my car is impossible. I'm sort of incognito, wrapped in a cotton dupatta with large sunglasses, but I still inspire the curiosity of passers-by who stop and stare at me. I need the black obscurity of a burqa here.

When I reach, the house somehow looks less grand than last time, or maybe I have grown accustomed to its imposing structure. It isn't a two-storied structure as I had thought earlier. The ceilings are very high—twenty-five foot Daniyal tells me later—which give the impression of height. Walking into the drawing room with Daniyal, I'm enveloped by a mellow, refreshing air. The walls are cool, almost moist to the touch. We have lost the art of making comfortable houses that are insulated against the heat with thick walls and high ceilings. Maybe they are too expensive and take longer to construct. I notice there are no air conditioners in Daniyal's haveli; they keep low lights on even during the day and thick curtains keep out the heat and light. Without Faraz around, everything seems more intimate, verging on clandestine.

I walk around the hall and the gallery, taking in the black and white framed pictures, and listening to Daniyal's stories—tiger hunts, coronation ceremonies, marriages, the durbar—till we reach the alcove with his great-grandfather's marble bust. You have the nose, I tell him. Yes, I mean to get it redone, he laughs. We enter his study cum library. Rare books and documents collected by four generations of the family line the three walls. I run my fingers on the faded green, maroon and brown spines with gold lettering.

'It must require a lot of taking care,' I remark.

'More than the books, there are private letters, documents and diaries written by the Nawabs and important officials. I'll have to burn them before I die.'

'Because they could destroy reputations, bring down the Empire of Great Britain? Do you really think it matters now? Why not donate them to the Raza Library for preservation and research?'

'It will always matter. History matters, which is why you're doing what you are doing. Anyway, the rest of the books will go to the library, but these documents are a matter of trust to be passed from father to son, away from nosy writers. So I plan to destroy them before I die.'

I sink down on a deep green leather sofa, and Daniyal sits on the revolving chair of his work desk.

'What if you die suddenly? Maybe it will be less complicated to give it to a trusted person, adopt a child or get married and have a kid.'

'Marriage… I almost got there twice, but it didn't work out. Now I'm in my fifties and can't raise a son.' I wonder if one of those instances involved Shezray.

'But why this insistence on sons? Can only men be trusted with secrets? I'm sure daughters can do just as well, even better.'

'That's true, of course, except, I don't have a daughter either.' Daniyal presses a bell, and a house help magically appears with water.

'Would you like to have tea or something cold?'

'Tea for me, please.'

'*Chai le ayiye*. I'm sorry I have been a bit busy lately, and I meant to ask—how is your writing coming along?' Daniyal shifts gears.

'I have, in fact, written three chapters, but I'm not sure if I can really get Hijab, you know. From Dagh's point of view, she was wilful, temperamental, even bitchy. I realized that she is always written by others—Dagh, Nishapuri and all the biographers—and now, I'm writing about her. But how did she see herself?'

'Do we ever know who we really are?'

'Maybe it's tougher for women to describe themselves, even now.' We are off on our soul-searching conversations—I missed them. I lean back.

'Tell me, why are educated women always on the defensive? Why do you all feel suppressed or oppressed?' Is there a little irritation in his voice? I bristle.

'Because several women *are* oppressed, at least in India, or they are repressed and not allowed to grow to their full potential. It's true even today.' Could he really be so divorced from reality?

'So men are the culprits?'

'I believe, it's patriarchy enforced by men most of the time; sometimes, other women and society act as agents of patriarchy.'

'That's why I don't like reading women authors from the subcontinent; they often write from positions of oppression. How much credence can we give to art that is born out of a certain position, justified or unjustified?'

'But what they write is the truth! How can you be so… so—'

'Were you oppressed or repressed as you say?' he cuts in.

Seriously, does he think I'm going on about myself?

'I think, and I might be wrong, that you had every opportunity to do what you wanted with your life.' Daniyal's chair is at a greater height, and I feel like I'm being analysed by a psychoanalyst.

'I had to take care of Gul, and I guess I just flowed along with the family. That's what we do across all social segments—willingly or unwillingly.' Why am I submitting to him, letting him judge my life choices?

'But you enjoyed teaching, I'm sure.'

'Sometimes, but it wasn't me.' It was more like my mother; I always wanted to write.

'Then, is it writing that defines you?'

'Perhaps… although I'm not sure that I would be able to write well anymore. It's been years since I even put together a sentence.'

'Faraz never asked you to take up teaching, and you didn't need the money in Dubai. So it was your choice. Then he didn't stop you from quitting now, even though you do need to help financially.'

Our Dubai home was so shiny and ordered that all the cracks were hidden, all the arguments seemed out of place. But here, the odd mixture of glitzy Dubai things, well-worn colonial furniture and flaking, damp walls might allow for real discussions, arguments, fights—an imperfect marriage exposed.

The lamp towering over Daniyal's seat creates a spotlight around him. His eyebrows are an inverted V over his half-closed eyes. I'm so used to mansplaining in my life that I don't even flinch, but I have had enough of his dissection of my life. You can't sum up a life so easily, I want to tell him, but don't.

'May I read?' I cut off the strand of the conversation, take out my diary and read out my first hesitant lines about Hijab. I think I have almost got her voice right, filtered from Dagh's letters and my own understanding of her. Daniyal leans forward like a teacher accepting offerings, nodding intermittently.

I pause. 'I decided to use the second person for her narrative. So it feels that I'm in conversation with her over the centuries that separate us. What do you think?'

Daniyal nods. 'It's working, it's working. I think it draws Hijab closer to the readers. This is probably the first time a woman author is writing about her so intimately.'

I'm filled with a gust of positivity. I didn't even think about sharing my draft with Faraz. Somehow I feel fiercely protective of it. It's still a fragile bundle of sentences growing and taking shape. But I think all writers need encouragement and support.

'It's a first draft, a beginning, and it's good. Hijab had a lot of obligations—a tawaif who had to support her family, but she made certain decisions despite all that—not stemming from the compulsions of her situation but from the strength of her character.'

'Exactly! It was because of her circumstances that she couldn't develop her full potential as an artist.'

'Are you also translating her ghazals?'

'Yes, I am. There are very few surviving lines from her. I don't think one can base one's evaluation of Hijab as a writer on just that. Not that I claim to be a judge of Urdu poetry.'

'As all poetry, it should touch the heart. That's the only yardstick you need.'

I confess my anxieties over getting my book published. I feel that the bigger publishers are biased towards male writers, there is gatekeeping, and good literary agents are unapproachable by new writers. An old colleague, a journalist, recently got a book deal, and I wrote to her congratulating her, feeling slightly jealous. I told her I was writing fiction, and she advised me to find an agent unless I want to self-publish. Daniyal rubbishes my view, giving examples of successful female writers and talking about the growing number of literature festivals, which have increased the readership and brought new writings into focus.

'You should write from a position of strength, not of weakness... Just a suggestion.' He hands me Dagh's biography and sees me off at the gate.

I carry his words with me on the bumpy rickshaw ride back and decide to look up Baba at his clinic. He hasn't visited us since the quarrel with Faraz. I miss him. Somehow, he can make every mess right—physical or financial. We become kids and let him take charge once we have finished rebelling. I know Faraz wants him to come home, and I'm the eternal peacemaker.

Baba's clinic is swarming with patients even though it's lunchtime. He'd have a quick sandwich and tea served by Seema, his assistant of fifteen years. Faraz detests Seema, and I tell him he's jealous. Seema, enveloped in a loose black abaya with swathes of scarf wrapped around her moon face, her lustrous eyes enhanced by a thick eyeliner, floats around with calm efficiency. We have watched her expanding unobtrusively under the abaya with her three pregnancies and their after-effects. Faraz is convinced that Baba once had a liaison with

Seema. He has been a widower for more than thirty years, so some quiet arrangements once Faraz was safely in college wouldn't have been unreasonable. Baba laughs at Faraz's veiled accusations. 'Rest assured, you have no brothers or sisters running around the town.'

Seema ushers me into Baba's chamber, where he reigns dispensing medicines, advice and home truths. There are three patients awaiting their turn while he examines a fourth one. No one is particular about privacy, and Seema quickly rattles off a patient's details and history. She is an extension of Baba's memory now that Baba tends to forget cases.

'If you're going to continue like this, you will die! Who is with him? Who is with him?' A skinny boy in drainpipe jeans falling off his butt steps forward.

'I'm not going to treat your father now. Please take him to another doctor. Next!'

He rings the bell to signal the end of the consultation, and the next in line jumps up to take his place.

Baba has always been an autocratic doctor, emotionally involved with his patients, most of whom are simple farmers or shopkeepers from in and around Rampur. He doesn't charge the economically challenged and helps them get medicines, but they have to follow his advice. What I love about him is that he does give a lot of time to each patient—asks about their family situation and counsels the caregivers.

I look inquiringly at Seema as Baba continues to scold the skinny boy.

'This man has cancer, and Doctor Saab had asked him to go to Delhi for treatment; he didn't, and now the cancer has spread,' Seema whispers.

'What now?' I ask her.

'He will go back and sit in the line again. Doctor Saab will cool down, call him in and try to help him. But it's a terminal case now.'

Seema sighs. There is desperation and sadness packed in the clinic on most days. Baba wanted to be a gynaecologist and even trained to be one, but a male gynae is not acceptable in Rampur. So he is a general physician, renowned for his diagnosis and the first stop for people who can't afford specialists.

Baba turns to me and waves away the other patients, who troop out and wait at the door. He asks me about my research. I tell him I had been to the Raza Library and complain that he hasn't visited us. We miss him and Jumbo. Baba smiles and says he'll come over for dinner. There is deep love between him and Faraz that I'm sure they will make up over qorma and pulao.

I start planning the dinner as I drive back. Qorma and yakhni pulao, or, maybe, mincemeat with besan roti. Faraz loves qeema, and qeema-besan roti-lehsun chutney is typical monsoon fare when the weather cools down and one can digest ghee-slathered rotis. Some of my most satisfying meals have been qeema-besan roti lunches with the rain pounding the garden. It would be a perfect make-up meal—too satiating and heavy for further arguments. I make a mental note to ensure that Meezan Bhai cooks large, thick rotis over low heat till they have golden spots to mimic those made on a wood chulha. These days, all meals end with Chausa mangoes.

Faraz is waiting for me at home. He's never back at this time.

'Where were you?' There is an edge to his voice, which I ignore. 'Gul was calling you up, and then she called me.'

'I was at the library.' The lie slides off my tongue more easily this time despite the stab of guilt. I shuffle in my bag for the mobile. Three missed calls from Gul. My phone was on silent.

'Gul is coming home.'

'In the middle of the semester! Something must have happened. What did she say?' My heart is a drumbeat in my ears.

'She just said she couldn't stay there even a day more. I didn't ask her anything; just calmed her down and arranged a taxi to get her back immediately.'

Dagh's Letter to Hijab

Dearest of Dagh,

Ae meri jan, jan se behtar, *o my life, dearer than my life. If I only possessed the magic of Prophet Suleiman, I would summon the winds and fly to you in an instant. I would come to you on the wings of the wind that flows with this letter. I can happily lay down my life for the joy of seeing your coquettish smile once more. I swear by my God, my love and desire for you that your invitation is a debt of gratitude upon my soul. My heart bows in reverence even more because you feel my pitiable state. I will lay my head on your feet, my beloved. I have endured all the calamities of this universe in this separation.*

It is impossible that you summon me and I ignore your sacred command. My ishq for you is above everything in my life. Yet even greater than my ishq is the sanctity of your izzat, your honour. A person cannot live without honour in this world. I live in dread that you would turn away from me; should that day ever come, it will be my last on this earth.

Those who know me understand this truth: When my heart inclines towards someone, it is for eternity. With each breath I take, my lips move to utter your name. I surrender my soul unquestioningly to this overpowering ishq for you. My words, my poems are offerings to the purity of our ishq. My heart holds no doubts, no misgivings against you for it is illuminated with the pure light of love. My feet are bound to tread the path of loyalty. All I pray for is that you reciprocate my love.

Dāgh kī yād meiñ Ḥijāb rahey
Sāth shoḳhī ke iztirāb rahey

May Hijab live pining for Dagh
Her coquetry consumed by tumultuous love

The Nawab, fearing that I would die if he denied permission, has granted me leave and I fly to my lover.

I pray that Allah smooths my journey to your threshold.

Yours ever,
Dagh
April 1882

Dagh Visits Calcutta

(June 1882)

Subaḥ se shām tak jamāl ke lutf
Shām se subaḥ tak wisāl ke lutf...
Wasl kī shab meiñ jalwey they din ke
Sar e māh thī ḥalq meiñ mu'azzin ke...
Muskurātey they lab jo dilbar ke
Khiley jātey they phūl bistar ke...
Ātish e ḥusn e yār kī garmi!
Bazm meiñ ek bahār kī garmī

From morning till evening I gaze upon her beauty
From evening to morn we relished our ecstatic union
The night of our love had the brilliance of day
The moon encircled us till the muezzin's call.
My beloved's lips smiled as she lay on love's bed
Her fiery bcauty as passionate as a spring garden.

—Dagh Dehlvi
Faryād e Dāgh (1882)

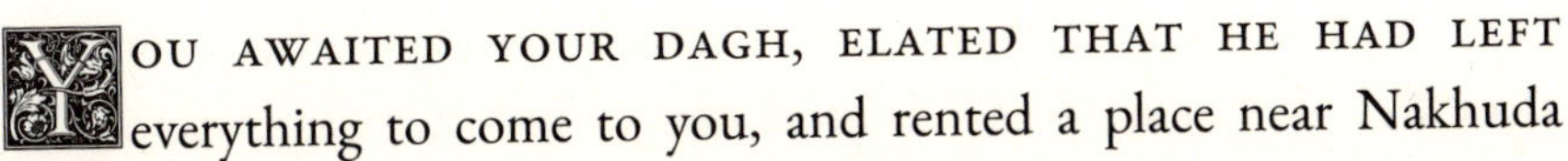

YOU AWAITED YOUR DAGH, ELATED THAT HE HAD LEFT everything to come to you, and rented a place near Nakhuda

Mosque for him. The rooms were befitting Dagh's stature. His coming to Calcutta would be a literary event of sorts, with mushairas and people thronging to his door. It was also near your kotha, so that he could come over, or you could stay with him again. Apa was holding her peace, calculating the benefit of this alliance. The kothas, mehfils and noble households were buzzing with the news of Dagh's arrival. Dagh wrote to you from all the stops on the journey—Awadh, Allahabad, and finally Azeemabad, which claimed him with an unending string of mushairas. Dagh revelled in the hospitality at Azeemabad and the mushairas held in his honour. People converged from all around to listen to him. You had expected him to stay there a while with his stepbrother, Mirza Shaghul. Impatient, you sent missives. How long would you have to wait? Azeemabad was so near, and yet, Dagh stayed there for a month. It was too hot to travel, Dagh wrote—'I have turned as black as your kajal!

Hameedan laughed. 'Apa, he was never fair, and now you have to grope for him in the dark. Don't trouble the poor old man in this heat!'

Dhūm hai ghar meiñ hamāre yār āta hai Ḥijāb
Beher e istiqbāl lab par jān e zar āney ko hai

Celebrations as my lover comes to my house, Ḥijāb
My soul readies to escape my lips in his welcome.

You laid these lines at his feet, and Dagh gathered you in his warmth and kissed your brow. He loved the house and decor you had so painstakingly prepared for him. Khuda Bakhsh immediately moved in with Dagh. He adored Dagh and happily fitted into his ambit of fatherly affection. Khuda Bakhsh had a passion for music, and Dagh encouraged him to learn from the best ustads and make a career out of it rather than hang around the kotha like Khala's son, Shafeeq. The latter was a wastrel and had taken to stealing from the kotha. Khala often hid his faults, which made him even more undisciplined. He was involved with a prostitute from Sonagachi, and, much to Khala's dismay, the girl was a Hindu. Dagh had come to know about the situation from Khuda Bakhsh and had taken it upon himself to counsel Khuda Bakhsh to keep himself away from such entanglements and focus on his music.

You knew Dagh loved elaborate meals and inviting people over for dinners. So you sent your old khansama, Attan, and his shagird (pupil) to give Dagh the best of Awadhi-style spreads. Attan had learnt to cook Awadhi fare from Khala and was especially adept at galauti kabab. He knew the thirty aromatic spices that went into producing the delectable dish, firm enough to make the patties, yet so soft that they practically dissolved in the mouth. Attan was a stickler for the correct meat and had even refused to cook his signature kababs if he didn't find the perfect mince. You knew Dagh relished raan, roasted leg of mutton, and asked Attan to prepare it to welcome him. The meat had been marinated for twenty-four hours—its tenderness assured by a precise measure of green papaya paste. Too much, and the flesh would turn putrid in the heat, too little, and it would be chewy. Attan also ensured that the marinade stayed chilled with blocks of ice. The aromatic blend of Awadhi qorma masalas seeped into the roast while Attan barbecued it over coals to give it a sweetish, smoky coal aroma. Dagh enjoyed the raan and remarked that it was close to the Mughlai style with its thick, rich curry. Rampuri raan kabab had no gravy, and the cooks there would skilfully stuff the raan with mincemeat and roast it over coals. You also got the Calcutta biryani cooked for him. It had whole potatoes along with meat in the layered aromatic, spicy rice. Dagh was taken aback—why the potatoes? You told him that Nawab Wajid Ali Shah's cooks had introduced this new vegetable to make a different biryani.

'Ah, such is fate that the Nawab of Lucknow has to economize with potatoes in his biryani!' Dagh shook his head, sighing. He didn't eat the potatoes. You picked them out and ate them with the dahi badas.

Your aversion to meat had been a long-standing rebellion, which baffled, angered and frustrated Apa. You were six or seven when Attan took you to the butchers. The visceral sight of slaughter had left you clinging to Attan in horror. From that day on, you refused to eat meat, turning your face away and clamping your lips shut. You could smell blood, you said. Apa tried to sneak in a piece of meat into your khichdi while it was on the boil. You spat it out, inviting a resounding slap. How would you grow up to be a lissom, curvaceous tawaif if you ate no meat? Anger, persuasion and pleas left you unmoved. Starve her, Apa commanded, and she will eat anything. They tried to feed you hilsa, the beloved Bengali illish that everyone enjoyed, but you were adamant—no meat because all meat had blood. After exhausting all options, they left you alone for a few years. Apa often taunted you on your scrawny figure, comparing you unfavourably to your pudgy playmates. She said your complexion would darken. When Husna, a girl Apa had purchased for kotha work, younger than you by six months, got her first period and you continued to be scrawny and flat-chested, Apa lost all patience. She caught you by your neck and stuffed your mouth with a kabab, cursing you. You threw up all over the dastarkhwan.

'Bring the tongs! I'll set this bitch right,' Apa yelled.

Khuda Bakhsh, loving the drama and happy to see you face Apa's anger, ran and got the tongs from the maid preparing rotis on the chulha.

'Look at your skinny arms. Who would want you!' Apa screamed and pinched them with the still-hot tongs as you shrieked in pain. She stuck your back with jangling ferocity till Khala forced the tongs out of her raging hands. You were starved and banished from eating with the family. Apa said looking at you picking on boiled rice and vegetables filled her with repugnance. Husna, feeding on the leftovers, was growing to be a curvy girl, while you, blessed with such bounty, chose to turn away. Khala invented vegetable curries and kababs mixed with 'warm' foodstuff—dry fruits, sesame seeds, melon seeds and spices. She got special medicines from the hakim to activate your inert hormones.

Much to the collective relief of the household, your body obeyed the dictates of growth and you finally bled. Apa predicted that you would remain frigid inside and would never have the hot-blooded passion that a successful tawaif should have to satisfy her patrons.

Dagh's presence in Calcutta was magnetic. The city, resplendent and cosmopolitan, embraced him. This was Dagh's second visit to the city. He had come with Nawab Kalb e Ali Khan in 1866; he found the city even more grand than on his earlier visit. Dagh's arrival had been announced in poetic circles and the nobility. Invitations to mushairas started pouring in. His baithak became the hub for poets, nobles and admirers as people flocked to meet him and spend time with him. He found the people of Calcutta cultured and affable and made hundreds of friends. Among his visitors was Abdul Ghafur 'Nassakh', the deputy collector of Midnapur, who had questioned Dagh's lineage in his tazkira, somewhat insultingly referring to him as the 'son of Chhoti Begum', implying that Dagh, who proudly wrote his name as 'Nawab Dagh Dehlvi', was the offspring of a junior begum of Nawab Shams of Jhirka and not entitled to use the grand suffix. Nassakh was your tutor and a regular at your kotha. You had expected Dagh to snub him, but he surprised you by extending a warm hand of friendship. Nassakh, charmed by Dagh's magnanimity, became a regular at all of Dagh's mushairas, and his son became Dagh's shagird. Dagh continued to write to Nassakh for years and often asked him to intervene in your frequent quarrels with Dagh. Nassakh was a typical British official, officious and correct. You privately accused him of being servile to the British. Dagh said Nassakh was redeemed by his love for Urdu poetry and his sensitive kalaam. He found Nassakh a man of old values, a wazeydaar—a reading that proved to be true. Dagh gave a lot of importance to lineage and family as a determiner of behaviour and attitude. He formed enduring bonds and kept in touch with friends and acquaintances all his life by writing numerous letters every day.

Dagh, you realized, was an open-hearted person. He harboured no grudges, even befriending known enemies and critics, and used to say *mulaqat ko to safai se*—cleanse your heart when you meet someone. You, on the other hand, were more guarded and suspicious of people, often judging them for their actions or reported words. Your outward geniality towards your clients was perfected over the years, but your unforgiving heart would never open to anyone you had once rejected. There were no two sides to Dagh's personality—he projected what he felt inside and was nearly always affable and generous to a fault. You were astounded at Dagh's innocent trust in people even after suffering reverses, mistreatment and insults throughout his life. Strangers who got to know him would feel loved, accepted and find comfort. Unlike his cousin, the great poet Ghalib, Dagh was never arrogant. You had heard that Ghalib's sojourn to Calcutta in 1828 for reinstatement of his pension was marked by tussles and conflicts with old friends and he made new enemies. Dagh only brought harmony and affection wherever he went.

He would often ask you, 'Why do you love me so? Dark and old as I am.'

You would laugh and reply, 'Yes, no one would like your face; it's you I love. I have never met a person like you.'

Monsoon rains swept through Calcutta, and Dagh enjoyed the salubrious winds, often going for moonlit drives along the Hooghly with you. He loved to watch the moon chasing the clouds on the bridge. The windows to his upstairs room were thrown open to the moisture-laden winds and the light spray of rain. Your life would forever turn back to look upon those days and nights as a time of contented happiness.

You often sat receiving guests in Dagh's salon, introducing him to the grandees, very much the mistress by his side. Every poet and connoisseur clamoured for his appearance at their mushairas. Dagh was kind and didn't refuse even the humblest invitations.

You loved his quick humour, which matched your impetuous repartee. He could lighten everything with a witty remark; only you had the power to crumple his heart with a serrated sharp word. Ah, give me your prolificity you sighed; just that, and I can give you my life, my words, my soul. I shall be forever your slave and write at your command, you promised.

Dagh was at his most prolific at that time, reciting and penning ghazals every day from the wellspring of his lived happiness. He made you sit in the room as he wrote. You were his inspiration, and you felt words emanating from your pen almost as effortlessly as his. A touch, a look, a shared thought would pull you towards each other in the middle of a sher. You would float into his ghazal and he into yours. His nights after the mushairas were yours, and you had stopped hosting soirées at the kotha during his stay. This time was for the flowering of your love, unfettered by fear from Nawab Haider and mean-minded remarks by Dagh's friends. The anxiety of the clandestine dissipated, and you relaxed in his arms, opening your heart to him. You observed his habits closely—his love for Indian attar, which he so generously sprayed on himself, and his abhorrence of drinks—you were his only vice, he said. *Yes, I and all the other tawaifs you have loved*—you couldn't resist the barb, even when it found its mark in the hurt of his eyes.

On one such pleasant evening, on the insistence of Nassakh, you organized a mushaira at your kotha. It was to be a grand event, with the members of Nawab Wajid Ali Shah's family arriving from Metiaburj along with his noblemen. You had helped to make all the arrangements, hoping that the mushaira would finally win you an invitation to one of the Metiaburj soirées, where you would sing under the benign eye of the corpulent Nawab Wajid Ali Shah. Metiaburj was the epitome of culture in all of Hindustan, and if Nawab Wajid Ali Shah invited you for a recital, it meant you had made your mark in the world of poetry, you told Dagh. He laughed, saying, 'Your heart is the only mark my poetry seeks.'

The mushaira was a great success, a convergence of all the renowned poets and grandees of Calcutta. Phaetons and carriages choked the road as guests were ushered in by liveried guards. Dagh was not well off, and Nassakh and you had financed the expensive soirée. Your presence there underlined your association with Dagh as his muse and lady love. When finally the lamp was kept before Dagh, signalling that he would be reciting his new ghazal, his words were for you and Calcutta.

Roknā dil ko ke shauq zulf e dilbar le chalā
Thāmnā mujh ko ke saudā merā sar le chalā
Ye ḥasīñ ye mehjabīñ ye shahar aisī lehar ba lehar
Dāgh kalkattey se lākhoñ Dāgh dil pe le chalā

My heart is swept away with the tresses of my beloved
This transaction of passion has numbed my reason
This town with its waves of luminescent beauties
Dagh leaves Kalkatta with his heart bearing numerous marks (dagh)

Nawab Kalb e Ali Khan's letter summoning Dagh back to Rampur came like a death sentence. It had been a little more than two weeks since he arrived—how could there be such little time for you? Dagh requested for a two-month extension of leave, which was refused. You tried to persuade him to stay back. Whatever I have, is yours, stay with me here, you reiterated. He was so popular in Calcutta that there were many who would happily sponsor him; together, you could make a good living. But Dagh was a faithful servant of the Nawab, indebted by the latter's many favours—Rampur riyasat had supported Dagh when he lost his father and again when his mother was expelled from the Mughal court. Besides, Dagh was a married man, and that was also an article of faith. Once again, he invited you to accompany him back to Rampur, but you couldn't leave your obligations towards your family and sever all relations. These were familiar arguments, fuelled by the pain of impending separation and the inevitable stalemate between you. Within a few days, Dagh left, feeling, he said, like a corpse leaving the city. He had to reach Rampur before Ramzan.

Is this how it will end, you asked yourself. For how long can this continue? As Ramzan fasts and sehri sounds buzzed around you and him in different parts of Hindustan, you heard of him writing a masnavi, *Faryād e Dāgh,* a plea from his grieving heart. Would it be an obituary to your love?

I put down my pen, not daring to disturb Hijab's presence. I want to reach across the years and tell her not to think of the future, for love has only beginnings and beginnings; to think of its ending is kufr, blasphemy.

كَشْمَكَش

10

Kashmakash (Perplexity)

Ham bhi kharīd lete tere zulm ke liye
Bāzār e dahar meiñ koi dil kī dukān nahī

Had they sold them in the bazaars of the world,
I would have bought a heart to endure your tyranny.

—Munni Bai Hijab
Tazkirā e qadīm shairāt e Urdu

GUL ARRIVES LOOKING EXHAUSTED AND BASICALLY PISSED OFF with everything. Delhi is 'savage', she couldn't stay there even for a single day, and she had had enough of the grind of med school; it is just not her. She collapses on the bed, ordering Meezan Bhai's signature cold coffee. I just hold her, thankful that no harm came to her.

Baba comes over that evening. It was supposed to be a make-up dinner, and now, it obviously becomes all about Gul. She whines about her problems to Baba—the dorm was 'so sus' (suspicious), the teachers hated her, and she hated medicine. Baba puts on his best bedside manner, listening and soothing her. Gul had only one friend there—Rita, an NRI from Saudi—and she had decided to leave, too.

'Maybe that's the reason you decided to leave, hmm?' Baba asks.

'Dada, I just don't see myself as a doctor.'

'Then what do you see yourself as?'

'I'm trying to figure out.'

'Figuring out? Then you will become a nothing like your father!' Baba gets up from the dining table. He just had one helping of the pulao!

Faraz gets all riled up at that, and suddenly, it becomes all about them. Faraz often regresses into a teenager with Baba, and today there are two in the room.

'You were happy enough when I was successful in Dubai. Now that I'm down and out, you are trampling all over me!' Faraz lashes out.

I gear up for the familiar posturing. What will Gul make of this face-off and the sudden transformation of the two men she loves into tornadoes. The dumpukht murgh pulao has lost its dum (steam) and is fast becoming cold and lifeless. No one even notices the stuffed chicken sitting gloriously atop the rice, which I had so painstakingly cooked in my iron pan and buried in the pulao at the time of dum.

'Business never succeeds! Tell me the name of any successful businessmen in our family or in Rampur—real businessmen, not shopkeepers. There are always ups and downs in business, and families are ruined. What you need is a good job and a salary at the end of the month. Now even Rukmini has left her job to wander around in the qila ruins!'

'Please don't bring Kuku into it. Let her do what she wants—it's her shauq, her interest. The school wasn't even paying her much.' Faraz defends me and dismisses my present and past careers at one go. True, the school salary was meagre , but that's not why I left. Does Faraz really feel that writing is a pastime for me?

'At least she earned enough to feed the family.'

'We are not starving, Baba!' Faraz counters.

'No, you're not, because you're borrowing money from everyone! You'll soon put this family into debt again.'

I'd no idea that it had started again, the borrowing from friends and distant relatives—the Dubai prototype of a slow-moving disaster wrapped in a shiny façade of dinners and parties for our debtors. The Dubai venture ended with us selling off business assets, except for a flat in Burj Khalifa—our plan B if nothing worked out in India.

Gul is sitting stunned. I take her hand. She had always lived with a nonchalant attitude towards money. In Dubai, we never felt the need to deny her anything because she was not a wasteful child, besides we could afford it. Leaving Dubai was a disruption in her life, but she didn't know the full story behind the move.

Faraz storms off, and Baba calms down to eat gulathhi, my masterpiece. He adores gulathhi and calls it a well-dressed kheer. It had taken me two hours to stir the rice, khoya and milk porridge till it was thick enough to set.

I had decided to cook gulathhi to occupy myself while Gul, exhausted from the journey, had curled up with Faraz to watch Netflix, the pacifier for all troubles. We had tacitly agreed to dissect her issues later, after she was more relaxed. Now, even more worries are heaped upon her. Maybe it is time for her to grow up.

'Where will we go after this?' she asks me that night.

'We are here now, and we have enough,' I say, holding her close.

I feel a desperate bleakness lodge in my heart. I want to ask Faraz—tell me whom you borrowed from this time; the people I have to be nice to. Should I leave it unquestioned and await the consequences like last time? Only now, I know the full breadth of disasters that can follow his reckless borrowing sprees. Gul's breathing deepens, and she turns away, snuggling her stuffed toy dog. I kiss her and get out of bed.

Faraz has gone for a walk to calm himself. To be fair to him, he had done well in Dubai; we had a large trading concern with four outlets and a lavish lifestyle. We'd barely saved anything, presuming that nothing would change. In hindsight, there had been signs—Faraz's moods and tense conversations with his suppliers. He didn't want to worry me and only confessed to the losses and debt spiral when it all came crashing down. We always had a place in Rampur to come back to. But where would we go now? I decide to speak to Faraz; maybe tomorrow.

For the next few days, I hedge the confrontation, giving excuses to myself—Faraz needs time after the face-off with Baba, we can't argue during the day because it will disturb Gul. Perhaps I'm scared of all that we have now splintering again, but I can't be as oblivious as I was the last time.

I used to work at the dining table, but Faraz has so many visitors throughout the day. I try not to listen in when there are raised voices or when he speaks on the mobile, though my shoulders knot up with anxiety. Gul's room—the only other air-conditioned bedroom—had become my sort of study, but I can't work there with Gul watching TV 24x7. I can barely get Gul to unpack. Faraz, as always, becomes the good cop and asks me to let her relax, so I end up settling her things in the cupboard. I can't write anything these days, and my head feels heavy with a build-up of unwritten words and unspoken stress.

I shouldn't have let it fester. A casual remark makes me snap at Faraz, and all the accusations and fears burst out in a massive showdown. I want to shatter this unreal peace, maybe break some fragile glass and crockery from our sham life in Dubai. The desire startles me—I was never a violent person. Faraz is adamant—he is doing what is right and accuses me of being unsupportive and over-anxious. You used to be such a calm, quiet person when we met, he says. I hurtle all his failures and deceptions at him—this is me now because of all that happened to us. It is liberating to have it out after months and even years of non-conversations. Thankfully, Gul is asleep.

❧

The remains of the fight still simmer in a corner of my brain as I get out of bed the next morning, sleep-deprived and overwhelmed with my powerlessness. Perhaps I need to be in an alternate mental space where I can envelop myself in my work and break the thought overdrive.

I don't give myself time to think it out—just get dressed, get into a rickshaw and reach Daniyal's haveli. Gul will anyway sleep till noon. I wear a saree, which I rarely do in the old town—it marks me out as the other, the saree-wearing Hindu woman. At least there are less inquisitive stares. The school was the only place I could wear the saree in my role as a teacher, but no bindi—that was only for Hindu women. I had made the mistake of putting on a bindi once and was told by an old teacher that if I were a Muslim, I shouldn't wear a bindi because it was a mark of the Hindus and my forehead would be shot with hellfire in the hereafter! Today, I wear a red bindi, unlike Mamma's big black one, and wrap the soft mulmul around my head and shoulders, a protective sheath.

Daniyal hides his surprise when he sees me walk in. I have broken two rules—first, I visited him alone, and now, I have arrived unannounced—and caught him in his olive green long shorts, T-shirt and sneakers, pottering around in his garden. He takes off his cap, his face sweaty from the sun, and apologizes for his casual wear. I tell him he looks great. He blushes, and I breeze past him into the study. He sits at his desk, gulps down ice-cold water and clears his throat, debating what to say. I settle down on a high-back sofa rather than the low sofa this time because I don't want him towering over me.

He swivels his chair towards me and I almost start talking about Gul and stop myself. I'm afraid I'll spill out everything if I open up now. I need to consciously occupy this place and cut off all the noise. I breathe in the wood-scented, slightly musty air of the study. Perhaps he can read my distress and says, 'If you feel comfortable, you can come and work here, away from your preoccupations at home. I'm out most of the day, busy with these blessed cases. I think Faraz will be fine with it. Even if you write five hundred words a day, you'll feel good, and there will be some progress.'

I thank him and tell him that I will take him up on the offer. I immediately decide not to tell Faraz because I know he won't approve. I need the peace and atmospheric beauty of this place to write. I'll be back by the time Gul gets up and has her very late brunch. Daniyal introduces me to Akhtar Bhai, his major-domo, who can make tea and snacks appear magically and soundlessly.

I read out my latest chapter to him to know how it sounds. Sometimes I find the work feels precarious and unsubstantial. I'm still looking at her through Dagh's lens and trying to find the real Hijab.

'I like the way you have made their relationship come alive. But I think you need to get more under its skin. There are some gaps…' he trails off.

'…as in every relationship.'

'Here they are just beginning to love, to get involved, but she doesn't write to him on her return from Rampur. Why? Then he writes that emotional letter, threatening to drink poison.'

'Maybe she wanted to be wooed like a normal woman and discover a love that wasn't transactional.'

'But the relationship *was* transactional in a way, as most relationships are. She was getting something out of it. He was her teacher, and the association brought her fame.' Daniyal peers at me.

'Hmm… she insults him when she writes from Azeemabad, and

things could have ended there. It was a huge risk if she wanted to capitalize on his fame. He was an influential man. I mean, she had guts for a nineteen-year-old girl! She is definitely not flattered by the famous poet's obsession with her.' I pause to write a note in the margin and carry on. 'I don't know... maybe she is scared of getting hurt again and was kind of pushing him away.'

'But he carries on loving her despite the hurt, and the love survives. So it's a complex relationship beyond social strata and age gap. And this is the complexity that you need to convey in your writing.'

'I guess all relationships are complex. Even a mother–daughter relationship. My mother... well, it wasn't easy between us.'

'And how did it affect your relationship with Gul?' Daniyal almost jumps in like he was waiting for that little chink.

'Okay, let's get back to Dagh and Hijab!' I snap. Daniyal looks startled at the snub.

'Sorry... it's just that... I don't want to go into my relationships here.' I try to soften the blow, blaming myself for inviting the question.

'Fair enough. So Dagh forgave her, and they carried on like most modern relationships.'

'Ultra-modern, I think, because they weren't even faithful to each other, which is the first rule of love—polyamorous they call it. But she knew what love felt like. Just read this sher written by Hijab. I feel so... impacted by it. I'm no judge of poetry, but I think she would have rivalled any famous male poet of the day, even Dagh.' I shuffle the pages of my notebook, find the lines and walk over to hand it to him. I stand expectantly beside him, leaning on the bookshelf, waiting as he recites.

'Dil meiñ jigar meiñ, sīney meiñ pehlū meiñ ānkh meiñ
Ae 'ishq terī sho'la-fishānī kidhar nahī'

(My heart, my eyes, my very being
What, o love, has your flame left untouched.)

Daniyal's voice savours the words, his head bowed over the page.

'What do you think?' I ask.

'*Shola-fishani*—can you visualize it? *Atish-fishan* is a volcano.'

I shake my head, though I understand. I want him to make the words real.

'It's this image of burning coals, raging with fire and bursting into little sprinkles.' He takes off his glasses and looks at me.

'Beautiful...' I say softly. We are quiet, lost in the intensity of the image, conscious of its glow.

'I should get back to my work,' I murmur, straighten up and walk back to the chair. Daniyal gets up saying he has to be somewhere and I should make myself at home on his desk and continue my writing.

Dagh's Letter to Hijab (1885)

Nek bakht, paak daman, be laos, O pure and unselfish soul, Munni Bai Sahiba Hijab,

May Allah keep you safe!

Forgive my impertinence; your complaint is baseless. The sky has fallen on my head. My teeth have fallen out, and you show your teeth in laughter! You didn't have the time to read my letter carefully, and if you did read it, you didn't try to ease my problem. If I die today, I'm sure you will celebrate. I had asked you to send me false teeth—the whole set for a man. Everyone knows that a person has thirty-two teeth. Even if you sent four or five teeth, I could manage.

I had also written to please let me know the price and the name of the dealer because some friends also require teeth. I'm hurt at your unsympathetic attitude! Please don't trouble yourself now, for I have found a British denture expert in Meerut. I waited long for your response; you hurt me by writing that your reply got delayed because you didn't have the time to write! My letter needed a prompt reply, but you feigned indifference and ignored my pleas. If you send the teeth now, they would be of no use to me.

Well, the problem of my teeth is now solved, but the pain in my knees is killing me. I thought it must be an old wound, but there is a pus-filled swelling. I go to and fro in a palanquin these days. I can't sit on the floor

for the royal durbar and Huzur Purnoor (Nawab Kalb e Ali Khan) asks me to sit however I feel comfortable. I'm worried. I was recommended a medicine, which did help me initially, but the pain is still there. For the past ten days, I have been in sheer agony.

You rule over your domain dispensing favours and punishments like the despotic Zamurrad Shah of dastans. A person would be close to you today and shunned the next day...

My masnavi, Faryād e Dāgh, *which I sent for you, was about you, your qualities and life. I was but a narrator penning 838 passionate lines in two days after my return from Calcutta. I didn't know that your sister, Bi Hameedan, would find fault with it. I didn't know she was even interested in my masnavi! I had posted a batch of ten masnavis but didn't receive even a single receipt. It looks like my faryaad (plea) has reached the house of God!*

O cruel one, I hope my masnavi affects your heart. I don't know what feedback you got, but I have received accolades from all readers. Most people feel that Dagh must be sixteen years of age!

I have a great desire to meet Khuda Bakhsh. Mashallah, he must have grown up by now. I also heard of his illness. Please write and inform me of his well-being.

Hafiz Ahmad Ali Khan Shauq has compiled a collection in which I had contributed the following sher:

Sab kuchh to ho chukā ye faqat intizār hai
Keh deiñ bigaḍ ke āp ke tumheiñ iḳhtiyār hai

After traversing all stages of love, I await
For you to surrender to my ardour.

How can I be so fortunate that Bi Hameedan should thank me for the masnavi I sent for her? It has been ages since I received letters from her pen. Her patron, Munshi Abdul Hameed, sometimes conveys her salam.

In response to this letter, please explain your preoccupations.
Rest all is well with me.

Despatched by Dagh Dehlvi,
From Riyasat Mustafabad Rampur
August 1885

Munni Bai Hijab, Calcutta (1885)

After investigating, I found that not only was Hijab an accomplished poetess with a published diwan, but she had also tutored several well-known poetesses of the time. She was one of Calcutta's most popular dereydar tawaifs. Her beauty coupled with her playful demeanour was entrancing; her music and soulful melodious voice had no equal.

—Wafa Rashidi
Bangāl mein Urdu

WHAT DOES DAGH KNOW ABOUT THE IZZAT OF A TAWAIF? He wrote that he honoured you with his masnavi. Does he not realize that the masnavi portrays you as a tawaif who dishonoured a patron by taking a clandestine lover? It has destroyed your reputation as a dereydaar tawaif of Calcutta. You came across as a cheap, two-timing Sonagachi randi. Was it sensitive to sell your most intimate moments? He paraded you naked in his tale of love, depicting you as a cantankerous, loose-tongued, venomous woman who hurt a sensitive poet's soul with her ill-considered words—a poet who persisted in his love for her. But the masnavi had entwined your name with Dagh's for posterity. You told Hameedan to write to Dagh and inform him that you shall never set foot in Rampur or meet him—your immediate reaction after reading the masnavi. Dagh wrote back to Hameedan complaining about your attitude. Hameedan read his letter aloud with a coquettish air,

'Listen to your heartbroken lover: I have heard that she has sworn on the Quran never to meet me. I'm convinced now, *Baiji ko lagana aata hai, lagaye rakhna nahi aata* (Baiji knows how to win a heart but not how to keep a lover tied). Hmm... he carries on, saying, "Please remember that I have never had relationships without the other person's consent. Why should I bother writing to my enemies? I'm ill and have little hope for my life. If you are a friend, pray for my recovery and forgive me if I have wronged you." Allah, Baji, how can you be so unfeeling? He is dying!'

You told Hameedan that this was not love—a few letters, a titillating poem. Love has to be lived. If he truly loved you, he would have come to you. It had been three years now. Predictably, the letters had waned until, one day, someone told Dagh that there was an obituary in a paper about a Munni Bai. In desperation, he wrote to you, and you assured him that you were alive and well.

Much changed for you in the intervening years. Dagh's visit and your alliance brought recognition for your poetry. Your kotha became popular, as did your ghazals. You were invited to Metiaburj mehfils—the pinnacle of recognition you craved. Nawab Wajid Ali Shah said your ghazals have a soul. Critics noted the unmistakable stamp of Dagh's style in your compositions; some whispered that they were probably written by him. None of Dagh's numerous male disciples suffered such accusations. Your new ghazals weren't even corrected by him.

You now had a rich Bengali zamindar, Niranjan Babu, a friend of Nassakh, as your patron. Apa said you were lucky to have him. It was a sort of marriage with the freedom to write and perform at mujras. Niranjan Babu enjoyed your body with the air of a connoisseur. You were a rare gem in his collection of tawaifs and singers, he told you. You had been with him for two years now. He was a generous patron and paid the bills for you and your family. He had many preoccupations, so you didn't expect him every night—a relief for you—but you always feigned complaints of his indifference when he came. You played the expected role of a tawaif and mouthed the oft-repeated lines—did these men really believe words of love and longing spouted by their tawaifs? You had become even more prone to episodes of overwhelming melancholy; you shut yourself off from everyone for hours. Sometimes, you didn't have the luxury and pushed yourself to sing and dance.

Then Dagh wrote, saying that he got leave from Nawab Kalb e Ali Khan to visit Calcutta because the Nawab knew Dagh would die without his Hijab. He called you 'paak daman', a pure woman, in his letter. You read and re-read Dagh's masnavi, picking out the words that spoke of you. How could a tawaif plying her trade be called ba-haya, a modest woman? Dagh's Hijab was faithful. You had never revealed your true self to anybody as you had to him—in that, you were faithful to him.

Dagh's impending arrival filled you with excitement. Nassakh told you that Dagh knew of your Niranjan Babu and was apprehensive, wondering how he would be received by you. Everything would be as before, even if it meant breaking off relations with Niranjan Babu, you told Nassakh. No honourable patron would continue his sponsorship knowing your relationship with Dagh. When you informed Apa that you were leaving Niranjan Babu, you steeled yourself for her wrath. Apa had begun weighing her words and consulting Khala before speaking to you—a subtle acknowledgement of your rising power over the kotha. She invited you to sit with her on the takht, her smile deliberate and practised—you knew it well as the one she reserved for difficult negotiations. She began by complimenting you, her voice laced with affection; then cloaking her anger in well-chosen words, she put forward her advice that it would be unwise to leave Niranjan Babu for Dagh's brief visit. You told her that for you, Dagh was above all patrons. There would be more patrons, you were still quite popular, but Dagh was coming to Calcutta just for you. There was nothing Apa could say or do to dissuade you.

Your anger at the masnavi dissipated, and you found yourself longing for Dagh's assurances of love beyond time, the familiarity of jovial references to his physical ailments and the laughter you could share only with him. You had missed his grand persona. He had become your muse, the spark your poetry craved. Of late, your lines had grown stale, your thoughts jaded, and only he could reignite passion in your words. You had several professional rivals who invited you to their homes and celebrated their family occasions with you—Malka Bai, Zohra Bai, Munni Bai of Agra. You were in awe of Malka Bai's legendary beauty; her compositions carried the weight of her heartbreak and betrayal—grief was etched in every note she sang. She had survived devastation and was now the toast of Calcutta; no grand mehfil was complete without her. The sheen of interest as Dagh's muse, the lady love he pined for passionately in his masnavi, was the only thing that kept your name up there. At mehfils, a local grandee would invariably quote a few lines laden with insinuations from the masnavi. Dagh had unclothed you in the eyes of the world.

Niranjan Babu gifted you a phaeton, and you often drove out to the Indian side of Chitpur Road. The white side was forbidden—a world apart, inaccessible and heavily fined for trespass. Later, Gauhar, the audacious new star, would drive on the white side and pay the fine of a thousand rupees with blithe insouciance. On your drives, you would often encounter Malka Jan. With her usual subtle condescension and insincere affection, she insisted that you call her Malka Apa because she was three years your senior. Sometimes she remarked on your absence at an important concert. You would lie that you had a sore throat, and she would click her tongue and ask you to be more careful, the laughter in her eyes catching your lie. She told you casually that Dagh had praised her kalaam in a letter; even the poet Akbar Allahabadi had praised her ghazals.

Nassakh Sahib had informed you that Malka Jan was compiling her diwan—a highly anticipated literary event. You envied her acclaim and her ability to channel her pain into art. It had been six years since the publication of your first diwan—a slender volume that had caught the attention of litterateurs. You felt the ponderous weight of your youthful lines now. A second diwan required about a hundred ghazals—a hundred heartaches to pen those lines.

Dagh wanted to live at the same house near Nakhuda Mosque where he had been put up earlier, but it wasn't available. You found another place right in front of your kotha. Dagh, unsure about your feelings for him and your current obligations, didn't want you to rent it for him. He wrote to his friend and fellow poet, Muhammad Abdul Razzaq Shad Lucknowi, to check if the house was suitable and to rent it for him. Razzaq Sahib informed you of Dagh's request. You understood his apprehensions immediately and allowed Razzaq to make the necessary arrangements. You had the place cleaned up for his stay. It would be as before—the two of you together in nights of love and unrestrained poetry. You bought several bottles of French perfumes as gifts for him, knowing he preferred Indian attars but determined to make him wear the perfumes for you.

He wrote to say that his deceased son's nursemaid, Naseeman, would look after the house and cook for him during his stay. The day Naseeman arrived, you told Niranjan Babu that you couldn't continue with the employment; he was expecting it and seemed apathetic. Emotions were never a part of the deal. Apa was livid.

'You have jeopardized the whole kotha. Will your Dagh Sahib pay for us? What about your oath that you would never set eyes on his face?' she thundered, disregarding Khala's intercession. You stormed out and shut yourself in your room. You wanted no claim on your body or mind for the brief time of Dagh's visit. Was it too much to ask? Dagh's house would be filled with guests, laughter and food; you would be the hostess beside him at the grand mushairas—his celebrated lady love for whom he had come all the way.

For now, this was enough.

رابطَہ

11

Rābtā (Ties)

Āj woh mujhse sar e bazm adā se boley
Tu shanāsā hai merā, main hūñ shanāsā terā

With élan he declared in a gathering
You are my acquaintance and I am yours.

—Munni Bai Hijab
Tazkirā e qadīm shairāt e Urdu

I'M PROBABLY THE FIRST WOMAN TO BE SITTING AND WORKING at Daniyal's desk. It must have been the official work desk for at least three generations of his family, a male refuge from the complexities of the zenana, a snug place to share secrets with friends and a backdrop for important meetings. Working here has now become my daily writing routine. It feels as if inspiration will only flow once I'm seated at the oak desk with my notebook and laptop in front of me. I leave my writing tools on the table—my inkpot and pens lined up neatly next to a paperweight and a crystal ink receptacle. I always write in the old style, with a fountain pen moving with the flow of my thoughts, forming letters that are mine, not a mechanical font on a screen. My writing diary, tucked in the drawer Daniyal assigned me, is my secret edged into his world. Sometimes,

I imagine Daniyal sitting on his couch and flipping through my hesitant scribbles. Although I have told him that he is welcome to read my work, whenever I discuss the story, he gives the impression that he is hearing it for the first time. The study has become the space where Daniyal and I converge to discuss about my work. But most days, he has already left when I arrive. I'm greeted by Akhtar Bhai and a tall glass of iced lemonade. I don't write anything at home; sometimes, I read to still my mind or to switch off the present.

Meanwhile, I have been desperately trying to find a literary agent. Perhaps I'm used to immediate publication from my years as a journalist. I do need an assurance, or some sort of hope, that my work will be published. Websites of publishing houses state that only a complete work of fiction can be submitted. I have written quite a few chapters and one can still hire an agent. Earlier, one could write directly to publishers in India, but now, most big publishers effectively work through agents—not the best ecosystem for a debut writer. So I have been writing to some agents, but there is no response. Daniyal says I'm being too impatient and just piling on more anxieties on my plate when I should focus on the book, but he has no clue about the competitive writing world. I need to work on that crucial next step, and if I land an agent or a book deal, it will be motivational. While reading announcements of book acquisitions on Publisher's Marketplace or Bookseller, I feel a mix of anxiety and envy. Very few debut authors land a good book deal. But journalists often get signed on by the big five. I tell Daniyal about every proposal, every rejection letter I receive—there is no one else I can talk to. At least he understands, even though he doesn't always agree with me or my feelings.

I call Akriti on my way back from Daniyal's, and we decide to meet at Domino's near Shahbad Gate. It's a long drive from her farm, but it's late afternoon and she is relatively free. I need her to unpack a lot of feelings. From the day at school when she stood up for me,

I knew she would be by my side forever. The past nine months, she has been a rock.

Sitting at Domino's waiting for Akriti, I gaze at the audacious, sparkling new Shahbad Gate. The grand arch of the old gate has been broken down to be replaced by a faux Mughal arch painted gold and white. It was one of the gates from the Nawab's times, leading into the city from Shahbad tehsil. Rampur had ten gates leading into it from different directions; they have all been torn down and replaced by gaudy, poorly designed arches. Faraz says the local contractors and politicians made crores constructing them. I miss the three scalloped Topkhana arches leading to the qila, framing the marble cupola of the Raza Library. An ugly mall stands there now.

The fact that a mid-sized town like Rampur has a real Domino's is incredible. Most of the restaurants have a women's section, but Domino's has done away with that. I see four burqa-clad women enjoying a huge pizza and talking in whispers. My saree shields me from their stares. Akriti comes in, or rather, blows into the restaurant, and we order a high-caloric fix.

'So, Gul is back. How is it going?'

'Gul is staying with Baba for a few days. I'm so relieved! There is so much going on, you know. Faraz and I…' I shrug.

With Akriti, no preamble is needed, and we fall into each other's confidences. She knows everything that happened in Dubai. I tell her it's happening again—the debts, the lavish drinking parties. I start recounting the old wounds till Akriti commands me to stop. It's not going to help and now we must think of Gul's future. Shutting out Faraz, won't help—you both must team up for Gul's sake, she says.

'It was never like this with us. Maybe I have less patience now. Why does Faraz need to play the provider and hide the ugly things from me? Then he tries to "fix" things with a picnic, a holiday or a dinner? I can't go on like this.' Whenever I brought up finances with him, Faraz would say that he was giving me enough to spend on myself and the household, and that's all I should care about. It just doesn't work for me any more.

Last week, he invited some friends to dinner at a five-star hotel in Moradabad. Daniyal was there, too, along with others I barely knew. Most of them were steadily getting drunk. In Rampur, drinking among Muslims is a shameful secret, even among close friends. Faraz was pleasantly drunk and flirting with me. It was Dubai times again, and I couldn't deal with it. Besides, it was so awkward. I realized that it wasn't considered 'proper' for women to attend such gatherings, and there I was, with a drink in hand—no one had brought their wives. Finally, I had shrunk into a corner, angry at Faraz for exposing me and at myself for playing along. The dinner must have been very expensive. I should have known what was really happening at that time.

I ask about Shubham, and Akriti tells me that they are consulting another psychiatrist at Vimhans, Delhi. He feels drowsy with the new medications, and Akriti has to help him with his assignments for his open school. He had to drop out of school, and they registered him for the open school exams. The way her shoulders tense and her gaze drifts away, I can feel her helplessness. Involving Shubham in the farm didn't work out though he loves animals. It's a low phase again and they have learnt to endure, she tells me. I know they try, but one can never 'get used to' having your child diagnosed as manic depressive, schizophrenic, autistic—all the terminology clumped together to be carried forever. I worry for Akriti's mental health as she takes most of the burden on herself.

'How's your book coming along?' We flow from one topic to another without pause. Sometimes it feels rushed; we always have less time.

'Please keep this to yourself—I have started writing at Daniyal's place. No one knows about it. I need the isolation and some peace.

And Daniyal… he is such a support. He helps me see things clearly and has such amazing knowledge. And sometimes… something he says just opens a new direction for my writing.'

'I get it—he's your mental fuck!'

I start laughing.

'He's hot!'

'Yes, he is! Maybe if it wasn't for Faraz and everything else, I would… I could, you know… think about him.' I surprise myself, then try to cover up with a light-hearted grin, but Akriti jumps at me.

'You already have, haven't you, you naughty Aunty Pussy. Hey, you're blushing!'

'Nooo, it's my menopausal hot flush.' We burst into girlish laughter.

'Okay, listen, for the next book club meet, Shezray wants to choose the book.'

'Does she even read? What is it, *Ain e Akbari*?' I'm relieved. I haven't yet strung Daniyal into my thoughts and words.

'No. It's Anuradha Roy's *All the Lives Never Lived*.'

'Can't we read any other title by Anuradha Roy. Do you know this one is about…' There is a tightness in my chest that I try to breathe out.

'Yes, I read the blurb. I tried convincing Shezray, but she's very keen on it. Think about it; it's bold of her to take this up. Listen, just play it cool. No one knows anyway.'

'Maybe I won't come to the meeting at all.' I could say I was busy with my writing or something.

'It's at your place, remember? Now just relax and don't think too much about it.' It's easy to brush it away like that. Even if no one knows, I don't think I can control my visceral reactions to the discussion. There is no way I can possibly sit this out. I feel trapped. Maybe we can change the venue, but Akriti says it might make things worse if someone has heard some vague rumours. I'll try to be completely passive.

❧

Gul has decided to stay in Baba-land, where Baba has installed Wi-Fi for her, and she has Jumbo—what more does a teenager need? She is an escapist like her father. Maybe she doesn't care, or like Faraz, when things get too much to bear, she decides to blot them out. Boundaries, she keeps telling me, are the way to survive. I'm sure Baba will try to persuade her to get back to med school. He often takes her to the clinic, hoping to inspire her with the suffering of the people. I seriously doubt that Gul or most of her generation (I do hope I'm wrong) feel anything beyond the digital world. Sometimes, I feel God was too tired to make them differentiated, or maybe he or she did his usual work, but we were too preoccupied to help them develop their individuality. We just threw them before screens and digital monsters and carried on with our lives. Gul is a brat—worse, a Dubai brat. The sweaty, crowded clinic must be freaking her out.

I visit her at the clinic en route to Daniyal's and find her looking lost, sitting with Baba at his desk while he scolds a patient. I take her out of the chamber, give her a pack of home-made brownies and tell her I miss her. I want her home.

'I'll come, but you guys are so icky!' A typical Gen Z accusation in their incomprehensible lexicon.

I invite her to the book club meeting. She rolls her eyes. Why would she want to hang out with a bunch of old 'yahoo boomers' reading books?

'That's what life here is like. Do you want to live in Rampur for the rest of your life? I would have never left Delhi. There is so much to do there.'

'I think I'll take a gap year and figure out what I want to do.'

'All your ideas come from your endless scrolling!'

'I want to go back to Dubai. I miss everything.' Gul's eyes fill with tears.

I'm tempted to tell her like Mamma, 'Stop snivelling. I don't want long faces!' But I think I have been too nasty to her already, and she is dealing with a lot. I give her a quick peck and tell her that I have to go to the library. She shrugs and returns to Baba's chamber.

For me, even today, moping around, crying, curling up in bed is a guilty pleasure. At least I owe it to Mamma that I always manage to get up and carry on. Even mourning Papa's death was not allowed. I used to cry in bed, missing him. I had to be soft because Mamma had decided to sleep with me. It wasn't out of love or shared tragedy. She was repulsed by her old bedroom, the bed she had shared with Papa. I felt suffocated. I would just wait for her to start snoring her open-mouthed snores and creep into Papa's bed. After a few days, I told her that I couldn't sleep because of her snoring, and Papa's bedroom became mine. There was a TV there, and I put on some funny movie that Papa and I used to watch together, snuggled into his blanket—which still had his musk scent—and went off to sleep smiling and crying. Mamma scoffed at my devotion to Papa. If I so much as mentioned him, she would feel offended and say, 'Who carried you in the belly, gave birth, fed you and wiped your potty-bottom? I devoted seven years of my life to you! Have you forgotten everything?'

The funny thing was that I didn't remember Mamma before she left us. I was six when she went away and I must have some memories. Was she a sad or a happy person? How did my days with her feel? Did she scold me and kiss me? My memories of that time are of the three of us—holidays, car rides, arguments—every memory with Papa in it. I have a feeling that she was indifferent to my needs, even though she was a stay-at-home mother at that time.

After Papa passed away, Mamma's paralysing coldness congealed my insides and my tears. All emotions were considered excessive and overdone. Mamma never touched me. Ever. At least not since she returned—which she was forced to since Papa was dying—and I could take care of my needs. If it wasn't for Papa and Ayah ji, I wouldn't have been held at all. I would have been destroyed.

I read somewhere that everyone needs a mother; if you didn't have a perfect one, you try to become one—a truth that defined my life. I held Gul close to my heart all the time. She needed me intensely for survival—a premature tiny, pink creature born a little more than eight months after marriage. Faraz laughed that Baba had valiantly defended my virginity when people commented at her birth. I was terrified I would lose her, forget to feed her, not hear her soft mewing cry in my sleep. Constantly swamped with exhausting anxiety, I would call Baba if Gul didn't feed or had a cold. He would come immediately, and putting Gul into his large, capable hands calmed me and her immediately. I would beg him to stay over till Gul was better, and he nursed her through all the distressing infantile ailments. He would say he was staying around for me, that Gul was a strong baby even though she looked frail. I wanted him to live with us permanently, but he valued his independence too much and loved the old house—he was born and lived most of his life there, as did his father and grandfather before him. Not even his love for us could tear him away from his home and his mohalla for very long.

Faraz would sometimes try to participate in the child-rearing, but he didn't have the patience for it and he hated my anxiety around Gul; maybe I edged him away—Gul was primarily mine. I poured all my physical and emotional love into Gul. When she started school, I was beset with illogical fears and would make excuses to not send her there at all. Faraz came up with the solution of working in Gul's school, and I agreed, even though I hated taking up my mother's profession. In short, I was an over-anxious, over-emotional, clingy parent—an antithesis of my mother. Faraz was the more balanced, practical parent, and when she grew older, it was to him she turned for advice and to vent her feelings; he has tremendous patience with her. I hope they talk it out and resolve things. She doesn't want to discuss anything about med school, and we decide to let her be for now. I don't know if it's a wise decision, but we certainly don't want to be accused of being 'cheuggy'!

Finally, Gul returns home with Jumbo, who makes himself comfortable on his round mattress in front of the TV, his chin resting meditatively as he watches Netflix. At least Gul stirs herself to feed him and take him out for a walk. It is so generous of Baba to part with Jumbo; the offspring is reasonably, at least intermittently, cheerful. Jumbo is a comforting presence and comes out of Gul's room in the morning to walk with me in the lawn. I find myself talking to him about my book over my morning coffee. He often gives me a baneful side glance, yawns and goes off to sleep.

Dagh's Letter to Hijab
(1885)

Meherban Dagh, qadardan Dagh, *My munificent, appreciative love*

Salamat raho, *May you live long.*

Mubarak! Oh, I'm such a selfish person—my desire is going to be fulfilled and I'm congratulating you. Sometimes I feel I shouldn't write to you at all and watch you being consumed by jealousy. But I can't help writing to you.

After a wait of three and a quarter years, Huzoor Purnoor (Nawab Kalb e Ali Khan) has understood that I would die if I didn't meet you. The day before yesterday, the Nawab commanded me, 'Go immediately to Calcutta. I don't think you will get well without going there. If you go there, you might return in 2–3 months. If you leave the world, how will I meet you again?' I accepted his offer with gratitude. My desire is to fly and reach you in two days, but I fear I'm not strong enough for the journey. The heat is overpowering. The hakim is making me drink juices of nilofer (water lily), khiyarain (cucumber, muskmelon), spinach, coriander and plum to reduce my fever.

To further complicate prospects of travel, this year Muharram and Dussehra are being observed on the same dates, and there are chances of a Hindu–Muslim conflict. Nawab Sahib has advised travel on the day of Muharram.

I hope all goes well for us. Do tell me—should I come unannounced or announce my arrival? Should I stay with you, or take up lodgings elsewhere? If you could find a house for me, it would be great. But inform me quickly; also let me know what I should bring for you from here.

Sab se hai terī ārzū badh kar
Ārzū se hai ābru baḍh kar

My desire for you supersedes everything
But your honour is above this desire.

I come with a broken heart, filled with helpless yearning. My honour is in your and God's hands.

I'm still troubled with my knee pain.

I don't want people there to know of my visit yet. Destroy this letter after reading it. Because of you, I have many enemies there. It would have been better if you had come to me, but you have taken on the role of the Qutub pir (Sufi saint) of Calcutta and cannot move from your station. I plan to stay in Calcutta for some time. I don't know what all I might require. Though your house is like my own, I think maybe you won't have time for me.

Salam
Passionately yours,
Dagh Dehlvi
29 September 1885

عقیدَت

12

‘Aqīdat (Respect)

Detey haiñ cheḍ-cheḍ ke kyūñ mujhko gāliyāñ
Samjhey hue haiñ woh mere muñh meiñ zabān nahī

Teasing and insulting me at will,
He believes I don’t have a voice.

—Munni Bai Hijab

‘YOUR CLOCKS DISAGREE ON THE TIME OF THE DAY,’ I SAY, glancing at my mobile. A huge grandfather clock stands in Daniyal’s study, and a wall clock hangs above the desk. Daniyal’s home has a number of old clocks ticking away in disharmony. They perplex me as I walk through the drawing room, the gallery and the study, noting their versions of time and get irritated by their odd ringing of the hours.

‘I wind all six clocks in my house every three–four days and then let them wander off in time. Some slow down but continue ticking and ringing in the time; some just stop. One stops at twelve, refusing to let the date change. I love the variability of time. Maybe you should consider keeping your mobile away while you work here.’ Daniyal seats himself on the high-back chair, leaving the desk for me—my space for now. I shuffle in the drawer, take out my notebook and pen. I never fill it up, just dip in the inkwell and write the old way. Daniyal gets up and starts winding the clock for my sake. We need to do nothing to ensure the correct reporting of time now; it's ever present in its perfect form in our hands.

A memory suddenly surfaces—when Mamma lived with us, she had total control over my time. All the clocks were set twenty minutes ahead.

As a child, I was hyper-aware of time—a false time. I remember always feeling that it was time to do something—go to school, have lunch, do homework, bedtime. Play till the hand is on six, Mamma would tell me. I would run back, overcome with anxiety, to check the clock hands. At some point, I don't recall when, I realized the fraud practised on my days, and I started adding back the twenty minutes she had spirited away. When she returned to us after many years (was it four or five?), she tried to reclaim the time that belonged to just Papa and me—searching through old report cards, pictures of birthdays and holidays without her, scribbled poetry, sketches and school essays lovingly collected by Papa. She tried to squeeze back into our lives. I never asked her about her years away from us and didn't answer her questions about ours; I exacted my revenge by coiling away from her, forever. After some time, she withdrew. We were two beings inhabiting the same space. For two years, Papa was there, bridging the spaces between us, and then he left because, as he put it, it was time for him to go. Mamma would have never returned if Papa hadn't been taken ill.

'Mamma used to change the time in all our clocks,' I say.

'You are still used to the time in the real world.'

'You're right. I have to be in a timeless zone to write about the past, though I still can't get myself to write of a time not lived in—at least not convincingly.'

'Then write of a lived time instead.'

'I don't have the courage.'

His lips flatten, he nods. 'Very few of us have that courage. At least you are writing. Perhaps one day, you will write the story you need to write.'

'Maybe... but I probably won't.'

'That's okay, too. For now, you can write this unlived story and try to inhabit it, but mind the tone. Hijab is not you. She should never sound or behave like you—I'm not saying she is; I mean your characters shouldn't be people in period clothing mouthing your lines.' As usual, he gives me a new perspective. I need to go back and weed myself out of Hijab. Daniyal sits around for some time, then leaves quietly.

❧

Faraz comes out of his self-righteous silence to persuade me to call my friends over for dinner. I don't want my book club members to become a part of one of his grandiose schemes; I feel protective towards my new friends and have no faith in Faraz. We end up having another tiff over the elaborate dinner Faraz wants us to host. Gul is back and I don't want the stand-off to continue. I can't be accused of being 'toxic' (or icky) again, so I finally agree. My friends are all adults and can handle Faraz's lofty schemes. My only condition is that Faraz won't borrow from any of my friends—he promises he won't. Suddenly, he is like a boy, eager to go out and play. I accept the truce; I need some mental peace to sort out Gul's issues.

When I invite everyone for dinner on our WhatsApp group, there are loud protests.

Akriti: *We are not a kitty party group.*

Vani: *Next we'll have restaurant dinners. LOL.*

Shezray: *Let's do potluck. Then the husbands can also be invited over and we won't have to rush back.*

Kuku: *Good idea! We'll have more time.*

Shezray: *Who knows they might end up reading a book!*

More snide comments follow. So we decide on a menu and delegate dishes. Daniyal doesn't respond to the chat, but we assign him a mincemeat dish. I'm sure he has read the messages. I will speak to him about it when I go there tomorrow; I hope he doesn't turn up his nose at the dinner idea.

Gul hates reading books and at one point I was convinced that I had a dyslexic child. But like Faraz, she loves party vibes. Vani is bringing along her college-going son, Vibhor; Shubham will also be there. Gul is very fond of Shubham; maybe Shubham will get along with Vibhor, unless Vibhor is as insensitive as his mother. Faraz and Dinesh could relax and chat in the guest room, which has a sitting area and a bar. I hope Ritesh and Daniyal don't ditch us to be with the boys. This is the first time we are hosting a dinner in Rampur, and I slip back into my Dubai-hostess mode, calculating who gets along with whom.

I offered to cook yakhni pulao because it should be served piping hot after being sealed to simmer on 'dum' twenty minutes before dinner. Baba always says one should wait at the table while the pulao is put on dum as dum literally means life, and if the dum steam escapes, the pulao becomes lifeless. I promise the members that I won't leave the meeting to fuss over food.

I could have left the yakhni pulao to Meezan Bhai, but I need to cook to calm myself. Actually, I'm not as anxious as I thought I would be because I received an email from a good—she featured in an article on lit agents—not great, lit agent. In short, I now have an agent to call my own. I forwarded it to Daniyal, who wrote, 'Congratulations, I'm happy for you.' I know he has his reservations.

With my lit agent-fuelled joy, I decide to make do-gosht pulao, based only on Baba's description. It's a brave choice to go recipe-less.

It might just fail, but I need this positive stress to counter my anxiety over the meeting. Baba told me that they used to have yakhni pulao with mutton pieces and chicken meatballs earlier, so it was do-gosht—meaning two kinds of meat, a typical Rampur dish. Now our pulao only has mutton pieces.

I prepare the mutton stock for the yakhni by boiling the meat with whole aromatic garam masalas, bay leaves, coriander seeds, fennel seeds, ginger, garlic and onions. 'Dulhan Begum, your izzat in front of your friends is at stake. Add this, too.' Meezan Bhai puts some more spices from different bottles and pudiyas in a muslin cloth, makes a potli and ties it up. He does his secret potli thing quickly; as usual, he doesn't want to divulge his special mix. Baba laughs when I complain about the secrecy. Rampur and Lucknow cooks keep their secrets, and a daughter-in-law is an outsider. Maybe he will share his recipes with Gul, who is from the family bloodline.

I felt I had *become* when I cooked my first perfect pulao—the satisfaction of meeting my family's fundamental need. I remember thinking, *Here I am, a wife and a mother.* Every grain was perfect, coated with a light sheen, spilling out on to the dish, free of clumps and yet soft and firm. Pulao is my small miracle.

I make the meatballs from chicken mince, fry them and let them stew in their own juices till they are completely done. I tell Meezan Bhai that they have to be placed on top of the pulao before it is put on dum. He is sceptical and gives me dire warnings against the erratic behaviour of meatballs. I tell him he is in charge of putting the pulao together because I will be too busy with the meeting. He grunts, a little pleased, and assures me that everyone will love my pulao.

By the time I have completed the pulao prep, it's time for the meeting. Gul is still in her pyjamas, her constant mode of dressing these days. At least she loves Akriti and Shubham and is looking forward to meeting them; otherwise, there would be no way to make her entertain the guests or to serve drinks and snacks. If she dislikes someone, she just sits and glowers, making her feelings only too obvious. With time, she will learn to veil her emotions. For now, I love to look at her transparent face, knowing exactly what's going on in her head.

Akriti brings her special chicken curry. She calls it Punjabi qorma, and I love it—reminds me of Papa's cooking. Akriti and Dinesh arrive early to settle Shubham. Shubham looks a little pleased to see Gul and she takes charge of him and invites him to her room. I don't approve of Gul's black T-shirt and jeans—it's too casual—but Faraz asks me to let it be. At least she has laid out the snacks on serving trays. We should be happy with whatever little these kids do, Faraz says. So I let it slide.

I laugh and tell Faraz and Dinesh to go to the 'naughty boys' room'. I know Faraz won't drink today; he never does when there are Muslim guests. But he will serve drinks to Dinesh.

Shezray arrives with a musallam raan cooked Rampur style—mutton leg stuffed with mincemeat and barbecued—on a large silver dish borne by her khansama in a white kurta pyjama walking behind her. It looks so perfect that I call Gul to take pictures. Shezray says that Fehmida Khala, Daniyal's mother, taught her khansama to prepare it. 'Khala' is an aunt; if the two families were so close, what was the impediment to their marriage, if there was any? I wonder why these two never speak to each other directly. There is always a mute salam by one, reciprocated by the other.

Vani has brought her 'utterly unhealthy chocolate layered pudding'. Vibhor looks like he has been dragged here by his parents. I introduce him to Gul, who stands talking to him, handing him drinks and snacks. She invites him to her room—he wouldn't like to be a part of a boring boomer discussion, she laughs. I'm relieved and surprised; Gul never takes an immediate liking to anyone. They must have something in common, or maybe she finds him hot. He is tall, skinny and pretty unremarkable. Maybe Gul likes those sorts; I don't know her type, if she has one.

Daniyal, holding a casserole gingerly away from his spotless kurta pyjama, is a quirky sight. I smile mockingly and ask him to introduce the dish. He says he has prepared the Rampuri darra-qeema himself—hand-chopped mince cooked in the basic spices with lots of green chillies. We set it all on the dining table, admiring and taking pictures. Somehow, the first reaction to food has become clicking pictures; we have forgotten to salivate. I hope Daniyal does not mention my visits to his house; I should have told him that Faraz doesn't know about it. But that would have made it sound clandestine, so I avoided the conversation. Somehow, I'm sure he has understood and won't bring it up.

'This looks more like a food fest than a book club meeting,' laughs Faraz.

'We are book lovers *and* foodies,' smiles Shezray.

'We had to add food for you guys,' I say.

I ask Meezan Bhai to take everything to the kitchen. I don't want anyone entering my decrepit kitchen, but Vani is already heading off there carrying her precious pudding because it needs to be put into the fridge immediately. Soon, everyone is in my kitchen fussing over their dishes.

'Okay, everyone, time for the meeting. We will come back to food later,' I say gently, leading them out to the drawing room.

Since it's Shezray's choice of read, she begins with an introduction to the book.

'The title is taken from Virginia Woolf's lines: "And all the lives we ever lived and all the lives to be are full of trees and changing leaves." This book by Anuradha Roy tells the story of young Myshkin, who was abandoned by his mother, Gayatri. It's said that she ran away with an Englishman; he was in fact a German artist called Walter

Spies. The story is based on real-life characters. We look at the story from the point of view of Myshkin, now an old man, as he reflects on this event that changed the course of his life.' Daniyal looks like he could break into applause; maybe I'm imagining his approval.

'Gayatri was in a terrible, unhappy marriage, and I guess in the 1930s, it was not possible to divorce. Remember how he throws out her paints? And why is it only a woman's responsibility to bring up children?' says Vani.

'But how traumatic for the child! His life remains stuck to the day his mom left him.' Akriti avoids my eyes.

'Yes. Myshkin lives his life going back to the moment. Imagine how such children deal with school and friends,' says Ritesh.

I try to remember the day Mamma left. They used to have fights when they thought I was asleep. Maybe they fought the night before she left. I just remember waking to a morning without her and knowing something had happened. Does a six-year-old feel shame? I remember Bhaskar and Divakar, the terrible twins routinely punished by every teacher, were the ones who said it first—'your mother ran away with her hero'—and the others joined in jeering. The children tittered; even my friends smirked. Akriti slapped Divakar across his face. 'Get back to your seats!' she shouted. She was the class monitor, the draconian dictator who wrote names on the blackboard and got kids punished. After I'd narrated the incident to Papa between sobs, he considered changing my school, where no one would know about Mamma, but I refused. I had Akriti now. She had asked the class teacher to let me sit with her. Like Myshkin, I was the abandoned kid; only, my mother had come back or had been called back to look after me because Papa was dying.

'I just can't understand women abandoning their children for career or for love,' says Vani.

'Why is "career" still a bad word, and why should it be an either/or situation?' questions Akriti.

'But why have children if you can't give them time? I think you have to give up yourself, your needs and desires to bring another individual to the world. I mean, both the parents have to do it,' offers Daniyal.

'By the way, this was before effective birth control and children, well... just happened. Even today, one might decide to have a child to... I don't know... support a relationship or to make things better? Anyway, I don't think it's ever easy to walk out of a marriage leaving your children. But sometimes... you have to think about yourself.' Shezray turns to Daniyal. Reading the book and discussing it must be excruciating for her; she stood exposed, inviting judgement for walking out of a bad marriage and leaving her child. Perhaps she wants to use this space to put her feelings out there. It is still brave.

I shake my head, trying to steady my thoughts. Maybe I have been shaking my head for some time; I feel everyone is looking at me. I take a deep breath and plunge in.

'Nothing, nothing can justify leaving your young child, even if it's with the most wonderful father in the world. Myshkin deserved an explanation. There was a schism... a void in his life, which he could never fill. It destroyed him.'

'But Gayatri did want to take him with her. He got late that day,' says Shezray.

'Then she should have postponed her departure.' I shrug.

'This was the 1930s. It was her only chance. She couldn't just catch another flight!' Shezray's voice scales a height we haven't heard.

'Well, then, she made her choice and...and goddamn her child!' I match her pitch and watch her curdle. I regret my reaction immediately. I shouldn't have been so insensitive towards Shezray—everyone has their story. A sudden heat prickles my hand, races up my arm and burns out from my head. I'm sweating, vaporizing; my ears still jangle from my voice. Shit, shit! I breathe deeply, and Akriti quietly hands me her cold drink. Everyone is frozen, but Vani, oblivious to social cues, carries on about the awful husband and Gayatri's letters to her son.

I look across the room. Daniyal's concentrated gaze is watching my unravelling. He nods slightly, and I feel sure that he has glimpsed my core and understood; perhaps he already knew. Later, I will look back at this moment—this sudden, improbable creation of 'us'.

'What would you have done?' Mamma once asked of me, a married woman with a child. She assumed I knew what had really happened—knowledge I didn't have. It was an opening I replayed in my mind for several years. I could have said so much—expressed my anger, hatred and hurt—and braved accusations of insensitivity. I had simply turned away, lacking courage to engage with the moment. But she knew that I would never leave like her. Never.

I excuse myself to check on the pulao and busy myself with frying the onions to a perfect golden crisp, adding the meat, then the rice, with just the right amount of stock. I wait for the correct time to place the meatballs, check the rice and consult Meezan Bhai. Finally, we seal the pot for dum. I slip back in when Daniyal starts reading, 'In my childhood, I was known as the boy whose mother had run off with an Englishman…'

The book discussion carries on longer than usual because we don't have to rush back home. Shezray participates in quieter, less passionate tones while I sit passively, getting up to fuss over the table and the pulao.

'How is your book coming along?' Vani asks me as I carve the mutton leg.

'The good news is that I've finally got a literary agent.'

'What does that mean? Please translate for us,' asks Ritesh.

'It means that if the agent finds a publisher, my book will be published.'

'But have you written it?' asks Akriti.

'Not completely. I just sent sample chapters and a synopsis, and she accepted. Which is huge for a new writer.'

'Wow! You're a writer already.' Vani claps.

'Cheers!' They are unselfishly happy for me; even Shezray shakes my hand, smiling. I'm aglow.

Munni Bai Hijab, Calcutta (1886)

Dagh was a practiced flirt. He caught the eye of the beauties and captivated them with his guile. He sent Qutubuddin Ashk to Calcutta to enquire about Hijab's well-being. Qutubuddin also visited Malka Jan, and she sent a copy of her masnavi to Dagh.

Dagh tried to ensnare Malka Jan, but she was an experienced, worldly wise woman and didn't get caught in his web.

—Tamkeen Kazmi
Masnavi Faryād e Dāgh mai Muqaddama

49 CHITPUR ROAD WAS AN ADDRESS THAT EVERY MUSIC AND poetry aficionado knew of, and if he had the means, would aspire to visit at least once. Malka Jan had bought all three floors for a sum of 40,000 rupees just three years after settling in Calcutta. Moving out of the cloistered gullies of Colootola to the wide roads of Chitpur was the measure of her success. She had decorated all three floors in different styles—the main performance hall in Mughal style, her salon for intimate guests in British colonial style, and there was a massive French bedroom. She showed you the renovations and changes in decor when you visited to celebrate Gauhar Jan's 'nath utrai' ceremony. Malka had laughed at your exclamations at the opulent gilt sofas and the heavy silk drapes in

the drawing room. The performance hall, double the size of yours, had mirrors till the ceiling, alive with flickering flames from a magnificent pale blue chandelier with a hundred candles at the centre; velvet masnads with bolsters all around a blue Persian carpet were the perfect setting for her performance. Malka had added four Italian marble statues of semi-nude Greek goddesses in the corners and low ornate tables for the huqqas. French windows with coloured glass panes opened to a balcony overlooking the wide street.

Malka often wore red, but today, her outfit was a subdued rose pink. She was the mother of the belle of the ball—the thirteen-year-old Gauhar Jan dressed in white lace gharara, signifying her purity. Her virginity would be up for sale today to the highest bidder. Gauhar still had the innocent chubbiness, the incipient double chin and a glowing English rose complexion. She had been accompanying her mother to mehfils, and her voice had been trained by ustads since the time she could speak. When she sang with her mother at Metiaburj, she caught the attention of Binadin Maharaj, the most illustrious proponent of thumri and Lucknow gharana, and became his pupil. She also learnt Bengali songs from Ramesh Chandra Das. It was said that when she came to her full form, she would outshine her mother. Her face was broader than Malka's delicate oval, still startlingly beautiful at twenty-nine, though there were shadows and pouches under her eyes, which she powdered over. It was rumoured that she was fond of her drink. You also drank occasionally to relax, especially after an exacting mujra. Malka told you that she was looking for a young, handsome prince or zamindar for Gauhar so that her path to womanhood would be pleasurable. It was a monumental occasion, and she had invited all the grandees and zamindars of Calcutta, the newly emerged bhadralok—the professional, English speaking Bengali babus—as well as the Nawabs and Rajas of nearby princely states.

As the mehfil began, Malka asked you to sit next to her. She always said you enhanced the allure of the mehfil. You felt you looked dark sitting beside her, even though you were quite fair by Indian standards. The floor lamp was placed next to Malka, illuminating her, while you sat in her shadow. You fidgeted with your green dupatta, it's too-garish tinsel made you feel like an imposter in the elegant room. Green was not your colour; it turned your complexion dull. You would have preferred a pink, but you somehow knew that Malka would wear pink and command the room with her resplendent persona.

The guests started arriving and were ushered into the hall. Malka welcomed them with an elegant salam, standing up and moving forward to greet a few, a seated acknowledgement for others. Sometimes, she would whisper an introduction to you—Nawab of such-and-such place. It was obvious that you didn't know most of them. Whenever you saw a familiar face, you would quickly touch your forehead in salam. A few nodded back, some turned away. You were conscious that you were trailing in the race for well attended mujras at your kotha. Invitations to mehfils were also dwindling, and Bablu, your agent and pimp, sometimes struggled to get you mujras. Sensing that you had nothing new to offer, the Metiaburj invites had also stopped.

The male guests, dressed in brocades and turbans, settled down on the elaborate floor cushions. Zohra Bai, Malka Jan Agreywali and all the celebrated baijis of Calcutta were seated on your side of the hall. They had brought expensive gifts for young Gauhar, kissing her brow and circling gold and silver coins around her head to ward off the evil eye. You knew that it was an outward show of friendship; they were competitors in a brutal market and kept a keen eye on each other.

Gauhar entered the hall, bent low in salam and took her place with the daughters of the baijis. You followed the envious eyes of the baijis. Their daughters could never compare with Gauhar's complexion, those hazel eyes under the magnificent brows, the nose ring gleaming on a chiselled nose. Tonight, the chosen 'nath babu', the highest bidder for her virginity, would remove the nose ring, and from then, on Gauhar would wear a nose pin and enter womanhood as a tawaif. Which one of them would have the pleasure of deflowering young Gauhar, you wondered, looking at the old and young men watching the dancing girls with naked lust and sipping English whisky. A sudden despairing nausea flooded you looking at Gauhar's excited, innocent face—did the child-woman know what lay in store for her tonight? You remembered the shock you had felt at the act and your struggle to keep your clothes on. You had been left in a room with a strange man with instructions to let him do what he wished with you because he would give you a lot of gifts and money. 'Don't you dare scream,' was Apa's warning whisper as she left. Terrified of Apa's wrath, you had gritted your teeth to bear the pain. Husna, the kotha maid, had no elaborate nath utrai ceremony but was unceremoniously bundled off to the first bidder. She had, after all, been bought at a low price from her family, who couldn't afford to keep her and found her expendable enough to sell and stave off hunger for some time at least.

Sometime during the mehfil, Malka Jan leaned forward and whispered through alcohol fumes, 'Your lover, Dagh, still pines for you, though he amuses himself by writing to old hags like me.' She fished out a letter from her purse and thrust it in your hands. You had first come to know of Dagh's cancellation of his Calcutta visit through Kamoni Bai, a budding tawaif of Calcutta, who was suddenly in correspondence with him. When Hameedan wrote to him, he replied saying that he had sent a telegram informing them about his change of plans due to his ill health. They hadn't received the telegram. Dagh asked Hameedan to arrange the return of his maidservant and send all the expense bills, which you might have incurred on his behalf, to Nassakh. He hadn't written to you after that, fearing your furious onslaught on his fragile ego. You decided to accept Maulvi Aal Ahmad's offer; it was impossible to look after the needs of the household without a steady income. Apa was right—you shouldn't have believed Dagh and put everything at stake. Aal Ahmad was more demanding than Niranjan Babu as you were the only tawaif in his employ. He was kind at times, and at times, brutal, as if his sanity depended upon venting his anger against the world on your body. It had been a long while since you had written a single line. Words congealed around your heart and clotted in your veins; the ambition of compiling a second diwan became a dream of a former youthful self.

Malka Jan sang first, after showing great reluctance. Leaning on the bolsters, the corpulent, old Raja of Karagarh threatened to leave if Malka didn't sing. He had been a patron of Malka Jan at one point of time.

'For you, Raja Sahib, from my diwan, *Makhazan e ulfat e Malka* (Treasures of Malka's Love).' Malka adjusted her dupatta, touched her forehead and began singing. Raja Karagarh sighed and shook his head, overcome by the poignant words of the ghazal. Malka's diwan had been published on 22 October 1886 to rave reviews. It had 106 ghazals, thumris and other compositions; many poets confessed to being moved to tears reading her lines. Dagh had once said that Malka had opened herself to suffering, which had bled into her words. It was whispered in the kothas that she suffered from malikholiya or melancholia—a word that defined inexplicable sadness and despair. Malka Jan was slightly drunk and flushed, which added to the allure of her singing. After refusing several encores and then giving in to the demands of her guests, she finally presented Gauhar, and the lamp was placed in front of her. You had noticed Gauhar taking a sip of wine with her friends, Badr e Muneer and Munni, in her room when you were exploring the house. She looked flushed, eager to be a part of this shimmering, glamorous world—she had sat on the fringes too long.

Gauhar's voice soared in a thumri set to Raag Malkaus, scaling its heights with impatient flashes of youthfulness, summoning the notes by punctuating the air with her pudgy childish hands—you were breathless at her daring confidence. Dhulichand, the renowned musical aficionado sat stunned; Shyamlal, a famous music patron, was waving his hands, mirroring Gauhar's gestures and shaking his head in ecstasy. Gauhar would soon be invited to the Dhulichand and Shyamlal concerts for solo performances. Apa had predicted that all the other baijis would take a back seat as soon as Gauhar came into her own. The grand dames of the time—Malka Jan Agreywali, Zohra Bai, Malka Jan Chilbila and you—were in their late twenties, and Gauhar Jan was in ascendance. Her contemporary, Janki Bai of Allahabad, could match her voice but not her looks.

There was much whispering in Malka Jan's ears by the servants of the aristocrats—proposals from the future patrons for Gauhar Jan. Malka Jan was smiling and nodding, her eyes glazed with brandy and the success of her daughter. The guests were ushered to the second-floor dining room for the feast. Malka had set up a long, ornate dining table holding an array of Indian and continental fare. Trained waiters were pulling back chairs and seating the guests. The baijis were ushered into another room with the traditional dastarkhwan, with Awadhi fare spread on the carpets. Malka Jan had cleverly separated her clients from possible enticement by her rival baijis. Insecurity over patrons was a quiet leitmotif running through their outward bonhomie. A closely knit community, they congregated for all important life events—birth, deaths, nath utrai—celebrating and mourning together and quietly gauging each other's success. They were a small coterie of Muslim tawaifs from Awadh, Agra, Banaras, Muzaffarnagar and surrounding areas, prized for their mastery over Urdu poetry and music. Patronized by Nawab Wajid Ali Shah, his family and other princely states and zamindars, charging high fees, they collectively looked down upon the Bengali Hindu and Bengali Muslim tawaifs, though, like Gauhar, the younger generation had learnt to sing Bengali songs to cater to the Calcutta clientele. Apa said that times were changing, and after the Nawab, they would all have to live and work undistinguished from Bengali tawaifs. The latter had a place in local culture, singing at temple ceremonies and other occasions and were preferred by Hindu babus. Only a select few Bengali babus, who loved Urdu poetry and wanted to show themselves as cultured elites, frequented the non-Bengali tawaifs. Malka, and now Gauhar, had the advantage of angrez parentage and spoke in English to the bhadralok officer class and English patrons. This was the reason for their success. They could demand an even higher price than you and other tawaifs. Gauhar sang in Bengali, Urdu and English. Later, Gauhar would become one of the first women singers to be recorded on 78 rpm records by the Gramophone Company of India and become a national sensation, her voice and compositions preserved for posterity.

The dining room hummed with talk and laughter. The guests and hostess became increasingly inebriated, laughing raucously and singing. Hameedan watched from behind the curtain and laughingly reported their antics to you. After dinner, she ran back to watch some more. By that time, you and the others had also finished dinner. Hameedan came back and whispered in your ear that she had overheard Malka's maid tell her that they couldn't find Gauhar. You went up to Gauhar's room—you had seen her lying on the bed with her friends, giggling uncontrollably—but she wasn't there. Malka came in stumbling down the stairs, asking her maid to hold up the lamp. She had decided on Kunwar Rai Jain as the most appropriate person to be Gauhar's first lover and patron; they were both young and would definitely take to each other. The bedchamber for the couple had been prepared, and it was time for the ceremony. After Kunwar Raj removed Gauhar's nose ring, they would be led to the flower-bedecked bed with singing and laughter like a newly married couple. The maid had gone looking for Gauhar because she was supposed to change into a red gharara for the ceremony.

Malka and you finally found Gauhar in a small anteroom with the old Raja of Karagarh. Gauhar flung herself into Malka's arms sobbing, terrified. You shrank back at the sight of the blood stains on Gauhar's pristine white gharara. Malka was screaming at the Raja, who was fumbling with his churidar, his bloated form struggling to get up, a sly, oily smile on his face. The maid closed the door, and you slipped away. There would be no ceremony, but you knew Malka would extract a heavy price from the Raja.

اِضْطِراب

13

Iztirāb (Restlessness)

Pūchho na hāl e zār merā tum se kyā kahūñ
Gum karda rāh e bāgh hūn yād e āshiyān nahīn

What can I say about my misery,
I'm a lost way not the memory of an abode.

—Munni Bai Hijab
Bahāristān e nāz

THEY SAY IZTIRAAB, A RESTLESS, BURNING FORM OF ISHQ, IS THE purest form of love—momentary and momentous, transient and eternal, manifesting on both spiritual and physical levels. It doesn't matter that ishq does not achieve its zenith; what matters is to love the very being of the lover and let that love define your life. It was this iztiraab-e-ishq that Dagh wished Hijab to experience for him and perhaps felt for her.

I'm pondering and scribbling in the time-ambivalent study, where the clocks argue over the time of the day. My mobile is left outside in the drawing room. I enter into another world. Maybe I need to be here to become myself; perhaps, as Mamma said, I'm shedding my skin again, snake-like, a timeless biological reflex. Mamma knew me; she had made me, and her cells still existed in my body.

When Daniyal leaves—I often pass him on his way out; perhaps a deliberate avoidance—I walk along the gallery, examining the pictures on the walls, and peep into the bedrooms. I'm like a little child exploring a secret place. Akhtar Bhai retreats to the servant quarters after serving me tea, and I feel comfortable wandering alone. It's for my research, I tell myself, to understand how people lived back then. Daniyal says the house was constructed during the time of Nawab Kalb e Ali Khan, that is the late nineteenth century, the era of Dagh and Hijab. Several changes have taken place since then, but the main portion of the house is the same—the arched verandas, the cool, dark bedrooms and the gold kamra, the drawing room. He occupies the mardana, the male-only portion of the house. The zenana section is accessible through another gallery, which opens up into a courtyard with more bedrooms on one side. They are all unoccupied now. Here, the women of the family lived their lives, gave birth, reared children, got meals prepared for the men, sang songs of happiness and sorrow.

Since the book club meeting, I have encountered Daniyal only once on his way out. Today, I arrived earlier, hoping to speak to him, but I was told that he had left even earlier than usual. Maybe he anticipated the conversation—he knew my lit agent had just dumped me. I read and re-read her email, in which she basically told me that there was no market for books on Urdu poetesses. She had pitched the book idea to first-rung and then second-rung publishers and got the same response. Perhaps this is why Daniyal didn't want me to engage with the publication side yet. Writing is fragile; it needs to develop in quiet places, and there was already so much noise in my life. I had forwarded the email to Daniyal; he hadn't replied. Unable to write, I call up Akriti for an emergency meet-up at Kareem's; I need lots of good food and a sympathetic shoulder.

When I told Faraz about my lit agent, and mentioned I was considering going back to my job, he looked up briefly from his mobile and said, 'It's your decision. I think writing is a tough thing to do.'

'You don't care about me!' I snapped, but he went back to a forward—fresh dirt on the government shout-out by a popular TV anchor. I wanted to tell him that I didn't feel comfortable with the idea of going back to school. There would be sly remarks, and they would most likely post me in a lower class as a substitute teacher, expected only to keep children quiet and pinned to the desks. I could try other schools, but it was mid-term, and getting a job would be tough. All I wanted was for Faraz to tell me to hang on, not to give up. It is always obvious what we need in a relationship at a particular time, but sometimes, we don't want to respond to the need. Faraz did not want the distraction of the emotionally disordered woman—the change that I know he feels in me. It was easier to wait for my exhausted, outward calm to return.

Akriti, in her wisdom, brings along Vani and Shezray to Kareem's. I know she is thinking of a support group for my writerly life, but I feel a bit let down—I wanted Akriti alone and undivided. So we are the book club girls hanging out together. We are ushered into a females-only section for purdah ladies. There is a group of women who have taken off their head scarves and are eating and laughing with abandon. One of them is trying to placate her howling baby by rocking him and shoving rice into his mouth. He spits it out every time and continues to bawl. The unperturbed mother keeps talking, shaking her torso to rock the baby, and feeds him some more rice.

'So basically, the publishers said my work is crap.' I break the news as soon as we settle down. It sounds trivial, almost funny.

Akriti and Vani pause in their perusal of the menu.

'What does your lit agent say?' asks Vani.

'That I have no style. The story is good but—'

'Did you pay her?' Vani frowns.

'Yes, I paid her 20k to trash my book and destroy my writerly dreams.'

'I thought so. You know, you never, NEVER pay the lit agents till they sell your book!'

One of Vani's clients is a lit agent, and she was cribbing about the so-called lit agents, who are fleecing new writers. Pramila, my lit agent, has a very stylish website with purple pages and flowers all over. She specializes in taking on new authors. Vani is looking indignant for my sake and explains that true agents charge 10 to 15 percent commission *only* when they sell the manuscript to the publisher.

'So, my client, Opparna Rai, tells me that these lit agents keep extracting money from new authors in the name of editing. Then, finally, they say the book is not selling and suggest self-publishing. So you put in more money. Opparna says self-publishing doesn't work because you need a marketing network and a sales team to sell a book well. You need a proper publisher. Not every book is *Fifty Shades of Grey*!' Vani explains.

She promises to connect me to the famous Opparna Rai. I have read about her, who hasn't; she is a diva among lit agents.

'You have been really brave in starting off on a new career at this age. I love the story. It's brilliant, and you will tell it,' Shezray smiles her sudden, brilliant smile and pats my hand. I feel I have been handed a gift.

'And don't even think of going back to that ridiculous school. Dump this Pramila. She is preying on your insecurities.' Akriti instinctively knows that I'm tempted to leave everything and get back to school. I feel near tears.

'You girls are the best!'

'We know, and now the qorma is getting cold!' Vani laughs.

'You are some nutritionist!' I laugh with her.

Kareem's is famous for its qorma prepared from a (as usual) secret recipe by Munna Bhai, the ustad of nearly all Rampuri khansamas. He is rumoured to have been a masalchi (spice grinder) in the royal kitchens. Munna Bhai is very old now, and his enterprising son, Naeem, has set up a Kareem's restaurant in the Civil Lines area, bringing the fabulous qorma out of the old town. It is finally accessible to us now. I call for chapli kababs to go with the qorma and tandoori nan. Kareem's chapli kabab patties tread the thin line between too firm and mushy-soft. Rampuris tend to look down upon over-tenderized and over-aromatic Lucknow kababs. Baba always says that chapli kababs are the original Afghani–Pathan kababs. I just love their rustic, meaty and no-frills taste.

That evening, an email from Pramila informs me that she has found the 'perfect editor' to 'rescue' my book and work with me to ensure it sells to a good publisher. Just as Vani had said, there is a thinly veiled demand for more money. The mail ends with an encouraging 'we will get there with some help'. I call up Pramila. She immediately texts back saying that she is in a meeting. She's always in a 'meeting' and never has the decency to call back. It's quite a confidence downer. Whenever I manage to connect with her—after several messages and missed calls—there's always a bratty child on the verge of or in the middle of a tantrum. I decide to break up with her over WhatsApp text. She calls up immediately.

'It's okay to be disheartened, dear, but your story holds so much promise! I believe you need a little bit of handholding. We are going to make it better,' she croons. I think she has locked herself up in her bathroom to escape the pesky kid—there is a bathroom echo. I can picture her sitting on the pot; I hope my ultimatum has not acted as a laxative.

'Ah, Pramila, I'm not disheartened at all. In fact, I've got another lit agent. Sorry, this didn't work out. I really need someone who's truly there for me. I can see you have a lot on your plate.' I listen with satisfaction as she semi-grovels and promises brilliant editing with the new editor. In fact, she says she is already in touch with a publisher. I thank her politely while typing a 'your services are no longer required; please release my manuscript' email.

Vani has already spoken to Opparna about me and shared her email with a warning that Opparna is on a strict diet and therefore very crabby. I wonder why lit agents are on such a short fuse. I'm sure they are nicer to well-known authors. I hope one day they scramble over each other to represent me. I compose a submission letter—the word makes me feel like a slave—and email Opparna with a synopsis and sample chapters. Opparna answers almost immediately—'Hi, I'll take this on. O'

I do my wide-arms Snoopy dance. Gul peeps in, laughs and joins me as I explain.

Dagh's Letter to Malka Jan
(1886)

O eloquent poetess, Beloved of Banaras, Pari of Calcutta, beauteous and miraculous Malka,

Oh, dear, why has God bestowed upon me a lover's temperament? Why am I not stone-hearted? I get infatuated if I see a stylish person. If the lady is well educated and writes poetry—that is death for Mirza Dagh! So I wrote of my state:

Raham āta hai apnī ḥālat pe
Paḍeiñ pathhar butoñ kī chāhat pe

I pity my state now,
May I be stoned for loving idols.

I had sent Qutubuddin Arsh to inquire about Munni Bai's well-being. When he returned, he gave me your masnavi. I can't find words to thank you. The masnavi is unique in its aspect—playful, flirtatious, worded in Hindustani but conceived in English style—an excellent composition. For a long time, I have heard your praises, especially from my stepbrother, Mirza Shaghul, and have been desirous of meeting you. I cannot come to Kalkatta because Hijab is an impediment. The people of Kalkatta are afflicted with such painful feet that they cannot come to Hindustan. There are many fine qualities of Hindustan that have not travelled to the east.

The virtue of your tribe is ink, your profession is freedom, and you are skilled in several arts. I'm surprised that you have never been to this part of Hindustan even for the pleasures of travel. Your writing is as fabulous as your shining future.

Oh, and I have heard that Munni Bai has developed a closeness to you these days. She must have spoken badly about me. Well, I also 'sing her praises'. Convey my salam to Gauhar Jan. I'm sure she must be an educated woman. Your house is radiant with the light of knowledge.

From,
Dagh
13 March 1886

Munni Bai Hijab, Calcutta (1886–1888)

Ya ilāhi nijāt gham se miley!
Wo sarāpa Ḥijāb ham se miley
Warna uskā ḳhayāl bhī na rahey
Ab hai jaisā ye ḥāl bhī na rahey

Oh, Lord, expunge me of this grief!
May I reunite with my Hijab,
Or efface her thoughts from my heart,
And reprieve my torment.

—Dagh Dehlvi
Faryād e Dāgh (1882)

It was just like Malka Jan to send her masnavi to Dagh, thus inviting correspondence, and then pass his letter to you. You invariably got to know of his many liaisons with tawaifs, both literal and physical—each as fleeting as they were fervent. The thought of him coming to meet Malka Jan was an insult. You shot an angry letter, warning Dagh that if he set foot in Calcutta to meet her, you would create hell for him. He was yours, at least in this city—the idea of him cavorting with Malka Jan or any other tawaif under your nose was intolerable. After he cancelled his Calcutta visit, you had come to know through Nassakh that Dagh had recovered and was attending the durbar, organizing literary gatherings—a shining star among the literati of the riyasat. He was probably loth to leave Rampur because of his recent dalliance with Chanda, a young tawaif who wrote under the cloying pen name of 'Chanda Piya' and had taken your place as his adoring pupil and lover.

Gauhar had disappeared after the brutal incident with the Raja; there were whispers and conjectures about her whereabouts. Apa said she had become pregnant and was sent away till she delivered the child. You couldn't get Gauhar's shattered, tear-streaked face out of your mind. But she was young and would forget about it; we always did—there was no other option. You realized with a shock that you had internalized Apa's words—the superimposition of thoughts and the inevitability of your life cycle as a tawaif swamped you with terror.

When you met Malka Jan at a concert organized by Dhuliram, she embraced and kissed you on both cheeks.

'You are my one true sister, you know that, na? I remembered later that you were with me when we found poor Gauhar. She had been drinking with the girls—something we never do before a performance. Singing is a prayer.' She touched her ears. You saw the dullness in Malka's eyes, and for the first time, felt a genuine warmth towards her.

'How is dearest Gauhar?' you whispered.

'She's recovering from the dreadful experience. I sent her to Midnapur for some time.' Gauhar's life path had already been decided; a little diversion could not alter the grand plan. Later, you would hear that Gauhar had a stillbirth.

'I wanted to give you this. How much he desires you, your Dagh! You are so lucky.' Malka pulled out a letter from her blouse and handed it over to you. 'It is still warm with your lover's heart.' She tinkled, patted your cheek and turned away to meet someone with a gay smile, the pallu of her heavy Banarasi saree slipping down, a trailing comet. She gathered it up, flung it back on her shoulder and walked away.

...I'm grateful to Hijab for meeting me in Rampur with a sword hanging over her head. With great faithfulness and love, she sustained our relationship; I visited Kalkatta for her. Our love and parting have become famous all over Hindustan through my Faryād e Dāgh *masnavi. When we parted, I knew there was no hope of reuniting. I am a humble servant of the Rampur riyasat. How could I stay in Kalkatta forever? How could I leave my employment—the source of my income and recognition? Baiji's stubborn insistence that she would never step into Rampur doomed our love. If she had come, it was possible for us to be together at least for a few months in a year. I'm a poor man, but I can host her stay. She keeps asking me to visit her in Kalkatta, but going there doesn't feel right. At my age, I can't bear any more grief and heartbreak. Seeing her with others would spell the end of my life. I wrote to her several times—numerous letters with pages blackened with the ink of my despair—till my fingers were ready to drop off, but she never came to me. After a long wait, I turned to others to amuse myself and she got employed by Maulana Aal Ahmad, and thus, vanished from my life.*

I'm a faithful lover, and I have yet to meet anyone who can assuage the wounds given by Hijab; long have I searched for such a lover. I have heard of your famed attributes, and I'm desirous of meeting you.

Dāgh ek ādmī hai garmā garam
Ḳhush bahut hoñgey jab mileñgey āp.

Dagh is a passionate and warm person
You would be delighted to meet him.

Although Kalkatta suits my purpose of meeting you, I cannot go there. Hijab has come to know of our correspondence and has written an angry, raging letter. In Rampur, she doesn't care whom I flirt with, but she cannot bear rivals in Kalkatta. Her jealousy knows no bounds...

Dagh Dehlvi
9 Aug 1886

The words cut into the precarious illusion of his love you had clung to, even though the ties between you were straining and tenuous. Apa always said, 'A tawaif's life is for a few years. *Umr ka khazana hota hai zindagi ka nahi*—the treasure of a long existence but a short life.' She made you hyper-aware of the transience of time and beauty.

A few months later, in 1887, you came to know that Nawab Kalb e Ali Khan had passed away. His successor, Nawab Mushtaq Ali Khan, was physically challenged and dependent on a Regency Council led by General Azamuddin Khan. The new Nawab was too frail to nurture poetry, and the general, an anglophile, had little interest in Indian languages. The literary circle so painstakingly established by Nawab Kalb e Ali Khan started collapsing, and ultimately, Dagh and several other poets and writers left Rampur in search of sponsors.

You remembered Dagh saying that the day his Nawab died he would become dar ba dar, a homeless wanderer. You heard stories of his travels to Agra, Lahore and Hyderabad in search of employment and mounting debts; he had to leave his wife in Delhi. Nassakh said that Dagh was reduced to asking his students for small loans to pay off the local grocer's bills. You forgave him.

Aal Ahmad remained your patron for two years, and you adjusted to the set patterns of life with him—after all, you were nearly thirty, an age of reduced choices and greater tolerance. At 500 rupees, he was a generous patron, but for how long would this largesse continue? Every year on your salgirah, the day of your birth, Khala would tie a knot on a silk skein to mark another year of your life and count them out loud.

Your music and poetry could have ensured a slipping toehold of relevance, but you had practically given up writing and singing—you had nothing new to offer at the mehfils and had withdrawn. The tempestuous fire that fed into your words and your performance was simmering down and the invitations to mehfils had also petered out. The middlemen who brought invitations and negotiated the price were rarely seen at your kotha. Hameedan would sing sometimes in the salon, but she wasn't as popular as you were. Apa cribbed about you giving up your music practice. There were still a few more years for you before new beauties and new voices drowned you out.

It was the beginning of an era of high popularity of Hindustani classical music. Thumris and bol-banao stylizing was becoming a masterful art created in the salons of aficionados like Shyamlal and Dhulichand. Gauhar had returned to join her mother in musical soirées. Malka was slipping deeper into a drunken stupor, but she had Gauhar in fierce competition with Zohra Bai and Malka Jan Agreywali. Gauhar, with her flamboyant dresses, her fluent English and stunning looks, had become the reigning tawaif. It was said that she knew twenty languages and could sing English, Bangla, Hindi and Urdu songs. She charged an unthinkable 2,000 to 3,000 rupees for a performance and kept learning from the top ustads of the time.

Abandoned women, 'fallen women', women who ran away from their homes, duped by their lovers, and childhood widows craving freedom—all found a place in Calcutta's burgeoning flesh trade. Some like Binodini had become famous theatre artists. Acting had never attracted you as a possible profession. Even the musical practice of dhrupad and thumri seemed like an imposition, though you loved music. It was the shape and sound of words, the feeling of syllables set into meters that delighted you. Poetry was your passion, and you were the happiest singing your own compositions and setting them to tunes. But you had always doubted the praise of poets and your patrons—even Dagh's appreciation seemed to be more inspired by your beauty than your words. You felt that you didn't have that rare genius, the talent to string the words into immortal ghazals.

Aal Ahmad's proposal of marriage felt more like a decree than a request. He had separated from his wife and had no children. All the grand moments your life had promised had already occurred. The brief allotted time for your shining was nearly over. You had seen too much of the world to expect eternal love and were practical enough to recognize the security he represented. Maybe he wanted to salvage your soul; he had mistaken your withdrawal from mehfils as penitence. You didn't drink on the nights he came to you because he hated your drinking. He offered to continue to pay for your mother's and your khala's needs, but you had to leave the kotha and live with him as his wife. It wasn't unusual for tawaifs to marry and withdraw into purdah. You had accepted that Dagh could not be a part of your life—marriage was never an expectation for he would never leave his wife or take a second wife. Brief stints of togetherness were all you hankered for sometimes, but that desire was also fading from your conscious mind. Maybe he truly loved you, at least briefly and despite his dalliances. But he had already forgotten you now, immersed in his struggle for survival.

You might regret it at some point of your life, but for now, marriage was the wisest step. Many tawaifs had married their patrons; noblemen always advised their young sons to employ tawaifs but never wed them. Apa, who had seen you go through your dark phases, rejecting concerts, your anxiety and self-doubt before a mujra, accepted it. You were over thirty, and there wouldn't be better offers. If Aal Ahmad left you, you would become what local people called chhutto, an unemployed tawaif to be claimed by any bidder for an hour, two hours or a night. Night after night, you would have to deck yourself, stand on the balcony and display yourself to the gawking passers-by; Apa would haggle over the prices like a madam for a common randi. Fear and vulnerability would shadow your nights.

You remembered one customer before Aal, who had fallen on you with such vicious hatred that you had screamed. Apa had burst into the room and prised him away from you. There would be others like that. After some time, no one would come to rescue you. They would come later to tend to your wounds. You could manage Aal with your wiles and tact; he was a simple person, given at times to physical cruelty. Apa said that was marriage—the acceptance of lack of choice. She blamed you for not birthing a daughter and choosing not to adopt one. You could never tell a girl, your daughter, to accept the glamour and torridity of this existence. It was your stubborn decision that you wouldn't live your old age like a parasite on the earnings of another. You had decided to break the chain and prayed to Allah to forgive your deeds. You were ready to let Aal salvage your soul.

کشیدگی

14

Kashīdgī (Estrangement)

Jab se suna hai ek wafāt o wisāl hai
Marne kī wo kḥushī hai ki jīnā muḥāl hai

Ever since I heard of reuniting after death,
Dying became happiness and living, an exile.

—Munni Bai Hijab
Tazkirā e qadīm shairāt e Urdu

I CHORTLE READING DAGH'S LETTER AND HAND IT TO DANIYAL. 'I was going through this letter. Have you seen this? It's priceless. Talking of physical conditions—weak knees, falling teeth—to your lover!'

'Maybe their love had transcended physical boundaries.'

'But you still need good knees to make love.'

'Hmm. Not necessarily,' Daniyal laughs. It's teatime, and Daniyal has walked into the study bearing the tea tray. He had promised to join me for tea and talk about the progress of the book. Most days, I have my tea absentmindedly while scribbling or reading.

I leave my desk to sit on the sofa and let the ceremonious stirring and pouring of tea take over. Daniyal hands me my cup and reads the letter aloud, smiling.

'I guess the poor tawaifs were used to entertaining men of all ages. Maybe they were sympathetic to human frailties.'

'But he was her lover, not a patron as such. Women accept ageing husbands but not ageing lovers. We want our lovers to be agile; otherwise, we might as well be married and faithful.'

'What if Faraz loses all his teeth? Would you still love him?'

'Probably. He's my husband.'

'Indian women!'

'Yes, very much so,' I smile.

We discuss Hijab's decision to get married, dictated by her age and 'marketability'. It is not very different from the choices women are still making—the balancing of salary, looks and family, a negative balance if the woman crosses thirty—especially in arranged marriages. We continue to have low expectations of marriage ingrained in our psyche across all strata.

I scroll through my WhatsApp messages and find a message from Gul: *At Nostalgia café with Vibhor.*

Gul is on a date with Vani's son! She is just sixteen, and that skinny guy with barely a face is in his final year of college. What is my child getting into?

Come home NOW! I text. I have to leave, I tell Daniyal. He doesn't ask me anything, just rings for Akhtar Bhai and asks him to get a rickshaw. I quickly drain my teacup and run out of the house. Gul had sent the message more than an hour ago, and I had left the mobile in the drawing room. I start calling her as soon as I sit in the rickshaw; she keeps cancelling my calls. I'm so frantic, I can barely breathe. I call Faraz to drop everything and come immediately. I tell him that we need to be together on this, or our only daughter will lose the plot. He complies, maybe out of guilt, and we wait for the errant offspring to return.

'What were you thinking, Gul? Why didn't you ask me? How dare you!' I start shouting the minute Gul returns.

'I asked Papa.'

'And he probably didn't even hear you! And this is Rampur!' I continue, becoming more illogical by the second while Gul looks at me with a wariness one would reserve for crazy relatives.

'We did nothing. Just had coffee at this shitty place. No worries; still a virgin.'

I choke. 'You're sixteen! It's not even legal.' I can't say 'sex' in front of her. I just can't think of sex in connection to her.

'I'm in college now.'

'Huh. You… you are nowhere! You're a college dropout. You need to think about your career, not boys.'

'Mamma… Ma, relax! It's perfectly normal to date. Most of my Dubai friends are in a relationship. You met Papa at college and dated him.'

'For god's sake! I was… nineteen, nearly twenty, and it was different.' I'm fuming.

'Listen, Gul. Your mother is right. I didn't think it through when you asked me. It's time to think of your studies, not get into a relationship. Anyway, you are far too young for that,' Faraz puts in. For once, we have tuned in together over the Gul situation.

'Okay, parents, relax! We just had coffee and talked.' Gul is exasperated and angry.

There is that stupid hot flush flaming up my body again. I shout out for water. Meezan Bhai always lurks outside the door when he hears loud voices.

Gul huffs off to her room, ignoring Faraz's attempts to smooth out the situation. Guilt snaps around my throat. I have been too busy with my writing and have ignored her issues. I was waiting for her to settle down before speaking to her. But she has been here for two weeks, and I still haven't made time to connect with her and sort out her mind. Neither has Faraz. For him, everything else besides his current preoccupation is blurry and insignificant; maybe I have been mirroring his attitude and Gul is out of focus for both of us.

Before I can turn my ire on Faraz and risk him calling me hysterical, which he always does when it comes to Gul, I call up Baba—my knee-jerk reaction to any Gul situation. Faraz frowns. I know he will walk out, but I want him here and pin him with a look. He starts pacing around the room.

Baba is the only one who has engaged with Gul and discussed her studies when she stayed at his place. I don't tell him about the 'date'—that would lead to another kind of conversation. I ask if he could use his contacts to get her admitted to one of the local colleges. The admissions are over, but they might squeeze her in through the back door. This is small-town India. Any graduation course would do; at least it will give her something to do during the day. If she doesn't want a career, we can marry her off after graduation.

I realize that I'm sounding unhinged. Baba doesn't flinch; he knows my worry when it comes to Gul. She is my fragile one, the child I felt would shatter with the slightest fever. When Mamma found out about my pregnancy, she said, 'You'll become nothing, like I did after I had you.' I just wanted to become a mother, obliterate my identity and pour all of myself into this little life.

'How can you give up on your daughter? She's bright. She's just confused with the changes in her life, and we haven't given her time to adjust. You don't want these horrible so-called colleges to destroy her future. I'm trying to persuade her to go back to her medical college.'

'But maybe she doesn't want to be a doctor!' I don't even know what she wants, what her interests are. She sings well, has a great sense of rhythm and she loved playing the Casio. In fact, at the book club meeting when she first met Vibhor, they were jamming on her karaoke system. Music brought them together. I hope she doesn't imagine herself in love with him.

'You underestimate her. She got 89 per cent in the class 12 boards,' Baba says then carries on, seizing the opportunity to go full steam on our parenting failures: we are not good role models, she has no desire to excel, we are too soft with her, giving her an easy life, et cetera. I roll my eyes, sigh and listen. The phone is on speaker for Faraz's benefit. He sits down with a thump on the sofa, legs crossed, a foot shaking with impatient annoyance. Baba is holding forth, interspersing his rant with '*Sun rahi ho*? Are you listening?'

'Haan, haan, I'm listening.' I keep haan-ing, and he carries on shouting into the speaker phone.

As soon as I get a breather, I say, 'Baba, Faraz wants to say something.'

'Humph, what can he say. It's his fault, too, not just yours.' I hand over the mobile to a scowling Faraz.

Maybe I should have done more—some helicopter parenting and hovering around instead of leaving her to her resources. I didn't want to be the prying mom. Gul gets up late, watching god knows what all night or maybe talking to that boy. I have started working at Daniyal's till five, the official closing time of the library. Gul skips dinner because she has now decided to practise intermittent fasting. She doesn't even want to sit at the table with us. Another relationship slipping into non-conversational mode. When did she leave my force field?

Faraz, as usual, has been engrossed in matters he doesn't want to share. When he is home, he is on WhatsApp, watching random people giving opinions on everything under the sun and reading forwards with the zeal of one controlling the world economy with the steady jabbing of buttons. Sometimes I hear him chuckle and ask him what's the joke. He forwards it to me.

Why should I be the only one on a guilt trip? I wait for Baba's call to end. Normally, I delay such conversations waiting for Faraz to calm down, but I'm relentless today. Faraz tells me I'm overreacting—it was just a friendly meeting. Gul called it a date to rile me.

'The date is a symptom of the problem, maybe a cry for our

attention. The point is that Gul needs to be taken in hand; we should give her direction or help her find direction,' I say.

'You… are talking like a writer now,' Faraz accuses.

'This is not about me. Listen, I feel we should try to enrol her in a private college in Moradabad. TMU is a nice college and just half an hour drive from here. I'm sure they can take in one late admission. The fee is just about 40 to 50k per semester.' I blot out my usual reaction to Faraz.

'We can't afford it right now. Not unless we borrow from Baba.'

'I can't believe we can't afford college fees, that too Indian college fees, for our only child. Has it really come to this?'

'I did pay her med college fees for the year. Maybe we'll get it back if she opts out.'

'I doubt we'll get much. It's a loss of one seat for them as well. If nothing's working here, maybe we should leave Rampur.'

'And go where? At least we have a house and land here, even though it's in Baba's name.'

'If we sell off the Dubai flat, we can settle in Delhi. Maybe you could take up a job or something.'

The Burj Khalifa flat must be worth a lot by now. We had bought it when things were going well in Dubai. Faraz falls silent and I realize that story is over. There were debts, he tells me, and he couldn't pay the bank loan instalments. I feel a breathless panic. There is no Plan B; we are in free fall.

'I know you're upset, and I feel like a failure.'

You *are* a failure, I want to scream. All those wonderful schemes he threw himself into, the optimism fuelled by the plush lightness of borrowed money. He just wanted to live huge, become larger than life, and it all needed to happen immediately. It never did, so the grand schemes multiplied with the promise of sudden exceptional leaps just lurking around the corner.

'He's so *hyper*,' Vani had whispered, her usual no-filter remark when she first met Faraz.

I was amazed that a relative stranger had to point it out to me—after nearly twenty-five years of being together and seventeen years of marriage—that this hyperactivity, which is a part of Faraz's personality, wasn't normal. What I mistook for dynamism and youthful optimism could well be ADHD or some 'deviant personality' disorder—terms I had skimmed through while Gul was growing up. I realized that Faraz was always in motion, restlessly moving around the room, sleeping in small bursts. Even at meals, he would quickly pile food on the plate and shovel it into his mouth, talking constantly if he was in the mood. If I were an artist, I would draw his face in a blur. I had read somewhere that we invent our partners and see them as we want to rather than what they actually are. After all these years, I could finally see him: he lacked the focus to succeed, to stick to anything. The conditions were not against him, *he* was the condition.

'The only way out is to pull in more money, or we go under.' Faraz looks at me warily. He can handle my anger, but my calm sharpness has unsteadied him.

'That's what you had said last time, and we did go under.'

'You don't understand business. It's a debt spiral.'

'I'm not dumb. The higher we go up the spiral, the harder we fall. I know that now, and it's not going to work.'

'What do you know about markets? You sit in the library all day and live in the past. I have to struggle to put food on the table.' Faraz is shouting now, pacing the room with sudden belligerent energy. He always had these angry outbursts and could be cruel with his words. I had ignored, justified them and forgiven him when he apologized. Most of the time, I rushed in to smooth things over with acts of atonement to restore the old equilibrium—the only balance I knew in our relationship. I sit it out and let him rant.

'Don't worry about food on the table. I'm going back to work now. In fact, if you'd been honest with me, I wouldn't have left.'

'Huh, what will your measly salary do!'

'It's enough to feed us but not enough to put my daughter in college. She'll have to miss a year.' I walk out of the room.

Munni Bai Hijab, Calcutta
(1888–1901)

Judāyī terī kis ko manzūr hai
Zamīn saḳht hai āsman dūr hai

Who can endure this separation from you,
The world is harsh and the sky afar.

—Dagh Dehlvi
Letter dated 5 September 1885

THE TINKLE OF ANKLETS, THE RESONANT BEAT OF THE TABLA, the dizzying trysts with raag compositions and the summation of words into meters receded from your life after your marriage. Yet, certain mornings, you would awake with the cadence of a ghazal in your ears; sometimes, you would catch yourself humming an old tune as you went about the monotony of household duties. You would stop abruptly, mutter a prayer to banish the evil Shaitan (Satan) from entering your life again.

Qazi Muhammad, an old friend of Dagh who officiated as Mohammedan marriage registrar, informed you that after nearly two years of wanderings and penury, Dagh finally found employment with the Nizam of Hyderabad in 1888. You were happy for Dagh. Qazi

Muhammad had registered your nikah with Aal. He had married several tawaifs to their benefactors and considered it a great mission of his life. Aal Sahib considered him a pious man and he was the only male besides your brothers whom you were allowed to meet.

Dagh came to Calcutta with the Nizam of Hyderabad and met Apa and Hameedan at the kotha. Hameedan said he looked well and gave fifty rupees to Khuda Bakhsh and invited him to come to Hyderabad. He could find work for him there as a musician. He was warm-hearted and loving as ever and inquired about your well-being. Apa was muttering later that it was because of him that you had developed an aversion for and finally left the profession of your ancestors. Hameedan said that you should have waited for another two years for Dagh. Another tryst, fiery and short-lived—but that part of your life was long forgotten. You smiled, thinking how Dagh loved and despaired your unpredictability and quicksilver temper—the side you curbed as a married woman.

There were periods of contentment in your marriage; you crushed your impulses to keep peace. Sometimes, your bottled-up frustration would explode into sharp words at the maidservants, Hameedan and Khuda Bakhsh. You hated the casual way your husband treated you—his coldness and masochism hollowed you out; you were used to being admired like a precious being. Apa said husbands were accustomed to having their wives with them forever, and it made them negligent. Though you had shunned your profession, it irked you to be a dependent; you had always been open-handed and uncaring about money, and it was galling to plead and wheedle for a few rupees. You accepted the powerlessness of a marriage—all beings are powerless before the will of Allah, bent down in prayer several times during the day and night attempting to erase the kinks in your thoughts. But some days, you still hungered to drive in an open phaeton along the river, singing and listening to music. Hameedan had been employed by Nassakh for several years. She said she didn't enjoy singing at mehfils without you and the kotha didn't feel the same. Even she, your most avid pupil, had stopped writing.

Aal hated your old tawaif ways. If you so much as flirted and laughed with him—all that had titillated him earlier—he would turn away in disgust. You are a wife now behave like one, he would say; I will come to you the way I want to and when I want to. You were supposed to lie supine to receive his seed—he was often punishing towards a body that had sinned—and take a bath immediately after the act to pray for an offspring. All the lessons of pleasuring men, of revelling in your beauty had to be forgotten. At least you were spared that sick, anxious feeling when you were left alone in the room with a new patron, of waking up after a night of passion and setting your appearance right, scrutinizing the mirror at the foot of your bed. You had started choosing your patrons, looking for kind, smiling eyes and even a paunch. Whereas you had the right to refuse then—Apa would never force you—now it was your duty to open yourself to Aal's and God's will. He was convinced that you would have a child from him, a son, which his wife was unable to give him. You were still young and fertile, and if you gave up the traditional contraception techniques you had used over the years, Allah would surely bless you.

You went with Aal to Syed Ali Shah's shrine, wrote your arzee, your request, on a piece of paper and tied it on the jaali around the tomb, lit a candle and sat whispering prayers at the foot of the grave. He was the 'Qutub Pir', the axis of Calcutta, and it was believed that he controlled its rise and fall. Aal Ahmad was a great believer in the power of Shah Sahib and fed hundreds of pigeons whenever he visited the shrine. You felt a sense of peace as you set your forehead to the saint's grave. Maybe Shah Sahib would grant you a son and make this marriage, your path to salvation, easy for you.

The years with Aal were measured by attending the annual urs celebrations at Shah Sahib's dargah. It was said that Shah Sahib was most magnanimous on the days of the urs. Every year, you and Aal attended the urs, gave alms and lit candles. Hope lingered for some time after that, then faded over the years. Aal blamed your wanton ways and the mysterious methods tawaifs used to avoid pregnancy. Apa snorted and said, 'If your husband was virile, he would have had children from his first wife. The fault lies with him, not you. You could have had children from anyone if you wanted support for your old age.' Even if it were true, you felt diminished.

Hameedan finally married a middle-aged zamindar. She said she was happy even though she was a second wife; she no longer contributed to the running of Apa's household. Khuda Bakhsh earned some money playing tabla at nearby kothas, but it was not enough to support the household. The kotha became defunct. Husna, after living at the kotha for most of her life, rented a hovel in Sonagachi and started working as a randi—the only option left for her. She had no gift for music and at the kotha she was employed to serve paan and drinks to the guests and entertained some customers. Shafeeq was married to a distant cousin and since he didn't work, he became another dependent for you. Besides Apa and Khala, your old Maulvi Sahib and his wife also lived at the kotha. They had come with Apa from Awadh all those years ago and had taught the Quran and Urdu to you and your siblings. They were your family, too. Where would they go in their old age? You felt the burden of their needs press down upon you. Aal was, in a sense, still a patron, contributing to the upkeep of the former kotha. He was happy that he had been instrumental in closing down a house of sin. He was rich enough to send money to Apa but tight-fisted to just send enough to feed her. It was sawab, a blessing, to give to the old and infirm.

عبادت

15

'Ibādat (Adoration)

Maza yehī hai ke tarfain se ho bechaiñī
Merey taḍapne ne unko bhī beqarār kiyā

An exhilarating restlessness mirrored in our hearts,
My tormented state disquieted him.

—Munni Bai Hijab
Bahāristān e nāz

GUL IS IN LOVE OR IN A HORMONAL CRUSH WITH THE WEAK-chinned boy, and my teacher's intuition tells me he is trouble. I hear her laughing and chatting with him, singing into her mobile (presumably with him on the other end) and emerging radiant from her room, hugging her newfound happiness. We have all ridden the wave, and one can only brace for it to crash. I want to throw away Gul's mobile and take her away with me somewhere—maybe to the hills, just a three-hour drive away. But I don't think her generation can survive being Wi-Fi-less for even an hour—my generation is no better now. Our senses now need constant entertainment, information and a relentless connection. Why did we decide that being connected and this perpetual information overload was a desirable state of being? I remember hovering around the landline phone, waiting for Faraz's call—the longing heightened by the wait.

Mamma was right in her dislike for mobiles, and for once, I agree with her, albeit posthumously.

There is no message from Daniyal. Not even a 'I hope everything is okay' after I rushed out of his house like it was on fire. I suppose that's Daniyal; he doesn't use WhatsApp and rarely messages. Maybe he respects my privacy or wants to stay away from whatever mess I'm in. It almost feels that he and his world are contained in another sphere, floating unconnected to my realities. I can enter it at will, but he will never puncture its skin unless I allow him to. I resist the urge to go to him and dissect everything surrounded by his calm. He would listen, maybe advise. But I know I would never do it; it would be disloyal. Perhaps he knows that, too. I long to be transparent, to let myself reflect on my face without schooling my features and words to the appropriate.

Meanwhile, my hormones and everything else are conspiring to give me sweaty, sleepless nights. Faraz complains that I thrash about, throw off the quilt, then pull it back, leaving him cold. During the day, I'm on edge with the hot flushes creeping up, ambushing me unexpectedly. Swallowing my pride, I meet the principal of Academy School, asking her if I could rejoin. I even blame my menopause for the sudden decision. She listens to me with a cat-like satisfaction as I practically grovel and informs me that she has already promoted Pankaj Sir to my position. Out of her 'fondness' for me and 'sympathy', she offers a position in junior school, where the pay is so meagre and I would vegetate and kowtow for years to get back to my earlier pay scale. I see her savouring the news she will spread through her coterie—I have come crawling back. Going to a rival school is an option, but no one hires in the middle of a session unless there is some unforeseen vacancy. Akriti suggests that I write articles. Two well-placed pieces might earn the same amount as a junior teacher's salary. I could also complete the book and hopefully sell it to a publisher. Sadly, as always, Baba is right—only the rich can afford to be full-time writers.

Emotionally drained from my humiliating expedition, I decide to go to Daniyal's and write the sacred 500 words, which all writing blogs prescribe for budding writers. I haven't written anything for days now. Resisting the urge to wallow in bed, I wrap a chador over my saree and take a rickshaw to Daniyal's house. I'm convinced of its energy field—my writing flows as a mental reflex after entering the stillness of the alternate world. The wind on my face is grassy and moist from last night's rain; I breathe in the hills.

Daniyal is ill with a high fever and hasn't eaten for days, Akhtar Bhai informs me mournfully as he ushers me in. No wonder he hasn't messaged; the clocks are unwound and frozen. Sitting at the desk, I try to write while I wait for Akhtar Bhai to leave for his afternoon nap. I need to check on him; it could be serious, and he hasn't seen a doctor. I slip into Daniyal's bedroom. He is sleeping on an intricately carved four-poster bed draped in gauzy sky-blue curtains straight out of a Merchant Ivory movie. In my wanderings around the house, I had never ventured here, respecting his privacy. A cool darkness and stale aftershave scent envelop me. I stand looking down at him—the crushed kurta pyjama askew and bunched up, an outstretched arm with curled fingers. There is a tiny flicker of his closed eyelid; he is aware of my presence but unwilling to acknowledge or disturb it, perhaps waiting. I climb on to the bed next to him, stretch out and close my eyes. Daniyal sighs and then breathes tentatively. I turn towards him. Men look like children in their sleep, vulnerable and soft. Strands of hair curl on his brow. I smooth them back, resting my hand lightly on his fevered brow. Resisting the urge to cup my palm on his flushed cheeks, I take my hand away. He opens his eyes and places his palm on my cheek; we stay there, connected. I edge closer, until our foreheads touch and close my eyes to feel the pulsating us created in that moment.

'You'll catch the fever,' he murmurs.

I shake my head. We lie there and drift off into a still place. My cool brow rests on his fevered forehead, his warm fingers entwine in mine, a transference of temperature, an osmosis beyond reason. We sleep for what seemed like hours, dreamless, floating in a shared magma. From Gul's point of view 'nothing happened', yet in those two hours we 'slept together', I could sense a fragmentation, a shift, a possibility. There will always be a before and after for us.

I wake with a start. Daniyal is burning up. I get out of bed and ask Akhtar Bhai to get some tea and biscuits for Daniyal, find a paracetamol in a drawer, hand it to Daniyal and make him call up the doctor. I gulp down my tea; I have to leave before the doctor arrives.

I'm conscious of something tearing up inside me as I sail past the now-familiar gullies, the corner paan-cigarette vendor, the shops spilling out to the street with their wares and men on their way to the mosque. I obscure my face with the edge of the chador. Can they see me? I have finally disembodied and need to hide this treasured disembodiment I carry inside myself. Has it begun, and where will it end? I ask myself as I heard Hijab asking herself—an infinity of lives and choices.

When I reach home, Meezan Bhai informs me with a disapproving look that Gul has gone out in a rickshaw. Gul venturing out alone in Rampur is a first. Last time, Vibhor had picked her up.

'Hello, Ma, we are having coffee at Food Plaza.' The airy tilt in her voice forbids questioning. They are already a 'we'. How dare she defy us and go like this! Should I rush over there and burst upon them in the manner of a possessive parent?

When I fell in love with Faraz, Mamma knew almost instantly. Those were the days of secret love letters. It still mystifies me how she found Faraz's letter. She was never into prying through my things like an over-caring parent, but she simply *knew* that something was going on. Calmly, she asked me who this boy was and if I was ready to settle down in this godforsaken 'mofussil' town in UP. Mofussil—the word had an alien, deplorable weight, and there was no Google to tell me what it meant. She tried her best to cheapen my love with her cutting words. Bristling, I turned away; I didn't give her the right to question me. She was the mother who abandoned me for her lover.

I was about eleven when Papa passed away. I spent years fearing that she would bring her lover home to live with us. In my pubescent imagination, he was a grizzly, hulking man who would crush Mamma under him and leave me a starving orphan. I would dread coming back from school and finding him there. With time, I outgrew those childish fears, but the terror of abandonment was a subcutaneous alertness lodged inside me. When I got involved with Faraz, I felt that fear finally dissipate. At that moment, I decided to marry him. It took us nearly eight years to get married—we dated through college and continued to be together till Faraz was settled with his career; then we waited for Baba to give in and accept me into his family .

Waiting for Gul to come home, I prepare my lines: no hyper-parenting, no hyperventilating. She will find me cold and biting, like Mamma. I will lay down rules with an icy resolve, which will throw her off balance. I call up Vani. For some reason, the boy's parents still have the upper hand. We women have writ fragility into our attitudes. Vani, predictably, says that we should let the kids enjoy themselves and connect.

'We're not that kind of parents, you know. As long as the children tell us what they are doing and where they are going, it's okay.' It's easy for Vani; she is not from Rampur.

'Vani, this is Rampur. Most people have never seen our kids, but they are curious enough to find out every detail.'

There would be snide comments about Gul and me, which would find their way to Baba. This was a place where often, brides' names don't even appear on the wedding cards—Mr so-and-so weds the daughter of Mr so-and-so—as if their identities need to be veiled, too. Perhaps I'm validating the system, but I don't have the strength to deal with all that now.

Vani suggests that the 'young ones' should meet at her place or mine. Her mom-in-law is home to chaperone them, and I have Meezan Bhai. It is definitely better than sitting in cafés. If I stay away, they might agree to meet at my place. I shudder at the thought of secret trysts in seedy hotels. It will all be my fault at the end—too modern, not a 'real Muslim'.

'Don't overthink this; it's not serious. Chill. Let's not make it bigger than what it is.'

I manage to give Gul some no-career-no-money kind of home truths in a calm voice when she floats in. I also announce the ground rules, which Vani and I had discussed, sounding exactly like my mother—bitchy and harsh. Gul whines, pleads, throwing the full range of Gen Z phrases at me—they were just 'vibing' and I was 'delulu'—and then shuts herself up in her room, her shoulders drooping with my injustices.

Mamma never deserved my whining or my demands. There was a choking anger bittering my throat when she spoke to me. Mamma's eyes look back at me from the mirror. We have the same features in, thankfully, differently shaped faces and bodies. I have to exonerate all the parts of me that are like her—the tone, the clumping of words, the betraying gestures, the thoughts she placed in my head. I'm plagued with chronic matrophobia—a desperate fear of becoming my mother.

Dagh's Letter to Qazi Sahib of Calcutta

Janab Qazi Sahib, Assalam Alaikum!

Your letter says that Munni wants to come to me but is constrained. If a person desires with all her heart, what is there to stop her? Please explain it to me in detail—what does she desire? I have explained my feelings to you. I'm not the same person as I was earlier, and she has changed, too. My love for her is an ancient desire, a pang that continues to disquieten my heart. If she comes to me, it will give me a lot of happiness in my last years. Otherwise, I do manage to amuse myself. But do tell her that though I have grown old, my attachment and desire for her remain unchanged. I want to possess her at any cost and to the limit of possibility—assuming, and I should be convinced, that she also desires to be with me with all her heart. If so, every constraint can be removed.

Didn't you tell her that Dagh is wasting away for her after all these years? My heart is filled with her thoughts and with a constant, restless desire for her love. When I remember those days spent with her, I'm overcome with excruciating pain. Qazi Sahib! I'm an old lover; I live looking upon the beauteous; I cannot explain my great love and how I pine for her. My eyes await her. Please write with the good news that she is going to come to me.

Why the delay? Tell her to come immediately. Every moment of my day is consumed by this waiting.

Dagh
Undated

عشق

16

‘Ishq (Love)

Burā kiyā jo kahā un se mudda‘ā dil kā
Ġhazab kiyā jo muḥabbat ko āshkār kiyā

Thoughtlessly, I unveiled my heart
A calamity, the revelation of my love.

—Munni Bai Hijab
Bahāristān e nāz

DID SHE LOVE HIM, I ASK DANIYAL. THERE IS A THRILLING hesitancy between us; we are careful not to disturb its shimmering evanescence, which lives with us and within us. Daniyal's gaze sharpens as he decides to gamble. I sense his unasked question in reply to my question and deflect it, just as he knew I would.

‘So, one biographer, Fareed Parbati, says Dagh was only planning on being a tamashbeen and amusing himself, while Hijab hoped for eternal love like Laila–Majnu. This was perhaps the reason for the problems between them right from the onset,’ I say, going back to my notes.

‘I feel, expectations from a relationship change. What we expect from a marriage, for instance, changes as you grow with experiences.’

'We have one letter written by Hijab to Dagh in which she asks him for money. I don't think we should base our understanding of her, or their relationship on this one letter.' I steer back.

'No, we can't. Things taken out of context can be misleading. A hurt wife might write a nasty letter to her husband; it doesn't mean that she detests him.'

'Maybe she did love Dagh in her own way, perhaps not with the same intensity—we are presuming here that Dagh, despite his dalliances, truly loved her. As a tawaif, she had been warned against such love. For them love was treacherous—though some tawaifs did settle into matrimony.'

'We're not talking of marriage; we are talking of love,' he interrupts, a quiet insistence.

'For an Indian woman, love and marriage are bound together. At least that's what we expect…' My voice peters away, hesitant.

'Hijab's life was all about love outside marriage, and that's where she was seeking love, maybe subconsciously, while avoiding its pitfalls.'

'I believe Dagh made her feel like a woman, a person with thoughts, a poet with creativity. That alone could feel like love… was probably love. A lot of things feel like love at different points in life; perhaps love reflects what we are seeking at a certain place in time.'

'So, according to you, love is bound by place and time. What about the timelessness of love that all the poets write about?'

Daniyal waits for a response he knows won't come—we are floundering in half-conversations, the unsaid clogging up. He tells me about *Roznamcha,* a daily journal, written by Iftikhaar Aalam Marehrvi, a man closely associated with Dagh during his years in Hyderabad. Apparently, only after reading it would I be qualified to debate the question of Dagh and Hijab's love. It also quotes letters written by Hijab.

And what about us? The question slips into my mind and reflects on my face. I quickly look away to silence it, but he has seen it. We are forever in conversation, Daniyal and I—in our voices, our thoughts and in the tenor of our bodies, with their slight leaning towards each other. Daniyal has started sitting with me in the study while I work. It's unsettling, this awareness of him and the shocking desire that overwhelms me suddenly—more tender than the hot flushes that sometimes seize me. He sits half-turned from me, his elbow on the arm of the sofa, his shoulder a firm line under his T-shirt, his long fingers caressing the page before he turns it. He wears T-shirts and jeans now for me—at least I think so. I wonder if he likes me in a saree, if he desires me. We have accepted the tension and the comfort of simply being together. Our feelings are a silence; maybe that afternoon was an illusion. We tread lightly, afraid of crossing the line to the next stage of love—from the safety of uns and ibadat to the intoxicating depths of ishq.

Daniyal gets up and walks to an almirah. He has a slight limp, which lends a graceful rhythm to his walk, as though every step is an acknowledgement of physical humility. It adds to his self-deprecating charisma. He once told me his leg had been crushed while playing polo in college. An old surgeon had set the bones back and saved the leg, but the limp remained. He still plays the game when he can. He hands me a letter in Urdu encased in a plastic slip—a rare letter from Hijab to Dagh.

'Oh, you had a letter from Hijab, and you were keeping it from me!'

'I wanted to see if you were serious about researching their love.' Daniyal smiles.

I take out and hold the letter in my hand. The paper has light brown spots, the penmanship in black ink is beautiful. I'm terrified it will crumble under my fingers, but I have to feel it. I slip it back into the folder and try to read it aloud in my now reasonably coherent Urdu:

Haji Sahib, Assalam Alaikum,

I received your letter brimming with your love. How is it possible that you call me and I refuse to come to you? I'm powerless to object and wouldn't dare refuse you. But there are certain limitations that prevent one from acting according to their desires. I wish with all my heart that I get relief from the issues that plague me here, grow wings and fly to you. But my problems are insurmountable, and I find I'm unable to sort them despite my best efforts. It wounds my heart deeply that as I brave these hurdles, you accuse me of being stone-hearted and unfeeling; you see my struggles as excuses. The events that I explained in my last letter are, in your opinion, fabrications, even though Qazi Sahib has written to you and confirmed them. Why should I repeat the narrative again and again? Where is your wisdom and understanding? Why do you stress on my coming to you so thoughtlessly! Be patient; very soon I will be before you and you with me.

Hijab

'So this is after she got married and Dagh approached her through his friend Qazi Sahib. We can make that out from the date—1901. By that time, Dagh was well settled in Hyderabad,' Daniyal says.

'Don't you think there are hints of tawaif talk? Like, "How could I not come if you called me," and "I wish I had wings," etc.'

'Hmm, Dagh writes in the same way. Maybe this kind of hyperbole was an accepted form of expression.'

'And why does Hijab call him Haji Sahib instead of using lavish terms of endearment like Dagh?'

'Maybe she wants to keep a distance from him? She was, after all, a married woman at that time.'

'Yes, and he should have understood that. How could he expect her to drop everything and run to him? She was just asking for time to settle her affairs; maybe there were divorce proceedings and family affairs she had to settle; she had a family of dependents she had to think of.'

'It's his love for her which makes him so impatient.' I leave his words on the table between us and silently re-read the letter, feeling its weight.

'I believe Hijab did love Dagh in her own way though she was looking at gaining from this alliance. She had a hard exterior and an attitude of practicality natural for a woman in her position. Maybe she wanted an assurance of his love. She had to take a leap of faith.' The unknown is an unlived territory to be lived; the familiar suddenly becomes comforting.

'Or, she had problems in her marriage, and Dagh was a possibility.'

'Who doesn't have such problems? It doesn't mean a woman will rush into the arms of any available man!'

He looks gratified at my tone, the sudden exposure of a simmering precariousness that lingers just beneath the surface.

'Not even when this alliance grants stability? Remember, Dagh was doing really well at that time. But like I said earlier, please don't impose your thoughts on Hijab. She wasn't a modern woman; she was a tawaif facing tough times. Maybe it wasn't love but opportunism. You have to decide after you research the whole story—we are still in the middle of it. You can keep this letter and decipher it at leisure—a keepsake for you.'

'A keepsake?' What did he mean—a memento from a time that one day would only exist in memory? I force a laugh, 'A 120-year-old letter! Wow. Thank you. Are you sure you won't ask me to burn it with the other secret manuscripts?'

Daniyal laughs and shakes his head.

I carry the letter and a strange transience home. Faraz is sitting with his drink. I feel an irrational guilt. I pour a drink for myself and sit beside him, wondering if we can talk. I speak about the new ground rules Vani and I have laid out for our children. He nods and tells me things are looking up for him. He had applied for a tender, which had been approved. Now he will easily get a bank loan. It's the beginning of something good, he says. I see him smile after ages.

'You are tense about the loan. I can see it on your face, Kuku.' The smile fades with a furrowing of the brow.

'No, that's not the thing. You are doing your best…' I try to sound convincing, placating.

'Kuku, I know you have no faith in me, but remember, I had set up a good business in Dubai, and we would still be there if… okay, forget it. I need you to be with me on this, Kuku. Tell me, what other options do we have? No one will give me a job now. The money we have will run out soon.'

I don't reassure him, I can't; not now.

That night, he reaches out to me, and I offer my body in sympathy, guilt and kindness. Can he sense my splintering?

Munni Bai Hijab, Calcutta (1888–1901)

Dagh might be old, but his attitude is still that of a young person. He is tall, broad shouldered and well built. His face is full and round with large mischievous eyes. I can't describe the laughing, sensuous playfulness in his eyes which penetrate the heart and endear him.

—Sayed Haideruddin Dehlvi
Sāqi Dehlvi, 1 March 1940 Issue

SUDDENLY, THERE WERE SECRET MISSIVES AND LETTERS. Qazi Sahib delighted in the role of a romantic go-between; you had confessed your marital problems to him. You were torn—you knew Dagh's reputation as a flirt, but he had kept in touch through friends and family, even after learning of your marriage. Was he a true lover or merely an embodiment of a tawaif's fantasy—a self-effacing, devoted admirer? Qazi Sahib informed you that Dagh's wife had passed away in 1897 and he was free now. Did Dagh offer marriage, or was it a few years of amusement? You had left all that behind, had continued to suffer through your marriage because you couldn't bear to go back to a tawaif's life—at your age, it would be annihilating. You were firm and told Qazi Sahib that you would only consider marriage.

Things had become increasingly bitter between you and Aal. He relentlessly accused you of barrenness—the scourge of your sins—and said that your womb was cursed and would bear no fruit. Diminished to a point where your husband could insult you and abuse your body at will, you had stopped going for Shah Sahib's urs—your fertility was beyond his power. Despite ten years of piety, Aal still did not trust you. When he wasn't home, you would seek solace in anonymity by wrapping yourself in a burqa and wandering faceless through the city. The clamour of bazaars drowned out the noise inside and calmed you, a brief reprieve. The tight circle of tawaif friends you had grown up with were out of your reach; Aal would come to know if you visited them, and it would ignite further quarrels. Even after all these years, if he found that you had gone out without his permission, he would turn his vicious rage on you, inflicting violence that left you battered and abused. You would lie that you had gone to meet Apa or Hameedan—your voice was your only defence, and you would retaliate by releasing your pent-up frustration. There would be days of bitter silence, and the quarrel would drag on, putrefy till he turned to you to fulfil his needs.

Aal's family had not accepted you, closing their ranks behind the first wife. Initially, there were some invitations to family occasions, prompted by Aal and the curiosity of family members. They wanted to see the famous tawaif and Dagh's ex-lover. You met the corpulent first wife, fortressed between the relatives, acknowledging your salam with a cold nod.

You were used to spending money on whatever caught your fancy—clothes, jewellery, food, curious articles—it gave you momentary joy. You were also generous in giving to the poor and your servants, but now, you had to justify every anna. Aal expected you to keep a meticulous account of household expenses, like all wives, and learn to live within your means. New clothes were only permitted on Eid, and if you wanted any jewellery, it depended on the pleasure of the husband. Though you were relieved of the effort of dressing up to please your clients, you still loved to get clothes made; your colour palette was always bright, and you embellished your garments with gold trimmings. Your old mujra clothes were put away because Aal didn't like you to dress in provocative outfits, and there were no occasions to wear your opulent ghararas. You now wore plain, loose cotton kurtas and pyjamas—simple garments that he approved of. Yet your pride in your beauty was undimmed; you dyed your hair as strands of grey started showing. Quietly, you tried to get back to writing again; some educated women from respectable families had started composing poetry. Your ghazals were your private sanctuary; they would never be published or recited in mushairas. You didn't even share them with Aal, who regarded all poetry, especially that penned by women, as an invitation to fornication. According to him, Islam forbade music because it was the devil's work. This hadn't stopped him from listening to your songs when he was your patron.

Dagh wrote to you:

O enemy of my life, my Hijab,

After a long, long wait your loving letter found its way to me. I read it several times, held it to my heart and pressed it to my eyes. You ask me to forget you; or if I can't forget you, you want me to change myself. Only then will you return to me.

Tu bhūlney ki chīz nahī ḳhūb yād rakh
Nadān tujhey kis tarah dil se bhulāyeiñ ham

Know that you are unforgettable
O innocent, how can I erase you from my heart!

All right, come to me, and together, we shall try to forget each other. I agree with all your conditions. Just come back to me!

Faiz ul Mulk,
Dagh Dehlvi
Hyderabad
20 March 1901

You smiled—only Dagh could express intense yearning with humour and familiarity. He still desired you despite everything and after all these years—you were stirred and flattered. Your core persona must have left a mark on him. His letters spoke of missing your laughter, the way it could banish all gloom; he even found your anger invigorating, although your words sometimes broke his heart. Aal wanted to suppress all that was inherently you because he couldn't deal with it. You had tried all these years to fit into the mould he imposed on you as his wife; it had dimmed your sharp edges—you didn't spring up in anger or burst out in laughter—but the essence of you, buried inside, still burned. You knew you couldn't fit into his life now, and Dagh was an option you could think about even though it needed courage to leave the familiar for the unfamiliar.

It would definitely be a more comfortable life for you and your family. Apa was unable to make ends meet because Aal's contribution towards maintaining your family had, over the years, reduced to a bare pittance. You couldn't curb your pride and beg him, so you secretly sold off pieces of your jewellery to keep her household afloat. It haunted you that Apa would have to ultimately sell off the two-floor house you grew up in and move into a hovel. Hameedan, slavish to her husband's needs, refused to ask him to contribute. Maybe marriages survived not on love but by limiting women's agency, forcing them to endure. Convinced of Dagh's love, you felt ready for a new beginning.

When you told Aal that you were leaving him, he was incensed—you were a tawaif after all, and he had been fooled by your inherent duplicity. After dramatic, ugly scenes, you finally returned to Apa's house and told Qazi Sahib that you wanted a divorce. Apa was appalled—they could barely survive with the little Aal sent them; what would become of them now? You were old and unsaleable. It was foolish to pin your hopes on Dagh; hadn't he betrayed your trust several times already?

Qazi Sahib, thrilled at your decision, told you that Dagh had been granted grandiose titles—*Dabir ud Daulah, Faseeh ul Mulk, Bulbul e Hindustan*—by the Nizam of Hyderabad. He was designated the Nizam's ustad and earned about a thousand rupees per month. Ladli Begum—his wife's niece, whom they had adopted as a child—and her poet husband, Saail Dehlavi had settled in Hyderabad and were supported by the Nizam. Some other relatives—a cousin, a nephew and their families—had also settled in Hyderabad but Dagh was unhappy with their grasping and uncaring attitude. He needed someone to ease his loneliness. Dagh had written, 'I want you in whatever way you wish, I'm ready to fulfil any condition.' He had last seen you in 1882 when he had come to Calcutta. You had changed so much in nineteen years, but he must have changed, too. He was nearly seventy, an old man.

You confessed to Qazi Sahib that you were worried about Dagh's association with tawaifs. It was reported that a beautiful, young tawaif, Akhtar Bai of Surat, was employed by him now. Qazi Sahib assured you that Dagh kept tawaifs because of his love for music and that he had no physical relations with them any more.

'Times have changed now. You can listen to Gauhar Jan on a record. Ask Dagh to buy that, turn the key and listen to the tawaif!' Qazi Sahib chuckled. 'Dagh has changed. He has wealth but no family life. There is no doubt in my mind that he loves you, or I wouldn't have dared to convey his letter to you. Why don't you go and meet him in Hyderabad?'

'I'm not a tawaif any more, I can't travel on my own or walk into any person's house unescorted. I have earned this respectability after ten years of marriage. I observe strict purdah now.'

'There is no harm if you go to Hyderabad with Khuda Bakhsh.'

'Please write to Dagh and tell him my conditions—I shall observe purdah from him till the nikah; I shall live in a separate house till then.'

پوشیدگی

17

Poshīdgi (Secrecy)

Chuptā nahī hai lākh tarah se chupāyieñ woh,
Mazmūn e wasl e 'eid bhī 'āshiq kā hāl hai

Love defies concealment belying her efforts
The lover's rapture betrays his state.

—Munni Bai Hijab
Bahāristān e nāz

GUL IS WATCHING SOMETHING ON HER LAPTOP; LOUD background music fills the spaces around her. She pauses it and looks up inquiringly. Maybe it's something she can't watch with me. There is too much casual sex in every show these days, so we all retreat into our own entertainment bubbles. I side-hug her and kiss the top of her head. She smells endearingly of Johnson baby shampoo. She finds it gentle for her hair. Her shoulders tense in my arms. I sit on her bed and start telling her the Hijab–Dagh love story. She relaxes, shutting her laptop. Faraz would be annoyed at me for filling her head with romantic nonsense when she is already infatuated. Suddenly, I spot a familiar-looking piece of fabric near her pillow—Mamma's favourite light green Bengali cotton saree.

'It's from Nanu's saree. I found it in her cupboard after she passed away and cut it up. It still smells of her. I sleep with it.' I want to be deified by my child, too. Every mother wants to be this divine persona for her kids, or maybe it's a cultural expectation. Gul has just found out that her father is a failure and that must have broken something in her. Mamma doesn't deserve her idolization, but there is her saree she has been clinging to.

I silenced the constant why's ages ago. I preferred not to know. Mamma once said that she wanted to tell me something—probably her version of truth which might unstitch my beliefs. She said, I was grown up enough to understand about Papa and her. It was right after the class ten boards, so I must have been fifteen.

'No, I don't want to know.' My words had an unmistakable clarity. I would never let her narrative transpose the memories of my father. I knew she hated him and only twisted, bitter lies would come out of her hatred. I didn't want her story when she had abandoned mine. I only wanted Papa's story, the one I was a part of. And so, the silence condensed around us, stretching till those last days in the hospital. She was aware of life draining from her body, of my cold, methodical tending to her needs; much like I imagined her caring for me as a child—feed one end and keep the other end dry. Her eyes glittered with that greedy desire to release a truth to shatter me. I thwarted her. The day she slipped into a coma, I sat beside her and watched her eyes, wide open, flickering with death's terror. The doctor and Faraz left me with her to whisper my goodbye; probably she could still hear. I bent close to her and told her about the day she left us and the humiliation that bled into my school and our lives. She was my shame, our shame. Something caught in her chest, a sort of choking, her eyes stilled—and then she was gone.

I had given away all Mamma's clothes, made a bonfire of her letters and files and donated her books to the college library. It was then that Baba handed me the dossier, heavy with secrets and labelled 'Divorce' in bold black ink. She knew I would throw away all her things and attempt to erase her from my life. She had to make sure the dossier found its way to me. I had kept it aside till the day I left my job.

It was Faraz's idea that Daniyal should host the meeting followed by a barbecue. He told him jovially that I could take on the role of the hostess. It is possible that Faraz, buoyed by his new venture, just wanted an evening of good food. He can be quite oblivious and self-absorbed, but did I really know him? I have to choose a narrative—a suspicious husband or a trusting one. Both are damning and played through the evening in alternating strands.

The weather has become crisp with an evening nip in the air—the perfect time for the first barbecue of the season. Daniyal had summoned a kababchi to prepare seekh kababs. Akhtar Bhai was making his Rampuri speciality—stuffed chicken dumpukht. I was assigned a qorma, Shezray, a yakhni pulao, Akriti snacks and Vani a dessert. We had fallen into our culinary roles seamlessly, with a tacit agreement to bring out the full qorma-pulao-kabab trinity at every dinner. Faraz and Dinesh come unabashedly for the eats and settle down in the drawing room with their drinks. Daniyal is a teetotaller, so Dinesh brings his 'mobile bar', and Akhtar Bhai is instructed to ensure a steady supply of snacks and ice. The meeting is held in the study, a perfect setting. But I'm on edge, feeling as if the walls will reveal my secret. I notice that Akhtar Bhai, undoubtedly instructed by Daniyal, is careful not to show any familiarity with me. Old retainers like him are used to keeping their master's secrets.

Daniyal has arranged the chairs in a circle around my work desk. I sit down at my usual seat, then get up, unsure, asking Daniyal if he would like to sit there instead. Relax, there is no seating arrangement, he says. I sink back, feeling the first tingling of a hot flush creeping up my neck. I want to jump up and run away. Daniyal calls out to

Akhtar Bhai to serve cold drinks. He can sense it coming; he has seen too many of these in this study. I would stand up suddenly, gulp iced water, throw open the windows and stand under the fan breathing deeply till it passed—normal episodes inter-folding into my day. When it would fade, after what seemed like ages, it left me drenched in sweat, exhausted and irritated. I secretly sniffed at my armpits. How can anyone find me attractive?

I take a long sip, letting the drink meander down my throat, cooling my insides, and breathe deeply. Opening up my copy of *The Sea of Poppies,* I begin to read aloud. Vani is unhappy with our three-month commitment to reading Amitav Ghosh's trilogy. She feels we should go for a thriller now. Shezray has ditched us with a last-minute excuse, and Akhtar Bhai has to prepare the pulao assigned to her. Maybe Faraz is right about Daniyal's involvement with her. She must have been a stunner and is lovely even now. Faraz claimed that there was a pregnancy and then the hasty marriage to a rich Saudi-based techie. I don't think Daniyal was 'ineligible' for the marriage as Faraz said; maybe the families didn't agree to the match over some ancient feud or a new one brought on by belligerent male Pathan egos. Did she continue with her supposed pregnancy, or was she scrubbed clean and offered up for matrimony? It is still open to speculation when the story is told. I told Faraz that the whole story was concocted because of his (and half the town's) unrequited crush on the beautiful princess.

Once, while working here, I heard a woman's voice murmuring in the drawing room and soft, muffled sobs. Peeping from the study, I saw Shezray speaking to Daniyal, who had his arm around her hunched shoulders. I retreated. Later, when Daniyal came to the study, he didn't mention the visit and I never asked him. This was before we had our slept-not-slept together intimacy. I wove several theories in my mind—she wanted to rekindle things with him now that she was free; she was torn between her husband and Daniyal; she was confessing the horrors of her marriage, hoping that he would take her back. Did he want her back, or had their love run the segment of time, if there is a time for love? Daniyal believes in timeless love, ishq. I finish reading, and we start discussing the book, marvelling at its recreation of an overlooked slice of history.

As has become our usual procedure now, after the book discussion, everyone turns to me with queries on 'what happened next' in the Dagh–Hijab love story. I update them on my research. They listen raptly to Dagh's journey to Hyderabad, Hijab's marriage, and finally, Hijab's arrival in Hyderabad.

'So contradictory, no? First, she's furious at him for writing about her in the—whatever you call that long poem—and then she acts so territorial!' says Vani.

'And she won't even let him have his pretty tawaifs in Hyderabad. Not fair!' Ritesh smiles.

'Well, she was known all over the Urdu-speaking world as Dagh Dehlvi's one true love. The others were fleeting; she was his eternal love,' I say.

'I doubt he could manage much action at seventy-plus. But he was definitely tawaif-obsessed,' laughs Ritesh. He has refilled his glass from Dinesh's bar and is more garrulous than usual.

'Remember the letter about his bad knees and false teeth!' Akriti whoops with laughter.

'It wasn't always about sex. You see, tawaifs were the only interesting women around—well-read, witty, and they could sing—something like a living, portable entertainment. Recorded music on the gramophone was making an entry—it wasn't popular, and people still preferred live performances. So, if you wanted music, you went to tawaifs or called them over. If you were wealthy, as Dagh was in Hyderabad, you could employ them on a salary and have them at your bidding,' Daniyal explains.

'Well, Dagh had physical issues. So I read this letter he wrote to an attar or perfumer in 1886 asking for aphrodisiacs. I guess perfumers also mixed meds like modern-day pharmacists,' I say, glancing at Daniyal, who nods slightly.

I read excerpts from Dagh's letters, saved in my files, as the seekh kababs are served with the hot, yellow chilli chutney.

'This is my favourite line from the letter to the attar—*Main ashiq mizaj hoon, dil mein har waqt aag lagi rehti hai,* I'm a lover by nature and my heart is always afire,' I smile.

'Tough to be a lover with such problems. Unless you believe in spiritual love—eternal, asexual ishq,' titters Vani.

'Which can also exist. Why have we been tricked into believing that only sex draws people close?' Daniyal says.

'Perhaps he found comfort with tawaifs because they understood and accommodated the ageing body,' I say.

'I believe Indian wives are even more accommodating,' Daniyal says.

'No, darling, they are simply… accepting,' Vani smirks.

Roznamcha: Iftikhaar Aalam Marehrvi

(22 January 1902)

Munni Bai Hijab has been in Hyderabad for four days. She was staying at Dagh Sahib's house. Once a tawaif, she had transformed herself completely. For the past six years, she had prayed namaz five times a day; she also performed extra prayers, the wazeefas, throughout the day and night. She fasted from the month of Rajab till the end of Ramzan, that is, two months in a year. Dagh Sahib remarked to his friends that in one or two years, she would become a saint. When she came to Hyderabad, Dagh Sahib presented her with a prayer mat and a rosary.

Mirza Dagh decided to call her 'Farishtan bi'—lady angel—and once said, 'In the heavens, the angels are exclaiming, "Ya Allah! In Dagh's house, there is an angel who has outdone us in her prayers and devotion." They marvel that humans can possess such capacity for prayer!'

Mirza Dagh told Hijab, 'Until you abandon your wazeefas and extra prayers, you cannot become human; and until you become human, you are of no use to me. Remember, I shall gradually make you leave all your wazeefas and let you pray only the compulsory prayers.'

Roznamcha: Iftikhaar Aalam Marehrvi

(2 February 1902)

Dagh Sahib dictated this letter to Qazi Abdul Hameed, the person who had helped reunite him with Munni Bai:

'Bi Farishtan and her brother are here. My house feels like the heavens with praying angels. But I'm a sinner and not an ascetic saint! Let's see what happens next. I have still not seen if it is truly her beneath the veil or someone else.'

Despite spending days in her company, Dagh remains doubtful of her true identity and unsure if this would work out. The dramatic change in her has disappointed him. He is intrigued, if not in love.

Hijab and Dagh, Hyderabad

(January–February 1902)

'Hijab, how do I know it's really you behind this hijab.' Dagh tried to peer through your veil.

You stepped back.

'Dagh Sahib, I thought you would know me. Don't you recognize my voice?'

'Hmm... but even Bi Hameedan has your voice. How can I be sure? Let me at least look into your eyes.'

'Then you will say Bi Hameedan has my eyes, too, and ask me to show my mole,' you laughed.

'Ah, the mole on your chin. I would sacrifice all my diwans for just a glimpse of it!'

'Listen, I'm not going to be seduced by your words. I'm now a purdah-observing, respectable woman. You can only see my face once we're married. If you're still unsure, ask Khuda Bakhsh. Surely, you haven't forgotten him too?'

'Khuda Bakhsh is like a son to me. How can I forget him? But he can also get caught in your schemes.'

'Ah, so I'm a scheming witch now? Are you afraid that you'll be tricked into marrying an old crone?' You laughed.

'And you're afraid that if I see you aged, I will turn away. Dagh is not the kind of a person to turn back on his word. But at least you'll have to relinquish your oath and show me your beautiful face.'

'I have not come here to break the rules of my religion. I have just been divorced, and as per the religious laws, I must observe iddat for four months. During iddat, I cannot meet any man who isn't family—they are namehram; you're also namehram till our nikah.'

'You will sit in iddat for that impotent pimp? He could barely bed you properly. What a farce of a marriage! I have a solution—you have to get a photograph clicked in Hyderabad. Until I see it, I won't marry you.'

You turned away in anger, your voice curt. 'It's time for my prayers. I can only meet you after the afternoon prayers.'

'Hai, Bi Farishtan, what will become of us? You have become a praying angel and turned my house into heaven. Alas, I'm but a sinner.'

'I was a sinner, too...'

'How we used to sin. I miss the sinning!' Dagh chortled and you were caught in the familiar warmth of his merriment.

'That Munni Bai is no more...'

'And you have stopped writing, so you are not Hijab anymore. So who are you? Munni Bai buried under another kind of hijab? It was Munni Bai Hijab I loved, and I will bring her back. Just pray five times like all Muslims and no extra prayers. What use are you to me as a Farishtan? I need you to become human.

'Rāh par unko lagā lāyeiñ to haiñ bātoñ meiñ
Aur khul jāyengey do chār mulāqātoñ meiñ'

(I have drawn her to love's pathways,
A few meetings will unbind her.)

Dagh guffawed and left.

Even though you had written to Dagh insisting that you would live in a separate house till the nikah, he had brought you to his residence in Mehboob Gunj. It was a double-storied house, and Dagh proposed that Khuda Bakhsh and you could live on the lower floor while his mardana—

accessible only to males—was on the first floor. When you protested, he said it was proper for you to stay in the zenana, the women's quarters, until everything was finalized. You were determined to observe four months of iddat when you wouldn't meet any males except your brother. As per religious law, this period clarified the paternity of a potential child; the widowed or divorced woman could only marry after iddat.

Dagh, of course, flouted all the rules of purda and spent most of his time after his durbar duties with you and ate all his meals in the zenana. After a lot of persuasion, you had agreed to forego purdah in his presence as you were going to be his wife soon. Khuda Bakhsh also joined forces with Dagh in persuading you. You allowed yourself to be cajoled and slipped back into your old bantering rhythms and humorous conversations with Dagh, even indulging in light flirtations, but drew a firm line at any physical relationship before marriage—you were not his tawaif. You had been apprehensive about Dagh finding you old and unattractive, but Dagh said his love and desire for you remained unchanged; besides, he had become old, too.

You cherished the time with Dagh. You started writing again and sang your new compositions, accepting his islah—rediscovering your voice and your words inspired by Dagh as your mentor. He was moved to tears listening to your compositions which you had penned during your torturous marriage.

Khuda Bakhsh, meanwhile, had befriended Iftikhar Marehrvi and other students of Dagh. He often spent his evenings with Dagh and his friends in the mardana, listening to their discussions. You told Khuda Bakhsh that he had to keep you informed about all the goings-on there. Dagh used to dictate his letters to Iftikhar in the presence of all his friends and students. The letters were copied, entered into a register and then posted. Sometimes, you would ask Khuda Bakhsh to get the register. He was a reluctant spy, but you knew that he wanted this marriage to happen—he loved Dagh, was impressed by his lavish lifestyle and wanted a stable life in Hyderabad with you and Dagh.

'If your Dagh Sahib keeps himself entangled with these tawaifs, he'll never marry me; we shall have no choice but to return. Do you want that? You have to keep me informed.'

Khuda Bakhsh, a simple man, worn down by the hardships of past years, became your ears and eyes in the mardana. Dagh's open nature was incapable of discretion—even if he asked Iftikhar to pen a love letter, he didn't make a secret of it. Dagh's evenings were usually spent listening to music at a friend's place, or Akhtari Bai would be called over to his house. Earlier, you would ask him to leave your rooms by sundown, citing iddat rules, but now you invited Dagh to the zenana after the evening prayers, engaged him with conversation, sang your ghazals. If he excused himself to meet his friends, you employed the old artful wiles of a tawaif, which delighted him—everything short of giving yourself to him.

You observed and appreciated the change in Dagh's dressing style. He had put away his Rampuri cap, Lucknowi-style sherwani, angarkha and the loose and voluminous pyjamas of his Rampur days. He now wore a pyjama of a slimmer fit with a white kurta, donning a sherwani and a Turkish cap when he went to formal gatherings. You found his Hyderabad durbar dress with a gold-trimmed coat and cap very grand. He was fond of the best in everything—clothes, food and attar. He believed in living life to the fullest. Beneath the exterior of indulgence, Dagh was known to be empathic and munificent. Khuda Bakhsh reported that he sent money regularly to some poor families through the post. He also wrote to several people—friends, acquaintances, students and family—inquiring about their well-being. He was disciplined and conscientious about his official duties; besides that, he had hundreds of students all over the country who sent their compositions for corrections, and he spent hours correcting poetry with red ink, then posted back the scripts. He even invited his old rival from the Rampur court, Ameer Minai, to Hyderabad and helped him secure a position at the Nizam's court. Dagh was incapable of jealousy towards fellow poets and appreciated talented writers without envy.

Despite his social and official obligations, he found time to compose, reciting verses extempore while his students scrambled to note them down and compiled them for his next diwan. He said being alone filled him with anxiety and he was always surrounded by friends and students. Once he laughed and said, 'I don't even want to be buried alone. If no one agrees to accompany me to the grave, I will take a photo; if even that is not possible, I will catch hold of the angel who comes to interrogate me after my burial!'

Though you enjoyed the freedom and ease of living with Dagh, his penchant for tawaifs distressed you. He assured you several times that his relationship with Akhtar Bai was musical rather than physical—he called her over to listen to her songs with his close friends, and it befitted his age and station to have a tawaif close at hand when he wished to listen to music. You were still insanely jealous of her or any other tawaif and would never agree to him employing them. You couldn't be Fatima, his first wife, accepting of his philandering ways—you lacked her patience and trust. You made sure that Dagh sent off Akhtari Bai, who was anyway getting romantically involved with his friend.

One day, you intercepted a copy of a letter Dagh sent to Nabi Jan, a tawaif, and summoned him into the zenana.

'Bi Farishtan, why this urgent desire to see me? Are you finally ready to break your oath of celibacy?' he teased, a mischievous twinkle in his eyes as he leaned back on the takht. Why couldn't he behave like a seventy-year-old?

'Dagh Sahib, I had only one condition for coming here—that you won't keep any tawaif in your employment.'

'I agreed to your condition and sent Akhtar Bai away.'

'And yet I find that she visited the mardana yesterday.'

'She had just come to pay her respects...'

'I have been a tawaif; I know how these arrangements work.'

'Hijab, I have told you—only you and Khwaja Moinuddin Chishti are my true loves. The rest are mere amusements.'

'There will be nothing between us till you stop writing such letters! What is this nonsense you write to Nabi Jan? "O lovely one, how can I meet, how can I catch a glimpse of you, and if I don't, how shall I live? I can't even hope that you would appear in my dreams."' You hold up the letter.

'Oho, it's a harmless letter admiring her picture.' Dagh sat up.

'Yes, and what admiration!

'Kab dekhney waloñ par khulā dil kā hāl
Khichwāi hai kyā sīna chhupā ke tasvīr'

(What lover could decipher your heart
So artfully you conceal your bosom in the picture.)

You flung the letter at a chuckling Dagh.

'Ah, I'm an old lover. Permit me some flirtation.' He got up and wrapped his arms around you.

You pushed him away, pouting. 'And what of the young girls who sit laughing with you in the mardana? I know everything.'

'They only come to talk and cheer me up, Hijab.'

'You don't need me, Dagh Sahib. Permit me to leave.' You touched your forehead in mock salam.

'My jan, you are more beautiful than all these women, even at this age.' He cupped your face to behold your beauty.

Roznamcha: Iftikhaar Aalam Marehrvi

(January–February 1902)

Bi Hijab's age now must be around 45 but she looks much younger. Her complexion is pink and white with large, black eyes and an aquiline nose. Her hair has greyed somewhat, which she camouflages with dye. She is of medium height, has a healthy body, a high forehead and takes a central parting in her hair. There is a beautiful mole on her chin; her cheeks are thin and slightly sunken. She often laughs out loud. She wears tight, silk pyjamas edged with gold trimming, a sheer crinkled scarf and a long kurta, which clings to her form, which she pairs with Delhi-made, embroidered footwear. She wears several rings on her elegant fingers, as well as gold bangles, a necklace and earrings. She eats vast quantities of paan, smokes huqqa and used to love her drink. Altogether, she is an alluring middle-aged woman.

مَمْتَا

18

Mamtā (Maternal Love)

Ham aur bīch meiñ āte haiñ un kī bātoñ ke
Unhoñ ne wa'da kiyā ham ne e'tibār kiyā

How can I contest his words?
He offered his vow and I, my faith.

—Munni Bai Hijab
Bahāristān e nāz

S*END SYNOPSIS. EDIT AND RESEND SAMPLE CHAPTERS. NOW!* Opparna's cryptic message beeps on my mobile. Something must have clicked, or maybe this is her usual drill. Anyway, the Grande Dame has deigned to give my manuscript her attention today. I decide to skip going to Daniyal's. Should I message and tell him? I haven't signed up for a daily appearance there. I tell myself to just focus and get my act together. Most of the writing blogs on crafting the perfect book synopses are written by American writers and tout a punchy, intriguing, almost casual synopsis that shouldn't reveal the ending. I jot down notes and begin composing the synopsis; I edit the crucial first chapters, obsessing over structure and every word choice. Have I found my writerly voice? Can the readers see Hijab clearly? Another message from Opparna—just a question mark.

Just sending, I reply.

I haven't written the complete novel, I write into her impatient, teeth-gnashing silence.

Never mind, just send!

Vani had warned me that Opparna is a Monday maniac and an aggressive workaholic. But if she takes on a book, she is sure to get a publisher. She looks formidable in her pictures—greying hair drawn into a severe bun, bare of make-up, crushed, (probably) organic-dyed mulmul sarees wrapped around her large form. She needs to be on a perpetual diet. Vani has found a long-term client.

By the afternoon, I send off the synopsis and three chapters. Relief washes over me like I have just fed a manuscript-devouring monster and bought myself a brief reprieve. I make myself coffee and relax. Gul wakes up and calls out to Meezan Bhai for coffee. I make some sandwiches and take her coffee to her room. She gives me a surprised smile, and I cuddle up with her. We have coffee together. I tell her how, in my imagination, Opparna is this paper-eating beast waiting impatiently for her next meal.

'It's nice to see you happy, Mamma.'

Do I look unhappy to her? Have I become a preoccupied, uncaring parent? I decide to stay home for the rest of the day and spend time with Gul. I suggest brunch somewhere, and Gul lights up, jumps out of bed to get dressed. She insists I wear something 'cool' for the girly date. It reminds me of our Dubai dates—shopping and her favourite pizza and ice cream treats at the mall. She needs me, and I have been too busy to give her time. Guilt circles in.

Maybe I will call Baba over for a khichda dinner—he cannot resist the spicy melange of meat and pulses. Hijab's persistent voice nags in my head, but I ignore it. If I sit with her now, this time will be lost. I set about soaking the oats, broken wheat and lentils in separate bowls. Meezan Bhai tells me that they need to be soaked overnight—you just can't decide to make khichda on the spur of the moment. But

I cannot spare another day. The grains better work out; I drain and re-soak them in boiling water. Faraz is home, too, but has to go for an afternoon meeting. In the spirit of reconnecting with the family, I try to approach Faraz. He is bent over a file. Grunts and vague replies follow. I hope he has registered that Baba is coming for dinner. I fleetingly consider the option of giving the spouse a tranquillizer-laced evening tea.

Gul and I make our first stop at the nursery to pick up winter flowering plants—the best part of being in Rampur is having a garden. She hates that but tolerates it because the next stop is the promised café. She even helps me choose the colours and do the maths—the number of flower beds and plants required per bed, what should go where, etc.—getting impatient as I decide on the blooms and weigh the survival ability of the saplings. Loaded with trays of petunias, dianthus, pansies and dahlias, we drive to Lady Bake Café. Gul had discovered it on Insta and tells me it's run by a scarf-wearing young girl and is the only café in Rampur serving actual coffee bean brews and lovely bakes.

I had hoped for an easy-flowing catch-up chat, like our mall-hopping days but Gul goes quiet suddenly. The excitement of the treat has petered out, and I have to keep talking to draw her out and fill in the pauses.

Gul interrupts my thoughts, asking about Faraz's work. I tell her what little I know. When things are not going well, Faraz closes up, like he did when we were dating in college. He would withdraw, almost becoming a stranger—a proverbial red flag I should have heeded. We dated for eight years before marrying, so there were a lot of red flags I ignored—I always laugh that after such a long courtship, marriage was the polite thing to do. Our relatively late marriage meant that I wanted to start a family immediately; I worried that I would be too old to have children.

Gul looks slightly happier, absorbed in her chicken burger. My heart melts with her childish delight in simple things. She is lucky to have Faraz's metabolism—she can eat anything without gaining weight; not that I would ever, ever body shame her, like my mother did with me.

'You're like your father. He also never shares his problems.'

'What's there to say, Mamma? I don't know where I'm going. I can't decide.'

'So why not look up career options online?' I wipe a blob of mayo on her chin.

'It's October now. This year is lost.'

'Maybe you can complete this year at med school. At least you won't lose a year. Maybe then you can take up some other paramedical line, and the credits can be added there.' Faraz is right; these kids have a sense of entitlement. We didn't bring up Gul to think rationally about money and waste. He has forbidden me to speak to Gul about the loss incurred because of the med college fees. No pressure.

'I hate it there. All those horrible cadavers! Imagine the first naked male I see is a dead one! Everyone is unhappy or sick.'

'Did anyone bother you there? Anything bad happened to you?'

'Ah, Mamma, it's not that at all. You just won't understand.'

She is retreating, clamping up again. I keep prodding.

'Okay, so why waste time? Take up an online course on something you love? It might actually lead you to a career path and help you find direction.'

She loved to paint—it wasn't outstanding, but we over-appreciated her—then she had that loud music phase. We bought her a guitar and a Casio, and she picked up basic skills at school. We were one of those eager-beaver parents who shower the child with all kinds of equipment and support if she showed even a tiny inclination in our fond belief that she was a prodigy. Parental expectations on an only child must have been so exhausting for her; it probably made her withdraw from something she loved. Parents never get anything right.

'I was thinking, maybe you could study music for a while. You know Rampur has a musical legacy. There is a Rampur gharana of classical music, which claims roots from Tansen,' I carry on.

'Who's Tansen? And Indian music is too boring!'

'What a typical Dubai kid you are!'

'Please don't start off on the burger-internet generation.' Gul rolls her eyes. Did I roll my eyes at my parents, or is it a generational thing? I want to ask about Vibhor, but the walls are up again, and we drive home.

I get busy getting the flowers planted with the gardener and then start cooking khichda. The oats and the wheat do take a very long time to cook, and Meezan Bhai gives me a long I-told-you-so lecture with stories of cooking disasters by women who didn't respect culinary rules. I take a shortcut by grinding all the cooked grains in the mixer instead of cooking them down, stirring and mashing for hours. They are supposed to have a mushy consistency. I ignore Meezan Bhai's disapproval and ask him to make the meat curry. Finally, we combine the curry and the mushy grains—it tastes good, though Meezan Bhai points at the odd grain of chana dal which resisted the mixie. I'm sure with the garnishes—fried onions, green chillies, ginger, coriander leaves and vinegar—it will be delectable. Baba was delighted at the invitation and the menu—he always asks what I plan to cook. I hope he likes it. I hope the khichda will take the edge off the dinner table arguments—you can't sustain much antagonism with a tummy full of khichda!

Baba arrives with Jumbo and a carton full of Jumbo paraphernalia. He is lending Jumbo to Gul again for a while. She already knows his routine and mealtimes. Gul is thrilled and keeps hugging Baba. After all the excitement, hugs and fervent barking, Jumbo settles down at Gul's feet much to her delight.

The khichda gets rave reviews. I have prepared a paneer dish for Gul, who hates the khichda. I try to coax her to have a spoonful from my bowl.

'Leave her, Kuku. Why should she eat it if she doesn't like it? She's not a baby,' snaps Faraz.

'But she should try it at least,' I insist.

'Papa, Mamma says I'm a lot like you,' Gul says.

'I was wrong. Faraz likes to try out new things,' I say to stop Gul from carrying on, but Faraz's eyes glint.

'I like to try out new things, too!' says Gul.

'So does your mamma, but she feels one should carry on with the old ways,' Faraz says, but I sidestep and get back to persuading Gul to have a tiny bit of khichda. Not today.

Faraz, probably uplifted by a good meeting, lets it go.

Baba is in fine form, launching into an anecdote about his father when he was the Nawab's physician and the latter's infamous temper—'*Nawab ka ataab*' as it was called. It is the oft-narrated family lore about his father's escape to Bareilly to save his life. Gul is fascinated by lived tales of grandeur and despotism.

'How could he leave his wife and kids? Suppose the Nawab killed all of you in his anger?' asks Gul.

'Papa knew the Nawab would never do that. It was a matter of honour. Papa had asked only one favour—the Nawab's vehicle should never be sent to our door.'

'What does that mean?'

'If the Nawab sent his carriage or car to your door, it meant you had to send your daughter to the Nawab's harem.'

'Whaat! OMG!' Baba loves Gul's reaction.

'Yes, such were the times. Papa knew that the Nawab would never trouble the women of his family. He only returned to Rampur after the Nawab passed away,' Baba says.

'Okay, so why did the Nawab get angry at your father?' Baba has a habit of telling a story from somewhere in the middle. We are all used to it and keep throwing in our questions.

'Papa refused to poison the crown prince on the orders of the Nawab. The Nawab felt that the crown prince had become too arrogant and might displace him, but that's another story. So Papa said he was a doctor who gave shifa (healing), not death.'

'Wow, so cool! For that, he gave up everything.' Gul is awestruck, and I know where the story is leading.

'They were men of honour, Gul, and you carry this bloodline. So you must become a doctor to carry on the family legacy.' Baba reaches for another serving.

'I don't know. I think I might do something in communication or music.'

'Gul Jan, that's shauq, not a career. You can still do your music, though in Rampur, women are not supposed to sing and dance.' Baba shakes his head.

'Why not? Just because in ancient times women who sang used to be tawaifs? So music is not a contribution to society? What about that Tansen chap?'

'Bhai, I don't understand these media careers.' Baba gets up from the table to wash his hands before the sweetmeat.

'There is so much more in the media than just acting!' Gul mutters, rolling her eyes, and I serve qiwami sewain. I'm rather proud that I used double the amount of sugar and the sewain didn't stiffen up but turned out to be soft and dripping with sugar syrup. Perfect! At least I can control some things.

Roznamcha: Iftikhaar Aalam Marehrvi

(25 January 1902)

Since Munni Bai had arrived, Mirza Dagh Sahib stayed for only two to three hours in the mardana. The rest of the time was devoted to Munni Bai. His friends took umbrage at this shift, and many stopped visiting him altogether. Mirza Sahib dictated a letter addressed to his friend, Nawab Hasan Ali Khan, who had not visited him for two days. He invited Mirza Hasan for patang-baazi, a kite-flying contest, scheduled for the next day. Mirza Sahib instructed me to write that he could not decide on many matters without consulting him and implored, 'Please come every day as usual.'

Nawab Hasan was a very egotistical and proud person; he often took offence at the smallest of things. Nawab Hasan wrote back saying tersely, 'Please excuse me from this daily attendance.'

Dagh Sahib wrote back:

'Nawab Sahib, you are wounding me with your words! Whatever happened was not intentional. I could give up a thousand Hijabs for your friendship and love. Please reply to my letter immediately and come over.'

Roznamcha: Iftikhaar Aalam Marehrvi

(6 February 1902)

During a gathering of close friends whom Dagh Sahib always consulted on personal matters, there was a discussion on Munni. One friend remarked, 'Mirza Sahib, you wear false teeth and colour your hair. Is this the age for marriage?'

Dagh Sahib replied, 'In common parlance, it will be called nikah, and Munni will be called my wife, but she will truly be my rafeeq, my soulmate and companion. I feel my advanced years; I wear false teeth, and have to colour my hair with mehndi every two weeks. Yet, my bed is decorated like that of a newly-wed with colourful, embellished net curtains. So, if all this is permissible in my life, why should I not have Munni as my wife? At this age, more than a wife, I need a sympathetic soul to share my life. I have come to understand this: the first wife is a wife, the second wife is a rafeeq (friend), and the third wife is a complication!' This quietened the company.

Hijab and Dagh, Hyderabad
(March–April 1902)

What was between them was wazeydaari and a desire for fun, which had nothing to do with love by any stretch of imagination. Both of them were strangely aligned in this endeavour—Dagh wanted to impress Hijab with his wealth, fame and his position at the Nizam's court, and Hijab was interested in enjoying his wealth.

—Fareed Parbati
Dāgh ba haisiyat masnavi nigār

IT HAD BEEN TWO MONTHS SINCE YOUR ARRIVAL IN Hyderabad, and your life had fallen into a set pattern. Dagh would complete his morning work and have lunch with you. He slept in the afternoon, then took a bath and changed into a fresh set of kurta pyjama for the evening. He often had evening visitors and would attend to them in the mardana and return to dine with you. You had reduced your long hours of prayers to maximize your time with him; you instinctively knew that his friends were opposed to your place in his life and resented the change in his routine. Dagh loved food, and you ensured that his favourite dishes were prepared for him. He had a cook who was adept at making Hyderabadi cuisine and you taught him Awadhi biryani and qorma, which Dagh preferred. You loved Hyderabadi khattey baigan and mirch ka salan but found their style of biryani missing the aromatic appeal of Awadhi biryani. It was the vast array of sweetmeats that held you enthralled—khubani ka meetha and badam ki jaali were your favourites, and you often dispatched Khuda Bakhsh to the bazaar for them.

Dagh introduced you to Khursheed, a close friend, and Iftikhar, Dagh's student who wrote his letters and roznamcha, and asked you to meet them unveiled. Nawab Mir Hasan Ali Khan, another close friend of Dagh, was a rich zamindar of Hyderabad who often visited Dagh and dined with him in the mardana. On one of his visits, he was told that Dagh was with Hijab and could not be disturbed; he felt insulted and stopped visiting. Dagh wrote to him, apologizing for the confusion and invited him to a kite-flying contest. Dagh's childish enthusiasm for contests—patang-baazi, kabotar-baazi (pigeon flying), bater-baazi (quail fights)—was endearing. You remembered the pachheesi and ganjfa card games you played with him in Rampur; Hameedan and Khuda Bakhsh would join in amidst great merriment. Hasan Sahib accepted the invitation, and Dagh asked you to come unveiled before him as he was not only his student but also a close confidant. You agreed to entertain his two gentlemen friends in the zenana right after morning prayers. After becoming a 'true Muslim'—as Dagh called you—you had started getting up for your late-night prayers and continued praying till sunrise. Like Dagh, you only slept in the hot afternoons. It was a sea change from the all-night singing mehfils and getting out of bed by late afternoon.

The morning of the patang-baazi was pleasant, with a light breeze. Dagh had asked you to get a late morning meal prepared to be served after the contest. A servant announced that Hasan Sahib was in the mardana. Dagh looked at you, and you nodded. He sent the servant to call Hasan down. The servant returned saying Hasan Sahib was saying Dagh Sahib must have called someone else to the zenana.

'My friend is upset because Khursheed Sahib has been allowed into the zenana. Hasan is my closest friend, but he is so jealous of Khursheed.' You joined Dagh in his laughter. Hasan Sahib appeared at the door, and Dagh leapt out of his chair and enveloped him in a bear hug, pulling him in with one arm around his shoulder. Nawab Hasan was possibly a few years younger than Dagh—a tall, elegant man, grey-haired, with a clipped, reticent moustache, dressed in a Hyderabad-style sherwani, tight pyjamas and a Turkish cap. Dagh formally introduced him, extolling his lineage—his great-grandfather, a high-ranking officer in Mughal emperor Aurangzeb's army, had been awarded a fiefdom in Hyderabad and had settled down there. Hasan Sahib touched his forehead in salam, and you responded warmly, welcoming him to the kite contest. His gaze dropped after a brief glance at you, and he sat down on the takht looking ill at ease. You were sure he heard Dagh mocking you as 'Farishtan Bi', and Hasan now judged you as a fading tawaif, titillating and enticing Dagh, first as Hijab the poetess and then in the guise of veiled piety. Where was the saintliness now that you were entertaining three men in your rooms? You wished you hadn't been laughing your old laugh when he was at the door. Dagh said listening to your laughter made the blood in his veins dance with more liveliness than life itself. Since you got back the sound of your old laughter, you wanted to use it at the slightest pretext. You adjusted your dupatta on your head.

The zenana drawing room had two large takhts with soft carpets covering them and bolsters to lean back on and chairs on the sides. Dagh sat down on one takht, and you made sure that your chair was at a distance from him. Normally, you would have sat beside Dagh on the takht.

'Ameeran Bi! Get some tea and huqqas,' Dagh called out to the maidservant.

'Our friend, Nawab Sahib, has his morning tea early, and if it gets a bit late, he gets really angry!' You were drawn into Dagh's teasing laughter.

Ameeran brought in the tea and simmering huqqas. Dagh said,

'Hijab, get the kites and strings out. Nawab Hasan will be on our side, and Khursheed Sahib will be our challenger. Let's see who wins!'

You brought out the kites and rolls of special sharp strings and put them on the takht. Hasan Sahib started examining the equipment.

'So, will we be able to beat Khursheed Sahib?' Dagh asked.

'He will lose all his kites today,' Hasan Sahib smirked.

The Awadhi biryani was ready, and you gave instructions to lay out the breakfast on the dining cloth spread on one of the takhts. There was mincemeat, kidney curry, mirch ka salan, parathas and eggs, along with the piping hot biryani. Everyone took their places around the food. After much persuasion, Khursheed Sahib, who had already had his breakfast, joined in. You liked Khursheed Sahib because he was a straightforward person and Dagh also adored his simplicity. But it was Hasan Sahib Dagh consulted on all matters personal and professional and confessed his deepest thoughts. He held Hasan in high esteem for his wisdom and balanced outlook. Though Dagh called you his rafeeq, soulmate, in reality, Hasan Sahib was his rafeeq.

You sat next to Dagh on the dastarkhwan and could feel Hasan Sahib observing your settling into the zenana, the signs of domesticity and your ease with the place. This house, given to Dagh by the Nizam, was your home now, and you had accepted your place in his life. Dagh paid for all the household bills and gave you sixty rupees for your personal expenses and some pocket money to Khuda Bakhsh. 'Does this mean I'm your employee now?' you had asked him. 'It means that you are going to be my wife and my rafeeq,' he had replied.

Looking at Hasan Sahib and Dagh laughing and joking, you had a distinct feeling that Hasan was avoiding your eyes and any conversation with you despite Dagh's efforts to make him comfortable with you and that he disapproved of you ensconced in the zenana. Maybe he was close to Fatima and found you an unfit, if not a despicable, successor. Your giving up the veil for Dagh was not a good idea, especially when your iddat was still continuing. Which genteel lady entertained her fiancé's friends to a kite-flying match in the zenana? Fatima Begum would have never done so. Though you were skilled at kite flying, you decided not to join the contest that day.

The patang-baazi on the roof was closely contested. Dagh praised your kite flying and tried to persuade you to join in, but you refused and watched from the sidelines, cheering as Hasan decimated Khursheed Sahib's kites. It became sweltering hot on the roof, and you retreated into the cool confines of the zenana, leaving the match at a crucial point. The shouts and cheers receded as you came down and sat waiting. If only Khuda Bakhsh were here, it would have been more proper; but he had started giving sitar lessons at a nobleman's house. He said he didn't want to be dependent on Dagh. The latter appreciated his efforts and recommended him to his friends.

You asked Ameeran to prepare cool almond sherbet with saffron and rose petals for the guests. Hasan Sahib must have presumed that you and Dagh had resumed physical relations.

When the men returned sweaty and jubilant, you asked Ameeran to serve the sherbet.

'Bhabhi Sahib, Nawab Hasan has composed a long ghazal about you and Ustad Dagh,' Khursheed Sahib said after gulping down the sherbet and letting out a long burp. He had started calling you 'Bhabhi Sahib', a title suitable for a brother's wife.

'You never showed it to me for corrections, Nawab Sahib! Is it a secret ghazal? Let's hear it,' Dagh insisted.

'I can't... I don't remember it.' Hasan shifted in his chair, blushing.

'Don't lie! You have memorized it. You recited it to me.' Khursheed was amused at Hasan Sahib's unease.

After a lot of argument and Dagh threatening never to correct his ghazals, Hasan cleared his throat, his eyes fixed on the floor, and began:

'Ye Ḥijāb āpkā go tūtney wālā hai zarūr
Roz e maḥshar pe āp ne ṭāla hai zarūr'

(Your modest veil will be surrendered soon
Despite your vow of abiding till Judgement Day.)

Dagh, who was leaning against the bolster, sat up and exclaimed, 'Waah, waah! You can see your prediction has come true. I have made Hijab be-hijab (unveiled) now!' He guffawed.

Rising abruptly, you left the room, shame and anger coursing through you. For them, you were a mere tawaif with an ephemeral hijab.

تسویر

19

Tasvīr (Image)

Kya tamāsha hai ke le kar ā'īne ko hāth meiñ
Dekh kar zulfeiñ wo āp balkhāney lagey

A vision she is, mirror in hand
Preening and swaying like her tresses

—Munni Bai Hijab
Bahāristān e nāz

'HELLO! HELLO! HAAN, IT'S ME, HAAN.'

It is Opparna Bansal! I croak out a hesitant hi and clear my throat.

'So, I have spoken to Hachette, Penguin and Bloomsbury, haan? They're all interested.' She pauses, crunching on something. The sharp, crackling munching sounds like bhujia. She must be perpetually hungry with the diet, and surely, she can't be allowed to eat fried bhujia. Maybe she is stress eating and cheating.

'*Aur tu kab complete kar rahi hai, haan*, so when are you completing it?'

'Ermm… I think…'

'How many words, how many, huh?'

'I think… about 40,000.'

'Okay, good. Add about 10k more and fatafat send it, okay? OKAY?'

'Sure, fine.'

'Chal, you take care, bye!'

Did she actually say Penguin and Hachette? Breathless, with my heart drumming a frantic beat, I rush to tell Faraz. He is shaving, the tap streaming hot water and steam with complete disregard to the planet. I turn it off and tell him the news.

'Of course, you should have all of them bidding for your book. Congrats! How much did she say it will sell for?' Faraz hugs me and gives me a foam-bestowing peck.

'Uh, I don't know. I mean, she's not sure.' It hadn't occurred to me to ask Opparna, and I don't want to appear juvenile. 'So she wants me to complete it quickly, edit it and send it off.'

'You have written just 40,000 words after working for so many days!' Faraz wipes off the foam and abandons the shave.

'Faraz, I can't just rattle it off. It needs a lot of research.' A heavy knot of dread settles in my chest—I have barely written 30k words (I lied), and I'm already feeling pushed.

'Nonsense. The game is to get at least one novel published each year to be out there. Look at all the bestsellers.'

There is a call from Opparna again! I brush aside Faraz's questioning look and leave the room.

'Listen, forget the ending. Just clean up and send whatever you have. We almost have a bidding!' Opparna screeches.

'Ummm... How much do you think it will sell for?'

'Arrey, it's a bidding, man. Anything up to five grand. But then, you're a new writer. If this does well, for your next one, it will be much more!'

'Omigod!' I blurt out and hear a chuckle.

I spend the rest of the day taking printouts and editing. It is a strong story, but I don't know how it will end—I'm still in the middle of it. Gul jumps around in happiness, helping me print and reading out to me. Faraz comes in and gives Gul a kiss.

'Now no one will disturb Mamma. She needs a proper study with a table and bookshelves—I will get that done. Meezan Bhai should not bother her. Gul, you look after the kitchen stuff.'

'Me! I have no idea!'

'You don't have to cook. Just tell Meezan Bhai what to make and what he should get from the bazaar. I'll give you the money.'

'If it's so easy, *you* do it. Dada looks after his household; it's not a woman thing,' Gul says with a twinkle.

'All right, I take care of Meezan Bhai; you have to look after your mom. Keep sending her coffee and things. Come on, it will be fun!'

They set up my work table—an old desk and chair from the store—in the guest room overlooking the courtyard. Faraz removes the ancient dressing table to make place for it. We don't need air conditioning anymore, so it's quite comfortable. Feeling like the proverbial hen, I sit and try to lay my golden eggs. I want to share my happiness with Akriti, but Vani got me the lit agent, so I end up sharing the news on the book club WhatsApp group. They are all thrilled for me, demanding signed copies and promising to go to the Jaipur Lit Fest as my entourage. Their buzz uplifts me, but underneath it, I feel a swamping fear—what if it's not good enough and is trashed by all the publishers? I'm exhausted but continue to work, dreading Opparna's call.

I call up Daniyal from the privacy of my new study.

'This is not business. It's art. You need more research before writing.'

'Don't you get it? Opparna is the best lit agent. She takes 15 per cent commission, which is a bit more than the others, but that's okay.'

'Have you met her?'

'No, but she is Vani's client.'

'And you are ready to trust your brainchild, all your work into her hands! What can I say—all the best!'

All I needed was some encouragement, and now I can't write with him brooding in his study. This has become too much like a marriage. What the fuck! Now I have two moody men in my life to simper around. I shrug off his image and try to return to my edits; his disapproval is a damp fog clamming my thoughts.

❧

Headshot! Opparna wants my headshots. Help! I write in the book club group.

Messages flood in—a flurry of excited questions and emojis. I don't know the publisher yet, but Opparna asked me to keep my high-definition image (headshot) ready for publicity. She is on to something big, she says. I hope it happens. I had sent the manuscript without an ending, and now this command has to be obeyed. I scream emojis at the exorbitant cost of hiring a photographer from Delhi suggested by Vani. He can't be a magician—I will look the way I look; I don't want to transform into a slim and fair entity. A writer can be herself. I look up pictures of famous writers—unabashedly wrinkled, confident and unfiltered. That's how I want to look, too. Filters make it difficult to recognize people in real life. Gul says unfiltered images don't exist. The phones have built-in filters, and people download more. We have become a race with filtered self-images.

Luckily, there is a local photographer who, according to Vani, is good enough. The next morning, I prepare to face the shooting squad. Gul and Vani have conspired to make me into an Insta celebrity. Gul tries to convince me that only Insta sells books and Facebook—which I look up sometimes—is for uncles and aunties. She has created my Insta account. Vani commands me to take off my red and black mulmul saree. The only thing we agree upon is outdoor shooting. I refused to go to the parlour for hair and make-up. I detest the geisha-style make-up, with those feral false lashes and fluffy curls. Vani has come armed with her tongs, straighteners and hair sprays. No makeover, just tidying up—I try to emphasize before submitting to Vani.

'Hair is EVERYTHING!' Vani declares as she teases my waist-length hair into waves. Gul asks Meezan Bhai to serve tea and snacks to the photographer while he waits for me to emerge.

'Mamma, don't worry, you'll really look glam with your hair done up.' Gul hovers around excitedly in the mini 'set' Vani has created.

I whine for subtle make-up.

'Of course, darling, it should be a fresh, no make-up look,' coos Vani, finishing off the waves with sprays and serums.

After much argument, I get one picture in my favourite mulmul saree before being forced into a loose beige top over black trousers. I manage to get some shots in a culturally appropriate short kurta. We shuttle in and out of the house—arguing, shouting and laughing. Faraz says I look very 'hep'. The young photographer is very amused. He does wedding photographs and videos most of the time—the blushing bride holding on to the embarrassed groom and the compulsory family groups around the couple. He moves around snapping away, instructing me to look up, relax, turn away, smile. My desk is dragged to the veranda—the room is too dark—and I sit with my pen poised, pretending to write. Gul shows me Insta pages of writers and celebrities. I'm too exhausted to protest when Vani hands me the pièce de resistance—a red coat. I feel like Santa's Indian handmaiden. Finally, it's over. I only request the photographer not to make me white. I want my dusky complexion. People should be able to recognize me in case I go to speak at lit fests.

'Ma, you don't realize how important SM is today.'

'What's SM?'

'Uff, social media. You must post every day to have followers. And you must lose at least ten kilos. Right, Vani Aunty?'

'Of course not! Look at Adele; she was quite plump—at least initially,' says Vani.

'I'm not going to do this again. We can keep using these photos forever.' But I will age drastically after menopause and will need another batch of photos. I sigh.

Gul is so excited and fussing over me, almost the way she used to be, that I want to give in to everything she says. *Where were you, and welcome back,* I think. 'Thank you,' I say, kissing her.

I have found guitar lessons for Gul in the Civil Lines quite near our place. They start at 8 a.m., and I rather like the middle-aged teacher. He exudes the right mix—cool and strict. I get strong teacher vibes. I wonder if Gul will stick with the lessons. She is very up and down these days. Maybe her moods reflect what is going on between Vibhor and her. He has returned to college, and hopefully, that story is over, though I can't be sure. Love at that age needs a physical presence. There is less of laughter over the mobile. I want to pull my child away from the roller-coaster love ride. I even explained to her that the music class costs us quite a bit—something we could barely afford. No more pussyfooting around the child now.

'Baba will throw a fit when he gets to know of it,' Faraz warns.

'Yes, he will. But at least she's up early and enjoys her lessons. She even practises in the evenings. It's nice. Besides, she needs to get away from the Vibhor story.' Faraz agrees that a diversion would benefit the ultimate fading out of the infatuation. He then switches the subject and tells me that he is starting work on a government-funded low-income housing project coming up on the edge of the city. It was with a lot of political string-pulling that he could get a tender and then the bank loan. Now the challenge is to keep the costs low and make a tidy profit from the work. Hopefully, more projects will follow, he says. This is his area of work, and he sounds confident and happy. I tell him it will work out, and he looks pleased, but the question rears its head—is our home a collateral to the loan? It's the only property in his name. I'm watching, balancing, reacting as thoughts, worries, stories, emotions chase around in my brain, but Faraz has his own axis.

I drop Gul at the 'Music Academy' at 8 a.m., sit for a while listening to her and then head to Daniyal's. I show the photoshopped pictures to Daniyal—the photographer refused to send my 'raw shots'. Faraz said he made me look too young—more like a 'floozie' than a writer. Who even uses the word 'floozie' anymore?

'Look, my nose has been almost painted over,' I laugh.

'If I were Dagh, I would keep these for inspiration.' Daniyal spreads the different versions of me on the table.

'And maybe offer me a naukri?'

'Yes, come and live with me.' Daniyal is still, watching his words seep.

Roznamcha: Iftikhaar Aalam Marehrvi

(21 April 1902)

Today, Mirza Dagh Sahib was very upset. When his friend, Meer Mardan Ali, asked the reason for his melancholy, Mirza said, 'Ever since Hijab has arrived, I cannot entertain myself by listening to tawaifs at mujras. Even if some tawaifs come to pay their respects , Munni gets upset. Love for beauty and music is intrinsic to my personality. How can I deal with this confinement?'

For a long time, the conversation continued in the same vein. Finally, Dagh said that he has devised a solution. He planned to organize mujras at his friend's place and cover the expenses himself. Dagh was a very determined person; he wrote to his friend, Nawab Hasan Ali Khan:

'Nawab Sahib Bahadur,

Bi Hijab insists that I dismiss Akhtar Jan from my service. I need to listen to music and call tawaifs from time to time. She opposes the large salary I pay to Akhtar Jan and insists that if I employ her, it should not be an exclusive engagement. How does one respond to such unreasonable demands? I have been trying to reason with her, but she is obstinate and unyielding in her resolve. She quarrels with me every day. I haven't listened to any music for the past two–three days, and it has left me feeling quite unwell. I have asked Akhtar Jan to perform at your place and will try to come over somehow. Please make the necessary arrangements. I also need your counsel on a certain matter of importance.'

Roznamcha: Iftikhaar Aalam Marehrvi

(27 April 1902)

In his passion for music, Dagh Sahib can be likened to Nawab Wajid Ali Shah, albeit on a smaller scale. He supports artists—sitar players, flautists, ordinary folk singers and tawaifs. His competence at the tabla and sitar are notable; he frequently plays a raag composed by Emperor Bahadur Shah Zafar. Since he moved to Hyderabad, he has consistently kept at least one courtesan in his employ, ensuring that his evenings are filled with music and enjoyment. In short, he lives a luxurious and opulent life. Since Munni Bai Hijab has re-entered his life, the daily programme has altered. Before her arrival, every evening was filled with music and mehfils. After evening prayers, he longed for music. Sitar players, employed by him, were called, the town tawaifs would visit him, and an impromptu musical soirée would be organized.

Though he did not favour the songs of Deccan tawaifs, there were one or two local tawaifs who would visit and entertain him with their talk for hours. Akhtar Bai of Surat was employed by him for two years at a hundred rupees per month. In the Deccan, she is considered as beauteous as a houri—pleasant tempered, of medium height and so spirited and vivacious that she can't sit in one place for long. Though she is too young for him, she had charmed Mirza Sahib with her style and repartee; he was completely enchanted by her. When she left Hyderabad for Surat for some time, Mirza felt depressed and sank into a melancholic state. Now after Hijab's coming, this vibrant world of music that defined Dagh Sahib's evenings has faded into silence.

Hijab and Dagh, Hyderabad

(May–June 1902)

YOU KNEW FROM YOUR ASSOCIATION WITH DAGH AND FROM the letters to Nabi Jan and Malka Jan that he had their pictures. You demanded to see his collection.

'I have no relations with these tawaifs. Why are you jealous of mere pictures? I have changed everything for you.'

'Now my face is the only one you will gaze at. Only I will fulfil your desires, but after nikah. My iddat is over, and I'm ready.' You smiled coyly and kissed Dagh's hand. He looked as happy as a child. Khuda Bakhsh told you that Dagh's friends, including Hasan Sahib, told Dagh that you had already placed so many conditions on him that once you were married, you wouldn't let him live freely. You also learnt that Dagh's adopted daughter, Ladli and her husband were opposed to the marriage. They were used to squeezing Dagh for extra money under different pretexts and knew that this would stop once you were Dagh's wife. Ladli refused to meet you, and Dagh said she would come around when you were wed, but you weren't so sure. Khursheed Sahib had also stopped visiting and made excuses when you sent Khuda Bakhsh with an invitation. Hasan Sahib visited when Dagh or you sent for him to intercede in your quarrels. You had to act swiftly before everything slipped out of your hand.

When Dagh asked you to get a picture clicked with him, you refused, saying that genteel ladies didn't get their pictures taken and you were no longer a tawaif. Besides, why did he want your picture? You were right there in front of him. Finally, Hasan Sahib was called to mediate, and he suggested that you get a single picture taken for Dagh's eyes only. You consented but only after demanding, in front of Hasan Sahib, that Dagh should destroy all the pictures of tawaifs he possessed. Dagh was reluctant, but Hasan retrieved the pictures from the study and handed them over to you. You took them out of the envelope and spread them on the takht, carefully examining them and reading the names and messages written at the back. Among them was one of you taken twenty years ago, which you had sent him. Dagh had written seven rubaiyat (stanzas) in honour of your beauty when he received it.

'Dagh Sahib, you have to leave even the thought of these tawaifs behind you.' You picked each one and kept tearing them into small pieces, watching his face freeze.

The photographer came the next day. You wore a dark pink silk churidar kurta ensemble paired with a striped scarf with tassels and gold trimmings covering your head—stripes added texture to a picture. You had adorned yourself with your jhoomar-teeka, and large hooped chand-balis swung from your ears.

'You look like a bride,' Dagh murmured, twinkling .

'Why are *you* so dressed up? I told you that I want a single picture.'

'You understand what we want?' Dagh looked at the photographer.

'Ji, ustad.' The photographer smiled, peered into his camera and asked you to sit on a chair. Dagh moved to stand behind you.

'Noo, Dagh Sahib,' you exclaimed, jumping up. 'I thought we had agreed. I'm leaving!'

'Dagh Sahib please sit on this chair behind the begum. Don't worry, he won't be in the picture,' the photographer assured you.

When the pictures arrived, mounted on ivory-coloured cardboard and covered with a wispy, translucent paper, you opened them eagerly and found Dagh in all the pictures.

'What is this! Can't I ever trust you?'

'Tum gar falak e ḥusn pe ho māh e munīr
Sāye ki taraḥ sāth hai Dāgh e dilgīr
Ḳhāl e lab e gulfām hai shahid is kā
Bedāgh na khich sakī tumhārī tasvīr'

(You shine brilliant in the firmament of beauty
Heart-struck Dagh accompanies you like your shadow
The lovely mole on your flower lip is witness
That your picture cannot be taken without dagh [blemish])

Dagh touched your mole tenderly. All your defences crumbled and you gave in to Dagh. It would only strengthen your relationship and prompt him towards a nikah. Apa had written to you caustic and desperate—'What is this zenana-mardana act? Leave the pretence of a purda-observing Bibi. It is not in your fate. Satisfy his needs. Get him to wed you.' You had to hold on to him with nights of gentle passion reminiscent of your earlier love.

The news that Apa had sold off the kotha, which she had bought after such hard work to establish you and Hameedan, came as a shock. Most of the money went into settling debts. Apa had set aside the remaining amount to sustain them for the next few years. Shafeeq had already sold off the chandeliers, mirrors and everything of value he could lay his hand on. They had moved to a small two-room hovel in a slum area populated by prostitutes and beggars. Poor Maulvi Sahib was forced to sleep in the veranda while his wife slept with Apa and Khala. Shafeeq and his family occupied the other room. Shafeeq had started plying a rickshaw to feed everyone. You had let Apa down and couldn't bear your family's suffering. The image of Apa living in a dilapidated shack after the resplendent kotha haunted you. You wrote to her, urging her to come to Hyderabad for your nikah. She was reluctant—calling the family was not a good idea; Dagh might change his mind after seeing so many dependents. Khuda Bakhsh agreed with Apa because Dagh would have to rent another place for them and his expenses would increase. You accused him of being selfish and uncaring towards your own people. You assured Apa that Dagh was committed to the nikah. Initially, he was busy with some important court matters, then he had to postpone because of Muharram—a month of mourning.

After a lot of arguments, Dagh had started giving you a hundred rupees. It irked you that he had employed Akhtar Jan for double the amount. Dagh wasn't tight-fisted. In fact, he was a spendthrift and lived a lavish life. Fatima Begum was a simple woman and never interfered with his spending. Things would be different once you were married. He gave a lot of money to singers and musicians, supported two organisations; about a hundred rupees were sent every month in alms to poor families. These days, your quarrels were only about money. Maybe Hasan Sahib also believed that Dagh shouldn't marry you, that you were a grasping woman out to fleece his rich friend. He pretended to be sympathetic to you, and you didn't have anyone else to confide in. You wanted your people around you now.

You were happy when, with Hasan Sahib's intervention, you were able to send for your family. Dagh said your family was his family now and he would care for them. Wasn't that proof enough that he would marry you despite his family's and friends' objections? You thanked Hasan Sahib profusely for procuring the rented accommodation. It was just a short ride away, and soon, the two parts of your world would come together. You told Dagh that they could set a wedding date once your family had settled in Hyderabad. The tension of the last few days melted away, and you found yourself humming the familiar cadence of your old ghazal.

Dagh's Letter to Nawab Hasan

Nawab (Hasan) Sahib,

You must have heard, but if not (perhaps you feign ignorance), let me tell you that Hijab has been annoyed with me for the past two days. She wants to call her relatives and dependents to Hyderabad. I refused her request in jest, and she felt hurt. A furore erupted, and now there is a tussle between us over this issue. You haven't visited me for the past four days. Please come and help me out as soon as you receive my letter. I tried telling her a thousand times that her dependents are most welcome and to send for them happily. There is no place in my house for them, but I shall rent a house. Maybe we can sort this out when you come over, and she will be mollified.

Dagh

Roznamcha: Iftikhaar Aalam Marehrvi

(30 May 1902)

This evening, Mirza Sahib said, 'Have you heard she wants a nikah? Her iddat is over now. I'm also ready for nikah.'

Barā e nām nikāley falak merey armān
Jo hai nikalney kī ḥasrat kahān nikaltī hai

O heavens, my desires were satisfied only in name,
The yearning heart can never be fulfilled.

Then he remarked that he had no teeth and was old, so what would he get out of the nikah:

Waqt e āḵhir huā magar ae Dāgh
Hawas e zindagī nahī jāti.

The end is nigh, o Dagh
Yet lust for life remains.

وَصْل

20

Wasl (Union)

Ai Ḥijāb unko g̱hurūr aur hameiñ bāt kā pās
'Aish o ārām idhar thā na udhar wasl kī rāt.

O Hijab, he was proud and I, honour-bound
The solace of fulfilment was not our destiny.

—Munni Bai Hijab

'DAGH'S BIOGRAPHERS CALL HIJAB A PARKAALA—A SPARK. I guess they meant that she was a sharp and manipulative woman. Of course, the biographers were males convinced that she was entrapping the old poet,' I muse.

'Maybe she was manipulative—she had to be. This marriage was also a matter of survival for her; plus, she had to think of her dependents,' says Daniyal.

We are back in the study, the set pattern—reading, writing and then discussing over evening tea—a comfort and a disquiet. I'm being pulled with an incomprehensible force to the house even as I sense a meandering towards the end of the story. I want to turn around and go back to collating, analysing and resolving facts and words, but the story has already been lived. Faraz was disappointed that I wasn't writing in the workspace he had created for me; I told him that visiting the library was essential at this stage.

'Then she should have been sweeter, kinder to him—basically behave like a tawaif not a wife! And she shouldn't have called her flock of relatives—that was bound to cause a lot of problems. So, clearly, planning the next move wasn't what she was doing. And she was really demanding and nasty towards him—look at how troubled Dagh sounds in the roznamcha,' I say, handing him the roznamcha pages.

'I have read these. You're right; she was behaving like a wife already. To me, she looks desperate.'

'So, if she was really a scheming woman, she would have waited patiently till they were well and truly wedded before calling her relatives or creating a hungama over tawaifs. But she trusted his intentions and she set aside her veil for him. I wonder if she, if they...'

'Had sex or hambistri, literal meaning—sharing a bed. Like us.'

'We didn't... I mean nothing happened...'

'You know a lot happened. Maybe we can't define it, but let's not pretend otherwise.' His eyes are hazel blazing suns.

Our souls have been standing naked before each other since that moment while life flows around us. Did Mamma feel like this with her lover? Was her passion so great that she could abandon us? Somehow, picturing my cold, apparently unemotional mother in a passionate relationship defied my imagination. Was there even a lover?

She accused Papa of gay relationships, adultery and tried to get a divorce; she wanted my custody. I read it all in the dossier. Divorce was denied by the court because Papa refuted her claims and she couldn't prove anything. Maybe that's when she decided to leave us. She never tried to take me with her, never sent for me. Maybe she was unsure of where she was going. The dossier with its true and false allegations and defence was a version of truths and untruths.

Did people know of her accusations? Papa had a number of friends, mostly men, who visited us—perhaps it wasn't considered proper for women to visit him. Some evenings, he left me with Ayah ji to visit his friends. He had severed ties with his relatives at some point; I have no memories of grandparents or aunts and uncles. It felt strange attending social events with Papa, and I kept close to him. Perhaps he felt shame and was just putting up a brave front; he saw the questions on people's faces and ignored the whispers. It wasn't a forgiving time.

Mamma could destroy, I knew that. When Papa passed away, she tried to chip away at my love and idolization of him with remarks—he was a gentle person but maybe he needed 'something else'; at least he loved you, and I knew he would care for you. I would always turn away from her insinuations, seething, wanting to scream at her. Perhaps in my subconscious mind, I already knew about Papa but was unwilling to forgive her for leaving. Once, right before she slipped into a coma, she said—can't you forgive me for those years. But I couldn't. Now there is a nothingness framed by the dossier's truth and lies and sadma, a grief distilled into the bones and inflicting my very cells. And yet, perhaps like all women, I flow on with the tide of life. I think there are two parts of me, and one part is enveloped in a conversation with a past that refuses to inhabit the past tense in its narrative.

I want to sit at Daniyal's feet and lay my lacerated soul there. I feel the physical and emotional snarl tightening around my throat and reach out to him, suddenly transparent. The wait tensing his body relaxes; I turn to his gentle caresses. 'Let me…' he whispers and unravels my saree. I twirl, the relief of unspooling where words and thoughts become an intrusion. My body will forever be haunted by the reverberations of that moment as we lie together in the solace of hambistri.

With Faraz, my sincere, gentle first love, there were promises of perfect moments in our future. Now, as the shadows and light chase across the ceiling of the ornate bedroom, I know our moment is unapproachable by thoughts of the future. Daniyal's words frame the perfection of our love:

Man tū shudam, tū man shudī,
Man tan shudam, tū jāñ shudī;
Tā kas na goyad bād azīn,
Man dīgaram, tū dīgarī

I'm you, and you are me,
I'm body, and you are soul;
Such that no one can say hereafter,
That you are other than me.

What happened to our book club? I miss you guys, Vani writes on our WhatsApp group.

Akriti: *Don't disturb Kuku. She is writing a masterpiece.*
Kuku: *Let's meet now at Lady Bake. It's four and we're all free. Come!*

Vani has just returned from a conference in Delhi. She must be dying to talk.

After some back and forth, we finally decide to meet at Mood Food because Akriti has been craving dosas. I have received three question marks from Opparna today. Faraz has Googled Opparna to bits and has decided I should be flattered that she is so invested in my work. But I don't know how my book will end. I can't fake it. Pramila used to say that I should be more 'biting' and 'breezy' in my writing and try not to tie a bow at the end. Some things desist closure—just let them be. That was a valuable lesson from our disastrous association.

Vani is bristling with news. She keeps hinting at it till the dosas arrive and we start dissecting and crunching them.

'Shezray has gone back to her husband!'

'What! I thought he was abusive,' I say.

'He's seriously ill with something.'

'So, she has gone to play nursemaid. Is it temporary ?' Akriti asks.

'No, I spoke to her, and she has decided that it's for good. All is forgiven, husband reformed, son happy.' Vani chomps her dosa.

'But... weren't they divorced?' I ask.

'Not legally. Just separated. Shezray walked out on him,' Vani says.

'I thought that was so brave of her. Maybe she went back because of her son. He must be a teenager now. They had been separated for three years.' I reflect on her choices.

Shezray went back to a son who chose being in Saudi Arabia over his mother and 'boring' Rampur. I choke on my anger. It must take a lot for a woman to walk out of a stable though abusive marriage. I miss Shezray's quiet sadness, her fierce love for Rampur and her ancient house. Although she got only a portion of it, she would have chosen her 'Samanzaar' over her husband any day. We talk of the compromises women make—for children, for marriage, for expectations. Akriti speaks of Shabnam, her beloved mare, and how tough it was to give up riding. She used to be an ace rider, had won several championships, and there was talk of going to an Austrian riding school. Then marriage happened, and though Dinesh assured her that she could continue with her riding at the farm, pregnancy and Shubham's issues erased that dream. It was such a vital part of her life and her identity.

Vani's mobile buzzes. She sighs, mutters, 'Our children will drain us,' and moves to a secluded corner to take the call. Vibhor is in Delhi these days, and Gul has once again started speaking to him for hours. I let it slide; at least she is engrossed in her music. She ordered a special USB mic from Amazon and set up a home studio. She plays her guitar and uploads tracks on Instagram. I follow her and like all her posts, even though I can barely fathom the captions and the barrage of emoticons she often leaves alongside. That's my only activity on Insta.

I notice Vani gesticulating and getting worked up as she speaks to Vibhor. She looks upset as she joins us.

'We need to talk.' Vani's voice is taut.

'You can speak in front of Akriti.'

'Gul has… Gul is in Delhi. With Vibhor!'

Her words diffuse and sink in. I make her repeat everything, trying to stay still as the details emerge. They had planned it together. Vibhor had sent a prepaid taxi from Delhi. I had left Gul at the Music Academy that morning. She must have taken the taxi at three, the time she usually takes a rickshaw home. I wanted to keep a known rickshaw to get her back. But it was just a kilometre away from our house, and Gul assured me she could manage. She had planned it well and had even taken my credit card that morning, saying she wanted to buy some junk food. Vibhor's friend had advised him to call Vani—Gul was barely seventeen, and it could turn ugly; he could be accused of kidnapping or molesting a minor. Vibhor got cold feet and called up Vani. I check my messages; Gul had bought something from McDonald's—the only outlet is en route to Delhi. I should have been more alert.

Vani is holding my hand and crying. Akriti calls Faraz and hands me the phone. Faraz is in Moradabad, and it will take him about two hours, maybe three given the traffic, to get to Gul. Her phone is switched off. Vani tells Vibhor to be with Gul until Faraz arrives. Vani and Akriti want to stay with me till Gul comes home. It will take six-seven hours, and I tell them I'm okay. I will wait it out with Jumbo and my thoughts.

I let Gul down. She had decided to graduate in music; this was what interested her, and it had good scope. She had explained her plan to us. She would enrol herself in a short course in music production in Delhi until the degree course started in March. She would learn recording, mixing and production of music tracks, as well as modern music technology, to set up a musical studio. Most musical academies offering such courses were abroad and very expensive, so she found a certificate course in Delhi and got accepted. There was no application fee, but she had to pay the tuition fees to get admitted. Faraz threw a fit, accused her of wanting to be with Vibhor and refused to pay the fee. He called it a money-making scam with no real certification. He was probably right; we ganged up and refused to let her join the course. It led to one of those loud, stormy arguments that I thought would be forgotten in time and added to the list of teenagerish tantrums. Except now, this won't be forgotten.

I wanted to support her music career path but had hesitated. Faraz's logic loomed large; he accused me of indulging her with music classes, not caring about where they might lead. Baba, pulled into the argument, came immediately, leaving his clinic and added his booming voice to it. Predictably, Gul stormed off to her room, but it didn't end there. I should have stood up for her, maybe deferred the decision, suggested an investigation into the course—she was looking at me for that validation. It would have given her hope, stopped her from turning to Vibhor and taking such a drastic step. But for some reason, I couldn't defy Faraz. His grip on worldly matters, and practical knowledge felt unshakable. At some point, we had divided the spheres and carried on living the years.

Dagh's Letter to Nawab Hasan

Nawab Sahib, Salam,

Hijab's needs cannot be fulfilled; before her relatives arrived here, she was comfortable with the same amount. She is anxious all the time. That sense of fun and humour, her laughter—so much a part of her personality—which I loved, have all but disappeared. She frequently squabbles over small issues. I often trouble you to reason with her. At my age, I can't deal with her stormy temper, though I do try my best to appease her.

You are aware of our problems. Tell me, what should I do? Yesterday, for a long time, she continued to fight with me over Akhtar Jan. You know music is not just my habit but my passion. How can I indulge in it with the constraints she has placed on me? I have sent conveyance for you. Please come immediately.

Ilāhi tu ne ḥasīnoñ ko kyūñ kiyā paida
Kuch unkī zāt sey duniyā kā intezām nahī.

O Lord, what purpose drives you to create beautiful women
They serve not your great world's work.

Dagh

Roznamcha: Iftikhaar Aalam Marehrvi

(8 June 1902)

Hijab had come to Hyderabad thinking that the last years of her life will be comfortable with Dagh. Dagh Sahib, a lover of beauty had initially thought of marrying her. But the situation on the home front made him change his mind. His family members created such misunderstandings that Munni Bai, whom her loved fervently through all the years, now fell in his eyes. A major reason for the rift was also her family from Calcutta. Dagh Sahib was estranged from them. The result was that on one side his family and on the other Hijab's family created such misconstructions that today there is a rupture in their relationship.

Hijab and Dagh, Hyderabad

(June 1902)

AS APA PREDICTED, THINGS BECAME MORE FRAUGHT AND UGLY barely a month after they arrived. You demanded more money for your family. How could he believe that all of you could survive on an amount that barely sufficed for you. Dagh said that he was paying the rent ; Shafiq should earn for himself and not become a dependent and you should learn to make ends meet; wives survived on much less. Where was the generous, loving and jovial husband you had visualized in Dagh? Maybe it was a mistake to get your family here, but if Dagh couldn't support them now, how would things work out after your marriage?

It angered you that he kept hedging the question of nikah. You often flounced off to Apa's place in a fit of rage swearing never to return, then came back—sometimes on your own when your anger subsided or sometimes at Dagh's insistence. You were aware that your comings and goings and fights had become the topic of conversation in the mardana. Khuda Bakhsh had already abandoned your cause; he blamed you for all the quarrels, asserting that Dagh Sahib was an even-tempered man and only got upset and annoyed with you. You prohibited Khuda Bakhsh from coming over—he was a traitor, spying for Dagh, and possibly, Hasan Sahib. Khuda Bakhsh was earning reasonably well from various music tuitions and lived with Dagh in the mardana; he didn't need your support.

Apa, Khala and Shafiq were crammed in a run-down house in the middle of the old bazaar but were relieved to be there after the squalor they had left behind. Yet it was far from the palace-like home you had envisioned. Hopefully, Dagh would get a bigger house he had applied for and then all of you could be together. But Dagh had hardly been welcoming towards them. He had visited them only once on your insistence and regarded them as a troublesome burden.

Apa's gaunt face was framed by a faded dupatta, and her finger massaged her gums with tobacco as she sat on the takht ruminating. She had lost so much weight that her skin hung in loose folds. She was incensed with Dagh's attitude and blamed you continuously for not being able to wrangle a nikah even when you were living in the same house with Dagh. But what would the two words—do bol—of nikah achieve? Everything could be undone by three words—talaq, talaq, talaq—uttered by a man. Khala counselled you to be less arrogant and more patient and loving towards Dagh; he was a good man, and when he died, he would leave a large inheritance for you.

'She couldn't keep her first husband after years of slavery,' Apa scoffed and predicted another failed marriage for you—if at all you managed a nikah. She told Khala that they should be prepared to head back. Aal wanted a son from me, the marriage would have ended whether Dagh had reappeared or not—you said to Apa. She shook her head dismissively and started her usual litany of your disastrous decisions and your foolhardy trust in Dagh even after her dire warnings. You wished you could silence her bitter words and still the shadows of her poisonous thoughts with a comfortable life.

Dagh's words to Hameedan resurfaced in your mind—'*Baiji ko lagana aata hai, lagaye rehna nahi ata.*' (Baiji knows how to attract lovers but cannot keep them committed to her.) Maybe he was right. You were living with Apa, enraged at a recent quarrel with Dagh when you got the news that Dagh was seriously ill with gout, his old affliction. Apa sensing an opportunity, urged you to immediately go to his bedside but you decided to send a servant to inquire about his health. Dagh sent back a sher:

Āp pachhtāeiñ nahīñ jaur se tauba na kareñ
Āp ghabrāeiñ nahīñ Dāgh kā ḥāl achhā hai.

Don't regret and abandon your tyranny
Don't be anxious, Dagh is well.

Apa threw down her fan and raged—'Go, you wretched randi. Your pride will kill us!'

You ignored her and sent the servant back with a letter:

Respected sir, Salam,

Your complaints are justified but it is difficult to control the heart. When Jamal Sahib told me that you were taken ill, I couldn't stop myself. I kept thinking if I should visit you or first send inquiries about your health. Jamal Sahib sometimes says such things as a joke. So I sent my servant to your place and found that you were really ill.

How can you think that I don't care about you? For you I left my watan, my home and I'm staying here. If you break my heart where shall I go? You don't even give me leave to return. How can I continue to live here under such circumstances? You feel that I'm cold towards you and I sense that I have no place in your heart.

But this is not the time for such talks. If you permit, I shall visit you to inquire about your health. I often see that you are not happy to see me—for this reason I felt the need to seek your permission first. Your family and relatives are also against our meetings.

With great respect.
Hijab
8 June 1902

That evening you set aside your wrath and went to Dagh. He was lying in bed groaning with pain. Hasan Sahib and Khursheed Sahib were with him. You touched your forehead in salam and sat down beside him, your eyes brimming with tears. Hasan Sahib and Khursheed Sahib begged leave to go, but Dagh asked them not to leave him alone. He turned towards you and said, 'Baiji, thank you for visiting me. As you see, I'm better now. You can stay for dinner, if you wish.'

'I have had dinner, thank you.' You touched your forehead and got up.

Roznamcha: Iftikhaar Aalam Marehrvi

(3 June 1902)

For the past two days Mirza Dagh Sahib is looking very dull and despondent. The reason for this is possibly another rift with Bi Hijab... Dagh Sahib is not at an age where he can deal with Hijab's difficult and tempestuous behaviour. These are antics of young lovers. But she doesn't realise this. She should respect Dagh Sahib's and her own age and restrain from such behaviour. She often becomes cold towards him and this affects him for several days.

Tonight Hasan Ali, Khursheed Sahib, Sirajuddin and I visited Dagh Sahib. Hasan Sahib asked—'What have you thought about Bi Hijab? I have noticed that you are preoccupied and worried. I believe the reason can only be Bi Hijab. If you really want to wed her, then why the delay? And if you have decided against the nikah then this dalliance is a cause of vexation for you; your family is also worried. We, as your friends, are upset because a vivacious person like you has become quiet and melancholic.'

Mirza Sahib replied, 'I realize that you all are worried about me and I value your love. As for my family, they were not worried when I spent freely and extravagantly. Now when I want to do a good deed, they are suddenly concerned. I understand their worry but my decision is firm.'

Everyone was quiet and Hasan Sahib changed the subject. After sometime, Khursheed Sahib and Sirajuddin left and Hasan Sahib returned to the topic.

'With great respect, I request you to reconsider your decision to wed Bi Hijab.'

Mirza Sahib smiled and said, 'As I explained, my decision is unchangeable.'

Hasan Sahib said, 'Nearly all your family members are against your decision. As far as I know, Ladli Begum opposes it too though she doesn't say anything out of respect. I fear there will be a lot of strife in your family.'

'You are right and after considering all this I have made my decision.' Hasan Sahib became quiet. Mirza Sahib looked at him and guffawed. 'My dear, innocent Nawab, you have spoken at length but haven't asked me what is my decision. My firm resolve is this—I shall ***never*** *marry Hijab. You haven't understood me. Dagh has suffered and learnt many lessons. If I had to marry her, I would have done so ages ago. There is much pressure from Hijab and the reason for our quarrels is the question of marriage. Nothing can persuade me to marry her. But I want my family to feel that I'm bent on marrying her.'*

Some other acquaintances came in and the topic was changed.

جنُوں

21

Junūn (Madness)

Hajv hai merey āgey wāh re lutf e bayān
Ḥazrat e wā'iz utar āyeiñ zarā mimber se āp

Such an eloquent denunciation of me!
Mr Preacher, step down from your pulpit.

—Munni Bai Hijab
Tazkirā e qadīm shairāt e Urdu

I DON'T KNOW HOW FARAZ HANDLED GUL ON THE WAY BACK. There must have been scoldings, accusations and waterworks. When she arrived, her face was streaked with the remnants of tears and exhaustion; I just held her stiff body wordlessly. Vani and Ritesh were there, discreetly disappearing somewhere inside when Faraz and Gul entered. After Gul retreats to her room, choosing only Jumbo for company, I come out into the drawing room. Vani keeps saying she is sorry, till I ask her to stop. It was not her fault. It was Gul's idea, her knee-jerk reaction to us, and Vibhor had decided to be a part of the plan. Vani starts off saying it will be okay and no harm done—her reassurances unspoken and pointed. Vibhor must have assured them. Faraz and Ritesh are outside, smoking and having a man-to-man talk. I watch them, their body language. Ritesh pats Faraz on his shoulder—it's fine, buddy, nothing happened; hymen still intact. Faraz's rigid back looks a bit relaxed now. Tacitly, we decide to forget about it and bury the episode in silence. It was a momentary lapse; after all, nothing happened.

The book club meeting had been planned earlier, and I didn't want to cancel it, though we all, except Daniyal, knew and decided not to mention the incident. Pretending, burying shame, unhappiness and guilt always felt easier for me; to acknowledge a rupture needed courage. I asked Meezan Bhai to prepare alu-gosht—he does it well. I don't want to cook anything. Alu-gosht, with its tender mutton pieces and potatoes soaked in the light, yet surprisingly nuanced flavours of the curry, is my edible balm for the soul.

For the past few days, Gul has been on a steady diet of coffee, sandwiches and all-numbing Netflix. Faraz asks me to leave her alone to sort herself out. That's what we did last time, I say. He blames me for my lack of foresight. I knew Gul was involved, yet I got her into music classes and gave her the freedom to move around unsupervised; I was too busy with a stupid love story and Daniyal to care about what was going on under my nose. His words burn into me. Maybe he knows, or suspects. Perhaps he thinks it is an episode, a possible lapse in our marriage; perhaps he can never believe we can be unfaithful to each other. I turn his words, his tone and expression in my mind. I want to scream, admit, hurl accusations, but guilt takes root, choking my voice. We won't talk about it. We let Gul be, we let each other be. We have always lived in an 'unexamined' marriage. I have become like Mamma, with her eyes far away from me even when she was with me.

'Mamma, you have multiple tabs open in your brain,' Gul had said once. My darling, your tab is always on the front screen, I want to tell her.

❧

Akriti arrives a bit earlier with Shubham and Dinesh. Shubham goes to Gul's room, and I hope she will relax with him. We settle down on our usual chairs. She is fine, she will be fine, I say. We are all in an echo chamber, convincing and assuring each other. Vani and Ritesh come in next. Everyone looks a bit frayed, subdued, like they have come for a condolence meeting. Even Vani is wearing dark blue. Shezray sends a message: *I miss you all soooo much.* I wonder if she is happy. I will speak to her someday; for now, I send heart emojis to stand in for me.

Daniyal knows nothing about the recent developments, and I realize I can't talk to him about it as yet. I haven't been to his house since the Gul episode. As usual, I offered no explanations—I wonder what he makes of my sudden absence. I have curled around my guilt, my anxiety for Gul, and retreated into myself. I wish he hadn't come; his presence is an intrusion and he can sense my rejection. His being in my home pulls the very atoms of my existence and reconfigures them into another permutation; like he has made me shift my gaze to look closely at a painting sideways, with eyes half-closed, so that the miniscule brush strokes, expanded and uneven, reveal another shape and the phantom layers underneath. I don't want it, not now.

'Okay, before we discuss the book, I have to tell you what happened at the end of the Dagh–Hijab story. Then we can bury Hijab.' I force a brightness into my voice. Everyone perks up, and I dive into the tale. I read Dagh's final letter and say, 'So, things didn't work out between them, and she went back to Calcutta. Dagh sent her a hundred rupees every month till he passed away. She must have barely survived on that. I wonder how she made ends meet after he passed away.'

'They say that Dagh was deeply bereaved. His biographer writes that after Hijab left, Dagh even gave up listening to music, his greatest passion. He stopped using attar. "*Mujhey kisi baat ka lutf nahi aata* (nothing interests me now)," he wrote. He complained of not being able to taste and enjoy good food. He died of heartbreak a year and a half after Hijab left,' Daniyal says, braising me with a quick glance.

'Heartbreak? I don't think so. He seems to have enjoyed himself thoroughly at the Coronation Durbar in 1903. Here he writes to a friend, Bekhud Dehlvi, "*Nahi miltien yahan hirni, tarasta hoon kababon ko* (there are no does here, and I long for kababs)." His friend lists all the dishes he prepared for Dagh and sends them to his camp. Doesn't seem like a heartbroken lover to me,' I scoff.

'Yes, the old man must have had another young tawaif tucked away somewhere,' laughs Ritesh.

'Personally, I feel Dagh betrayed her and broke his promises. Hijab and her family were so vulnerable, and he just let them go back. It was so callous of him! It is said that Dagh's attitude changed because his relatives accused her of immoral behaviour—the easiest thing to do against a tawaif. She wrote to his friends from Calcutta professing her innocence; perhaps Dagh was convinced or felt guilty and started sending her money.' The gritty, vulgar end of the love story infuriates me. Maybe there was never a love story.

Daniyal shakes his head and says, 'Hijab was his one great love, and he lost her. Nothing else mattered; it was just the chatter of life going on.'

Over alu-gosht, Akhtar Bhai's chapli kabab and nahari, which Vani got from a new restaurant, we speculate on Hijab's possible fate. She disappeared from the pages of history and floated away into obscurity and possible penury. What happened to old tawaifs who didn't have daughters to support them?

'Maybe she employed tawaifs and set up a kotha again?' suggests Ritesh.

I shake my head. 'One of the tazkiras says that she returned to Calcutta and became a gosha nasheen—literally living in a corner, a recluse.'

Daniyal tells us that Gauhar Jan, the most famous gramophone artist and the richest tawaif, died in penury and lost all her properties.

He has a letter written by Gauhar Jan to Nawab Hamid Ali Khan, begging him to ask his treasurer to withdraw his case against her. She had borrowed money from the treasury. She wrote that her eyesight was failing and she could not sing. Nawab Hamid wrote back, granting her reprieve for six months. But for Dagh's masnavi, Munni Bai Hijab would have been one of the thousands of tawaifs who had struggled, shone briefly and perished namelessly.

I want to ask Hijab: Did you give up, were you driven to take your own life rather than face the daily indignities that life offered? Somehow, I can't believe that of her. Maybe a last bid at chasing the old dream—matrimony and security? How can I end your story in this telling, where I have suddenly become powerful and powerless at the same time.

'I'm going to Kolkata with Gul,' I tell Faraz that night, surprising even myself. Faraz accuses me of being impractical, but this is the only way to end this story. This tab must be closed.

Hijab's Letter to Dagh
(1903)

O benevolent one, may you live long!

I have sent three letters to you, but you haven't replied to even one of them. I had asked for money, which you didn't send. How am I going to finance my expenses? Anna gave me a hundred rupees and told me strictly not to expect any more from you. God only knows how much you sent to me—I only got this paltry amount from her. I'm very angry with your relatives. They are my enemies, and I'm sure they distribute all the money amongst themselves... may Khuda destroy my enemies.

Hijab
18 June 1903

Dagh's Letter to Hijab

Respected Madam,

I have conveyed my wishes through Nawab Sahib. Don't expect any more money from me. The rent is my responsibility; your clothes and other expenses are paid by me. Then why is a hundred rupees not enough for you? Your running debts from everyone is not good. It is humiliating for me. Tell your people to look after themselves and not become a burden on others.

I have asked Khuda Bakhsh to visit you even though he is estranged from you. Consider him my representative there. I know there are differences between you brother and sister, but try to be more tolerant. I will send Nawab Hasan to speak to you. I cannot understand the cause for this sudden change in you. God only knows the reason for your one-sided decisions. Tell Nawab Hasan clearly what your intentions are. If you have decided to go back to Calcutta, then say so clearly. I have no objection to the plan. I have arranged for everything according to your wishes and will continue to do so. Even after all this, you are leaving in anger, then who can stop you...

Dagh
Narsimpet

Hijab and Dagh, Hyderabad

(July–August 1903)

'KHUDA BAKHSH, I HAVE FED YOU WITH MY OWN HANDS, AND FOR years, you have lived like a parasite on my earnings. And now, you repay that debt by spying on me? I just said I'll go back to Calcutta in anger, and you had to write to Dagh in Narsimpet about it?'

'Baji, I can swear on anything that I wrote nothing about Calcutta.'

'Then it must be that accursed Nawab Hasan or that Anna who has been given charge of sending me money. That old witch! She comes here, sits around chatting and goes and tells everything to Ladli. I'm surrounded by enemies!' You struck your forehead in rage.

The past year, your tenuous relationship with Dagh had become increasingly brittle. Ladli, Anna and other relatives had dared to spread vile rumours against you—it was so easy to slander a tawaif. You were hurt that Dagh didn't even attempt to defend you. Maybe he believed them or was using it as an excuse to remove you from his life. You could sense when their talk found its target from Dagh's turning away though he was too decent to say anything to you. In fact, Ladli and her clan's behaviour had made you even more adamant to hang on—though the idea of your marriage had become a fast vanishing dream.

You called Hasan Sahib and showed him the letter from Dagh sent from Narsimpet where he had gone with the Nizam's entourage for a hunting expedition. The rent for the house hadn't been paid for months and he had refused to send more money. What were you supposed to do? Hasan Sahib said that Dagh had written to him complaining of the relentless heat of Narsimpet which made him ill and irritable. He loathed wilderness and hated living in tents; he was unable to eat the meat dishes prepared from hunted animals and had no interest in hunting but as the Nizam's employee, he had to endure the torturous conditions.

He told you that Dagh had also asked him to negotiate with the landlord to accept half the rent and evict your family. You were stunned. How could Dagh be so cruel? You read the damning line from the letter, which Hasan sahib, in his wisdom, handed to you:

> *'I will agree to pay half the rent when he (the landlord) evicts the family immediately.'*

You had broken down then, crying in front of Hasan Sahib. Where would you all go? You had threatened to go back to Calcutta, but that was to the tender lover you once knew. There was no place to return to in Calcutta. Shafeeq might find a hovel for you all. Soon, everyone would come to know of your state; your old tawaif friends would tut-tut over your fall from Dagh's grace, avoid you and carry on with their lives.

'Hasan Sahib, please write and tell Dagh Sahib that I won't go away till he comes back. He called me here with the promise of nikah. I was a married woman, and he sent all those letters through Qazi Sahib, asking me to leave my husband. I was unhappy, but at least I was secure and had some dignity. I called my family here because of his promise. They left everything, sold off their household things and came here. Is this a game he can play?'

Fragments of sentences from those passionate letters flitted through your memory.

'Bibi, don't be so disheartened; Dagh Sahib must have written this in anger. Life is not easy at the jungle camp, and his health is suffering...'

'Even so, I have decided now that I shall go back only when he returns. I have to make arrangements for my family there, so all I'm asking for is more time.' You shrugged off the pitying look in Hasan Sahib's eyes.

Hasan Sahib offered money to tide over your immediate needs. You refused. Dagh would accuse you of humiliating him again. You would all starve to death at Dagh's door if need be. But the hundred rupees were enough to stave off death.

Khala was extremely upset and angry. She could foresee the disasters in store for the family. For the first time, the aunt who had always protected you from Apa's blows, turned against you, spewing venomous accusations—what was the need for such pride at your age? Her spite bit into you. She urged you to throw yourself at Dagh's feet, use all the skills of a tawaif to seduce him and grovel for a nikah. Otherwise, they would have to pimp Shafeeq's young wife and daughters to survive—better you than them because you were used to selling your body.

'It is all black magic and talismans by that witch Ladli Begum,' said Apa. This was the only explanation for Dagh's volte-face. She proposed a visit to the mausoleum of the Sufi saints Yusuf Baba and Shareef Baba. Dagh also had a lot of respect for the dargah. It was said that they had come from Syria and worked in Emperor Aurangzeb's army, spreading the Sufi teachings of Moinuddin Chishti in Hyderabad.

You had lived at the shrine of Moinuddin Chishti at Ajmer for two months and fasted for forty days—a routine of fasts and prayers prescribed for cleansing and for the fulfilment of worldly desires. Had Sheik Moinuddin sent you to Dagh, and to what end? Maybe it was fated that your ego and pride should be decimated. How could Yusuf Baba help you where Moinuddin Chishti had failed before your abysmal fate?

'Allah has a plan for everyone, and you will be guided through Yusuf Baba. Miracles have occurred with faith and prayers,' said Apa.

The day verged on a downpour as you trudged with Apa and Khala to the tomb. Apa said Yusuf Baba's shadow was sheltering them from the sun. You spread two chadors as offerings on Yusuf Baba and Sharif Baba's twin graves and placed your forehead on Yousuf Baba's grave, praying.

'Bibi, you can't do that! Baba doesn't like women touching his grave.' A wizened old man with grey dreadlocks dressed in a dirty kurta pyjama shouted at you. You shrank back. The old man, eyes blazing, advanced towards you and raised a thick bunch of peacock feathers and brushed both your shoulders with the fan.

'Get up now and go! Baba is very angry at you!'

'Forgive my daughter. She is in great trouble. How can she repent?' Apa cried.

You stood rooted to the spot as the man continued to brush your shoulders with the feather bundle with increasing ferocity—a steady beating tattoo of pain on your shoulders and back. A scream erupted from your throat, and you sank to the ground, hugging yourself, clutching your sides in a self-huddle, trembling and wailing. Apa cast her body over yours, shielding you and screaming, 'Forgive my sinning daughter!'

The old man, his eyes rolling back in a trance-like state, said in a guttural voice, 'Go away! Go away!'

It started raining as you stumbled out of the dargah. Your burqa was drenched and clinging to your battered body; your tears mixed with the raindrops shattering your face. You felt hollowed out and brimming over.

The skies poured endlessly through that night. Wrung out emotionally, you had lain down as Khala blew prayers on you till you stopped shivering. Apa poured her acid words on you, '*Aurat ka wujood hi kya hota hai, mard ka wujood hota hai* (a woman has hardly any identity, only a man has an identity).'

You slept with her words heavy on your chest, a fitful, anxious sleep, waking and sleeping with the wetness of tears on your face. The rain was a relentless, punishing tempo, hammering the roof. You must have dozed off. A loud thud startled you, and something fell on your side-turned cheek like a stinging slap. Sitting up with a scream that turned into a choking cough, you inhaled the grainy dust filling the air and scrambled out of bed. A piece of lime and brick-dust plaster had fallen on your face. Your tears set the grit on your face, and your body was embalmed in wet mud as you tried to grope your way to the door. There was another rumble as stones and bricks started falling near you. Crouching near the bed, you felt a brick hit you on your back. It seemed that the very skies were pelting stones on your sinning head. The continuous screams, blending with the dull reverberations of the falling roof, must have been yours. You stared unbelievingly at a pile of rubble near the bed. Another brick fell near you. Someone was at the door with a lamp. There were screams of 'Ya Allah!' and 'Munni!' as Shafeeq came in, picked you up and half-carried, half-dragged you out to the veranda. You spent the night huddled with your family, waiting for more disasters. That morning, like bedraggled survivors of a calamity, you and your family left the house and went to Dagh Sahib's residence.

Khuda Bakhsh informed you that Dagh Sahib was back. He was resting in the mardana, tired from the journey and feeling unwell. You awaited him in the zenana. All that had transpired between you would now be wiped away. It was a misunderstanding created by others to break your relationship. He would tease you, laugh, and nothing else would matter.

'Arrey, you go to him. You are a tawaif and know how to charm men. Don't deny him anything. Give him relaxation. Your anger and pride will ruin us all!' Apa lamented.

But you wanted Dagh to call you to him.

'Even if he calls you, do you think that ungrateful wretch Khuda Bakhsh will tell you? These villains, Hasan and Khursheed, will persuade Dagh Sahib to send us away. Go and place your damned forehead on his feet!' Khala urged.

Unbidden, the words arranged themselves in perfect meter on your lips:

Bazm e dildār meiñ aghyar kā mujhe hai Ḥijāb
Qasad kyā dil meiñ hai ab kyā hai irāda terā

In my beloved's gathering, I veil myself from strangers
What is your heart's resolve, what are your intentions now.

Dagh's Letter to Nawab Hasan

Nawab Sahib, salam,

I'm a person who expects good behaviour, not impediments, in my affairs. How can the house be repaired in this rain?

Bi Hijab has descended upon us and is waiting desperately for you. Her house has fallen down, her life was saved, and the house is being repaired. There is no place in my house now.

Pray for me.

Faseeh ul Mulk Dagh Dehlvi
31 July 1903

جستُجو

22

Justujū (Search)

Adū ke kehne se mujhko zalīl o kḥwār kiyā
Sazā ye iskī hai maine jo tumko pyār kiyā.

You demeaning me at the behest of my enemy
Was my punishment for loving you.

—Munni Bai Hijab
Tazkirā Shairāt e Banglā

I WANT TO WALK THE COLOOTOLA STREETS WHERE HIJAB lived. Perhaps I will find her house or some information about her there. The tazkiras say that she returned with her family back to Calcutta. How did she survive, and where did she live? When and how did she die? Contacting historians, writers and reading academic papers have yielded no answers.

'It's going to be a useless and expensive trip,' Faraz warned me. I retorted that I shall pay out of my savings or the book advance I hope to get if and when we manage to sell the book. Perhaps I'm being impractical, but I want to embrace my impracticability. Gul and I check into an Airbnb she found for us. It is centrally located and surprisingly reasonable. More importantly, the food is just great even on our shoestring budget. Gul scours Insta for hidden gems and goes crazy over Royal Restaurant's biryani and chops and Flury's baked goods. She has declared that Kolkata is a foodie heaven and she could visit again just for the eats. Unlike me, she has a great sense of direction, has mind-mapped the city, navigating its chaos armed with technology and a sense of adventure. She loves to be in charge of the trip with her Google Maps and Uber allies. I was apprehensive that the Dubai brat would turn up her nose at the crowds and the filth.

I meet Debojeet Bandhopadhyay, a theatre aficionado associated with Academy Theatre Archives, at Flury's over coffee and cake. Debojeet ji tells me that the tawaifs from Lucknow and north India lived in the Colootola area—which is now Maulana Shaukat Ali Road and Ezra Street. But there are no records for most of the houses. Sometimes, the tawaifs were just given a house to live in by their patrons; they were often thrown out after the death of the patron. I search Google Maps—it lies close to Rabindra Sarani Road, which was earlier Chitpur. The Nakhuda Mosque is on the road. This must be the area where she lived!

We take an Uber to Colootola; I wanted to see it in the evening and at night. I worry about Gul's safety and ask the taxi driver if it is safe for us. He assures us that we will be safer than in Delhi; the Bengalis respect women. Debojeet ji had told me that the construction of Central Avenue in the 1930s had made the area accessible. Maybe Hijab was alive to witness this change in the geography of her city.

Seeking directions from the shopkeepers, we walk towards Colootola Street. Colootola unfolds as a bewildering, congested street, cacophonic with rickshaws, cars and motorcycles weaving past in a constant blur. Shops line the street, with two or three upper stories used as living quarters. Between uninspired modern constructions, the colonial relics with grand arches, fluted columns and characteristic wood-slatted windows cling to their crumbling glory. Overhead, masses of electric wires radiating from poles crisscross in a tangled web. Clothes are left to dry on balconies—cotton sarees and the typical blue-checked lungis. Politicians and Goddess Durga smile from billboards, colourful and jarring, and wish us a happy Durga Pujo. Gul clicks pictures to post on my Instagram when my book comes out. She points and laughs at an old building that houses 'The Charming School'. I love the curving wrought-iron parapets edging the verandas of colonial-era houses; some arches have scalloped edges with coloured glass panes. Did the tawaifs lean over these balconies to attract customers, their laughter merging in the evening air as their gaze followed the carriages down below. Perhaps Hijab was one of them sitting there smoking a huqqa.

I ask an old maulvi about tawaifs. Yes, the tawaifs from Lucknow and Uttar Pradesh, the dereydaar tawaifs, used to live on the street and the street used to be filled with music in the evenings. Now, most of the old tawaifs have moved to the Bow Bazar area; they are modern tawaifs and perform to film songs. A shopkeeper from a neighbouring attar shop leans into our conversation.

'Most Muslim tawaifs left this area after Partition. There were a few left. We threw them on the streets and chased them out in 1992. We wanted to purge our street of their filth!'

I watch his face curve into a pious smirk. He must have been a teenager at the time of the 'purge', standing there jeering at the helpless, humiliated women gathering their belongings. Did Hijab leave for East Pakistan after 1947? She must have been in her late eighties at that time, if she were alive. Was her spirit still fiery to crave another chance at life in a newly carved country?

One house catches my eye, and its grand decay beckons me inside. Maybe the ghostly presence of Hijab living within me invites me to see her world, to stand in the place where she probably spent her early years of heady success. Ignoring Faraz's warning echoing in my mind—he would be annoyed at me for taking Gul to such decrepit places—I give in to Hijab. We enter a high monogrammed door;

a carved wooden staircase winds over our heads. Beneath it, an old man dozes on a narrow bed. We ask for the owner and are directed to the first floor. I imagine Shafeeq standing here in his crisp white angarkha, bowing in salam and ushering the grandees up the stairs. I trail my hand on the wood of the banister, smoothened by more than a century of eager visitors. The wooden planks of the stairs creak under me. I point to the brass knobs placed on them, very like the knobs on the grand staircase at the Raza Library, to ensure that the carpet is held in place. The worn-out and rotted carpet must have been removed at some point.

Wajiuddin, the present owner, runs a wholesale business on the first floor. The rest of the floors are on rent. When I explain my quest, he invites us in. His grandfather had bought the place from a tawaif who had decided to migrate to Pakistan sometime in the 1950s. He hasn't heard of Hijab. But appreciates their contribution to Hindustani music. They supported the musicians, innovated and popularized the thumri, dadra and other styles.

We walk into a large central hall leading to smaller rooms on each side. Gul whispers that this must have been the mujra performance hall. The doors leading to the balcony have coloured glass embedded in wooden frames on the arches. The glass is broken in some places and patched up with cardboard. Enormous cardboard boxes are piled up on one side—goods for dispatch. A large desk, important with scattered papers and bill books, unwashed teacups, encircled with grimy white plastic chairs, is placed under a single ceiling fan.

I conjure up a resplendent carpet, low diwans and bolsters all around the hall. At the centre of the ceiling, there still hangs the brass skeleton of a chandelier with a single broken glass shade. The brass is dulled enough to be thought of as worthless. I erase the harsh light of prosaic electric rods and illuminate the hall with the soft glow of tens of flames from the chandelier and the many-armed floor lamps. I fill the room with the chatter of girls as they prepare the room, dusting the diwans, placing huqqas and pandans near the seats, the musicians settling into their diwan on the side, tuning their instruments. Now the girls light up the lamps with tiny flames, the chandelier is lowered and they set little flames dancing in the red glass lamps, tinting the room in a rosy hue. A rustle of ghararas, the tinkle of anklets and a wave of rose, khus and sandalwood attar perfumes as Hijab and Hameedan walk in with Apa. Now Hijab is sitting in front of the musicians, synchronizing her voice with the strumming of the tanpura, a preparatory alap, while Hameedan twirls gracefully, her hands raised like a dancer's prayer. Apa inspects the arrangements, going from one diwan to another, settles the brocade bolsters before she takes her place on her diwan facing the entrance, the wideness of her smile carefully calibrated to the wealth and social standing of the guest.

I turn to the arched doors leading to the balcony. The setting sun is glinting a play of reds, blues and greens on the floor. I open the three doorways, step out on the balcony and quieten the impatient horns of smoke-belching cars, the zooming motorcycles meandering between them. This is where Hijab sat on some evenings, watching the bustling traders and babus in their white kurtas, angarkhas, horse chariots and phaetons trundling below. Did she await a lover with promises to hold her forever? I turn around and find my shadow drawn on the dusty floor. Gul's shadow joins mine as she looks down at the road. We stand there framed by the arch—female shadows claiming their place.

We thank Wajiuddin and walk towards Rabindra Sarani Road. The white domes and minarets of the Nakhuda Mosque stand before us. Dagh could easily walk to Hijab's house within minutes, I tell Gul. Right next to the red-stone Nakhuda Mosque is Saleem Manzil, a five-storied dilapidated building, which was bought by Malka Jan. This is where Gauhar Jan lived, learnt her music and held sway over the hearts of Indians as the gramophone queen. I tell Gul about Gauhar

Jan. She must have interrupted her singing at the call of prayer from the mosque.

Dagh rented a place in front of Nakhuda Mosque during his first visit. There is an old three-storied building in front of the mosque, which now houses the Amenia Hotel and a musafir khana, a guest house, with a massive, arched doorway, which opens into a flagstone courtyard. There are rooms around the courtyard, with a running balcony overlooking the courtyard. Biographers say he lived on the first floor. Knowing Dagh, he would have gone for prayers at the mosque—for a few at least. Was this the place that Dagh and Munni lived in those early days of miraculous togetherness described by Dagh in his masnavi?

'It is here, in this moment I want to be forever,' Daniyal said once as we lay together, and my mind had echoed his desire and the unsaid impossibility of it. Most days, I get up with a sense of tormented despair at not being near him, unable to look up and find him turning around to see me watching him; his soft reassuring 'hmm' in answer to my 'hmm?' I scour my brain, my heart and all my senses to find shame. The boundaries of marriage, love, covenants have been smashed—for what? Desire, a temporary madness fuelled by unstable hormones—is that all? Will I look back and feel remorse and seek retribution? Can I bear the accusation in Gul's eyes? Do I want Faraz to know? How will this end? I'm wretched, I'm inconsolable, and yet I carry on. It amazes me, this business of life. I am a great dissembler; all mothers have to be. I'm living in a constant present—as one present unfolds after another, forever.

When I come across some new information, I want to call and discuss it with Daniyal. But we barely ever spoke on the mobile or sent messages. Our need to connect is always three-dimensional. We need the sight, feel and sound of each other—an urgent but calm desire. A part of my brain follows Daniyal's rhythms throughout his day. You must be in the garden tying up your dahlias with flints to support their flowering heads; now in the study, one elbow on the armrest, your long fingers hesitating, waiting for the page to complete what it has to say before turning it over. We are together in an embrace in some dimension of time. That part of my brain has been mapped out for you, Daniyal. It will always be like this while the chatter of life is lived. I know that now.

مَوت

23

Māut (Death)

Hamārī na'sh ko thokar lagāke usne kaha
Hamārey āney kā kya kḥūb intizār kiya

He kicked my corpse and said
O, how you waited for me.

—Munni Bai Hijab
Bahāristān e nāz

'PARKAALA'—THE WORD RINGS OUT IN MY MIND. THE TAWAIFS were called 'atish e parkaala', which literally meant a spark from a flame but denoted a smart, calculating woman. The sparks from a hundred flames lived, burned merrily and were extinguished here. Where were the tawaifs buried? A separate burial ground away from the pious? Or did they finally find a place with mothers, wives, sisters and daughters whom they barely ever met in their lives? Debojeet ji says that there was a time when tawaifs were not given a decent burial and were simply thrown into the Hooghly; but if they had a rich patron, they were given a grand burial. The thought sends a chill through me—Hijab would not have found patrons when she returned.

I meet Dr Shahid Saaz, a researcher who is compiling a compendium of Calcutta tawaifs. He didn't find Hijab's diwan or any new writings by her in Hyderabad libraries. We both have the same handful of ghazals by her, even though she was a celebrated singer and poetess of the time. Shahenshah Mirza, a member of the royal family of Awadh, tells me that most tawaifs from Lucknow were Shias. 'Maybe you can check out the old Shia qabristan in Munshi Bazar? Kajjan Bai was buried there, so maybe they took Hijab there, too. There is a female caretaker there, Sultana Begum. She will help you.'

The Munshi Bazar graveyard is the oldest Shia burial place near the Sealdah Station. I check on Google Maps; it's a forty-minute walk from Colootola. Hijab could have been buried here, that is, if she returned to live in the area around Colootola. If she had donned a hijab again, the pious might have gathered to bury her. Sultana Begum, a thin, middle-aged woman who took over this strictly male profession after the death of her husband, walks us through the ancient and new graves. The oldest surviving grave is that of a hakim who died in 1909. I read out the old tombstones in Urdu, brushing away the dust to trace the lines. Janab so-and-so lies next to his faithful ahliya—husbands and wives choosing to be buried near each other. Maybe the tawaifs edged into the periphery as they did on earth. Sultana Begum says that the old graves were reused over the years because of the limited space. I keep walking and reading tombstones—the old, mildewed ones and the sparkling whitewashed new ones, the painted steel placards—till Gul asks me to stop. Maybe Hijab was never buried here; maybe no one bothered to mark the grave, or her grave now has layers of new, respectable bones on top.

Debojeet ji finds eight recordings by a Munni Jan of Allahabad dating 1906 in Michael Kinnear's volume, *The Gramophone Company's First Indian Recordings 1899–1908*. The date corresponds to her return from Hyderabad. Munni was from Lucknow, I remind Debojeet ji. He says that the tawaifs moved from one place to another, 'borrowed' from their current sponsor. Calcutta tawaifs went for performances and lived for long spells in Delhi and the United Provinces. There could be a mistake based on that; or perhaps Hijab with her undaunted spirit decided to record her songs for posterity and climbed out of poverty by becoming a living voice. I like to believe this of Hijab.

Gul sleeps with me, her nose pressed to my back, her pudgy hand touching me. We talk late into the night. Gul says Hijab would have loved me because I'm as bold and determined as she was. She wonders if Hijab could ever find happiness with the choices she had to make. I listen to her now grown-up talk. The best fallout of the otherwise failed trip is Gul turning back to me with her confidences, her laughter and her whining. She tells me about Vibhor, her trip to Delhi and her plans. I listen, promising not to judge her as she talks her heart out. We shall figure it all out, I tell her; I know she believes I will. What will she say if I confide in her?

I take Gul with me to libraries and archives; she helps me search through stacks of magazines and newspapers for articles, obituaries on Hijab. We can't find any trace of Munni Bai Hijab anywhere. She had really become gosha nasheen. I explain the word to Gul.

'I wish I could become gosha-whatever. Vibhor has ghosted me.'

Looking at my clueless face, Gul explains what ghosting entails.

'First heartbreak is tough,' I say.

'Second. You never knew about my first love,' Gul winks.

'Congratulations, then. You know how it goes now.'

'Did Nanu run away with her lover when you were a kid?'

I feel off balance. My lips frame a question, then a denial. I have the power over the truth or projecting an unchallenged truth.

'I don't know…I mean, I don't know if there was a lover. She wanted to divorce Papa for other reasons but didn't get the divorce. Maybe she wanted to go away somewhere for some time… to find herself. Sometimes, you have to do that…'

'So I went away…'

The words scrawled in light pencil strokes, hesitant, pleading, on the last page of the dossier. There was the forward tilt of Mamma's writing but none of its neatness, as if she was unsure that they would ever find an understanding and would fade away. She possibly wrote it when she was ill and she knew she would not make it. She was ailing for a long time and didn't know she would have the time to tell her story—her version of our tangled reality. She knew I would turn away from it, and I did—as I always did. She had left me, a six-year-old, and cut off from us. Her revenge against Papa was greater than her love for me, or there was a lover competing for her love. Either way, love or hate, I lost to a bigger emotion.

'Were you happy without her?'

'Oh, yes, we were, but then she came back!' I laugh.

'I know you couldn't forgive her.' I was surprised that this self-absorbed child could observe our estrangement. Mamma was always so tender and loving with Gul. She came to live with us in Dubai uninvited, ignoring my cold behaviour just to be with Gul. She didn't want to miss out on Gul's growing years. Faraz compensated my indifference by being welcoming and kind towards her. I speak of Mamma, voicing my feelings and disillusionments, careful to not destroy Gul's memories of her. For the first time, I'm looking back, placing her in the past.

'You know, Mamma… I think she just did the best she could.'

هجر

24

Hijr (Separation)

Kahuñgā dāwar e maḥshar ke āge ḥashr meñ bhī
Ki 'umr bhar usī kāfir ko maiñ ne pyār kiyā.

Even on doomsday I will declare before God,
That all my life I loved this unbeliever.

—Munni Bai Hijab
Bahāristān e nāz

I DRIVE TO MEET BABA AT HIS CLINIC. HE DESERVES TO KNOW about Gul and Vibhor. I need his blustering energy, even if he turns around to blame me or both of us. Baba is explaining gently to a burqa-clad woman that there is no hope for her husband. The woman's eyes are frozen with stoic acceptance. She leaves and Baba gestures to Seema to stop the patients for a bit. His back is slumped, his lower lip juts out, and his eyes are suddenly hidden under the craggy white brows.

'I know.' He pauses and looks at me. There is a watery sadness in his eyes behind the thick spectacles, or perhaps it is a trick of light. 'Gul called and told me everything.'

We discuss Gul for some time. He has given up the hope that Gul will take up medicine. Maybe it was not to be, and he was just pushing her into something that didn't interest her, he admits. I nod and assure him that Gul will find her way and we all have to support her through it. He asks about my trip to Kolkata. I start talking about my research there.

'There wasn't much I discovered, but it somehow didn't seem futile. I could stand in the place where my character lived her life. I can complete my book now.'

He rolls his pen back and forth on the prescription pad in search of words to prescribe; then clearing his throat, he says softly, 'Rukmini, Faraz will have only himself to blame if he loses you.'

Turning away, he rings the bell, and Seema sends in three more patients. Baba says that he doesn't need new-fangled tests and scans to tell him about his patients. He has inherited the gift of knowing what ails the body. I get up, give my chair to the patient and take the usual rickshaw to Daniyal's house.

I gather my things—the spare iPhone charger, the purple ink pot, my diaries—objects have a habit of finding their own space. There are safety pins, a hair clutch—nothing as romantic as an earring in the bedroom; there are a pair of lurid yellow and magenta flip-flops that Daniyal had bought for me. I had laughed at his endearing colour blindness. It still bothers me that he cannot see the world in shades of colour visible to me. I didn't have to wear my high heels all day; there was no need to appear taller than I was. I had the perfect height to reach Daniyal's heart and feel his chin resting on my head, his heart in mine.

'You can offer these chappals to other guests. I mean…' I trail off.

We extinguish, our words turn viscid, and we fall back on the banal—packing up and summoning a rickshaw. Daniyal hands me my fountain pen, his gift to me—I wrote my book in longhand with it, dipped, not filled, with purple ink—and steps aside as I walk out of the study.

The unseasonal, illogical late October rain is pounding the courtyard. The weather will change now to a bitter winter. I hand a 500-rupee note to Akhtar Bhai, and he touches his forehead in salam. I wonder if he will keep our secrets in this town where nothing can remain hidden. Wrapping my saree over my head and around my shoulders, a borrowed umbrella shielding me, I negotiate the courtyard towards the gate. I hand back the umbrella refusing to take it with me. Akhtar Bhai asks the rickshaw driver to pull up the hood, even though it is cracked and will drip. Daniyal is drenched, his curls lying flat over his head. He touches his forehead lightly and clasps his arms behind his back. The rickshaw draws away. I can't see him; the rain descends like sheets from the skies.

Glossary

Arzee: an application or request.

Awadh: an erstwhile princely state under the British colonists in North India.

Babu: master.

Bhadralok: a Bengali term denoting the educated and influential class that emerged in Bengal under the British colonial rule.

Burqa: an outer garment worn by Muslim women which covers the body and face.

Chaar maghaz: the seeds of watermelon, cantaloupe, cucumber and pumpkin. The seeds are powdered and mixed into curries.

Daneydaar: grainy texture.

Dastan: stories or epic tales, generally with an oral tradition.

Dastarkhwan: a long piece of cloth spread over a carpet or bench on which the food is served in Muslim households.

Diwan: literary works by a poet.

Dupatta: a long scarf generally worn by women across the shoulders, sometimes covering the head.

Farishtan: lady angel.

Farshi payjama: voluminous pants which trail on the floor.

Ghazal: a form of ode or poem on spiritual or romantic love comprising of at least five couplets.

Gher: the common central courtyard of a mohalla with a group of houses originally belonging to members of the same tribe or clan. The Pathan tribes who settled down in Rampur created round courtyards as open spaces for weddings, funerals and daily baithaks.

Halwa sohan: a sweet made from wheat germ flour.

Haveli: a palatial house belonging to a nobleman or an elite family.

Hijab: a veil.

Hijr: separation from the beloved.

Huzur: lord and master.

Iddat: a period of waiting that a Muslim woman must observe after the dissolution of marriage, whether by divorce or death of the husband. The primary purpose is to confirm the paternity of an unborn child. The period varies according to circumstances. After iddat, the woman is free to remarry.

Ishq: all-consuming spiritual and emotional love.

Jaali: a mesh.

Kadhi: a chickpea-flour savoury custard, usually with dumplings.

Kafir: unbeliever; one who doesn't believe in God.

Kahaar: palanquin-bearers.

Kalima: Islamic verse for accepting the faith.

Kayastha: an upper caste among Indian Hindus known for their historic role as scholars, scribes and accountants.

Khandani: from a renowned lineage.

Khichda: a dish made from grains, pulses and meat.

Khubani: apricot.

Khuda Hafiz: a farewell; may God keep you safe.

Kotha: house of courtesans on a terrace.

Maika: maternal home of a married woman.

Mardana: the male section of a house.

Masnad: a large cushion seat, a seat of honour.

Masnavi: a long, narrative poem written in rhyming couplets.

Maulvi: a learned scholar.

Mazar: a shrine or tomb.

Mehfil: a gathering or assembly, a concert.

Muharram: an Islamic month. Some Muslim sects observe mourning for the martyrdom of Hazrat Husain, the grandson of Prophet Muhammad, during this month.

Mujra: dance and singing performance by tawaifs.

Munshi: a title given to a secretary or assistant to an official in colonial India.

Musahib: companions, often paid for their role.

Musallam: literally means whole. Dishes prepared from whole chicken or mutton use the prefix.

Mushaira: an assembly where poets recite their poetry.

Nashteydaan: a large tiffin with several sections.

Nath: nose ring.

Nikah: Islamic nuptials.

Parda: veil.

Patang baazi: a kite-flying contest.

Qadardaan: one who values or appreciates.

Qayamatnaama: a letter or missive that spells doom.

Qazi: the position of a judge or magistrate in a court in Islamic states or in the Indian subcontinent.

Qorma: a rich meat curry.

Ramzan: a holy month in the Islamic calendar for fasting.

Randi: prostitute.

Shayara: poetess.

Sher: Urdu couplets.

Sonagachi: the largest red-light area in Kolkata.

Taar gosht: a rich meat curry prepared in Rampur. The layers of oil on top of the curry resemble golden threads or 'taar'.

Takht: wooden bench, royal seat.

Tawaif: a courtesan, female entertainer accomplished in music, dance and poetry belonging to the Indian subcontinent.

Tazkira: a collection of biographical notes on poets, artists, etc.

Urs: literally means marriage. Urs is celebrated at a Sufi shrine on the death anniversary of the Sufi saint as the spiritual union with the Divine.

Veshya: a prostitute.

Wisaal: a meeting with the beloved.

Waah-waah: exclamation expressing approval and appreciation.

Waleema: a reception banquet after Muslim marriage.

Wazeydari: appropriate, polite behaviour; to give due respect to a person.

Zabaan: tongue, language, dialect.

Zamurrad Shah: a despotic, villainous character from the epic Hamzanama. He was the enemy of the Islamic forces and their hero, Ameer Hamza.

Zenana: the female section of a house.

Bibliography

Urdu

Aasi, Abdul Bari. *Tazkirat ul Khawateen*. Lucknow: Munshi Naval Kishore nd.

Ali, Mohammad Nisar. *Sawaneh Umri e Dagh*. Lahore: Islamiya Press, 1905.

Ansari, Alif. *Shairat e Bangla: Hayat o Khidmat*. Kolkata: Shab Noor Publications, 2001.

Arshi, Imtiaz Ali, ed. *Khutoot e Dagh aur kuchh Dagh ke mutalliq*. Rampur: Rampur Raza Library, 2019.

Dehlvi, Dagh. *Gulzar e Dagh: Deewan e Awwal*. Lucknow: Naseem Book Depot, 1973.

Dehlvi, Dagh. *Masnavi Faryād e Dāgh*. Foreword by Tamkeen Kazmi. Lahore: Aina e Adab, Chowk Anarkali, 1957.

Dehlvi, Nawab Mirza Khan Dagh. *Yadgar e Dagh*. Compiled by Kalb e Ali Khan Faiq. Lahore: Zafar Sons Printers, 1984.

Faizuddin, Munshi. *Bazm e Akhir*. Delhi: Urdu Academy, 1986.

Faruqi, Shamsur Rahman. *Kai Chand they Sar e asman*. Penguin Books, 2006.

Haidari, Akbar. *Qadeem Shairat e Urdu*. Jammu: Jammu and Kashmir Academy of Art, Culture and Languages, 1996.

Kanwal, Ibne. *Bazm e Dagh*. Delhi: Deptt of Urdu, DU. Kitabi Duniya, 2020.

Kazmi, Tamkeen. *Dagh*. Lahore: Aina e Adab, 1960.

Mahli, Shahid, ed. *Dagh Dehlvi*. New Delhi: Ghalib Institute, 2001.

Marehrvi, Ahsan. *Jalwa e Dagh*. Hyderabad Deccan: Shamsi, 1902.

Marehrvi, Ahsan, ed. *Insha e Dagh: Mirza Dagh ke Khaton ka Majmua*. Delhi: Anjuman Taraqqi Urdu, 1941.

Marehrvi, Sayed Rafeeq. *Zaban e Dagh*. Lucknow: Naseem Book Depot, 1956.

Mehdi, Sayed Mohammad. *Munni Bai Hijab* (A Play). Allahabad: Anjuman Tehzeeb e Nau Publications, Art Press, 1978.

Nigar, Dagh Number 426 (1953).

Noori, Noorullah Muhammad. *Dagh Dehlvi ki sawaneh hayat aur kalaam par tabsira*. Hyderabad: Azam Steam Press, 1355 (1936-37).

Parbati, Fareed. *Dagh ba haisiyat masnavi nigar*. Delhi: Educational Publication House, 2010.

Raliyaram, K.L. *Mirza Dagh*. Lahore: Educational Publishers, 1939.

Ranj, Hakim Faseehuddin. *Baharistan e naz*. Lahore: Majlis e Taraqqi Adab, 1965.

Saaz, Shahid, comp. *Deewan e Malka Jan (Makhazan e ulfat Malka)*. Kolkata: Asbat o Nafi Publications, 2020.

Zaidi, Sayed Muhammad Ali. *Mutala e Dagh*. Lucknow: Nizami Press, 1974.

English

Anonymous. 'Baiji Culture of Kolkata during Colonial Period: A Review.' *Lokogandhar: Journal of Folklore Studies*. https://lokogandhar.com/baiji-culture-of-kolkata-during-colonial-period-a-review/.

Banerjee, Sumanta. *Dangerous Outcast: The Prostitute in Nineteenth-Century Bengal*. London, New York, Calcutta: Seagull Books, 1998.

Bhatia, Nandini. 'How Courtesans Were Not Merely Entertainers, but Cultural and Political Influencers.' *The Hindu*, May 14, 2024. https://www.thehindu.com/entertainment/how-courtesans-were-not-merely-entertainers-but-cultural-and-political-influencers/article68148722.ece.

Courtney, David. 'The Tawaif, the Anti-Nautch Movement and the Development of North Indian Classical Music.' Chandrakantha.com. https://chandrakantha.com/articles/indian_music/tawaif/.

Gandhi, A.K. *The Dance of Freedom: From Gungroos to Gunpowder*. New Delhi: Fingerprint Publication, 2024.

'The History of the Colonial State and the Unmaking of the Tawaif.' Feminism in India, March 23, 2022. https://feminisminindia.com/2022/03/23/the-history-of-the-colonial-state-and-the-unmaking-of-the-tawaif/.

Jafa, Navina. '*Lost Histories of Tawaifs*,' 2006.

'The Jaans of Calcutta.' The Calcutta Chronicle. https://calcuttachronicle.co.in/the-jaans-of-calcutta/.

Jha, Shweta Sachdeva. 'Eurasian Women as Tawa'if Singers and Recording Artists: Entertainment and Identity-making in Colonial India.' *African and Asian Studies* 8, no. 2 (June 2009), 259–78. DOI: 10.1163/156921009X458118.

Kinnear, Michael S. *The Gramophone Company's First Indian Recordings, 1899–1908,* Popular Prakashan, Bombay, 1994.

Neville, Pran. *Nautch Girls of the Raj*. New Delhi: Penguin, 2009.

Oldenburg, Veena Talwar.

'Lifestyle as Resistance: The Case of the Courtesans of Lucknow.' *Feminist Studies* 16, no. 2 (Summer 1990), 259–78.

Sampat, Vikram. *My Name is Gauhar Jan: The Life and Times of a Musician*. New Delhi: Rupa and Co, 2010.

Williams, Richard David. 'Songs Between Cities: Listening to Courtesans in Colonial North India.' *Journal of the Royal Asiatic Society* 27, no. 4 (2017), 653–56. https://doi.org/10.1017/S1356186317000311.

Acknowledgements

I'm grateful to my Rampur Book Club mates—Samina, Sara, Raspal, Dr Mehmood, Sofia, Musarrat, Farah, Shibani, Paikar, Yasmin, Arshiya, Nupur, Preeti and Rahul—for accompanying me through my writerly journey as cheerleaders, critics and friends. I have taken the liberty of weaving their traits into the book club characters with a generous sprinkling of creative imagination. Our story continues over books and food!

To Anuradha Roy for reading my work, allowing me to include hers in my novel, and for her generous words of support. To Neelum Saran Gour for her guidance and clear-eyed critique. To Rana Safvi, Ira Mukhoty, Saif Mehmood and Sara Rai for reading my manuscript and their encouragement. To all the writers whose novels formed a rich backdrop of the book club discussions. To Kanishka for always being a friend and sage in my literary journey.

As all scholars, I owe a debt of gratitude to Rekhta for its yeoman's service in archiving rare Urdu texts, and to Rampur Raza Library for preserving Dagh's witty, emotional letters and poetic works. I am also deeply thankful to the scholars and archivists who preserved these voices, and to Hijab herself, whose artistry inspired this exploration across time.

In Kolkata, the 'Faqr e Hindustan' that Hijab cherished, I'm indebted to Debojit Bhattacharya who guided my explorations and offered insights into the history of the tawaifs and the city. I'm profoundly grateful to Dr Shahid Saaz for his research assistance and for sharing invaluable letters written by Hijab. To Shahenshah Mirza for oral history on

Calcutta tawaifs and for assisting my attempts to find Hijab's grave. To my friend Afreen for introducing me to such generous exponents of knowledge.

Dagh composed his shers extempore. So when a friend complained about having to sit with his huqqa, lie down, get up and then write, Dagh remarked: 'It seems to me that you don't write sher, you give birth!' That is my kaifiyat too, and I thank the Hachette team for helping me bring my labour of inspired love into the world. To Thomas Abraham for his steadfast faith in me and my work. To my editor, Abhivyakti Singh, for her wisdom, perceptive comments and patience in shaping the manuscript. To Riti Jagoorie, Abhishek Roy and the exceptional Marketing and Publicity team for ensuring that the book will take its first firm steps and find its way to readers. To Amit Malhotra and Rishika Kapoor for the fabulous, irresistible cover and for their patience with my ideas. To Vinita Nayar for copyediting and Parul Sharma for proofreading, to Sumaira Nawaz for peer reviewing, and Ajith Iyer for the beautiful typesetting. It certainly takes a small village to birth a fully-formed book.

Special thanks to Asad for his help in translations and for being a reservoir of creative thought I could freely access. To Taran for being my go-to literary emergency speed-dial person. To my nieces, Iram and Maryam—my first razor-sharp and loving critics, and Yusra, my guide into Gen Z–ism. To Mani, my aunt and critic, for her constant engagement with my writing.

To my husband, Qamar, for his continued encouragement and pride in my work, rivalled only by my mamma, my inspiration. To my children, Nadir, Gaeti and Rahima, for their unflagging championship. Your DNAs are entangled in mine and you are in all my books—a fair warning. To my siblings, Irmeen and Saleem, for their love and faith in me. And, most importantly to Baba, S.M. Mehdi, for inspiring me to research and write the Hijab–Dagh love story with his atmospheric play, 'Munni Bai Hijab'.

'Khan doesn't write women only as damsels in distress; she writes them as women who challenge.' – *Scroll.in*

The Begum and the Dastan

TARANA HUSAIN KHAN

ALSO FROM HACHETTE INDIA AND TARANA HUSAIN KHAN

Lined with grandeur, tragedy and fantasy, Tarana Husain Khan's odyssey maps the social, political and religious contours of 1897 Sherpur with the fascinating and strong-willed Feroza Begum at the centre of the storm.

On an evening not too many evenings ago, the blue-eyed Feroza, flouting her family's orders, attended Nawab Shams Ali Khan's sawani celebrations at the Benazir Palace. Tragedy coloured the night when she found herself kidnapped and withheld in the Nawab's harem—bustling, tantalizing and rife with sinister power play. As tyranny and repression tightened their hold inside the royal walls, at the Bazaar Chowk, dastangoi Kallan Mirza enchanted his listeners with the legend of sorcerer Tareek Jaan and his chimeric city, the Tilism-e-Azam, where women were confined in underground basements.

Misfortune and subjugation link eras when Ameera, Feroza's great-granddaughter, is restricted to her house and finds solace in her Dadi's retelling of Feroza's tragedy. When Ameera's circumstances begin mirroring the strife and indignities pervasive in 1897 Sherpur, she must reflect if society has shifted enough for women and their choices.

Written with careful flamboyance and striking evocativeness, *The Begum and the Dastan* is a world imbued with love, splendour and heartbreak, only saved by the women who refuse to play by the rule book.

Praise for *The Begum and the Dastan*

'Straddling themes of gender and sectarianism, of royal autocracy and republican apathy, *The Begum and the Dastan* resurrects the lives of women behind the purdah, telling a moving, even tragic tale of pride, loss, courage and determination, as well as that unyielding human capacity to subvert tyranny through art and the power of stories.'
– Manu Pillai, author of *The Ivory Throne* and *Rebel Sultans*

'Tarana Khan weaves a tale full of razm, ishq, ayyari aur tilism, war, love, trickery and magic—and takes us on a fascinating journey into the life of a nineteenth-century begum. The author's familiarity with the male-centric, feudal milieu and her meticulous research of the period brings to life a story of a woman and her story of love, loss and betrayal. The dastan with its use of two timelines keeps the reader in its grip throughout as it brings out the lives of a young girl in present times hearing the story of her ancestress.'
– Rana Safvi, author of *Tears of the Begums* and *In Search of the Divine*

'A captivating novel that shows Tarana Khan's masterful insight into the human heart, complexities of love and tragedy. Framed through published and oral histories and dastans, the novel introduces Feroza Begum, a highly memorable heroine, through whose life we are pulled into the richly regimented life of the nineteenth-century Nawabi culture.'
– Musharraf Ali Farooqi, author of *The Story of a Widow* and *Between Clay and Dust*

'Evocative writing that summons the soul of the feudal past, rich with history and romance and heartbreak.'
– Namita Gokhale, author and Sahitya Akademi awardee, 2021

'A moving and affectionate account of a late nineteenth-century heroine, both shackled and emboldened by life in a North Indian court. The novel skillfully shows how the modern, in this colonial era, could take the form of a violent conservatism, especially in relation to women. The shattering and often cunning refashioning of women's lives is Tarana Husain Khan's fascinating subject.'
– Anjum Hasan, author of *A Day in the Life*

'The story prompts the question: How can one write history without condoning it? In *The Begum and the Dastan,* history is an inspiration, a tool and an anchor, but it is not a justification.'
– *Scroll.in*

'[Khan] has done an incredible job of combining fiction and history with a delicate hand of imagination. The story lives with you long after you have read it.'
– *The Daily Guardian*

'Her novel sought to present historical fiction not from the perspective of the man as most dominant narratives do, but strived to represent the tale from the voice of female characters and their version of history. Khan ardently elaborated on the prejudices faced by women in the nineteenth century, the ones that women are still victims to today and the need for the rise of consciousness in these turbulent times.'
– *The Telegraph*

'A magical realism journey into the old feudal nawabi culture weaving two eras... The magic of the novel will surely survive for long.'
– Salman Khurshid, *The Wire*

'This is an immersive novel, remarkable for the thoroughly Muslim world it creates.'
– Anil Menon, *The Hindu*

'With Feroza Begum, Khan seeks to examine how women thrust into this life of purdah, filled as much with glamour as with subversion, found the will to love and rebel, and sharply questions how far we have stepped out of similar oppressive structures in the present context.'
– Firstpost

'... Khan accomplishes much: A flavour of Nawabi daily life, Rohilla military culture, the Sunni–Shia tensions mixed in with colonial influence, and, ultimately, the women representing each of these categories.'
– Deccan Chronicle

'... rhythmic, mellifluous and near hypnotic quality of prose. Khan's smooth grafting of the flamboyance of Urdu Dastan to the Anglophone narrative lends Feroza Begum's tale a compelling power. It is an exquisitely rendered, splendid story which you can read at leisure. The book, indeed, is an unputdownable page-turner.'
– The Book Review

'*The Begum and the Dastan* by Tarana Husain Khan has the ability to create enchantment with her words... Characters sparkle with such brilliance.'
– Frontlist

'Document[s] the stories of women history forgot, who lived in Rampur and shaped the history of the town.'
– SheThePeople

'...a haunting tale of a grand city and its women unfolding in three main narrative strands from the 19th century until the present.'
– Desi Books